Praise for Mylo Carbia and
VIOLETS ARE RED

"*Violets Are Red* is the most wickedly entertaining novel we've seen in years. Set as a modern-day fairy tale in New York's posh Upper East Side, it's like *Sex and the City* meets *Misery*, but with a fantastic twist ending you won't see coming—an ending so good, you'll wind up reading the whole book twice . . . It's the best horror-thriller novel of the year."

— *Top10Novels.com*

"Carbia's latest effort is tied with Stephen King's *Outsider* for best novel coming out this year due to its killer 'evil wife versus young mistress' theme and insane twist ending. We think her style of thriller-horror writing is so strong that with only two published books, she still makes our list of the best horror authors alive today."

— *BestHorrorAuthors.com*

"Just read the first few pages and you'll see why Mylo Carbia is making headlines. Her refreshingly vivid writing style, coupled with her ability to conjure interesting characters inside fast-moving, suspense-filled plots, makes *Violets Are Red* more than just a great read, it's perhaps, the greatest battle of 'wife versus mistress' ever told."

— *Great-Novels.com*

"She's the next Stephen King."

— *Horror Society*

"A new powerhouse author is here to stay."

— *Boston Globe*

"Mylo Carbia is truly *The Queen of Horror.*"

— *Examiner.com*

"A dazzling, sophisticated horror tale that breaks the rules of every genre."

—*Latino LA*

"Hollywood's top ghostwriter grew up in a haunted house and she wants to pay it forward."

—*Daily Offbeat*

"Not since Quentin Tarantino or Diablo Cody have we seen anyone break the 'writer nerd' stereotype in such a big way."

—*Nobby's*

"[Carbia] has a crisp writing style with multi-dimensional characters and a firm grip on plot structure. We will certainly be on the lookout for other books by Ms. Carbia."

—*Ginger Nuts of Horror*

"It's like nothing else out there."

—*News United*

"Screenwriting wunderkind Mylo Carbia makes a triumphant return."

—*Broadway World*

"We think Mylo Carbia is the best new author of the year."

—*Great-Novels.com*

VIOLETS
ARE RED

Coming Soon from Mylo Carbia

Z.O.O.

THE WALK-INS

YORUBA

THE QUEEN OF HORROR COLLECTION

THY BE SHUNNED

DAUGHTERS OF MARIE LAVEAU

TERLINGUA

VANDERBILT
PUBLISHING

2814 Grande Parkway, Suite 111
Palm Beach Gardens, FL 33410 USA

WWW.VANDERBILTPUBLISHING.COM

VIOLETS
ARE RED

MYLO CARBIA

VANDERBILT
PUBLISHING

Copyright © 2018 by Mylo Carbia

Published in the United States of America by Vanderbilt Publishing LLC, 2814 Grande Parkway, Suite 111, Palm Beach Gardens, FL 33410 USA. WWW.VANDERBILTPUBLISHING.COM

Library of Congress Cataloging-in-Publication data is available upon request.

Print ISBN: 9780996565233
Kindle ISBN: 9780996565240
eBook ISBN: 9780996565257

Edited by Melissa Gray
Cover Design by Perla Enrica Giancola
Cover Photo by Steven Khan
Interior Photo by Dawn V. Gilmore

Mylo Carbia "The Queen of Horror"
WWW.MYLOCARBIA.COM

EMAIL: fans@mylocarbia.com

Twitter: @MyloCarbia
Facebook: /AuthorMyloCarbia
Instagram: @mylocarbia
Goodreads: mylo_carbia

ABOUT THE BOOK

FORTY-NINE-YEAR-OLD Violet Ramspeck is the envy of Manhattan's Upper East Side. Wealthy, witty, and childless, she harbors secrets of self-destruction, devoting all of her time to others as an artistic socialite turned trophy wife.

Without warning, Violet discovers her adoring husband of twenty-four years is having an affair with a twenty-three-year-old bartender who is an exact, younger replica of Violet. Upon learning of his plans for divorce, Violet's inner sanctum deteriorates as she morphs into a sadistic captor of the naked, strong-willed, millennial mistress in the basement of her expansive townhome.

Meanwhile, Violet's prisoner—Allegra Adams—spends every waking moment trying to escape her luxurious prison. She soon discovers her mental games prove more effective than her physical attempts to run, challenging everything

Violet has ever known about her husband, her values, and her sanity.

The epic struggle between two flawed women fighting over the same man is profound.

Lovers of Grimm's fairy tales will enjoy this fast-paced, psychological thriller. With unforeseen twists and turns, the shocking ending will have readers talking about *Violets Are Red* for years to come.

WWW.VIOLETS-ARE-RED.COM

ABOUT THE AUTHOR

MYLO CARBIA is a Hollywood screenwriter turned #1 bestselling author widely known for her work in the horror-thriller genre and trademark of surprise twist endings.

Ranked 7th in the "Top 10 Horror Writers Alive Today," and among the "Top 250 Most Influential Authors" by Richtopia. com, her award-winning writing style has been described as "A perfect mix between Stephen King, M. Night Shyamalan, and Quentin Tarantino, but infused with a signature female sharpness that is all her own."

Born in Jackson, New Jersey, Carbia famously spent her childhood years writing to escape the terrors of growing up in a severely haunted house. By the age of 17, Carbia was already well established as a prolific young playwright. By the age of 30, her very first screenplay was optioned only 28 days after completion, earning Carbia a three-picture-deal, and the cover of *Hollywood Scriptwriter* in 2003.

Soon after, Carbia moved to Manhattan and quietly penned numerous television and film projects under her production company Zohar Films—earning the nickname 'The Queen of Horror' and the reputation of being Hollywood's top horror film ghostwriter.

In 2015, Carbia left ghostwriting to join the publishing world. Her debut novel, *The Raping of Ava DeSantis*, hit #1 best-seller in four categories, and won multiple awards including the prestigious 2016 Silver Falchion Award for Outstanding Achievement in Fiction.

Today, Carbia lives with her husband and son in Palm Beach, Florida. She absolutely loves writing novels and plans to release at least seven more titles over the next several years.

WWW.MYLOCARBIA.COM

FOR KURT LUND,

Semper Amare

"If you marry a man who cheats on his wife, you'll be married to a man who cheats on his wife."

—Ann Landers
Advice Columnist (1918-2002)

"Do I need to defend that I am a decent woman? I sure hope I don't. I know I am."

—Angelina Jolie
The Today Show, 2005

ONE

I AM SMART. *I am beautiful. Brooklyn born, Manhattan-raised. Marymount, Juilliard, Columbia—all the best schools New Daddy's affluence could buy.*

I married well. No, I take that back. I married 'nouveau-riche-hall-of-fame' well. At least that's what my dead mother-in-law declared at my bridal shower. God piss on her soul.

Forty-nine law-abiding years on this Earth, yet here I stand, dreading the scandalous, crass things the fake news media will label me.

A lunatic kidnapper?

An insane interrogator?

A jealous murderer.

Never once realizing . . . I am her fucking savior.

Not one of those reporters will ever experience the bursting heat inside one's chest when faced with the choice between death and life. But here I am. Standing in my own nightmare, staring at my own truth . . .

Of what I have done.

Of what I have become.
Of what will be my legacy.

Violet Ramspeck's thoughts stopped at the word *legacy*. She stood, dumbfounded, in the commercial-size walk-in refrigerator of the basement of her enviable Upper East Side townhome, wearing a royal blue, sequined gown and silver crystal platform shoes.

It was an enigmatic choice of wardrobe for nine fifteen in the morning, but Violet didn't care. Nor did she mind that her copper-red hair was dripping wet, or the red lipstick smeared across her chin, or the trembling ankles above her aching feet, absorbing the abominable scene stinging her amber-brown eyes.

Just then, Violet's right Christian Louboutin heel gave out—a blowout strong enough to knock her off balance, summoning both arms to quickly jump into motion, like a surfer nailing a wave.

Once sure-footed, she continued staring at the object in the corner of the chilly room. It was a plain burlap sack large enough to cover a small calf. But there was no cow inside that unmistakable, baby-shit-brown, stained sack. It was something more precious. Something loving and caring, and once full of dreams, that was now nothing more than discarded garbage.

The sack managed to stay upright, though slanting somewhat to the left, with sprouts of fresh, long, cinnamon-red hair dangling from the cinched top.

Violet cautiously approached.

She unraveled the thick, braided rope that held the top of the sack closed, carefully removing the hair to avoid tangling it.

She slowly pulled down the neck of the bag, revealing a white, solid mass, when a scene from *The Little Mermaid* flashed before her mind's eye.

Now a pale forehead was visible, though curtained by thick, cinnamon-red bangs. Warm to the touch, the skin was youthful, having never tasted Botox, Juvéderm, or Restylane in its life.

Violet continued pulling the sack, unearthing a set of closed eyes over a classic nose, chubby cheeks, and a blemish-free chin. The young woman's face was heart-shaped, like a Roman cherub, clearly in her early twenties and oddly sanguine given the circumstances. She sat unconscious and upright, undressed from the neck up, face free to the cold air, mouth gaped open like an over-achieving fifth-grader proudly showing her dentist not a single cavity could be found.

Violet peered over the young woman's face, examining it closely. She ran her right hand from the top of the girl's head to the side, behind her ear, and then checked her palm to see if any blood remained from the drag across the concrete basement floor.

Magically, there was none.

Violet crouched over her reluctant houseguest, intimately breathing inches from her mouth, merging with the young woman's soured breath, believing it was the only way to experience a person from the inside out. Before last night, she had only seen pictures of this naive, ignorant millennial. She knew her name, her birthday, where she was born, where she worked, how she lived, and whom she befriended, but most importantly . . . She knew the man she slept with.

Because he was Violet's husband.

As Violet hovered, the young girl's mouth began thrashing from left to right. Her tongue began swooshing in circles, creating minimal saliva that had long dried up. Still unable to move her body, she gradually opened her large, round, pea-green eyes and focused on the blurry vision responsible for the overpowering perfume accosting her newly awakened olfactory senses.

"Would you like a smoothie?" The fluorescent light from the ceiling cast a halo around Violet as she spoke in a maternal tone. "You must be starving."

The young woman's face violently contorted as she drew a deep, life-giving breath . . . And released an eardrum-piercing, primal scream.

TWO

YES, IT'S TRUE. The Upper East Side is God's favorite neighborhood in New York City. Its tree-lined, residential streets safeguard both the *newly coined* and *silver-spooned* alike.

Scores of first-generation millionaire bankers, brokers, entrepreneurs, stylists, artists, actors, and singers proudly call this Manhattan neighborhood home, living side by side with old money surnames considered American royalty—Getty, Morgan, and Rockefeller, among them.

Indeed, it is a unique neighborhood that houses extraordinary people from every corner of the world, from the pampered Egyptian pharaohs at the Metropolitan Museum of Art to the wealthiest *one percent of the one percent*, shielding them all from the faceless ills of society.

Crime, poverty, homelessness—all invisible here.

Even Mother Nature showed favoritism when Hurricane Sandy spared the neighborhood in late October 2012. Upper East Side residents remained dry and retained electricity throughout the catastrophic storm, while other neighborhoods were savagely unplugged and shoved underwater without fresh food or warmth for weeks. In fact, the Upper East Side served as a gracious hostess for surrounding vicinities, forcing impatient locals to wait in restaurant lines for up to three hours, for it was the only place in Manhattan serving meals warmer than fifty degrees.

With so much television and cinematic exposure—*Breakfast at Tiffany's, The Nanny, Sex and the City,* and *Gossip Girl* to name a few—one would think the Upper East Side was a large place requiring a street vendor map to be sold outside the IRT Lexington Subway line. Instead, it is very small, comprised of only two hundred thousand people (eighty-nine percent of which are Caucasian), and approximately three dozen wealthy vampires (whom the mayor still counts as diversity), living harmoniously in a near-perfect 1.76-mile rectangle, bound by the invisible socioeconomic walls of 59th Street in the south, 96th Street to the north, Fifth Avenue in the west, and the East River in the east.

The smaller sections of Lenox Hill, Gracie Mansion, Carnegie Hill, and the bastard child no one ever talks about—the working-class area of Yorkville—also have reputations quite different than the more famous Gold Coast of Museum Mile.

As with every other neighborhood in New York, the Upper East Side has a distinctive personality. In this case, *a sharp mind, steel balls, and a cheating soul.* And like other playgrounds that nest the rich and famous, the Upper East Side does a terrific job of hiding its most sinister secrets.

Violet Ramspeck sat quietly next to a first-floor window inside Dr. Simon Cohen's office, conveniently located on the corner of East 83rd and Park Avenue. As usual, she was ten minutes early for her appointment, walking straight past the empty reception desk, and into the comfy patient chair that was more welcoming than she would care to admit.

Violet was a privileged, educated, and graceful middle-aged woman. But unlike the *beige women* in her neighborhood, she was also bold, artsy, and outspoken—the kind of best friend who wouldn't hesitate to verbally point out the caviar stuck between your teeth at dinner.

Against cultural etiquette, Violet now wore the same lime-green Armani dress she strutted the month before at her husband's fifty-third birthday party at *Le Cirque*. A vibrant, colorful contrast to Dr. Cohen's stale, 1970s era office that had thwarted more than twenty lipo-junkies from slicing their wrists while waxing.

Fortunately, the Upper East Side is as empty as a hooker's Bitcoin jar every weekend during the summer. Now that Friday had arrived, everyone who's anyone was already on their way to the Hamptons, making it rather easy to sneak back and forth into Dr. Cohen's office without being spotted by anyone other than the local dog walker and his crew of four-legged pageant beauties.

The warm afternoon sunlight striking Violet's alabaster face was a harsh reminder she had forgotten to put on her usual 100+ sunscreen earlier that morning. The bright light deeply contrasted her smoldering, darkly lined eyes that peeked through wisps of long, copper-red bangs—the signature piece of her 'long in the front, short in the back' hairstyle that had become her trademark decades ago.

Violet was a master at the sophisticated squint. It was a gaze so alluring it allegedly made First Lady Melania Trump jealous when they briefly met outside the Met Gala in 2013.

Violet's striking eyes wandered outside, to the blooming red and yellow tulip bed on the sidewalk, when a dark-skinned woman dressed in uniform came into view, wheeling a blonde toddler sucking a lollipop.

Walking at a quick pace, the nanny was forced to stop outside Dr. Cohen's window when the toddler tossed the lollipop into the tulip bed and laughed hysterically.

At that moment, a pure-white Persian cat bounced onto Violet's lap. Its bright green eyes sparkled like Colombian emeralds.

"Sparkles! You're still here," she exclaimed.

The oversized cat purred with glee, circling in Violet's lap before sitting down.

"Do you think she remembers me?"

"Of course, she remembers you. You're one of her favorite patients," said a frail male voice with a thick Jewish accent from several feet away. "Sparkles never forgets a pretty face, or a kind heart."

"That's so sweet, Dr. Cohen, thank you." Violet petted the cat with fervor. "I can't believe she's still here after so many years." Violet ran her finger against the cat's crystal-studded collar. "How old is she now?"

"Old enough for me to lose track." Dr. Cohen chuckled as he carefully angled himself into his chair. "How have you been, dear?"

Violet hugged the cat closely, unafraid of Sparkles's white hair transferring to her dress. "I've been better. I've been worse. We're always in flux, aren't we?"

"Yes, dear. From beginning to end. Especially at the end." Dr. Cohen's miniscule, gray head was now shielded by the large, winged crest of his brown leather throne.

A faint noise from the window turned Violet's attention back to the nanny outside. After bending over, fishing the lollipop out of the tulip bed and wiping it off, the nanny returned the candy to the smiling child, who immediately threw it into Park Avenue with more laughter.

The nanny's face melted in annoyance. She was tired. She was miserable. She wasn't interested in playing childish games that afternoon.

Violet adjusted the five-carat, cushion-cut, canary diamond on her ring finger. "Do you believe in Hell, Dr. Cohen?"

It was a startling question, one that slipped out before she could catch it—like the cold air escaping through a small gap beneath the ancient air conditioning unit beside her.

"I know you've been through a terrible ordeal," he replied. "I'm not sure if you're ready to discuss such heavy topics."

Violet remained steadfast. "I asked if you believed in Hell, Dr. Cohen."

"Why? Is it the woman outside who's bothering you?"

Violet shook her head. "My question has nothing to do with her."

"Then, what is it?" He adjusted his round, wire-framed spectacles.

Violet leaned forward. "Hell. It's *here,* on Earth. Isn't it?"

Dr. Cohen slowly shifted his decrepit, worn body against the fractured leather. "Well, it all boils down to one's faith," he replied with polite authority.

"But I'm asking you. What do *you* think?"

Dr. Cohen rearranged himself as if he were about to give a long speech. "Well," he said in a drawn-out, New York-Jewish accent. "Hell is a concept that means many different things to many different cultures. For example, in my faith, Judaic mystics believe in a spiritual place called *Gehinnom* that differs some-what from your Catholic depiction of Hell."

Violet listened intently. Her expression was inquisitive yet stoic, with classic features as immovable as an antique por-celain doll.

"Our Hell is in some ways like—" He looked at the cracked ceiling to find the right analogy. "Our Hell is like God's professional dry cleaning service."

Violet tilted her head. "Dry cleaning service?"

"Yes, or washing machine—whatever image makes more sense to you . . . But in my faith, every time a person does a good deed, it cleanses his or her soul. Removes the stains, so to speak. Elevates our vibrational inner being just a little higher, closer to God."

Violet's squinty eyes opened wider. "Go on."

"But every time we do something wrong, albeit to another person or to ourselves, even if no one is looking, it leaves a little stain on our soul."

Violet was more confused than ever.

"So, if a person's spirit isn't ready to ascend to Heaven upon death, it goes to the dry cleaner's first—"

"This genie place?"

"Yes, *Gehinnom*. There, it gets thrown around at an intense spiritual heat to remove its sins, and cleanse the soul in preparation for entry into Heaven at a later date."

Violet drew a troubled breath. "So, Hell is temporary?"

"In some ways, yes. But I'm a very old man and far from a religious scholar."

His warm smile of yellow teeth still brought Violet comfort.

"I think I understand now. Thank you."

"But, as many Jews believe even to this day, if you completely and fully repent before you die, the whole process of Gehinnom can be avoided."

"Just like Catholicism."

Dr. Cohen gestured his hands. "Not exactly. You can't just say a few Hail Marys and be done with it. One would have to truly repent his or her negative actions in life, and then go out and do one's very best to make amends to those they've harmed. It's a much more thorough process than simply repeating a few prayers."

Violet did not like his answer. "I disagree. I don't believe that's how it works."

Dr. Cohen crossed his legs. "Then what do you believe, Violet?"

She vacillated on sharing her opinion. "I believe Hell isn't a location, per se. I believe it's an energy force. Something that sticks to your soul, grows stronger over time, and refuses to leave. Like a virus. Or a plague."

Dr. Cohen shrugged his hobbit-sized shoulders as if to say, *maybe.*

"And I believe it's right here. Surrounding us . . . Stalking us . . . Living inside our bodies, waiting to strike."

Dr. Cohen shifted his weight and let out a paternal sigh. "Let's talk about the real reason you would like to resume therapy, Violet. You know, I'm quite happy to see you again." He smiled. "I'm just surprised that you've come back to see me after all of these years."

Dr. Cohen first met Violet at the age of twelve, when her step-father insisted she start therapy to deal with the tragic death of her birthfather one year earlier.

Violet's real father, Roger Chamberlain—a well-known free-lance writer for major fashion magazines—suffered a heart attack in the back of a taxi while stuck in rush-hour traffic on the Brooklyn Bridge. Like any other child who suffered the tragic loss of a parent, Violet was immediately crushed by the death of her father. But for her, it was exceptionally heartbreaking having witnessed his death firsthand.

One snowy Wednesday afternoon in early December 1980, Violet and her father were on their way back home to Brooklyn after enjoying a matinee performance of *The Nutcracker Ballet* on Broadway. They were recapping the amazing dance sequences, speaking of holiday travel plans, and exchanging ideas of what to buy Violet's mother for Christmas, when Roger began sweating profusely. Five minutes later, he grasped at his chest, demanding the taxi driver hammer the pedal to the Brooklyn Hospital Center.

But the driver was unable to move. Sandwiched between thousands of cars, stuck behind a Port Authority truck that had stalled in the stagnant, holiday traffic.

After a few heated exchanges with the foreign driver, Roger eventually stopped talking. He slumped down to the floor in the back of the cab. Violet panicked and cried hysterically as the driver screamed CPR instructions in a language she could not understand.

Sadly, Violet was forced to stay in the motionless taxi while the driver yelled for more than two hours. She continued holding her father's stiff hand, knowing intuitively that he had already passed right before her eyes.

In light of that awful memory, Violet was always grateful she had the privilege of hearing his last words before he lost consciousness—on the dirty floor of that disgusting, smelly taxi. She wished it would have been something profound, like "Tell Mother I will always love her," or "Always follow your dreams," but instead, his dying words were as practical as his IBM Selectric II typewriter: "Call my editor at *Vogue* and tell her my article will be late," he garbled as his eyes shut forever.

Violet knew she would always remember that line.

And to this day, every time she walks past a newsstand proudly displaying a copy of *Vogue*, it pierces her heart.

Soon after Roger's death, rumors circulated he was secretly bi-sexual—rumors that were all but confirmed by the gaggle of openly homosexual design assistants wailing at his funeral. Years later, close friends speculated he was one of the first to contract the unnamed "gay virus" that killed off nearly half of the fashion industry at the time. This was, indeed, a rumor that ripped apart young Violet to her core. A rumor she could never acknowledge to be true. Yet despite the violent whispers, she continued to cherish her father's memory in every way, especially the memory of his unusual bedtime reading ritual.

When not flying around the world attending fashion shows, Roger would spend most of his days sleeping, and most of his nights writing, only taking breaks when Violet was preparing for bed. As she snuggled into the sheets, Roger—who proudly considered himself an unorthodox parent—would sit on a stool beside his only child and read aloud his favorite book, given to him by his German grandparents. It was a one-off, handwritten English translation of the first and second volumes of *Grimms' Complete Fairy Tales* first published in 1812 and 1815.

As a young girl, Violet loved hearing the original, unedited, incredibly violent versions of fables she had grown up with: *Little Red Riding Hood, Snow White, Hansel and Gretel,* and lesser-known tales like *The White Snake, The Golden Key,* and *Simple Hans*—all secret versions of stories no other children were privy to. Of course, Walt Disney had sanitized and popularized several of these famous fairy tales, but no other children in her fifth-grade class knew the real story of how Cinderella's stepsisters sliced off parts of their feet to fit into the golden (not glass) slipper, or how Rapunzel got knocked up, out of wedlock, by the prince who sneaked into her tower, or how Snow White's *real* mother ordered the huntsman to "stab her to death and bring back her lungs and liver as proof of your deed," and was later forced, at her daughter's wedding, to dance in hot iron shoes until death.

The original, *first* edition of Jacob and Wilhelm Grimms' masterpiece was not even commercially published in English until 2012, and was never intended to be a children's story-book. Instead, it was meant as a historical collection of crude, life-teaching fables that were *about* children. Somehow, families were still drawn to reading it to their offspring, and after severe critical pressure, the Brothers Grimm revised the tales and released another six editions—each one more conservative than the next—so that the seventh and final version, the one most frequently read today, had relatively little in common with the first edition.

And that's why Violet loved her father's book.

It was rare. It was raw. It was not to be read by children or seen by the nuns at school. Until adulthood, Violet would secretly read each tale over and over, memorizing her favorite stories just as her classmates would memorize passages from the Bible. To her, this book was her Bible and the only thing that kept her connected to her father.

Only six weeks after Roger's death, Violet's mother, Elsa Cane Chamberlain, a former British runway model, who, in her youth, resembled a ginger Brigitte Bardot, remarried a man by the name of John "New Daddy" Williams.

New Daddy was a sweet, rotund, wealthy real estate developer with a toupee modeled after Elvis and a laugh as hearty as a rodeo clown. The day after their quickie wedding in Vegas, New Daddy moved Violet and her mother to his Park Avenue apartment, located between East 79th and 80th Streets on the Upper East Side.

Violet, still grieving, was happy her mother had picked a man who clearly preferred women this time, but she wished she would have waited until summer break before drastically changing their lives.

Violet had a difficult time moving mid-year from a public school in Flatbush to a uniformed private school that mainly educated ladies whose last names were plastered on libraries throughout New York.

As warm as her building staff and school's reception was, Violet felt like an outsider for more than a year. She even had trouble transitioning from sleeping on a convertible sofa in the living room of her Brooklyn apartment, to sleeping inside a canopied queen bed in New Daddy's five-million-dollar palace in the sky.

Of course, Violet recognized this was a fortunate turn of events, since the death of her father left her mother penniless, but like any Powerball jackpot winner can attest: change, no matter what the direction, can still be stressful and traumatic.

Years later, Dr. Cohen and Violet reunited the day after her sixteenth birthday, when her all-girls school-acquired obsession with weight, and the resulting dance with bulimia, took a serious turn, causing a small rupture in her esophagus and a week's stay in Mount Sinai Hospital.

After thirteen months of therapy sessions to deal with her destructive self-image issues, Violet resumed a normal adolescent life, and to Dr. Cohen's credit, graduated from Marymount School of New York with honors.

But the worst thing that ever happened to Violet Chamberlain Williams Ramspeck took place eleven years ago, at the age of thirty-eight.

After a thirteen-year struggle with fertility—including twenty-two failed IVFs—came the fantastic news of an infant available for adoption in the Jingxi county of Guangxi province, China.

After a month-long trip to the impoverished village of Xiuan, Violet and her husband celebrated the homecoming of ten-week-old, Briar Rose Ramspeck, with no less than three baby showers—the final one being so well attended that it made *Page Six* news.

Tragically, only twenty-two days after her joyous arrival, Violet suffered the unimaginable heartache of waking up to find Briar Rose dead in the bassinet beside her . . . a horrific, natural death caused by SIDS, according to the Manhattan County Coroner.

Violet's suicide-attempt the night of her daughter's blockbuster service at the Frank E. Campbell Funeral Chapel was considered quite understandable, if not expected, by Manhattan's top gossip mongers. Her subsequent bulimia relapse garnered much attention and, eventually, a neighborhood-wide intervention for Violet to seek therapy once again.

Luckily, with Dr. Cohen's help, her physical ailments quickly healed as she went from a death-defying eighty-nine pounds on her petite five-foot-four frame, to a healthy one hundred sixteen pounds after only six months of therapy.

Within eight months, Dr. Cohen helped Violet resume her busy schedule as a Manhattan socialite, to roaring, silent applause.

Dr. Cohen angled his bushy gray eyebrows as he searched for a way to dig deeper. "Why have you come back to see me, Violet? Are you maintaining healthy habits or—"

"My husband wanted to divorce me for a younger woman."

Dr. Cohen was taken aback. "*Ram?*"

Despite being a highly lauded professional, it was difficult for Dr. Cohen to remain objective. Balthazar Edward Ramspeck, III—affectionately called "Ram" by his dearest friends— was not the sort of gentleman to fall into the second wife flytrap. An affair? Perhaps. A fling? Definitely. But leaving Violet for another woman would cost him millions, something the notorious trust fund cheapskate would avoid at all costs.

"What makes you so sure?"

"Many things . . . Mysterious lawyer meetings. Late-night text messages. I even found a Cartier receipt for a sixty-three-thousand-dollar necklace that I never received."

"Oh. I see."

"And he's putting our home on the market."

Dr. Cohen curled his old-timer mustache. "Your town-house? On 78th?"

"Yes."

Dr. Cohen shook his head. "Perhaps he sees it as a selling opportunity? The market is quite good for sellers this year."

"Dr. Cohen," Violet said in a pedantic tone, "you and I both know he loves that townhome. It's been in his family for generations. We've lived there our entire marriage. Now, all of a sudden, after twenty-four years, it's too big for him?"

"Have you found out where he wants to move?"

"I think he's buying a two-bedroom, two-bath penthouse in one of the newer buildings in the high 80s. By the Second Avenue subway line."

Dr. Cohen held his chin. "Moving to an apartment can be quite a change, but it's not necessarily evidence that he wants to leave you forever, Violet. Perhaps he's concerned about retirement and wants to downsize. Save money."

"Don't try to placate me, Dr. Cohen." Violet leaned in, facing her mentor. "You know Ram. You know how tight he is with money. He won't even splurge for a second home in the Hamptons. If he sells the townhouse, he'll ship the proceeds offshore, and leave me forever."

"Does he know *you know* about his plans to sell your home?"

"No."

Sparkles the cat leapt off Violet's lap and dashed into the kitchen as if she were late for a meeting.

"I see."

Dr. Cohen remembered how astute Violet's husband was with finances.

As one of the first investors in Andrew Carnegie's U.S. Steel Company, the Ramspeck family of Scotland had earned its place in American royalty . . . And with a birth name as pretentious as *Balthazar,* Ram was cursed with the fear of failure, knowing he could never sell hot dogs at Yankee Stadium and walk out alive.

"So, do you have any advice? On what I should do?" pleaded Violet.

Dr. Cohen knew that at the age of forty-nine, Violet was sadly approaching her Manhattan first wife expiration date. He cleared his throat. "Where is Ram now?"

"He's in Europe. He's traveling on business until Labor Day."

"Good . . . That means we'll have about three weeks to work together until he returns. Unfortunately, I must leave around that time as well."

"Really? So soon?"

Dr. Cohen gently grabbed Violet's hand and hobbled with her to the door. "We'll discuss everything in greater detail next week. But for now, please know I would like to see you as much as possible before I leave."

"Definitely. I'll be here every day if I can." She smiled. "Thank you for coming out of retirement for me."

"My pleasure. I know you're greatly concerned about your husband, Violet, but you should know I am most concerned about *you* and your health. So, I must ask this one last question before you go. Truthfully, how are you handling this?"

She paused. She looked through the open doorway to the empty hall, thinking of the last image she saw before leaving for Dr. Cohen's office: a *young, naked, red-headed woman chained by the neck to the radiator, defecating over an orange Home Depot bucket.*

"Given the circumstances, Dr. Cohen. I think I'm doing rather well."

Violet beamed.

THREE

BRAND NEW LISTING ~ $24,900,000
A SOTHEBY'S INTERNATIONAL REALTY EXCLUSIVE
13 EAST 78TH STREET, UPPER EAST SIDE, MANHATTAN 10028

FIRST TIME ON *the market in 89 years!* Built in 1903 by the notable design firm of Nardi-Balson, this exceptionally constructed seven-story townhouse is owned by a prominent family and situated in one of the most coveted blocks between Fifth and Madison Avenues. Located just steps from Central Park, this magnificent 40-foot-wide, 19,880 square-foot, 26-room mansion has undergone complete renovation with unparalleled finishes and the finest craftsmanship, including a complete resurfacing of the white neo-classical exterior. The interior features neutral colors throughout, teak floors, soaring ceilings, hand-carved mahogany paneling, Italian trompe l'oeil accents, gold leaf trimmed fixtures, and intricate plaster friezes. Enjoy a magnificent, wood-paneled, two-story library, eat-in kitchen, garden breakfast room, and a dramatic formal gallery with a majestic, Carrara marble staircase with over-sized landings and sculpted black iron railings serving all seven floors. The residence offers unparalleled design details, including a four-person elevator, custom lighting, Venetian plaster walls, over-sized windows, eight bedrooms, twelve bathrooms, and six fireplaces. The private full-floor master suite on the top floor includes a 1400-square-foot private terrace, oversized dressing room, and double windowed bath. On the third floor, three guest bedroom suites share a tranquil north-facing terrace. The sixth floor is an entertainment center featuring a cinematic screening room designed by Jacques Lousay. The second and fifth levels serve its occupants with a fully equipped gym, ballet room, six laundry machines, staff quarters, and extensive storage. But the pièce de résistance of this one-of-a-kind home is the fully equipped, full-floor, finished basement that was converted into a state-of-the-art shelter by its current owner after 9/11. Lined with soundproof, three-foot-wide lead walls certified to withstand a Level 5 terrorist or radiation event, this masterfully designed safe room includes a separate solar-powered emergency generator, custom-designed commercial-sized walk-in refrigerator and freezer, shower/bath combo, media center and kitchenette, and is equipped to safely house and feed a family of five for up to three years. It's the ideal home for both survival and entertaining in modern times. Quite simply, it's Manhattan perfection.

OPEN HOUSE BY APPOINTMENT ONLY
SUNDAY, AUGUST 12TH
10:00 AM - 2:00 PM
CALL PENNY SLOVASKI AT (212) 256-1945
FOR MORE INFORMATION

FOUR

ALLEGRA ADAMS covered herself with a soft, army-green blanket as she tried to sleep on the finished concrete floor of Violet's basement. She sat up briefly, pulling her wavy, waist-length, cinnamon-red hair out from underneath her bottom, now that it was knotting in the back and becoming quite uncomfortable to sleep on.

She was convinced this was a nightmare.

She thought if she could just force herself to fall back asleep *while dreaming*, she would wake up in her crappy sixth-floor Yorkville walk-up, stoned out of her mind, laughing with her roommate about how wasted she was the night before. The whole scene she imagined back at her apartment played out in her head, over and over that morning . . .

"Oh, man, you should have seen the fucked-up dream I had last night," she imagined telling her roommate, Chloe, while wearing her favorite Victoria Secret sleep shirt and matching panties. "It was insane! I mean, I was stuck in this crazy freezer or something, totally naked but covered by this big sack thing—you know, the kind we used during field day races in gym class? But I was freezing my ass off, locked up in this wicked cold room, when some crazy lady—"

"What did she look like?" Chloe, a tall, thin light-skinned African-American woman who resembled a young Tyra Banks, would ask.

"In the face, she looked like that red-headed chick from *Mad Men*, but she was much skinnier with a buffed body like Madonna, and had this 'rich lady' haircut that was like—"

Allegra ran her hand up the back of her head.

"Like the *Long Island Medium*?"

"God, no, more like . . . Victoria Beckham."

"Who the hell is that?"

"Or that blonde lady on Fox News."

"They're *all* blonde on Fox News. And why are you watching that racist shit anyway?"

"You know, it's really short—almost shaved in the back—but from the front it has long bangs?"

"I have no idea who the fuck—Forget it."

"Okay, so this lady in my dream took me out of my big sack, and she was strong as hell 'cause I couldn't move my body at all, and she dragged me into this warmer room just outside the freezer. So then I sat there, totally naked, pubes to the world and everything, while she went inside a big toy box and grabbed this fucking dog collar and put it around my neck—chaining me to this old radiator."

"A *human* dog collar? That's BDSM dreams right there."

"Yeah, I know. I read *Fifty Shades* too, Chloe. Anyway, I kept asking her why I was there, and she wouldn't answer me. She just kept saying 'you must be hungry' and 'you need to eat,' but I sure as hell didn't want any food, 'cause I couldn't even move my mouth. Then I was slowly able to talk, and begged her for some clothes, which she didn't give me, but she did go into the toy box and threw this huge military blanket at me instead, and a bucket, in case I needed to pee."

"That's fucked up, girl . . .What the hell did you take last night?"

"I know, holy shit, right? No more mollies for me."

"No more for me neither." Chloe would chuckle as she grabbed the purple bong from Allegra's bedroom end table and exited. "I'm staying organic."

The thought of Chloe's one-liners made Allegra smile as she rolled the large blanket around her body, making herself into a burrito so the hard, concrete floor would feel more comfortable beneath her bones. *At least it's warmer in this room*, she thought. Ignoring the fact that what she was rehearsing to tell Chloe when she woke up featured one, big, significant lie.

Allegra did indeed recognize the woman from her nightmare, but she couldn't tell Chloe who she was. Hell no. That would violate the NDA. Allegra had never seen her in person, but she knew her image well from Facebook and Google. She had studied every bit of that woman's face and body. Comparing every limb, lip, and breast to her own.

Comparing every dress. Every purse. Every smile.

She had slept in her bed.

She had used her toilet.

She had tried her expensive shampoo in the shower.

She had sampled her perfume and borrowed a pair of black, spike heels.

Yes, Allegra was fully aware of the woman at the center of her nightmare. Her guilty conscience, she was convinced, was the cause of this marathon hallucination.

Now if she could only wake up and make it to work by noon.

Wake up, Allegra. Wake up!

FIVE

VIOLET ENTERED the formal gallery of her townhome, tossing a set of keys into a large crystal bowl on a sculpture stand nearby. She stood at the entrance, studying each line and crevice of the twenty-foot ceilings suspended over the intricate white marble and black railing staircase, as if she were seeing it for the first time.

When Violet married Ram, this home—a wedding present from her in-laws—was so breathtaking and gigantic she was almost afraid to touch anything, a fear properly instilled by Catholic schoolteachers, who threatened the wrath of God for handling anything pretty when visiting Manhattan museums in her youth.

But over time, all new toys—big, small, expensive, or cheap—get old. They get boring. The body ignores them as the eye no longer sees it, or generates a thrill as it once did for the owner. It's the reason why wives keep getting younger, yachts keep getting bigger, planes keep getting fancier, and why one exotic car never, ever seems to be enough. After twenty-four years, Violet had also taken the beauty of this magnificent home for granted, ignoring its enormous size and grandiose splendor until the moment her husband threatened to put it on the market.

Violet walked deep into the foyer. She caught her reflection in an antique gold-leaf mirror, realizing she had been wearing a chest full of Sparkles's hair the entire walk home. While brushing off her dress, she spotted the main housekeeper, Rosa Hernandez, in the adjacent library, dressed in her usual tan-and-white uniform, with bright pink earbuds attached to an iPod.

Rosa was vacuuming, almost dancing, to the Salsa music blasting so loudly from her ears that Violet could hear it in the hallway.

"Rosa!" said Violet as she waved her hands. "Rosa, I'm home!"

But Rosa did not hear her, still dancing on the Persian rug in the library.

Violet smiled and continued walking toward the kitchen, near the back of the main floor. Her eyes scanned the staircase for her second housekeeper, Octavia Matamoros, but she suddenly remembered Octavia had left for Honduras earlier in the week to care for her elderly mother, who had been diagnosed with Stage IV colon cancer, and had less than a month to live.

As Violet entered the open-floor kitchen, she placed her fuchsia Chanel purse on the breakfast bar and headed straight for New Daddy's favorite appliance.

She swung open the double-wide, Sub Zero refrigerator that was smartly camouflaged in the wall, perfectly matching the mahogany wood cabinets behind it. The interior was spotless with barely any food, just the way Violet liked it, disgusted by her mother's habit of cramming items to the edges that always resulted in spoilage and gluttony. New Daddy was half Italian and insisted Violet's mother keep boatloads of food on hand at all times. But Violet thought a refrigerator should look like a high-end clothing store. It should be sparse. It should be special. It should display each meat, vegetable, and fruit like it was one of a kind, because it was, unlike the discount retailers that crammed its plebian mass-manufactured merchandise wall-to-wall.

Now that it was approaching three o'clock in the afternoon, Violet was famished but had already decided she was saving her remaining calories for dinner. She reached into the easy-access door and removed a large bottle of Smart Water. When she finished drinking it, she placed the empty bottle next to her commercial, four-figure VitaMix blender and opened the door to the adjoining walk-in pantry.

Unlike the refrigerator, the pantry was stacked floor to ceiling with package foods, like a mini *Bodega*, with boxes and bags of cereal, cookies, chips, dips, and more. While in there, she grabbed a package of double-stuffed Oreo cookies and a warm bottle of Coca-Cola—items she would never let Ram keep inside the kitchen, which was completely off limits to his terrible eating habits.

An ominous steel door with a lighted keypad was at the other end of the pantry.

Violet punched in her eight-digit code to gain access. It was easy to remember, perhaps too easy for anyone to figure out in case there was ever a break-in. She punched in 05-16-1994— her wedding date, and perhaps the happiest day of her life. It was the day she considered her official anniversary—the beautiful, romantic Monday morning she and her husband quietly eloped to New York City Hall before their big Catholic wedding ceremony at St. Patrick's Cathedral, and Loeb Central Park Boathouse reception, held only twelve days later.

Violet proceeded down a short staircase to arrive at the second steel door requiring a code. This date, however, would be much harder for an intruder to guess. She slowly touched the pad, keying each glowing number with faithful reverence: 03-15-2007.

Another date Violet would never forget, for it was the day she found her daughter, Briar Rose, permanently sleeping in her bassinet. A day she would give anything to forget.

The lock buzzed as the small light above the keypad turned green.

As Violet passed through the second door, she climbed down a final set of steep stairs, into a large, windowless room that looked like the inside of a submarine. It had walls lined with custom-fitted, industrial steel cabinets and a dark gray, finished concrete floor slightly angled inwards toward the small, silver drain in the center. To the upper left was a butcher-block, six-person dining room table and an open kitchenette with a sink, microwave, and stove. In the lower left corner stood a king-size bed, and a large-screen TV and DVD player. At the end of the stairs was a plain door leading to a shower/bathroom combo. To the right were two more ominous steel doors requiring codes: one that guarded the walk-in refrigerator and the other, its twin walk-in freezer.

One of the large cabinet doors was slightly ajar and revealed hidden shelves filled with canned foods of all sizes—beans, relish, corn, peas, spinach, chicken, tuna, and Spam. Next to it were a dozen, fifty-gallon plastic drums, stacked three rows high to the ceiling, marked DRINKING WATER. And beside it, stood a plain, rectangular wooden box, the kind often found in attics to store old toys or family heirlooms.

Violet always thought spending time in the basement (or *safe room*, as Ram called it) was like living inside of Costco. It was a doomsday shelter he created in the months following September 11th, when three of his best friends were among the six-hundred and fifty-eight employees at Cantor-Fitzgerald who perished in the terrorist attack, while Ram was in Hong Kong inking a new joint venture deal for the investment firm.

Near the white bathroom door stood a defunct, black cast-iron radiator, which was out of sync with the rest of the room, but remained bolted to the floor because Ram could not bring himself to remove it during renovations. It was a rare, antique piece of art, with painted gold leaves on top of its black metal exterior; an important part of his early memories growing up as an only child in that glorious home.

As Violet quietly stepped off the staircase, Allegra lay sleeping on the floor, still chained to the extravagant radiator above her, wrapped in the army blanket like a banana in a plantain leaf. She was sound asleep, lightly snoring, exhausted and drained from the unspeakable event that took place the evening before.

Violet gingerly approached her with Oreos and Coca-Cola in hand. She stood over Allegra's head, wearing the same platform shoes she had worn several hours earlier, when she dragged Allegra's paralyzed body from the walk-in refrigerator ten yards away.

Violet inched closer to Allegra, crouching down to wake her gently, when she spotted an open drawer in the kitchenette nearby.

Wait, I didn't—

At that very moment, Allegra sprang from beneath the blanket, plunging a steak knife into Violet's left foot, recoiling as the knife slipped from her sweaty grip.

She then dashed up the stairs, naked and free from the dog collar, hammering the steel security door, screaming for help. "Help me! Somebody, help! Get me outta here!"

Violet lifted her foot, barely feeling the shallow stab wound. She quickly took note of the minimal blood, and began removing her shoes one by one.

Allegra frantically moved from pounding the door to yanking the large steel pull as she screamed incessantly for help.

But the door did not move.

After a pause, she noticed the lighted keypad on the right and screamed louder, hoping her voice would go where her body could not. "Help!" she yelled in a screeching, high-pitched tone. "Somebody, help me!"

Violet gawked at Allegra's large, round, bare ass that jiggled as she struggled with the door. But to her dismay, not an ounce of cellulite could be found.

Allegra's infinity tattoo crowned the pale outline of a thong bikini bottom, confirming Violet's theory of how tramp stamps and tan lines speak volumes about one's character. But from the back, it was Allegra's gorgeous, naturally red hair that deserved all the attention. Waist-length, thick and glossy—it was hair so amazing, it made extensions jealous.

"No one can hear you scream," said Violet in a condescending voice.

"Fuck you! Let me out of here! I want to go home!"

"The entire room is soundproof," said Violet as she gestured her arms like one of Barker's Beauties from *The Price is Right.* "Behind all these steel cabinets are massive lead walls designed to keep out nuclear radiation. So unfortunately, no one can hear you scream. Not even if one pressed one's ear against that door."

Allegra slowly turned around. Her blunt bangs and innocent face conveyed the expression of a remorseful child. "What do you want with me?" She used one hand to cover her vaginal area, and the other to cover her large, natural breasts. With her tiny waist and flowing red hair, she looked like a stage reenactment of Botticelli's *Birth of Venus* painting.

Violet scoffed. "Don't even bother trying to cover yourself. I've already seen every inch of you. And you're not that special, I can tell you that."

Allegra bit her lip. "Why am I here?"

Violet was surprised. "Do you remember anything from last night?"

Allegra shook her head.

Violet opened her squinty eyes wider. "Not one thing?"

"No."

"What's the last thing you remember?"

Allegra looked around the room, trying hard to recall the evening before. "I was, like, on my way to Carl Schurz Park . . . That's the last thing I remember."

"*Amazing*," said Violet under her breath.

"My head hurts like hell. I don't even know where the fuck I am!"

"But you do know *who* I am, don't you?"

Allegra's eyes turned downward. "No."

"Then why haven't you asked me my name?"

"I'm sorry. I mean, like, I don't know who you are. What is your name?"

Violet scratched her head aggressively. "All of you damn millennials are full of shit. You know *exactly* who I am!"

"No, I don't! You must have the wrong person!"

"Please, Allegra. Spare me the amnesia routine."

Allegra spoke softly. "Where am I? Who... Who are you?"

Violet angled back, hand on hip. "My name is Mrs. Balthazar Edward Ramspeck, III. You're at my home, 13 East 78th Street."

Allegra gasped.

"I thought you would recognize the address. Welcome back."

"Why are you keeping me here? I haven't done anything—"

"I just want to talk."

Allegra's baby-doll, pea-green eyes filled with determination. "I can't stay here. I want to find my clothes and go home."

"Not until you tell me what I need to know."

Allegra grabbed the stair railing tightly. "You can't, like, just keep me here! Kidnapping is illegal. People will start looking for me!"

"I'm sure they will."

"I mean, people go to jail for this!"

Violet chuckled. "*Yes,* obviously."

Allegra tried to hide her distress, knowing a person without fear of punishment is more dangerous than a pack of rabid wolves. "What are you gonna do to me?" She looked at the steak knife lying on the floor.

"Hmmm . . . Let's see." Violet bent over and picked up the knife. "How about you come down here and we'll discuss it."

Allegra toughened her stance. "You know, I could totally kill you with my bare hands if I wanted to. My brother was almost a Navy Seal. He taught me everything."

Violet erupted in laughter. It was a laugh so forced and inauthentic, she sounded like a Disney animated villainess. "Really? Did he also teach you how to break the combination of a Rutger-Boone nuclear power plant grade steel door so you can escape after I'm dead?"

In that instant, Allegra's hopes melted.

"There are two doors on the way up. Each one with a different code."

Allegra's eyes hit the floor.

"What was that, little girl? *No?* I didn't think so."

Allegra bowed her head.

"I am one of only two people in the world who knows the codes to get in or out of here. More importantly, I'm the only person *in this room* who knows the codes, so it would be in your best interest to *not* piss me off any more than you already have."

Allegra slowly descended the stairs.

"That's right. Move it, little chick-chick . . . Come back to your pen."

"I want my clothes."

Petite and barefoot, Violet greeted Allegra at the landing.

Wide-shouldered and voluptuous, Allegra towered over her by six inches.

Violet's squinty, amber eyes stared at Allegra's large, natural breasts. "I know you think you're more desirable than me." She looked down Allegra's soft, naked body. "I know you think you're sexier than me, prettier than me, and wiser than me. But *you're not.*"

Allegra felt Violet's anger like a sound wave blasting through rock.

"Because if you were, I would be the one chained up in your basement, not the other way around." A spray of spittle fell onto Allegra's cowering face. "Consider this your one and only act of mercy. . . You, insignificant, *basic bitch.*"

Allegra rolled her eyes and shrugged defiantly.

Violet exploded. "Don't ever fuck with me again! Do you hear me!"

Allegra reacted. "Okay."

"Do you understand?"

Allegra nodded *yes.*

Violet wiped the blood off the steak knife onto her dress and held it up in the air. "Apparently, I'll need to do a better job at locking shit up, won't I?" She walked over to the kitchenette and replaced the knife in a drawer.

"I promise, I won't be any more trouble," Allegra mumbled, realizing it was her only chance at survival.

"Why should I believe you?" asked Violet from the kitchenette.

"I know why I'm here."

Violet turned.

"This is about Ram, isn't it?"

Violet threw her head back in sarcasm. "Finally, a girl remembers."

Allegra wiped her bangs sideways. "Ram and I are only good friends. *I swear*, I mean, I won't ever speak to him again. I don't want anything to do with—"

Violet rushed into Allegra's face and started screaming. "No, you're dead wrong! Allegra Renee Adams, born February twenty-fifth in Albuquerque, New Mexico, at three thirteen in the afternoon! This has *nothing* to do with my husband!" She spit as she yelled, standing inches from her face. "This has everything to do with you, and your sinister plan to break up a happy marriage, all in the name of greed!"

"But I—"

"I don't want to hear it!" she exploded, trembling as she screamed.

Allegra was terrified. She finally looked deep into Violet's half-shut eyes, suddenly realizing her captor was severely mentally ill.

She fought the urge to tell Violet how wrong she was. She never cared about the money. It was Ram—the warm, loving, generous, smart, incredible lover—who had won her heart over.

Violet picked up the dog collar from the floor and inspected it. Regrettably, she had left the tiny key in the small Masterlock in the back of the device.

Once again, Violet placed the collar around her prisoner's neck, but this time, she turned the key tightly and removed it. "This stays with me," she said, dangling the key in front of Allegra's nose.

The steel chain between the collar and radiator was long enough for Allegra to move freely in a three-foot circumference, but was too short to reach the stairs, or more importantly, the toilet, only a few more feet away.

Violet kicked the orange Home Depot bucket closer to Allegra. "That's all you'll get for now." Feces and urine splashed at the bottom of the bucket, filling the air with a pungent aroma.

Allegra sat down on the floor and buried her face into her knees.

Violet grabbed the blanket. "And for that little stunt, I'm taking this back."

"Come on! Please don't! That's all I have!"

Violet ignored Allegra's whining. She snatched her platform shoes from the ground, and limped back up the stairs.

At the top of the landing, Violet keyed in the code, using her body to shield the numbers from Allegra's view, and opened the heavy door. "Maybe next time, you'll think twice about fucking somebody else's husband," she said with poetic flair.

The door slammed shut.

The room was now completely silent, except for the low whirring sound of the electronic lock resetting itself. After six long seconds of silence, Allegra let out a large cry.

She finally realized this was definitely not a dream . . .

And that only *one* of her two biggest secrets had been discovered.

SIX

TWENTY-FIVE-YEAR-OLD Chloe Sinclair scrolled through
her phone in the crowded waiting area of the Nineteenth Precinct, located on East 67th between Second and Third Avenues.
She was wearing a pair of cut-off jeans too short to display
in public, and a yellow tank top that brightly contrasted her
brown skin and light green eyes.

"Sinclair!" announced a female police officer. Her platinum *Flock of Seagulls* hairstyle gave away her age.

"Yes, that's me."

The policewoman refused to smile. "Officer Martinelli will
see you now."

A uniformed policeman with cartoonish large ears sat at
a wooden desk across from Chloe. The cavernous room was
filled with other officers taking reports from civilians.

Chloe could barely hear herself think against the chatter.

The officer shuffled papers on his desk. "Okay, I read your statement. Looks like your roommate didn't come home last night. Correct?"

"Right, she didn't come home last night, or anytime today. She didn't even call out of work, which is really bothering me because Saturday is her biggest day for tips. Like, she never, ever, misses the weekend. Even her boss said I should come here and talk to you guys."

"Is this unusual behavior for . . . " His eyes searched the paper.

"Allegra."

"Here it is. Allegra Adams, twenty-three. Do you have a recent picture of her?"

Chloe handed him her phone.

"Do you have a printed photo of her?"

Chloe shook her head, as if she'd never seen a photo on paper before.

The officer looked down to the screen. It was a photo of Chloe and Allegra in bikinis at Coney Island.

"That was taken last month," Chloe told him.

He leaned on one elbow as he passed the phone back to her. "Now, I need you to be honest with me or we're all going to waste a lot of time here."

Chloe was intimidated by his tough persona. "Yes?"

"Does your friend have a habit of doing this?" he asked with attitude.

"Of doing what, exactly?"

"Staying out all night. With men. From Tinder, Grinder, Finder—whatever you kids are using these days."

Chloe puckered her lips. "Well, Allegra isn't *really* my friend, like in a BFF sort of way. We really aren't that close. She's more like, just my roommate and sometimes we hang out. I mean, she's a really nice person, maybe *too nice,* actually—we didn't fight or anything, we just weren't buddy-buddy, you feel me?"

"That's not what I asked you."

"Right, well, Allegra does go out with guys, and sometimes stays overnight, but this time was way different. It was totally weird."

"How so?"

"Usually, when she has a date with her boyfriend, she gets totally glammed up to go out with him—"

"She has a boyfriend?"

"Yes, and he's got serious bank. Probably somebody famous too, because she's never allowed to take selfies or talk about him."

Officer Martinelli grabbed a pencil. "What's his name?"

"Mr. Big."

"You mean from the show?"

"Yes."

"You mean Chris Nolan, the actor who lives around the corner, or are you referring to the character he played?"

Chloe was embarrassed. She forgot how many famous people lived in the neighborhood. "Well, I mean the character. Because that's what Allegra called him. She loved pretending to be like Carrie Bradshaw living in the city. She isn't creative, by any means."

"I can see that." The officer scratched his head. "Do you know what Mr. Big looks like? Any pictures on her phone?"

Chloe slumped her shoulders. "No, he didn't allow Allegra to take pictures of him."

Officer Martinelli raised an eyebrow. "Is this guy even real?"

"Well, she always has tons of cash now after being, like, dead broke for months, and she showed me a ruby necklace he bought her for her birthday. I think it was from Cartier? It looked real to me."

"Okay. Go on."

"So, over the last three days she's been, like, totally depressed. Something was really getting her down. I think she may have been fighting with him or something."

"She didn't share any details with you?"

"No. Allegra is, like, super private about stuff."

"Okay."

"But then last night, at about five thirty, she was getting ready to go running at Carl Schurz Park when she got this weird call on her cell. Something about it made her *really happy*. I asked what was going on, and all she said is that it was really good news."

"Then what?"

"Like usual, she just grabbed her headphones and rushed out the door without saying goodbye to me."

"And you think Mr. Big was the one who called her?"

"I don't know, probably. Can't you look up her phone records and see who called her around five thirty?"

"Yes, I could, if we had reason to suspect she was missing. But right now, I think we need to give it a little more time."

Chloe was disappointed. "Why? She missed work. She's not answering my texts. Something's wrong."

"Tell me, Miss Sinclair, the last few times she disappeared with Mr. Big, what did she say to you when she got back to the apartment? Where did they go?"

"Uh, well, last time he took her on a private jet to Miami for dinner."

"For dinner?"

"Yes."

"A three-hour flight just to eat Cuban food?"

"Yeah, something like that."

"Well, that seals it for me." Officer Martinelli put his pencil down. "Look, this happens all the time. Young, good-looking women meet old rich guys at the high-end hotel bars, then go halfway around the world on the spur of the moment and forget to bring their phone chargers. They can't even call their roommates to let them know where they are because nobody memorizes numbers anymore."

"I get that, but—"

"If you still haven't heard from her in seventy-two hours, come back and file a report. In the meantime, call her parents and let them know not to worry. Where do they live?"

"I don't know—they're, like, both dead."

"Great, even better. No need to worry anyone at this point." Officer Martinelli stood up. "Have a wonderful day, Miss Sinclair."

Chloe rose from her seat feeling like she had been scolded. "Thank you, Officer."

"Thank you for being a concerned citizen." He smiled as he pointed to the exit in the distance. "And, remember, if you see something, say something." He leaned over the desk and whispered, "Sorry, we have to close every interview with that statement now."

"Sure . . . Totally get it.

SEVEN

AN ULTRA-CURVY, middle-aged woman with equally big, over-processed hair, stood on the top step of 13 East 78th Street. She was wearing a professional blouse and miniskirt too tight for her figure, fidgeting with Food Emporium shopping bags filled with cheap champagne and orange juice.

Standing next to her was a younger brunette, dressed in a similar silhouette with hair swept up in a bun. She was calm and graceful, balancing an enormous wrapped tray of sandwiches that would topple any other lady her size.

They walked through the open, crescent-shaped, cast-iron gate until they reached the front door of the neo-classical townhome.

The eighties blonde grabbed the brass lion knocker and whacked it with gusto. "Remind me when we get back to the office to order a lock box for this listing." Her *Lawn Guyland* accent floated above her words like a cheap ocean breeze from Vinnie's Seaside Restaurant and Bail Bonds.

"Will do," replied the brunette.

Rosa answered the door in her maid's uniform, and hot pink earbuds permanently affixed to her square head. "May I help you?"

"Good morning. You must be the housekeeper?"

Rosa returned a look that said, *no shit.*

"Super. I'm Penny Slovaski, and this is my assistant, Laura Welch. We're from Sotheby's International Realty."

"Oh, yes, the house call is today," replied Rosa in a more welcoming tone. "Mr. Ramspeck mentioned this to me on the phone. Please, come in."

Inside the kitchen, Penny and Laura worked feverishly to set up for the Open House.

Penny poured a mix of Cook's champagne and orange juice into champagne flutes, placing each mimosa onto the black granite island in the middle of the floor.

"Pssst. Laura. Did you see this blender?" She pointed to the stainless steel VitaMix on the counter that was twice the size of a normal blender.

"Yes, I caught that. I have one of the cheaper ones at home. Cost me a week's pay, but I would marry it if I could," she replied, while building a Coliseum of tiny sandwiches from Dean & DeLuca on the breakfast bar. "I don't think I could survive this city without juicing at least three times a week."

Penny popped the cork off another bottle of champagne, wincing so quickly that her over-sprayed hair almost moved. "Did you see the Austof-Reed knives too?"

"Oh, no, where?"

"Right next to the blender. Aren't those things almost three grand a piece?"

Laura stopped her catering duties and walked over to a gleaming set of knives housed in an enormous black wooden block. She pulled out an eight-inch meat cleaver with a blade so luxurious, it sparkled in the overhead spotlights. "Now why would a New Yorker even *need* this? I use my kitchen to store office supplies."

"I know, right?"

Laura carefully replaced the blade in the block and returned to her sandwich display. "I would be shocked if anyone shows up today."

"Well, anyone with twenty-five million to spend on a house is in the Hamptons today."

Laura paused. "So why are we doing this now? Shouldn't we wait until September?"

"Trust me, the seller is *extremely* motivated. I can't risk losing an eight-hundred-thousand-dollar commission by sitting on my tush and doing nothing all August," replied Penny before taking a swig straight from the champagne bottle. "How's the media campaign going?"

"I've already booked space in *The Times*, *The Post*, *USA Today*, *Forbes*, Zillow and Trulia. The ads should keep running through the end of the month."

"Good. I really want to 'wow' this client."

"Any special reason, single lady?" Laura grinned.

"Well, he *is* kind of cute," replied Penny. "And about to be single," she whispered like a bona fide yenta.

"What does he look like?"

Penny turned to the sky like a lovesick teen. "Well, I only met him a week ago—right here as a matter of fact, to sign the listing agreement—but even so, he was incredibly charming and magnetic. Like a comic book character."

Laura smiled. "Which character?"

"Uh, what's his name. The sexy, bald guy in a business suit who runs the world?"

"*The Hitman*?"

"No. He's from *Superman,* I think."

"Lex Luther?"

"Yes! That's it. That's who he reminds me of." She motioned a high-five mid-air. "Lex Luther from *Superman*. Thank you."

"Too bad, I prefer men with hair."

"No, I do too, but this bald shtick looks *great* on him. He's very tall, like six-four, with pretty blue eyes. And he wears these seriously nerdy, black-rimmed glasses, like he's trying to downplay his hunkiness. Oh, and I can tell he lifts weights too because his chest was practically bulging under his dress shirt."

Penny let out a deep sigh.

"I think you need to get out more."

Penny snorted. "Ha! I think you're right."

"So why is he selling?"

Penny looked around the corner to see if Rosa was within listening distance. "I can only tell you in confidence, of course, because he swore me to secrecy." She leaned over the island and spoke in a loud whisper. "His wife left him. They're getting a divorce after twenty-four years together."

"Sweet."

"Hey, I know divorce sucks, but if people didn't do it, I wouldn't have a job."

"Agreed." Laura stole one of the mini-sandwiches. "So, do you need my help finding a bachelor pad? Fifth and 57th is giving out new BMWs with every signed contract?"

"No, I wish." Penny leaned over again. "I would kill for a double commission, but sadly, he's moving out of the country—which is also confidential, I might add." Penny lowered her voice to the point of miming. "The house staff doesn't know they're out of a job soon."

"Where's he going?"

Penny cupped her hand around her mouth, whispering louder than most people speak. "Scotland."

Laura's eyes lit up. "I bet he's looking at castles."

"Oooh, I never thought of that. Castles are nice."

"Yes, very nice."

"But how long is his second-wife waiting list?" Penny burst out laughing and returned to a normal speaking volume. "I promise I'll introduce you, but only after the closing."

"Deal."

Rosa entered the kitchen with three young men dressed in impeccable black suits, with beads of sweat hanging from their brows. They were all in their late twenties with light eyes and slicked-back hair—looking eerily similar to one another, although not close enough to be related. The only thing that differed among these three little pigs were the color of their ties: mint, yellow, and pink from left to right.

"Sorry if we're too early," said the pink tie. "We're from Coldwell Banker."

"It's never too early to sell a house," joked Penny. "Mimosas?"

"Yes, thank you," they said in unison, each one reaching for a champagne flute on the granite island.

"Previewing for clients, I assume?"

The mint tie reached for a sandwich and ate while Penny spoke.

"Absolutely," replied the yellow tie.

"Do you have any buyers in mind, or are you gents just looking?"

"We all have buyers in the market right now at this price range," said the pink tie.

"I have two," said the mint tie, while chewing.

A gleam struck Penny's eye. "Super. Please sign in and I'll show you around."

———

After thirty-two years in real estate, Penny Slovaski felt like a leper around younger, more aggressive Manhattan-bred brokers who built client lists overnight by soliciting their parents' tennis partners. But unlike the robotic Stepford realtors multiplying across town, she was a hard worker. *A closer.* The kind of person who would stop their Maserati in traffic to pick up a dollar bill on the side of the road, and she had the investment portfolio to show for it.

As the Sicilian and Jewish daughter of two wedding cake bakers from the South Shore of Long Island, Penny joked about "not acquiring the soft edges" that typically emerge for the newly prospered. She never married, and earned lots of money—an average of two to three million a year in commissions—but failed to harvest an ounce of class to match it. And no matter how many online etiquette courses she completed, Penny simply could not hide the fact she was not born into wealth. And for everyone who knew and loved her, somehow, it was okay.

"We're almost there," huffed Penny as she hiked up the staircase in her sausage-wrap skirt.

"Let's take the elevator on the way down," said the yellow tie.

"Yes, please," said the pink tie.

"Penny, why is this priced so aggressively? Twenty-five million seems way below market value for a townhome this large," asked the mint tie.

"I think you'll see why in a moment," she replied.

Penny and the brokers finally exited the grand staircase and arrived at the open, double door entrance to the master suite occupying the entire seventh floor.

Inside, the room was spacious, and unexpectedly decorated in dark shades of green, brown, and red. The focal point was a massive chandelier adorned with handmade, blood-red glass roses. Directly behind it, stood a row of heavy, dark brown silk curtains that led to an outdoor terrace bejeweled with hundreds of red, orange, and yellow potted flowers, as well as a phenomenal view of Central Park.

The furniture was dark rosewood carved in the fashion of Louis XVIII, including a carved, roll-top writing desk, and an armoire that cleverly hid a seventy-five-inch flat screen television inside. The walls were adorned with old English paintings of scenes from *Little Red Riding Hood*, but the pièce de résistance was what occupied the entire right side of the room.

There stood a double king-size bed fit for royalty, canopied in red and green curtains, hosted by four enormous tree-trunk bedposts with bare branches that appeared to hold up the painted open sky.

"Wow," said the pink tie. "Straight out of a nightmare fairy tale."

"Husband didn't have much of a say here," muttered the yellow tie. "This is definitely the work of the Big Bad Wife."

"Borderline creepy, but okay," said the mint tie. "The asking price makes sense now."

"It's the most creative room in the house, although not very modern," said Penny as she walked over to the terrace. "Now you see why we decided to leave out pictures of this room online. I'm sure the new owner will tear out everything anyway."

"That bed is spectacular. Is any of the furniture for sale?" asked the pink tie.

"All of it is, except the artwork and sculptures."

"The new owner will *definitely* need custom linens made," added the yellow tie. "Can't find sheets at Nordstrom's for that monstrosity."

"Better yet, come and see this," Penny led the brokers through the room.

The men followed her outside into the blistering heat, bracing for the direct sun setting early in the sky.

"Shit. I forgot my sunglasses in the Uber," said the yellow tie.

"Bummer, those were limited edition," said the pink tie.

Penny picked a flower from the garden. "A beautiful reminder that Central Park is literally in your backyard."

"I wish it were facing west, but it's still enchanting," said the mint tie.

"What's the square footage for the terrace?" asked the yellow tie.

"Fourteen hundred."

"What about the closets? The client I have in mind is very particular about going larger," said the mint tie.

"Understandable." Penny maneuvered around the brokers as she made her way back into the cool, air-conditioned room. "There's a traditional walk-in closet for him, but for her . . ." She smirked. "Wait until you see this."

Penny approached the carved wood archway that led to a feminine space featuring a circular, red velvet sofa in the middle, and an open case displaying Violet's prized collection of eighty-two antique porcelain dolls, all dressed as *Little Red Riding Hood*.

As the pink tie entered the room, he was jolted by the collective stare of the doll collection. "*Damn!*" He covered his heart. "Why do people even collect those things?"

"I hate dolls," said the mint tie.

"Clowns are worse."

In jest, the yellow tie hissed and crossed his index fingers like a GQ vampire slayer. "I command thee to go back! Go back to your toy factory, evil ones!" He cried out, mocking his colleagues' fears while the others inspected the room.

All but two of the Little Red Riding Hoods were more than a hundred years old, in various sizes with different hair colors, but one doll in particular caught the yellow tie's attention.

This doll was slightly older and larger than the others, sitting neatly in her red cape and plaid dress near the center of the display, with golden hair gracing her round, aging face. Her large blue eyes were the kind that fluttered and moved when you grabbed her, and as the yellow tie moved closer, she appeared to stare right through his soul.

As he leaned in toward her, his heart began racing—moving so closely his breath could be felt upon her delicate, alabaster skin.

"Creepy little girl," he whispered, nose to nose.

The doll winked in reply.

Holy shit!

He jumped backwards.

The doll slowly closed her eyes, then reopened them.

Her painted red lips curled upwards in a quarter-smile.

"I'm done here—Let's go," he said in a strong voice.

The others ignored him.

Penny gestured her hand. "As you can see, this dressing area offers plenty of room for the mistress of the house to get ready."

"It's beautiful," said the pink tie.

"I'm serious, let's go."

"And this is just the appetizer. Wait until you see the main closet." Penny lowered her voice as she approached the closed door. "There's enough storage for seven hundred shoes."

"Now we're talking," said the mint tie.

Penny reached for the shiny brass knob, turning it vigorously. Nothing happened.

"It's locked?" asked the pink tie.

Awkward silence.

The yellow tie looked over at the doll. She was no longer smiling.

"I guess it's locked, or off limits . . . or maybe both." Penny made a silly face. "I saw it last Friday when I previewed the home, so I know it's amazing." She yanked the knob one last time. "Sorry, Gentlemen. I'll send you photos."

The yellow tie now had zero interest in the home. He was thunderstruck, still processing how a doll could have communicated with him like that. But he refused to leave the group tour, too scared to walk down the staircase alone.

"Given the bedroom, we're sure the closet is outrageous," said the pink tie.

"Thank you for understanding." Penny masked her embarrassment. "How about we finish previewing the rest of the home?"

Thirty minutes later, Penny and the brokers returned to the kitchen.

"So like I said, there's lots of potential with this property. Most of the renovations have been done on the lower floors, but the upper floors need a professional decorator from this century, if you know what I mean."

"I agree. Beautiful place," said the pink tie.

"Reminds me of Caesar's Palace on acid," said the yellow tie, trying to remain in the conversation.

"Well, it definitely needs updating, but that will be reflected in my client's offer," added the mint tie.

Penny silently bounced for joy. "Super."

"And it's never been on the market before?"

"No, the same family has owned it for the past eighty-nine years."

"Impressive. My buyer will love that," he said, pleased with what he had seen thus far. And for twenty-five million, he knew there was plenty of leeway in his client's budget to renovate and redecorate as much as she desired.

"So, does anyone have any final questions?" asked Penny.

"I want to see the safe room Richard keeps telling me about," the pink tie requested. "The MLS said it's designed to withstand any sort of attack?"

"Yes, it's been certified as a level five shelter for all natural and man-made disasters—except for flooding, I believe—plus it comes with three years' worth of food and supplies."

"Nice selling point," said the mint tie. "I'm surprised we don't have more in Manhattan."

Laura, who had been near the front door waiting for buyers, returned to the kitchen.

"Has anyone else come through?" asked Penny.

"No, not yet. It's quiet."

"Good. Can you stick around while we check out the basement?"

"Sure."

"I'll stay here with Laura," said the yellow tie. Still uneasy, he reached for a mimosa on the granite island and drank it down in two large gulps.

Penny grabbed her notebook from the counter and led the two other brokers to the pantry door. "The owner is out of town, so I haven't seen this yet. Fortunately, he gave me the codes last night."

"Classic," said the mint tie. "I love secret rooms."

Penny and the brokers marched through the food utopia, enjoying the sweet and salty smells of lipo-worthy junk food in the air.

"Oooh, I smell Oreos," said Penny.

"I feel like James Bond in a Frito Lay factory," joked the pink tie.

"You look like him too," said the mint tie.

When they arrived at the first steel door, Penny ruffled through her notebook, searching for the code. "I wish I had my glasses. I can't even read my own handwriting anymore." She struggled to see her notes. "Okay, here it is."

She touched the lighted keypad and entered the numbers as she referenced back and forth to her notebook. As soon as she was finished, the low whirring sound of the lock opening pleased her. "First try, Gentlemen."

She grabbed the large steel handle and pushed the heavy door open. There, in front of them, was a corridor with another set of dark steps, and a second security door twenty feet below.

"Double door entry? Very cool," said the mint tie.

"Why did they make stairs so steep back in 1903? It's a hazard, I tell you," said the pink tie.

"Because there weren't any personal injury lawyers," joked the mint tie.

The corridor leading to the safe room was dark and lifeless, like a torch-lit hallway in a medieval castle. It was cold. Mildly freezing. With only two dim, yellow emergency lights highlighting the path below. As they stepped forward, they looked at one another, barely able to decipher each other's bodily features. Suddenly, the door behind them closed automatically. The soft buzzing sound of the lock resetting pierced through the silence of the corridor.

"This is disturbing," said the pink tie.

"What New York basement *isn't* disturbing?" replied the mint tie.

"Oh, we'll be fine," assured Penny. "I've seen hundreds of these secret passages in my career. Wealthy people have so many skeletons to hide."

BANG!

They all jumped.

"What was that?" asked the mint tie. "It sounded like it came from the safe room."

"I thought the doors were soundproof?"

"They are," replied Penny. "I have no idea what that was."

"I'm not scared," said the pink tie, sarcastically.

"No one else is down here," added Penny. "Let's move forward."

They continued descending the steep staircase, grabbing on to one another's shoulder given the low lighting. Finally, they arrived at the second steel security door.

"Let's just peek our heads in there and leave," said the pink tie.

"Why is it so damn cold? Is it supposed to be this way?"

Penny ignored the question. "Just a minute here." She looked at the notebook again, straining to see the pages in the poor light. "I can't see the numbers."

"What if it's Ratzilla making that noise?" asked the pink tie, fully aware that well-fed rats living in isolation could grow as large as small poodles. "Let's go back. I'm freezing."

"No, I really want to see this," said the mint tie. "It will only take a few seconds."

Penny finally began keying the numbers into the lighted pad. She waited for the red light to turn green.

Nothing happened.

"Can you see your notes?" asked the mint tie.

"No, not really. Can you try it?" She handed him the notebook.

The mint tie repeated the numbers as he entered them.

He waited a moment, then pushed the handle.

The door did not move.

"Maybe I was off by one number," he said as he looked between Penny's notebook and the keypad. "I'll do it again."

The mint tie keyed in the code.

He waited.

He pushed.

Nothing.

The pink tie shrugged his shoulders. "Let's go back."

Penny knew the mint tie's client wouldn't formally make an offer unless he saw every inch of the house. "No, let's try one last time," she said as she switched places with the mint tie and entered the code once again.

Penny slouched her shoulders in discontent. "Nothing."

Simultaneously, all three realtors looked back up the stairs at the security door leading to the pantry, taking note of the lighted keypad beside it.

"Wait. We need a code *to get out*?" asked the mint tie.

"You're kidding," said the pink tie.

"Hey, I'm sure it's the same combination for both sides," reassured Penny. "Besides, if we get stuck, they know we're down here. Laura will notice we're missing."

"Does she have the code?" asked the mint tie. "Otherwise, she can't get in."

Penny hid her anxiety. "No, she doesn't, but let's try it first, before we start worrying."

The pink tie was now at the front of the line and led the others back up the stairs. They quickened their pace, hurrying in the dark to the first landing.

Penny passed her notebook up the line.

"Is this the only combination he gave you?" asked the pink tie.

"Yes."

He slowly pushed the numbers on the pad, then grabbed the door handle . . .

And shoved it—bouncing back from the effort.

"You have to pull the handle. Not push it," said the mint tie. "The door swings this way."

The pink tie followed his directions, pulling the steel piece with his body weight.

Nothing happened. "I think it may be a different code to get out, Penny."

"This is ridiculous," grumbled the mint tie. He reached inside his pocket and pulled out a cell phone. "Of course, no service down here. *Puurfect.*"

Penny concealed her growing concern. "How about we—"

SNAP!

Pitch-black darkness. The emergency lights went out.

"Jesus Christ!"

The pink tie began banging on the door. "Doug! Are you there? Can you open the door?"

The others called out behind him. "Laura! Can you hear us?"

"Doug, we're stuck in here!"

The pink tie thrusted his large fist as hard as he could. "Doug!" he called out sternly. "Open this door!"

Twenty seconds had passed . . . No one came.

The three felt for one another in the dark as they tried to remain calm.

"I need a drink," said the mint tie.

"I need a new career," said the pink tie.

Penny was resolute she wouldn't let this fiasco jeopardize the mint tie's offer. She closed her eyes and channeled maternal energy as she whispered in the dark. "Let's try not panic. They'll notice we're missing soon. We'll all be fine."

The mint tie untucked his dress shirt in preparation for a substantial stay. "How long do you think it will take the Fire Department to break down this door?"

"I have no idea," said Penny softly.

After a good five minutes of meaningless conversation, Penny and the two brokers carefully arranged themselves on the top of the stairs, each finding a spot to sit while the darkness enveloped them.

"I would kill for a scotch right now," said the mint tie.

"Me too," added Penny.

"You know what's funny? I enjoyed the dark as a child," admitted the pink tie. "Yet here I sit with my eyes closed, fearing how long this will take."

"I'm sorry, guys, this is all my fault. I promise I'll make it up to you," said Penny.

Suddenly, the low whirring sound of the lock opening filled the air.

"Hallelujah," exclaimed the pink tie. Still closest to the door, he rose quickly and felt for the handle.

The whirring sound continued to buzz through the air for five long seconds, like a taunting bell of freedom barely within reach.

The light turned green.

"Open it!" yelled Penny.

The pink tie pulled the steel handle with all his might.

The door opened.

Strangely, no one was on the other side. Just the warm, delicious shining light of the snack-infested pantry.

"Thank God!" shouted Penny.

"That doesn't make any sense," said the pink tie.

As they re-entered the pantry of hope, the three shared a unified sigh of relief, straining as their eyes adjusted to the new dazzling light.

"I was stuck in an elevator once, but this was way worse," said the mint tie. "There's no 'call for help' button in a basement."

"Why would the door magically unlock like that?" asked the pink tie, still curious.

Penny quickly changed the subject. "Hey, it's okay, fellas, we made it! It was only a couple of minutes in there. Like a game. You know, when we were kids?"

Laura reacted to the frazzled group dumping into the kitchen. "Is everyone okay?"

"We were stuck between the security doors," said the mint tie.

"And then the lights went out . . . Creepy as hell, I tell you," said the pink tie.

"Agreed," said the yellow tie, munching on a sandwich.

The three basement survivors marched across the kitchen and grabbed mimosas.

Penny lightly tapped Laura's shoulder. "Please call Mr. Ramspeck and confirm those safe room codes," she said gravely. "I also need Hector to look at those security doors. I don't care what it costs to fix them."

"Sure, I'll call Hector now, but it's like three o'clock in the morning where Mr. Ramspeck is staying. Do you want me to wake him up?"

Penny was annoyed. "You know what, let's just skip showing the basement until Mr. Ramspeck returns, and we get it checked out by a professional."

"Why? What happened?"

Penny clenched her teeth in a fake Connecticut smile. "I'll fill you in later."

The pink tie snatched an open bottle of champagne, poured a glass, and downed it in one shot. "I'm sorry, but that was *way* too much for me. I'm done for the day."

Realizing this uncomfortable incident would cockblock offers from the Coldwell Banker Boys, Penny was determined to have them leave the Open House on a happy note. She turned to the audience like a well-trained game show hostess. "On that adventurous note, you all have my business card, so please call or e-mail me any time, day or night, if you have additional questions, requests, or concerns. Also, please send me any written offers ASAP. I have three more serious buyers touring the property later this afternoon, and I would love to put this listing *under contract* first thing tomorrow morning."

Laura raised her thinly tweezed eyebrow. "We have more people coming?"

Penny continued. "So, if you have a cash-buyer in mind, I cross my heart and promise I will work my seller until we get an insane deal for your client. This way we can close in thirty days, cash our fat commission checks, and move on to the next conquest." Penny looked like a bad gymnast who just nailed a dismount.

The brokers appreciated her worthless pep talk.

The yellow tie raised his glass in the air.

"Good plan . . . Hear, hear!"

EIGHT

ALLEGRA REMAINED standing, naked and chained in the basement prison, staring at the top of the stairs, hoping whoever was out there would feel her presence and come to her rescue.

She had the undeniable feeling that someone was outside that steel door, someone other than the crazy woman hell-bent on holding her captive. She didn't know *how* she knew, but she knew it as well as she knew her own skin. Perhaps her intuition had grown stronger over the last seventy-two hours—a sixth sense developing as a survival mechanism. Either way, she knew there was a liberator on the other side of that vile door.

For the past ten minutes, she had screamed and screamed for help, knowing her voice would not penetrate that door, but hoping the energy of her desperation would. She tried her best to make loud sounds, throwing the only item she could reach—the orange piss bucket—around and around, then finally lobbing it directly at the door, praying it would make a reverberation detectable by the angel standing on the other side.

The smell of the emptied contents of the bucket, putrid and foul urine and feces on the floor at her feet, made Allegra so nauseated, she vomited for a second time in her space. Now, she had shit, pee, and puke as her only companions, and reminders indeed, she was still here.

Ready to survive.

NINE

VIOLET SAT BY the brightly lit window in Dr. Cohen's office. But this time, she had remembered to apply sunscreen under her makeup, as she mindfully prepared for her afternoon appointment. She wore a tight, cobalt blue, ruffled Tom Ford dress that highlighted her protruding collarbone and perfectly sculpted arms. Her legs were crossed, proudly displaying her boney kneecaps and bright yellow YSL shoes that nearly glowed in the otherwise gloomy office.

Her seething eyes wandered to the window, focusing on a rusted, Dodge Charger illegally parked outside. She stroked Sparkles the Persian cat, zoning in and out of attention.

"So you *have* been sticking to your food plan?" asked Dr. Cohen.

"Yes."

"And you didn't skip any meals or regurgitate them?"

"No."

"Excellent." Dr. Cohen scribbled a note on his yellow legal pad.

She turned away from the vehicular eyesore. "Aren't you going to ask me how my weekend went?"

Dr. Cohen's bushy gray brows rose above his round glasses. "Certainly. How was your weekend, Violet?"

"It was terrible."

"Why? What happened?"

Violet looked outside again, focusing on the passenger side door dent that was the size of a garbage can. "A few realtors came to my home yesterday and held an Open House. Luckily, only a few people came to see it."

He sighed. "So Ram officially put your townhome on the market?"

"Apparently."

Dr. Cohen touched his chin. "Is your name on the deed?"

Violet's eyes darkened. "Nothing was ever put in my name. Everything is owned by his piece-of-shit trust fund."

Dr. Cohen flinched. He was uncomfortable with her language, believing she was still twelve years old. "And where were you during the Open House? Were you friendly to the visitors?"

Violet smiled like the Cheshire Cat as she stroked Sparkles's back. "I locked myself in my bedroom closet," she said, looking down at the cat's crystal collar. "Most of the time."

"You didn't interact with the real estate agents?"

"No, I just stayed in my closet for four hours and made sure no one wanted to buy my home."

Dr. Cohen reacted. "But, Violet. Ram has the—"

"I couldn't stand it!" she screamed.

"Violet—"

"Do you know what it feels like to have strangers in your home, Dr. Cohen? Looking at your most intimate belongings, making fun of your bed, and calling you awful, insensitive names like 'the big bad wife'—" Violet aggressively tucked her long bangs behind her ear. "—I don't want *anyone* in my home. Not yesterday. Not ever!"

Dr. Cohen shifted in his chair. "I understand, Violet, but technically, it's his decision."

"No, I'm not selling! I won't let him sign the paperwork!"

Dr. Cohen motioned his hands for Violet to calm down.

After a long session of heavy breathing, she complied.

"You must try to stay calm, Violet. Stay disciplined. You cannot control the actions of others, but you can control your own reaction."

"That's bullshit."

Dr. Cohen wrinkled his nose. "Next time there's a prospective buyer in your home, you should go outside for a walk in Central Park. It will be good for you."

"Have you been outside in the last decade? It's a hundred degrees out there. Global warming is everywhere. People are melting in Central Park *and* getting wrinkles."

"You need fresh air, Violet."

"I prefer to stay indoors."

He wrote another note on his legal pad.

Violet angled her chin in a smart-ass fashion. "Have you ever been married, Dr. Cohen?"

By now he was accustomed to her erratic change in conversational direction. "Regrettably, no," he said as he finished writing. "Why do you ask?"

"It's just . . . The end of a marriage, it's a *very* peculiar thing."

"In what way?"

Violet hesitated to answer. She turned her attention back to the clunker outside, which now had a bright orange and white parking ticket attached to the windshield.

"Go on, Violet. This is why we're here." He placed his legal pad and pen on the coffee table between them. "Why is the end of a marriage so peculiar, in your opinion?"

She turned back to Dr. Cohen. "It must be what people go through before they die on a plane crash."

He reflected. "That's an interesting analogy. Tell me more."

She shifted her athletic-ballerina body, crossing her lean legs in the opposite direction. "Sometimes I think about what it must be like right before a plane goes down."

Dr. Cohen leaned in.

"People just sitting there chewing grass like emotionless cows, having light conversations about what they'll do when they land . . . Where to eat, how long it will take to catch a cab, hoping Aunt Susie will see them outside baggage claim, laughing at the flight attendant's gigantic ass as she bends over and serves the people in the aisle across from them." Violet wiped the corner of her bright red lipstick. "They've lifted weight restrictions on flight attendants. Did you know that? They're huge now."

Dr. Cohen shook his head, disappointed. "No, I haven't noticed. I haven't flown in ages."

Violet touched the hem of her dress. "See, everyone on a plane is happy to get where they're going, even people who are on their way to see sick relatives or attend funerals, they're just glad to be surrounded by family."

"Hmm. Interesting perspective."

"Being on a big jet is pure, blissful silence." Violet straightened her posture. "All a passenger hears is the meditative hum of powerful, roaring engines whipping through the clouds between baby cries and adult snores . . . Like a sedative that easily puts patients to sleep." She leaned towards Dr. Cohen. "All is perfect and normal until . . . *BOOM!*"

She flailed her arms.

Sparkles jumped from her lap.

"A large bang immediately shifts everyone's reality. For a second, strangers stare at one another. 'What was that?' one stranger nervously asks her seatmate, as if he had more information than she did. 'It must be nothing, otherwise the captain would make an announcement,' he replies, faking a reassuring smile.

"*BOOM!*

"An unexpected hundred-foot drop.

"The strangers look at each other in panic.

"Someone screams, '*There's a hole in Row Ten!*'

"The plane drops in free fall.

"Your stomach fills your throat.

"The shrieks of hysterical women bore a hole inside you.

"The yells of small children follow the women.

"Then comes the worst of it: The men. The guttural, low-pitched howls of dozens of fathers, brothers, and sons wailing in harmony are what shut down your ability to cope.

"Men are *not* supposed to cry.

"It's a sound so disturbing—so rarely heard—your spirit will remember it for a thousand lifetimes." She caught her breath. "That's when you realize it's the end of your life and the next *unknown* phase will soon begin."

Dr. Cohen was always impressed with Violet's talent for melodramatic monologues. "All very true." He paused. "And poetic. It's perfectly normal to feel a sense of loss—even death—upon discovering an affair."

Violet was surprised. "It is?"

"Yes. We refer to it as *betrayal trauma*."

Violet had no idea psychiatry had invented an official term for being traded in for a newer model. "Really?"

"Yes, it's very similar to PTSD—post-traumatic stress disorder."

Violet shot him a look. *I'll be dammed.*

"And similar to the five stages of grief, there are seven stages to betrayal trauma: shock, denial, obsession, anger, bargaining, depression, and acceptance."

Violet was impressed. She recognized she had already experienced many of those phases and was clearly shipwrecked between anger and obsession. "That makes a great deal of sense to me."

Dr. Cohen removed his glasses. "When a person discovers evidence of betrayal by someone they love, the brain experiences a sudden loss of oxytocin—the same hormone released when mothers bond with their babies—which is why you are experiencing genuine feelings of loss and depression. And with time, your brain will adjust. You will be able to conduct your life as you had before. A new normal, so to speak."

The window-mounted air conditioner beside Violet erupted in loud banging noises.

Dr. Cohen was silent, waiting for the noises to cease.

The brief, wordless void saddened Violet.

Her eyes fell to the floor.

She began tracing the brown and beige geometric pattern in the carpet with her finger, running along its lines from her yellow shoe to the glass coffee table, around his chair, next to the overstuffed bookshelf . . .

"How did you find out about the affair?"

. . . then to the magazine table strangely placed near the door . . .

"Violet?"

"Yes?"

"Are you still with me?"

She returned to the conversation. "Can you repeat the question?"

"How did you know Ram was having an affair?"

Violet angled her head like a rooster. "I found out a little over two months ago. On June seventh, to be exact. Which was a Thursday."

"Go on."

"That morning, I met my husband in the kitchen for coffee as usual, around seven thirtyish, maybe seven forty-five, and we exchanged our plans for the day."

"What were they?"

"His plans?"

"And yours."

"Well, he was rambling on about a meeting he had later that afternoon with his internal auditors. It was something he dreaded in preparation for a merger with an Asian trading partner," she said, dragging each word like a disobedient child. "The usual."

"He is merging his trading company with a partner?"

"Yes, something along those lines. I stay out of his business affairs as much as humanly possible." She glanced outside, noticing the ugly car had left after its scolding. "His business dealings bore me to death."

"And you? What were your plans for that day?"

She inhaled deeply. "My plans were to take a ninety-minute dance cardio class with my trainer on East 84th at nine, then afterward, walk over to David Barton on Madison and meet my other trainer for floor work at eleven. My goal was to be home by twelve thirty, so I could make my Autism fundraiser meeting by two o'clock. After that, I had scheduled an early dinner at Café Boulud with my girlfriends from Pure Yoga. It was Gretel's birthday—her second birthday, really. She was celebrating her breast cancer remission."

"Typical day, I presume?"

"Yes, it was." She attempted a smile.

"So then what happened?"

"There was this moment while I was speaking and he just smiled at me, which was our little way of acknowledging our previous night of making *good* love." Her eyes fluttered. "We make love at least three times a week when he's home, keeping the passion alive with a little Viagra and Perrier Jouet before bed."

Dr. Cohen nodded his head.

"When you've been married as long as I have, it's in the small moments you know you've found the kind of enduring love that morphs from infatuation to passion to true love and back again, never getting old or stale, despite the changing times and our changing bodies. Although Ram knows I would *never* let myself go."

"I'm sure he appreciates your efforts."

"Yes, he does. I know he does. Even though he doesn't say it very often. Because what Ram and I have is a love you can count on, something you don't even question after a while. Like air, it's a love just there to breathe anytime you need it, without having to work for it, or worry that it will disappear one day. It's just there forever until one of you dies."

"Unconditional love."

"Yes."

"And do you think he has ever been unfaithful in the past?"

"I don't know. Maybe. Twenty-four years is a long time. Ram is a man like any other. He's handsome. And charming. Plus he frequently travels for business so I'm sure he's had a few unemotional dalliances here and there. Beautiful, single-serving strangers he meets in Hong Kong. Sydney. Buenos Aires. But I doubt it happens more than once every few years and it has *never once* affected how he treats me, or our marriage. Not one time."

"So, Ram continued to treat you well?"

"Yes, like gold. My friends were jealous about how easy I had it, or so they thought." She stared at her bright yellow shoes, remembering the night he bought them for her. "Ram was my Prince Charming. He had never said a negative word to me, or yelled at me, in the twenty-six years we've known each other. Not until last Thursday night, of course."

Dr. Cohen purposefully avoided talking about the night she was referring to, choosing to start at the beginning of the affair. "So, what was different about the morning of June seventh?"

Violet inhaled deeply. "It was getting closer to eight o'clock, which was the time he had to leave, and I was asking his opinion about an appropriate gift for a woman celebrating cancer remission. Then, out of nowhere, there was a *boom* on the plane."

"Meaning?"

Violets eyes hit the floor. "Ram accidentally spilled coffee on his lucky tie and left abruptly to change it."

Violet's eyes began tearing.

"Take your time."

"Then, when I turned to grab another cup of coffee, I accidently knocked over his iPhone to the floor. It fell hard and bounced a few times—I was *so scared* I had damaged it right before his important meeting. So, I slammed my mug on the counter, grabbed it from the floor, and inspected it closely for damage."

"Was there any?"

"No. Fortunately, he had a heavy-duty case on it, but—"

"Go on."

"While it was in my hands, this text message appeared center screen."

"And what did it say?"

Violet's amber eyes turned black as coal. "It said: *Hurry! I need to suck your cock before breakfast.*"

Dr. Cohen was embarrassed. "And the sender's name?"

"The screen said *Tom Wilson*, but then a second text message came in."

"And what did that one say?"

Bile rose up Violet's throat. She fought back the familiar urge to purge. "It was a picture."

"Of what exactly?"

"It was a selfie of a young redhead lying topless on a set of white sheets. Her mouth was showing off her pierced tongue like a porn star, waiting for him."

"So *that* was the smoking gun."

"Yes."

"Oy vey." Dr. Cohen picked up his legal pad and pen. "Give me a moment to catch up on my notes here."

Violet turned away so he could not see the tears welling in her eyes.

She reflected more about the picture, about the moment she saw Allegra for the first time. She remembered the sharp pain—a foot-long railroad spike in the chest—that deflated her lungs, weakened her knees, and clouded her mind simultaneously. In that moment, reality shifted. It became dreamlike. Something Violet experienced only one other time in her life . . . The morning of March fifteenth, when she spent ten minutes shaking and screaming for her baby to wake up.

Violet wept.

"And you had no reason to suspect Ram was having an affair prior to this event?" He nudged a box of Kleenex sitting on the glass coffee table by her shins.

"No, not one clue . . . The plane just went *boom*." Violet reached down and grabbed a tissue.

Dr. Cohen was sympathetic. He knew how fragile she was, despite her bravado. Ram was indeed the rock she had leaned on for years—particularly through the death of her daughter and multiple life-threatening bouts with bulimia. "What did you do? After you saw the picture of the girl?"

"I put the phone back on the counter where he left it. Then my feet glued to the kitchen floor. I froze. I froze right in place. I couldn't breathe."

"And when he returned, did you say anything?"

"No."

"He must have noticed something was wrong?"

"No, he didn't. He was in too much of a rush to see his whore—plus, my mind was spinning and spinning."

"Did he notice you read his texts?"

"No, that's the strange part. He must have some sort of app that automatically deletes them after they appear on screen. I don't think he even knows she sent that picture."

"Then what did you do?"

"Nothing."

"He must have noticed your reaction, Violet? Perhaps the tone of your voice?"

"No, he was in and out of the kitchen in a tremendous rush. I just kissed him goodbye, like I always do, and wished him good luck with his auditor meeting."

"I see."

They sat silently for a moment. Looking at each other, like two strangers on a plane trying to figure out what to do next.

"What is your goal in restarting therapy, Violet? Are you trying to decide—"

"I want peace."

"Peace of mind?"

Violet sat up straight. "Ram tried to leave me for a twenty-three-year-old bartender. That's right. *Twenty-three.* That's fucking young enough to be our daughter."

Dr. Cohen exhaled loudly.

"The worst part is that she looks exactly like me, except she's much younger and fatter. She's *real trash*, Dr. Cohen. A certified, trailer park hooker."

"How do you know all of this?"

Violet hung her head low. "I only know some bits and pieces about the affair, but not everything. I know who she is. Where she lives. Where she works. But so many details are missing, and it's *driving me insane.*"

"What exactly is making you feel this way?"

Violet looked at the broken ceiling light above, suppressing her urge to cry. "All I do is think about her. About them, about how they met, about how it started. What could I have done differently? Why *this* girl? How long has it been going on? I imagine them fucking in a hotel, fucking on her bed, fucking in *my bed*—endless, endless questions drilling teeny weeny pinprick holes in my brain, one by one by one . . . And that's why I'm here. I feel like I'm going completely mad— that I have to know *everything* about their relationship, every single moment, every kiss, every detail, before I can ever move on, yet the only two people in the world who know the truth will *never* tell me!"

Sparkles circled Violet's foot and laid down beside her.

"Yes, you are right. Only two people know the complete truth, and often neither one is willing to share it. Which is why you *must* let the details go."

Violet bit her lip. "I swear to you, I'm trying, but I can't."

"And as difficult as it is for you to hear this right now, your irrepressible spirit has survived much worse. You can survive infidelity."

"Survive?" Violet scoffed. "*Survive* infidelity? No, Dr. Cohen. No marriage ever *survives* infidelity."

Violet rose menacingly out of her chair.

"A wonderful, loving marriage dies the minute one spouse finds it has been betrayed by the other. Dead on the spot. Do not resuscitate." She sat back in her chair. "Once the truth is revealed, it takes the wind out of that person, making them beg to wake up from this terrible ordeal."

"Yes, I can imagine."

"If, and only if, the betrayed spouse can survive the shock, mourning, anger, hatred, desperation, and for whatever noble reason, the couple tries to save the dead marriage by burying it in a *Pet Cemetery*, it will only return as something else—something more sinister. It may look like the same marriage on the outside, but in truth, it's never, ever, ever the same thing."

He wrote vehemently on his legal pad.

"I want this pain inside my chest to stop hurting, Dr. Cohen. I don't think I can take it much longer."

The look in her eyes made it clear she was ready to do anything to end it.

"Now, Violet, you've stared at this abyss before. You've climbed out of that murky swamp once, and I assure you, you can do it again." He carefully rose from his brown leather throne, circled the table, and gave her a warm, paternal hug. "I'm very glad you came back for therapy. I think it will help you tremendously."

Violet sobbed in his arms. "I agree."

"Just don't do anything impulsive, Violet. We still have a few weeks before I leave." He released his hug. "Be strong. Be patient. And we will heal your broken heart together."

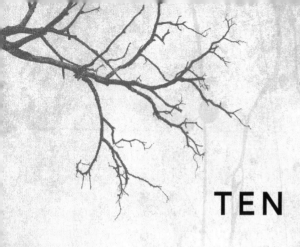

TEN

ALLEGRA SCRUTINIZED her naked body, surprised at how quickly her auburn pubic hairs were growing back, and how her stomach and thighs were widening from the exclusive diet of gas station fare. She rolled on her side, noticing a red sore the size of a pancake forming on her hip. *It must be from lying on the floor,* she told herself. *You need to move. Keep your strength. You will get out of here.*

If she wanted to kill you, she would have done it already.

That morning, Violet had tiptoed into the basement with a bucket and mop to clean up the dried mess of urine, feces, and vomit Allegra had made the day before.

Violet did not say a word while she cleaned, holding her breath as she awkwardly mopped back and forth around Allegra's sleeping body, unsure of how to properly use the unfamiliar cleaning apparatus. Instead of smelling rank and foulness, Allegra's nostrils were invaded by cheap lavender-scented bleach, a welcome exchange on any occasion.

When Violet was done, she left Allegra another gift, this time a plastic grocery bag filled with a roll of toilet tissue, a package of Pepperidge Farm Milano cookies, a roll of paper towels, and two small bottles of Mountain Dew before quietly exiting the forbidden door.

Now that it was afternoon, Allegra searched the room for things to be grateful for. It was a mental activity taught by her hippie grandmother to lift plummeting spirits.

She was grateful for the food and drink, as unhealthy as it was, for it was plentiful and delivered frequently, keeping her from becoming hungry like POWs or Jewish prisoners during the holocaust. She was grateful to not be physically harmed, in serious pain, or maimed. She was grateful to have a pee bucket—and now toilet paper and paper towels—that she used to make a quasi-blanket. But as she thought about it, Allegra was most grateful to have light. Yes, light. For the alternative in a windowless room filled with New York-sized roaches, rats, and mice would be unbearable. As thick as the lead walls were, the mere presence of thousands of pounds of food and water was a beacon for the toughest vermin in the city. Having light at least minimized the fear of her surroundings, and would let her know exactly what species of tiny teeth were gnawing at her big toe while she slept. But the light was on twenty-four hours a day, causing Allegra confusion as to how much time had passed. Was it morning? Was it night? She had no idea as each hour elapsed, bringing her closer and closer to Ram's return.

She looked over to the king-size bed, plainly dressed in ivory flannel sheets, wishing she could sleep on it, even if for only one night. An hour. Even fifteen minutes. And with that thought, her comforting feelings of gratitude quickly dissipated.

Her mind wandered again, now struggling to remember the details of last Thursday night. *The big night.* The night she can no longer remember, and Violet refuses to discuss.

The week leading up to that day was sharply detailed in her memory. Even the morning and afternoon of that day was as clear as a mountain spring. But past six o'clock? That was a total blank. All Allegra could remember was that it should have been a *great* night, for it was the same evening that Ram phoned from Beijing with the news that would forever change her life.

From the beginning of their relationship, Allegra struggled with the thought of being Ram's mistress. She hated that word, preferring to be called his *girlfriend* instead. She never thought it was glamorous, or prestigious, or an honor. Despite the gifts, dinners, trips, and money, his marriage was the one thing that kept her from sleeping with Ram for two full weeks. She knew from day one he was married, so she held out. But all it did was make matters worse. For in their sexless courtship, they got to know one another intimately and fell in love.

Once that happened, there was no holding back. Allegra unleashed her experienced-beyond-her-years sexual prowess, and Ram was hers in body, heart, and mind. But guilt quickly set in, for she had witnessed the immense physical destruction of marital affairs firsthand.

Back in New Mexico, Allegra's stepfather, Denay Morton, was the only man she had ever known and loved. She did not know her birth father, or even anything about him, other than he was a married, traveling businessman who tricked her mother into having sex in the bathroom of *Posh* nightclub. Or he was a nineteen-year-old carnival worker—the two most likely candidates according to Allegra's mother.

Denay was the only father she had ever known; a good man, with dark brown skin and teeth so perfect Allegra once believed he was the *real* Tooth Fairy.

Although poorly educated, he provided for Allegra's unemployed mother, brother, and little sister as best he could, working late nights and double shifts at the local Seven Eleven—even managing to qualify for the chain's exclusive manager trainee program without having finished the ninth grade.

While he was away in Albuquerque for a week, he met another woman from a neighboring store, a light-skinned lady eighteen years his senior, with a grown son and a mortgage in good standing.

Within a month, Denay left Allegra's mother, who was already in the process of self-imploding, moving his belongings out of the trailer, while her mother was out looking for drugs and her siblings were away at school.

Denay had raised Allegra from the age of two, yet when he left, he took everything they owned, including their bunk beds, and failed to say why. Instead, he wrote only two words on the back of a U-Haul truck rental receipt and taped it on the front of their bedroom door:

GOODBYE KIDZ

She remembered that day in stunning detail. It was three days after she had turned nine. She came home, alone, the first one of her siblings to return from school. She opened the trailer door and immediately noticed the kitchen table was missing, the counters were cleaned of cooking gadgets, and the carpet was soiled with dust that had been hiding behind the missing furniture.

For an entire decade afterward, she watched her mother bounce from man to man as she spiraled into heroin and alcohol abuse, a never-ending opera that ceased with a merciful overdose on the streets of Albuquerque at the age of thirty-seven.

Allegra was twenty-two years old when her mother, her only parent, died.

She gathered whatever savings she had left from bartending at the local sports bar, packed what she could into her ripped *Hello Kitty* suitcase, and left everyone she knew to take a Greyhound bus to the theme park of hopes and dreams: New York City.

As happy as Ram's call made her last Thursday night, the two weeks prior to Allegra's blackout had been a neck-jerking, emotional ride on the relationship rollercoaster.

It started with Ram sneaking out of his office early to enjoy a romantic lunch on Madison Avenue before heading to LaGuardia for a two-day trip to Boston. After their meal, they strolled down the sidewalk, walking arm in arm, planning their next getaway to Bermuda after he returned from his month-long trip to Asia on Labor Day.

While they were walking, Allegra caught sight of something in the window of Vera Wang Bridal that turned her head faster than *The Exorcist.*

It was a strapless, solar white gown with a glittering diamond bodice and a tulle skirt at least ten feet in circumference. It was, by far, the most beautiful Princess wedding dress she had ever seen, and it showed on her naïve, hopeful face.

Allegra bounced wildly with joy, excited to even *see* the dress. But when she turned toward Ram, she saw something unexpected.

A look of pure *pity.*

Right then, she knew Ram would never leave his wife and marry her. She was destined for a lifetime of spending holidays alone, living in the shadows of a world of privilege she would get to taste but never fully consume.

After a tearful goodbye, she returned to her apartment and scoured the Internet for statistics regarding cheating men and divorce. She read time and time again that only five percent of unfaithful husbands married twenty years or more actually leave their wives for their mistresses. *Five percent.* Meaning ninety-five percent of husbands stay with their wives, even if the discovered affair cracks the marriage and leads to divorce many years later.

She was shocked the numbers weren't higher, and continued to search longer and found no statistical evidence in her favor.

When Ram called the next day to ask what had made her so upset, Allegra explained how she noticed his reaction outside Vera Wang and garnered the courage to ask him to release her so she could find someone to marry and start a family with.

She never called it a break-up. How could she? They never fought and were happily in love. So, instead, she referred to it as a "merciful uncoupling."

After a few hours of contemplation, Ram agreed. He returned from Boston and met Allegra one last time to make love. They cried together as they said their goodbyes, holding each other in bed for no less than three hours, ending the evening with a cinematic kiss that made the final scene of *Casablanca* look cheesy.

The next day, they were officially back together.

But only a week later, they had the worst fight of their relationship.

After four days of unpleasant phone calls and exchanges, Allegra received the best news her ears would ever hear. As she was in her apartment preparing for a run, Ram called her from Shanghai and shared his decision to file for divorce. Even more, he promised a "huge ring" and a proper "one-kneed proposal" just as soon as he returned to New York.

Ecstatic beyond measure, Allegra would have run directly to his townhome and jumped into his arms if he wasn't so far away when he called. But instead, she went for her planned run in Carl Schurz Park. It was a great session, or so she thought, running hard along the East River as she always does to her favorite tracks—Justin Beiber, Selena Gomez, Lady Gaga, and Katy Perry—while visualizing how she would look in that Vera Wang dress for her spring wedding.

That was the last thing Allegra remembered before meeting Violet in the basement.

She looked around the sterile room, thinking about Ram, not believing how much she missed him. He was the reason she was there, yet she didn't care. She loved him and he loved her. She knew he would be home in a few weeks, and if she could survive long enough, without too much damage, he would be hers forever. She thought he might even come home sooner, or at least, call the police. Sometime soon, he would worry that she wasn't answering his calls or texts. Somehow, he would know his wife had gone mad and this would all be over within a few days.

Perhaps even a few hours.

The silver lining, of course, would be that no matter what she endured, as long as there was no permanent damage to her body or mind, she would win in the end.

She would be a hero. She would be famous. She would get a book deal.

And an exclusive interview with Anderson Cooper on CNN.

But the best part was no longer having to watch Ram fight a lengthy divorce to marry her. Once they came to her rescue,

Mad Violet would be sent away to prison, without *any* of his fortune, and they could marry quickly, without interference or obstacles.

Allegra recognized Ram loved her enough to give away half his money, and in turn, this was her sacrifice for the two of them.

Everything happens for a reason, she repeated to herself multiple times. *If I survive this, I'll be able to survive anything. And once this is over, she'll be locked in prison for years.*

Then the thought hit her like a Japanese bullet train:

If I killed Violet, it would be self-defense.

No questions. No trial. No jury.

She would be, like, totally out of our lives forever.

ELEVEN

ALLEGRA'S ROOMMATE, Chloe Sinclair, was no stranger to bargains. In fact, if clearance hunting were a sport, she'd own a hundred shiny shopping bag trophies by now.

Growing up on the south side of Chicago taught her many things, but the lesson she valued most was learning from her Community Center mentors that the key to happiness was to discover what you love, then find a way to earn a living from it.

During the day, Chloe was a successful commercial actress. Her pale green eyes, naturally curly hair, and tawny skin made her a perfect candidate for the ubiquitous, *smiling urban girl* role found in almost every ad on television today.

Chloe easily booked cereal ads, wireless phone ads, and mattress ads in particular, and earned SAG sanctioned royalties each time they aired. She was fortunate enough to never go more than a month without booking work, but she was well aware of the mercurial nature of commercial acting and was determined to set up a second source of revenue that would last well beyond her twenties.

For this reason, Chloe had created an eBay business called *Chloe's Closet* about three years ago. In this short time, she became a Top Rated Seller with more than a thousand five-star reviews and repeat customers from all over the world.

To create inventory, she spent her evenings after auditions scouring the Upper East Side's finest thrift shops, bargain stores, and sample sales, often purchasing designer shoes, clothing, and accessories at a quarter of the price at which they originally sold.

August was always the best month to find deals. Stores dumped millions in inventory to make room for the fall and winter collections arriving in UPS boxes by the truckload.

At her second callback for a Verizon ad earlier in the day, Chloe caught wind of a forty-eight-hour clearance shoe sale at Urban Outfitters, located near the busy intersection of Third Avenue and East 86th Street.

As she entered the store, her heart pounded, fantasizing about what she may be able to score. Last time she was here, she landed five pairs of Jeffrey Campbell shoes for $14.99 each. Since they retailed for $249 she was able to unload the tiny, size 5 beauties for $99 a piece. Although she never made big money at this gig, she was always able to cover her rent. And to a single person living in New York, that's all that matters.

Chloe, wearing a white tank top and cut-off jeans, was on the lower floor of the store, crouched down, rummaging through the clearance shoe rack stacked neatly in the corner.

A Goth sales boy wearing skinny jeans so tight he looked hungry, eagerly approached her. "Can I help you find something?"

"No, I'm cool. Just browsing."

"All right. I'm Greg. Call me if you need me."

The Goth boy recognized Chloe and hovered over her, lamenting his need to reorganize the display of shoes she was terrorizing.

Just then, Chloe's phone belted a loud text tone.

She continued digging.

It *dinged* again.

Annoyed, she snatched the phone from her back pocket.

Her light eyes widened as she realized it was a text from Allegra . . .

HEY CHLOE! OMG!
I'M SURE YOU MUST BE WORRIED!!!
                    ALLEGRA? WHERE THE F RU?
I'M IN MEXICO!! I GOT MARRIED!!!
:-) !!!
                                WTF??
                                TO MR. BIG?!
YES!!!
                    WHEN RU COMING HOME?
I'M NOT.
WE BOUGHT A HOUSE DOWN HERE!!!
IN GUADALAJARA
                            WHAT IS THAT?
I KNOW! I'M THE REAL CARRIE BRADSHAW NOW!
                    WHAT ABOUT UR JOB?

BOBBY IS PISSED!

TELL HIM I QUIT.
I'M RICH AF NOW.

WHAT?
WHY DON'T YOU CALL HIM?

HE DOESN'T TEXT :(
I DON'T WANT 2 SPEAK 2 HIM.
WILL YOU TELL HIM?

YES, HE'LL B HAPPY 4 U!
OMG! WELL, CONGRATS!
I WAS SO WORRIED.
I'M SUCH A DORK.
I WENT 2 THE PO-PO

CALL THEM TOO!! PLEASE!!
I'M TOTALLY OKAY!!
AND HAPPY!!

SEND ME A PIC OF THE RING!

IT'S BEING MADE NOW
WILL SEND LATER

SEND ME LOTS OF PICTURES!
POST THEM 2 FACEBOOK

CAN'T. NO INTERNET HERE.

WHAT? BARBARIC!

IT'S GORGEOUS HERE!
SO PEACEFUL
BIG MANSION IN THE JUNGLE!!

WHAT KIND OF DRESS DID U WEAR?

I'LL SEND PICS LATER
I'M DRIVING

DO U WANT ME 2 SEND UR STUFF?

ONLY MY PICTURES + JEWELRY
YOU KEEP MY FURNITURE
SELL MY CLOTHES
I HAVE DESIGNER STUFF NOW!!!

I'M SO GLAD UR OK!

OF COURSE. I'M FINE!

IS ANYONE ELSE WORRIED?

JUST BOBBY.

BUT I'LL CALL HIM.

THANK YOU!!

TELL THE COPS I'M OKAY!

I WILL

NO SERIOUSLY

I DON'T WANT MY BRO & SIS TO FREAK!

YOU HAVEN'T CALLED THEM?

I WILL AFTER.

WHAT ABOUT MY LEASE?

I CAN'T SWING 2K ALONE :-(

I'LL SEND YOU CHECK 2MRW

MY RENT FOR THE YEAR

UNTIL JAN?

YES!

YOU ROCK!

OMG THANKS!!!!

OF COURSE! I'M RICH NOW! ;-)

YOU CAN DO AIR BNB

OH YEAH, THAT'S RIGHT.

COOL.

WELL, DON'T BE A STRANGER.

I PROMISE, I WON'T!

I'M SO HAPPY 4 U!!

ME TOO!

HAVE FUN!

COME BACK 2 VISIT!!!

I WILL!

TTYL :-)

Chloe rocketed from the ground amidst the mess of shoes and hugged the Goth sales boy.

"Uh, are you okay?"

"I'm friggin' awesome! My missing roommate's been found! She's been gone for, like, four days and I thought she had been Craigslisted, but she just ran off to Mexico and *got married!*" She shuffled her feet. "I'm so excited!"

The Goth boy raked his hand through his skater bangs.

"Right on, YOLO."

TWELVE

LOCATED ON East 61st Street between Madison and Park Avenues, the interior of Sotheby's International Realty's Upper East Side office was exactly how one would imagine it: elegantly appointed woods, glass wall offices, modern lines, and empty hallways.

Out of the one hundred forty-four agents who consider it home base, only thirty realtors had stayed behind for the summer. The rest had moved to the Hamptons for the season to watch polo matches with clients patiently awaiting the return of fall weather.

Laura Welch, wearing a black-and-white polka dot dress, popped into Penny's fishbowl office. She zoomed in on the empty mesh chair in front of three enormous Apple computer monitors. "Crud!"

She jogged over to a neighboring cubicle, where a tan man with salt-and-pepper hair worked industriously on his laptop. "Good morning, Armando. Have you seen Penny?"

"I think she's here." He shifted his eyes. "Yes, I saw her in the break room about ten minutes ago."

Laura marched to the rear of the office, passing rows of empty work dwellings, littered with crayon drawings and pictures of celebrity clients. As she neared the entrance, she spotted Penny sitting alone, reading *The New York Post* while enjoying a cup of tea and crumpled coffee cake from Starbucks.

"We're late! We had a nine o'clock Skype meeting with 13 East 78th. Remember?"

"What time is it now?"

"Nine eighteen."

"Shit!" Penny grabbed her tea and abruptly left with Laura.

Penny and Laura sat across from one another at a black, piano-finish conference room table.

The eighty-inch flat screen floating above them displayed an attractive, bald man in his early fifties, with dark-rimmed glasses adjusting the unseen camera lens before him. His broad shoulders dominated the frame, covered by a silk dress shirt that matched the sky blue eyes partially obscured behind his glasses.

The Asian-inspired furnishings and double beds in the background hinted he was broadcasting from a luxury hotel room overseas.

Seeing him for the first time, Laura thought Penny was right: Mr. Ramspeck did indeed resemble Lex Luther. But after studying his golden tan, angled face, masculine cleft chin—and unfashionable black-rimmed glasses—she concluded he was part Clark Kent as well.

"Can you hear me okay?" His deep voice sounded as smooth as a seventies radio DJ.

"Yes, we can hear you perfectly, Mr. Ramspeck," replied Penny. "What time is it in Singapore?"

"Let's see here." He leaned out of frame. "It's nine twenty p.m."

"Same day?" asked Laura, smiling, fully ignoring her boss's request to stay quiet.

Penny shot her a playfully evil look.

He smiled. "Who was that?"

Laura's panties melted at the sound of his velvet voice. He was much sexier than she'd ever imagined.

"Oh, that was my assistant, Laura Welch."

"Nice to meet you, Mr. Ramspeck," she replied off camera.

"Same here," he said hastily. "So how was the Open House?"

Penny squared her shoulders, taking center stage. "Well, I think it was very well attended. We had a nice turnout, considering it was ninety-five degrees outside, and the brokers who previewed—"

Ram interrupted. "Did we receive any offers?"

Laura shook her head *no*.

Penny spoke with her teeth partially closed. "Unfortunately, no, not yet."

"Why not?" Ram was serious.

Penny hesitated. She did not want to share how much the monstrous tree-bed and disturbing doll collection turned off buyers. "There was a great deal of positive reaction to the home. I'm expecting an offer any day."

His rapid-fire questioning continued. "How many people showed up?"

Laura mouthed the number six.

Penny lifted her big chest. "Sixteen, I believe. I have to check the guest book."

"I thought we priced it to sell quickly? It's worth at least thirty million, if not more."

"I believe it's perfectly priced, Mr. Ramspeck, even those who saw it mentioned—"

"But no formal offers?"

"Well, it's been on the market for less than a week," implored Penny. "Homes in this price range usually take a few months to close."

"Well, drop the price, then."

"I would advise we wait for that, Mr. Ramspeck. It would make us look a little too desperate, and attract the wrong sort of buyer."

"Any buyer with twenty-five million in cash is the right buyer," he said with subtle dominance. "My wife is driving me crazy over this. I need to move on with my life as quickly as possible."

"Yes, we totally understand," said Penny.

"What about the newspaper ads. Has anyone called?"

Laura nodded her head *yes*.

"We have a showing later today, as a matter of fact."

Laura referred to her papers. "Two o'clock. Bram Peterson from Corcoran."

"Did you hear that?" Penny looked back into the camera.

"Yes," replied Ram. "Tell the buyer's agent there's a bonus of two hundred and fifty thousand to the first qualified offer that comes in by close of business Friday. That includes the two of you."

Penny and Laura exchanged looks of confusion.

"On top of our commission?" asked Laura timidly.

"Yes."

"Well, super, we'll get right on it," replied Penny.

Ram came closer into focus. His sky blue eyes were now more prominent than his glasses. "Penny, your e-mail mentioned you had a problem showing the safe room? Do you think that has anything to do with the lack of offers?"

Penny rocked her huge breasts. "Oh, no, actually." She attempted to laugh. "Most people are concerned about the living areas, not where they would sleep during the end of the world." Her head rolled toward Laura, immediately recognizing what a stupid answer that was.

"And the code I gave you didn't work?"

"It did on the first door, but not the second."

"I see." Ram leaned back in his squeaky desk chair, placing his wide hands behind his tan, hairless head. "Right, right . . . There's a second code for that door. My wife made me pick two dates we would both remember, and for the life of me, I can't remember the second one. It was so long ago."

"May I ask why the doors require codes for both sides? It just seems a little odd," asked Laura off camera.

Penny immediately shot her a look of disapproval.

"Oh, we had no choice. Those doors were originally designed to be used in high-security power plants, not private homes." He smiled.

Penny scratched her head. "Is there any way we can reset the codes when my electrician goes out to see it tomorrow? Or maybe we can call the manufacturer?"

Ram considered her suggestions. "Hmm. Probably not a good idea. My wife is the only one who uses that room, mainly to store her arts and crafts. She's already not speaking to me since I've put the house on the market, so naturally, I don't want to piss her off even more."

"Happy wife, happy life," said Laura faintly—suddenly remembering they were getting divorced.

"I completely understand," replied Penny. "Can *you* ask your wife for the code? We'll be very careful to show the house around her schedule."

"Yes, just as soon as she answers my calls," he joked. "I don't think my wife will be helpful in that department. As a matter of fact, I would avoid her while showing the house."

Penny and Laura exchanged looks.

"Have you met my wife, Violet, yet?"

Penny shook her head. "I only know what she looks like from the photos on the walls."

"Good. She's a real sweetheart when you get to know her, but I've seen Violet turn vindictive when she's angry. And she's rather angry about me selling the house."

Laura scrunched her face and curled her fingertips, impersonating an *evil queen* off camera.

"I should also mention I let go of the house staff as of September first as well."

Penny was surprised. "So, the housekeepers know you're moving out of the country?"

"Yes, they do. And I promised them a year's severance and excellent references, so if you detect any more dirt than usual, please let me know."

"Definitely."

"And if we need to hire a cleaning crew to come in before showings, just do it and send me the bill."

"Great idea." Penny lightened. "Oh, and regarding the safe room? How about you e-mail me a list of all the dates you can think of—birthdays, anniversaries, whatever—and I will try to figure out the code to the second door myself?"

"Brilliant. Consider it done."

"Should I call off the electrician until we get the dates?" asked Laura.

"Yes," replied Ram. "I can also e-mail you the 3D plans of the room we made as part of the renovations. At least you can share it with prospects, until we're able to get the doors open again."

"Oh, that'll be perfect," replied Penny as she looked at Laura holding two thumbs up.

"Anything else?" he asked forcefully.

Penny looked over to Laura, who was shaking her head *no*.

"No, sir. That's it for now."

"Good, because I literally just checked into my hotel after flying twenty-four hours straight. This Brexit nonsense is causing global havoc with my trading companies. Lots to sort out over the next several weeks."

"Completely understand, and again, thank you for your precious time. We'll be in touch soon with good news."

"Good night, Mr. Ramspeck," chimed Laura in a sing-song voice.

"Enjoy your day, Ladies." Ram reached into the corner of the frame and shut off the camera.

Penny let out a deep sigh. "Well, that was pleasant. Scary, but pleasant."

"He's a nice guy," added Laura.

Penny readjusted her tight skirt. "The wife is going to be a problem. Did you hear what he said?"

"About not letting her near buyers?"

"Duh, yeah."

"Do we need her signature for the sale?"

"*Nope.* Thank goodness for gold-digger-lockboxes," said Penny, rising from the table.

"Trust funds rule."

"Let's go call our broker list and tell them they have seventy-two hours to send me an offer. Tell them if it closes by the end of the month, we'll toss in a hundred-thousand-dollar bonus."

"But he said—"

"No, Laura. That's our *final* number. Not our starting bid."

"Oh, I see."

"Plus, we'll get better referrals if we sell this listing by Friday *and* save him money. So call all the big boys." She clapped her hands. "Let's get to it."

Laura gathered her belongings, then paused. "You know what's sad? I never saw someone so desperate to dump a gorgeous mansion in my life."

Penny leaned in closer. "You'd be surprised what rich men do when they get addicted to cheap pussy," she whispered. "It's like crack. Well, technically, two cracks." She laughed.

"But who are we to judge, right?" Laura pumped her arm in jest. "*Ching-ching!*"

"That's right, baby. *Ching-ching!*"

Back in the hotel room, Ram closed the lid of his laptop, grabbed his iPhone from the charger, and anxiously dialed a contact.

After several rings, the voicemail picked up. "Hey, it's me, Allegra. You know the drill." The tone was loud and long.

"Darling, it's Ram. Where are you?" He stared at his reflection in the mirror. "I need to hear your voice, so call me. It's the tiny green icon on the bottom, in case you've never seen it before," he said playfully. "No, seriously, darling. I'm worried sick you may be injured or in the hospital. Just let me know you're okay." His face was drained and ragged. "Goodnight."

Ram ended the call.

He plugged the phone back into the charger.

He removed his glasses.

He placed his elbows on the desk.

And buried his face in his palms.

Forgive me, Violet.

Please forgive me.

THIRTEEN

VIOLET STARED at her bare, makeup free reflection while sitting on a bench in her ivory marbled bathroom. Her hairline was unattractively high—severely pulled back by the white headband made of the same Egyptian cotton that covered her freshly showered, emaciated body.

Gazing at her own reflection, she was unrecognizable. A wash. Almost invisible. Without colored foundation, false eyelashes, or contouring tricks to define each finely chiseled feature, she was as plain as homemade yogurt. Ordinary. Generic. Tasteless. Now that her long copper-red bangs were pulled back, all that stood out against her colorless skin were the awful, dark red, *Joan Crawford* style highly arched eyebrows she regrettably had tattooed on her face years ago.

She leaned into the bright lights of her movie-star-dressing-room mirror, carefully studying each tiny wrinkle that emerged overnight. She peered deep into her surgically lifted, amber eyes, like a suicidal Broadway actress convincing herself to take the stage for the thousandth time.

Violet knew what she was planning for that day would be difficult. She wondered if she had the courage. The strength. Or the stomach to complete her mission. But if she did not start the process now, she knew she wouldn't have time to finish.

As she continued her internal pep talk, the gold iPhone plugged into the wall beside her rang, a pleasant tone of wind chimes and bells.

The picture of a smiling dark blonde in her late thirties appeared on the screen with the words LISA HOROWITZ above it.

Violet did not answer.

Instead, she closed her eyes and smiled, waiting for a small gray box to appear. Once it did, she clicked on the button that led to a long list of unheard voicemails.

Violet listened to the message on speaker:

"Hello, pretty lady! It's Lisa again." Her sweet, nasal voice was contaminated by a thick Jersey accent. "Honestly, I don't remember if you said you're traveling this month, or is it next month you're in Palm Beach visiting your parents? Ugh. I can't remember a thing with this crazy *twin mommy brain* syndrome. But, I digress." She hollered at two small children making a mess in the background. "So, anyways, we're all wondering why you missed the Autism gala last week. What happened? Are you sick?" She screamed orders to a nanny in the room. "Sorry about that. The boys are throwing Legos everywhere. Anyways, Ursula said you didn't look well that morning at Pure Yoga, so we're all just assuming you're under the weather. But if you're feeling better, I want to invite you and Ram to Jack's seventy-fifth birthday party this Saturday at our Bridgehampton house. It's a *Cowboys and Indians* theme, so please come in costume, but don't pick Pocahontas because that's what I'm doing." She giggled. "I've got the long black wig, the buckskin outfit with feathers—everything. Anyways, I don't think you've been to this new house yet, have you? Well, it's fabulous. We have a huge pool and ten guest rooms, so let me know if you're coming and I'll reserve one for you and Ram." A child wailed in the background, forcing Lisa to speak faster. "We have so much to catch up on, Violet! I hate having my best girlfriends scattered during the summer. I miss you! Let's chat soon."

Violet smiled warmly as the message ended.

She left the vanity and entered the dressing area.

While she was gone, another gray box appeared on the screen of her phone:

YOU HAVE 23

NEW VOICEMAILS

Violet walked the busy block of East 86th Street between Lexington and Third Avenues.

It was one of her favorite places to shop in that she was never recognized by her friends too afraid to walk west of Park

Avenue, and it was the closest thing the Upper East Side had to a Union Square vibe.

Each day, thousands of young people crammed this little area, most of whom would disappear into the hidden subway entrances after visiting the five-floor New York Sports Club, the three-story Barnes & Noble, the two-story H&M—or eating at the perpetually packed Shake Shack burger joint, which attracted nearly every movie-goer heading to the two movie theaters nearby.

Violet crossed the street, landing in front of Sephora without trouble. She was fully made-up, wearing a pair of dark sunglasses; a fitted, white Donna Karan dress; bright aqua heels, and an orange Hermes shopping tote—a stunning summer outfit for any woman, and it looked particularly amazing on her petite frame.

She entered the store.

She roamed through the colorful displays of makeup with club music throbbing above her: Dior, Clinique, Hourglass, Laura Mercier, Bobbi Brown, and Smashbox, until she found the kiosk she was looking for, Marc Jacobs Beauty.

Surrounded by three occupied, overly made-up salespeople dressed in jet-black army uniforms, Violet searched the bottom drawer stuffed with boxes of lipstick, finally pulling out one labeled RED RIDING HOOD 408.

She removed her sunglasses and placed both the lipstick and her glasses into her orange shopping tote, turned around, and walked straight out the door.

The security sensors near the front door did not go off.

She smiled as her face hit the bright, sunny street. She had scored her favorite red lipstick without a second thought. She then J-walked diagonally into Victoria's Secret.

There, at the entrance, was a huge poster of their latest model with angel wings, teetering above a circular table with hoards of lace panties in various colors and sizes.

Violet lifted one pair, stretching it between her hands, knowing its full covered bottom was much too large for her tiny frame. She checked the size, confirming her suspicion, and then inconspicuously shoved a handful of panties from the table into her bag.

She continued browsing, waltzing over to a wall of cotton nighties. One in particular caught her eye. It was cornflower blue, with two thick straps, a deep v-neckline and below-the-knee hemline outlined in white lace. It was at least four sizes too large for Violet. Yet again, a perfect addition for her bag, which she finished filling and quickly exited out the door.

Back at the townhome, Violet tossed her full orange tote onto the kitchen counter, opened the refrigerator door, and pulled out her first meal of the day: a bottle of Kombucha Tea.

She heard Rosa and Octavia, who had returned from Honduras the evening before, arguing in Spanish on the second floor. She shook her head, unable to understand their grievances, but happy to know there was always someone home to keep her company.

As she grabbed her tote and entered the pantry, she picked up more snacks for Allegra, this time Doritos and Dr. Pepper. She entered the codes, descended the dark stairs, and appeared at the top landing of the basement.

She saw Allegra sleeping down below with narrow rows of paper towels covering her yellowing skin. Violet used her body weight to push the steel door behind her. "Time to get up," she said loudly, carrying the tote and snacks in her hands. "It's almost lunchtime."

"What day is it?" asked Allegra, barely awake.

"That's not your concern. You need to stay focused on what really matters."

Allegra wrinkled her nose in confusion. "What do you want with me?" She inched up the wall behind her, pulling her chained collar along the way, into a sitting position.

Violet shook her head like a disappointed schoolmarm. "As I've already said several times, I just want you to answer a few questions."

"Then ask me," she said weakly. "Let's, get it over with."

Violet glided down the stairs like a beauty queen that could fire-walk in five-inch heels. "We will, but first I've brought you a present."

Allegra raised her eyes.

Violet pulled the cornflower blue nightgown from her tote. "You've been so good lately, I thought I would give you this."

Allegra held out her hands. "Really?"

Instead of handing it to her, Violet tossed the nightgown onto the dining room table. She then pointed at the bed in the far corner. "I'll let you have the nightgown, plus a pillow and blanket, if you answer me one question."

Allegra was agreeable. After lying naked for five days, on a cold, hard floor, a thin blanket and cheap pillow would feel like Buckingham Palace. "Sure, ask me what you want."

She regretted those words just as soon as they left her dry, chapped lips.

Violet pulled a chair over from the dinette and sat directly in front of Allegra. She dropped the shopping tote at her feet and crossed her boney legs so tightly, it looked as if she were double-jointed.

She leaned forward, connecting eye to soul. "Why did you pick my husband?"

Allegra paused. "I don't know what you mean?"

Violet leaned in closer. "Out of the millions of single, eligible men in Manhattan, why did you fall in love with my husband?"

Allegra rolled her head in a half circle. Her blunt red bangs now covered most of her eyes. "This is just a serious misunderstanding, Mrs. Ramspeck."

"You can call me Violet. We're friends now."

Allegra was skeptical. "Like, your husband and me, we're just acquaintances—nothing more. He's a customer at my bar." She looked Violet square in the face. "I swear to you, nothing's ever happened between us."

"You're *sure* about that?"

"Ask Ram, he'll tell you. He just comes to my bar a few times a month and has, like, a couple of drinks. He's just one of my regular customers, that's all. Ask him."

Violet thrust her shoulders back into the chair and crossed her legs in the opposite direction. "So, let me rephrase my question, since you apparently did not understand it the first time."

Allegra braced herself.

"Why did you pick *my husband* as your lover? What drew you to him?"

Allegra sat up taller against the wall. She coveted the nightgown on the dining room table, dying to cover her body with something other than a paper-towel blanket. "I wish I had a better answer for you, Mrs. Ra—I mean, Violet. But I don't. This is just a major misunderstanding. I promise you."

"I see."

"Call Ram and you'll see. I'm not his girlfriend."

Violet tilted her head, silent.

"If you let me go now, I promise I won't call the police. I won't tell anyone, like, not even Ram. I'll just leave here, pack up my shit, and move back home to New Mexico. I just need my clothes and my phone. That's all."

Violet's eyes morphed into black slits. "Now, why would you do all that if, as you say, Ram and you are just friends?"

Allegra sighed. "I can see our friendship has, like, totally offended you."

Violet burst with laughter. "*Offended* me?"

"Yes, it's a really easy mistake to make and everything, but no harm, no foul. Let me go right now and I'll be out of your life forever."

Violet sharpened her gaze. She licked her new red lipstick, and leaned in closer. "So why did you choose my husband?"

Allegra motioned to talk, but then stopped. She felt as if she were arguing with a new character from *Alice in Wonderland* called Mad Violet.

"I honestly don't know what you want to hear."

Violet scoffed, leaning back in her chair. "Do you like fairy tales, Allegra?"

Allegra's eyes widened, as if Violet could hear her thoughts. She cleared her throat. "You mean like *Frozen*?"

Violet half-heartedly nodded her head. "Close enough."

"Yes, I've seen those movies."

"Have you ever heard of a fairy tale called *The Virgin Mary's Child*?"

Allegra shook her head *no*.

"Of course not, Disney hasn't butchered it yet." She rolled her eyes. "Well, lucky for you, I know the story very well . . ."

Allegra slouched down, not sure of where the conversation was going.

Violet straightened her shoulders. "Once upon a time, there was a woodcutter who lived in terrible poverty with his wife and only child. They were a couple so poor, they could no longer afford food and had no idea how they would provide for their beautiful three-year-old daughter."

Violet elongated her neck as she spoke in a professional narrator's voice.

"One morning, the woodcutter was so stressed out by his dire situation, he went into the forest to chop wood and pray. And while he was praying, a magical woman appeared before him. She was seven feet tall, with long, dark hair and a glowing crown above her head."

Violet reached her hands above her head, changing her voice with each character.

"'I am the Virgin Mary, mother of Jesus Christ,' she said to him. 'Because you are a good man, but so poor and needy, bring me your daughter, and I'll take her with me to Heaven to look after her.'

"After careful thought, the woodcutter accepted her offer. He fetched his child and gave her to the Virgin Mary, who took her up to Heaven in an instant.

"Once she arrived in Heaven, everything went well for the young girl, who was soon consuming all the candy and cookies her heart desired. Her clothes were made of stars and gold, and the little angels enjoyed playing with her.

"On the child's fourteenth birthday, the Virgin Mary had to go on a long journey. But before she went away, she summoned the woodcutter's daughter and said 'Dear child, I am trusting *you* with the keys to the thirteen doors of the

Kingdom of Heaven. You may open twelve of the doors and enjoy all the marvelous things inside. But I forbid you to open the thirteenth door that this little key unlocks.' "

Violet held an invisible key in the air.

"The maiden agreed and promised to obey her commands. Soon after the Virgin Mary departed, she opened the twelve rooms and enjoyed all that lay before her: Each room housed a treasure and an apostle in glowing light.

"After she had finished opening the twelve doors, she became bored.

"For a long time, the maiden refused the temptation to open the thirteenth, forbidden door. But after several weeks she could no longer take it, so she opened that door as well. And as it sprang open, she saw the Holy Trinity sitting in golden fire.

"In amazement, she touched the golden flames with her pinkie finger. When she did, the finger turned golden. Horrified, she immediately shut the door and ran away. Her heart continued pounding and wouldn't stop until the next morning.

"Several days later, the Virgin Mary returned from her trip and asked the maiden to return the Keys of Heaven to her. As she passed them along, the Virgin Mary looked into her eyes and asked, 'Did you also open the thirteenth door?'

"'No,' the maiden answered.

"Then the Virgin Mary placed her hand on the maiden's heart and saw that it was pounding. Now *she knew* the girl had disobeyed her commands and opened the thirteenth door.

She looked into her eyes and asked the question again. 'Are you sure you didn't open the door?'

"'I'm sure.' The maiden denied it a second time.

Then the Virgin Mary glanced at her pinkie finger, now golden from touching the fire. Now *she knew* she was guilty. She said, 'Dear child, you have disobeyed me *and* lied. You're no longer worthy to stay in Heaven.'

"In that very moment, the girl sank into a deep sleep and fell back to Earth. When she awoke, she was lying on the ground in the forest, surrounded by woodland creatures. Her mouth had been locked shut so she could never utter another word, and her hair had grown so long it covered her naked body like a cloak.

"She lived in the forest alone for a year, scrounging for grubs and berries, until a king who had been hunting came upon her. He thought she was quite beautiful, so he asked if she would like to see his castle. Since she had lost her ability to answer, she simply nodded her head. The king then pulled her onto his horse and brought her home to his magnificent castle.

"Soon the king fell in love with the mute stranger and made her his wife.

"The next year, the queen gave birth to a handsome son. But during the night, the Virgin Mary appeared in her bedroom and said, 'If you tell me the truth and say you unlocked the forbidden door, I will give you back your ability to speak, without which you will not be able to fully enjoy your life.

But if you don't confess, I shall take your baby with me to Heaven.'

"But the queen was stubborn and once again denied opening the door. So the Virgin Mary took the little infant and disappeared with him.

"The next morning, when the baby was no longer in the castle, a rumor circulated around the village that the queen was an ogress in disguise, and had eaten her own child. The king, still in love with his wife, proclaimed that anyone spreading the rumor would hang for all of the townspeople to see.

"Another year had passed, and the queen gave birth to a second handsome son. Once more the Virgin Mary appeared in her bedroom and asked the queen to confess. But she refused, and the Virgin Mary took her child to Heaven once again.

"The next morning, when the second baby went missing, the king's advisors openly accused the queen of being an ogress and demanded she be executed for her godless deeds. The king ordered them to keep quiet, and continued to live his life as if nothing unusual had happened.

"In the third year, the queen gave birth to a beautiful little princess, and the Virgin Mary once again appeared before her. But this time, she took the queen and her baby to Heaven, where she saw her two sons, happy and playing with a globe of the Earth. Upon the sight, the Virgin Mary asked the queen to confess her mistake and stop lying, but once again, the queen wouldn't budge, and the Virgin Mary sent her back to Earth without her third child.

"Now the king could no longer restrain his advisors. They were certain his wife was evil, and since she could not speak, she could not defend herself. Consequently, she was sentenced to death—to be burned at the stake for her sins—in front of the townspeople, who were convinced she had *eaten* her three beautiful children.

"As the queen stood in fear, tied to the stake, the fire enveloping her feet below, she thought to herself, 'Before I die, I would like to confess to the Virgin Mary that I did indeed open the thirteenth door in Heaven. I've been so wicked by denying my actions all this time, and ask The Virgin for mercy.' Just as she was thinking this, the clouds of Heaven opened above her, and the Virgin Mary descended with the two sons and infant princess in her arms. The fire disappeared from her feet, and the Virgin Mary handed the queen her three children.

"The king and townspeople cheered at the sight. And from that day on, the queen could only speak the truth whenever her mouth opened, and lived happily ever after."

Violet smiled nostalgically.

She gently grabbed Allegra's left hand, kissing the top of it softly like a prince meeting a maiden for the first time. "So I ask, once again, do you confess?"

Allegra was puzzled by her gesture. All she could hear was Ram's deep voice saying: *If my wife ever asks you about us, deny it. Always deny.*

She felt sorry for Violet. "Like, I don't even know what you want me to say—"

In one swift action, Violet swung her meat cleaver in the air, then swooped down, slicing the pinkie finger from Allegra's unsuspecting hand.

The finger bounced twice on the floor, rolling toward Violet.

Allegra screamed. She screamed at the rolling finger in disbelief. She screamed at her four-fingered hand, gushing blood.

Violet picked up the small digit with chipping green nail polish, and hoisted it in the air, like a jeweler grading a diamond. As she did this, her face changed. It hardened.

The smell of animal musk filled the room.

Her breathing accelerated.

Her eyes closed.

Her jaw extended.

She dropped the tiny finger . . . And swallowed it in one glorious gulp.

Allegra was shocked.

Aghast. *Terrified.*

In the face of such disbelief, the stinging pain of her wound all but disappeared.

The lunacy of what she witnessed, stopped her breath.

Her heart.

Her sanity.

The smell of fear filled the room.

Violet reached down into her bag. She tossed Allegra a white roll of gauze. "Wrap it tightly or the bleeding won't stop," she said politely.

Allegra caught the roll, in awe of the monster sitting before her.

After a few seconds, she frantically unraveled it with her nine remaining fingers. *Wake up, Allegra! This is only a dream.* For this had to be a dream, or Allegra knew she would die at the hands of Mad Violet.

But it wasn't a dream.

Violet's stomach growled as it wrapped itself around the foreign meat. She wiped her mouth in excitement, accidentally smearing the red lipstick across her lips.

She now resembled an insane clown with a smile that matched the bloodstains on her dress.

Allegra began hyperventilating.

Tears fell from her baby doll eyes, while clear snot ran from her nose.

Violet returned an evil smile. "So, now you know the rules of this game, little girl. Answer a question truthfully, win a prize." She held up the shiny, three-thousand-dollar meat cleaver. "Lie to me again, and I will dissect the truth, piece by piece."

Allegra could not make eye contact. Instead, she kept wrapping and wrapping the gauze between the bleeding hole and her palm as she wept.

Violet rose slowly from her chair. "Let me ask you this question one last time: why did you choose my husband?"

Allegra shivered. Her child-like eyes looked up through her bangs. After a pause, she hiccupped before she answered, "Because he was a gentleman."

Violet lowered her lids and smiled, enjoying the brief moment of victory. She reached into her tote and placed the bag of Doritos and bottle of Dr. Pepper at Allegra's feet.

She made herself comfortable in the chair and gracefully re-crossed her legs.

"Good. Now tell me the story of how you two met."

FOURTEEN

SCORES OF bespectacled, hipster fashionistas crowded the entrance of the flagship store of Warby Parker, located on the corner of East 82nd Street and Lexington Avenue. The two-story building had recently opened, restoring the high-end Lascoff Pharmacy that had occupied the iconic corner for more than a century. Given its provenance, the architecture was stunning for a modern retail outlet, with oversized arched windows, dark wood moldings, terrazzo floors, and a vibe that was quintessential *Williamsburg meets the UES*.

Chloe and Allegra, wearing red and beige down coats respectively, were crammed shoulder to shoulder as the front door opened, and the well-behaved crowd of bargain hunters flooded the store.

"Why am I even here? I don't even *wear* glasses," said Allegra. "There's, like, a hundred other Black Friday sales we could be killing right now."

"Are you kidding me? They never have a two for one sale. As in *never*."

"Ugghhh."

"Plus, you can get a pair with no prescription and wear them to look smart."

"I work at a bar. Why do I need to look smart?"

"Their sunglasses kick ass too. Just check it out."

As they crossed the threshold, the crowd disbursed slightly, each person running to a different section of the open floor. The walls were lined with lighted shelves and mirrors, cradling exclusive Warby Parker design specimens—organized by style, shape, and purpose.

Allegra wandered the store, grabbing a pair of square, tortoiseshell acrylic frames and placing them on her face. She laughed when she caught her reflection. She thought she could easily be cast as *Ariel* in an undersea library porn video.

"Those look amazing on you," said Chloe, who was trying on a pair of round, red frames nearby. "What do you think about these?"

"You look like a talk show host. You want something a little more fuckable."

Chloe continued searching.

Allegra had just returned the tortoiseshell glasses to the shelf when a tall, bald man in a black wool coat bumped her shoulder.

"My apologies, darling," he said in a deep voice.

"No worries. It's ridiculous in here."

"Honestly, I hate crowds," he continued, smiling as he turned around. His square, dark-rimmed glasses suited his masculine, angled face perfectly.

"Me too," said Allegra. "My roommate made me come for moral support."

"My wife keeps nagging for me to choose a new style," he said, touching the corner of his lens. "I don't even know where to start." His low, sexy radio voice cast an invisible net, garnering Allegra's full attention.

She placed her hand on her chin. "Hmm. Honestly, the ones you have on now look amazing."

"Really?" he replied in a confident tone.

"Yeah, definitely stick with that shape. It totally works with your face. If you go with anything else, you'll look too *Big Bang Theory*."

"So you don't think these are outdated? Too Buddy Holly, 1950s?"

Allegra chuckled. "I have no idea who the hell that is, but hey, if he looked anything like you, he must have been hot."

Ram was taken aback. He did not expect a young girl as pretty as Allegra to be so loose with compliments. He extended his hand. "My name is Ram."

"Excuse me?" The cacophony of the crowd made it difficult to hear.

"I said my name is Ram. Like the animal."

She extended her hand. "I'm Allegra, like the allergy medication."

He chuckled. "Very nice to meet you."

"Same here."

"So, do you live in the neighborhood?"

"Yes. I'm on Second Avenue between Eighty-Eighth and Eighty-Ninth."

He raised his eyebrows. "Wow. How's that subway line construction going?"

Allegra smiled sarcastically. "It's the reason I'm out of my apartment as much as possible."

He smiled back. "I can imagine."

"How about you? Are you local?"

"Yes, I'm on Seventy-Eighth."

"Cool."

"I live at 13 East 78th to be exact. Between Fifth and Madison."

Strangers flaunted their addresses on the Upper East Side like Berkin bags and Bentleys. Because the lower the house number, the closer they lived to Central Park. And an address starting with *Thirteen* was a gold digger flag for old money.

Allegra's eyes lit up. "Oh, very nice."

Ram noticed. "Would you care to join me for breakfast?"

Allegra was impressed with his forwardness. "Excuse me?"

Ram moved in closer, pushed by shoppers behind him. His broad chest almost buried Allegra's face. "I'm having breakfast at the diner nearby. Would you care to join me?"

She spotted Chloe feverishly trying on sunglasses on the other side of the floor. She then looked at Ram's gold wedding band on his left hand, and his friendly, sky blue eyes. "What the fuck. It's just breakfast, right?"

"Yes." He smiled.

"Let me go tell my roommate I'm leaving, and I'll meet you right outside."

"Sounds good."

Ram turned to exit, while Allegra wormed her way to Chloe at the end of the store.

"I'm taking off."

Chloe was trying on a pair of blue sunglasses. "Why?"

"I just got invited to breakfast!"

"With who?"

"Some dude I just met who lives between Fifth and Madison."

Chloe jerked her neck. "What? Get out of here! Go, go, go!"

Ram and Allegra sat in a mustard-yellow booth at the Lexington Candy Shop—an old-fashioned luncheonette located one block north of Warby Parker on the corner of East 83rd Street. He was dressed in a long-sleeved navy-blue shirt. She wore a body-hugging, green-and-red plaid sweater.

"Is that cashmere?" he asked. "It's beautiful."

"Oh, God no. I totally wish."

An elderly waitress arrived wearing a white, fifties-style uniform. She held an order pad in one hand and a yellow No. 2 behind her ear.

"I dig the Buddy Holly glasses," she said, smiling.

Ram looked at Allegra, laughing. "See?"

"Looks like a sweet daddy and daughter breakfast. What happened? Did Mommy dump you guys to go shopping?"

Allegra wrinkled her nose. "Uhh, we're not . . ."

Ram just smiled. "I'll have the big breakfast special with rye toast. Make the eggs over easy. Extra sausage."

"Orange juice or coffee?"

"Coffee, please. Black."

"And you, doll?" Allegra continued staring at the menu. The waitress turned back to Ram. "Look at all that gorgeous hair. What happened, did she steal yours?"

Ram chuckled. He was immune to hack bald jokes.

Allegra lifted her eyes. "I'll have the same, just make it scrambled."

"And toast?"

"Yes, please."

"Coffee?"

"Sure. With cream and sugar."

The waitress leaned in and whispered, "Nice to see a girl who eats bread in this town. I'll put your order right in."

As the waitress left, Ram readjusted his large body in the uncomfortable seat. "She's a trip."

"Totally a tour."

"Have you eaten here before?"

"No." She smiled. "Like everyone else, I live in a five-block bubble."

"Me too," he added. "I've lived here my whole life, and I think I've been north of Ninety-Sixth Street maybe three times."

"Crazy, right?"

Their eyes met.

"So, do you, like, usually take strangers to breakfast?" she asked.

"What stranger?" He looked around the restaurant. "We're already friends."

Allegra batted her eyelashes. "You don't even know my last name."

"Let me guess. It's Smith."

"No."

"Jones."

Allegra laughed. "No, but you're getting closer."

"Lipchitz."

Allegra giggled. "It's Adams. Allegra Adams."

"Sounds colonial. Like you should be sewing flags for a living."

She smiled. "And you? What kind of name is Ram?"

"It's a nickname."

"For what?"

"Eugene."

She laughed. "No, it's not."

"Sheldon."

"Come on, you're playing—"

"Morty."

Allegra continued laughing. "No, really. What's your birth name?"

Ram looked coyly into her eyes. "Why do you want to know?"

"Because I don't have breakfast with strangers."

Ram diligently looked around the restaurant, as if he were a spy expecting enemies. "It's Balthazar. Balthazar Edward Ramspeck the third."

Allegra laughed out loud. "Now you're being totally ridiculous."

Ram held his coffee cup. "Honestly, that's my name."

Allegra slapped the table. "Like, nobody names their kid that! They would totally get their ass beat on a playground."

Ram turned serious. "Not where *I went* to school."

Finally, she saw in his eyes he was telling the truth. "Oh, my God. I'm being so rude."

"Not at all. It's just a name."

The waitress returned with two coffees and left abruptly.

"I know it sounds ridiculous to most, but it's an honorable family moniker, nonetheless."

Allegra was embarrassed. She just offended the hot, rich guy who was nice enough to buy her breakfast.

They sipped their coffees in silence.

"So, you said you were married?"

Ram nodded his head. "For nearly a quarter century now."

Allegra wasn't happy to learn he'd been married longer than she'd been alive. "Any kids?"

"No."

Allegra was pleased. At least there were no bratty stepchildren in her possible future.

"So, uh, where's your wife? Shouldn't she be helping you in the shopping department?"

Ram lifted his cleft chin. "She's with her parents in Palm Beach for the holiday. They're getting up there in age, so she didn't want to miss Thanksgiving with them."

"Why didn't you go with her?"

"You haven't met my father-in-law."

Allegra conceded. "Are *your* parents still alive?"

"Sadly, my mother passed away in her sleep three years ago."

"I'm sorry to hear that," she said, knowing how difficult it was to lose a mother.

"It's quite all right. She was ninety-one. She had a great life. Plus, she was rather old when she had me. I'm a *change of life baby.*"

"Oh."

"But my father? He's ninety-six years old and still kicking it with his girlfriend in Morocco. Or is it Monaco this year? I can't remember."

"Is that in Texas?"

"Not exactly." Ram laughed. "My father has this quest where they rent a manor in a different country every year. It's his version of RVing."

"Very interesting."

"I think it's a great idea, actually. I'd do it myself it I weren't so rooted in New York."

Allegra sipped her coffee. "So, what do you do for a living exactly?"

"I'm a business owner."

"What kind of business?"

He was hesitant to answer. "Well, I do a few different things."

"Like what?"

Ram drank from his mug. "My biggest company is an Asian goods import/export firm. But I also have a significant stake in a restaurant chain throughout Mexico and South America, a pharmaceutical packaging plant in Puerto Rico, and a chemical manufacturing plant in Croatia."

"Oh. I was, like, expecting you to say you owned a mattress store or something."

Ram smiled.

"That's a lot of responsibility."

"And a great deal of travel as well."

The waitress arrived with their plates. "Here you go, Annie . . . And here's yours, Daddy Warbucks."

Ram and Allegra exchanged a look, holding their laughter inside.

"Let me know if you need anything else," said the waitress as she left.

"We will, thank you," he replied.

Allegra dug into her food as if she hadn't eaten for days. "I love breakfast."

"Same here."

"I could eat this twenty-four seven," she said, chewing with her mouth open.

Ram was tickled by her unpolished personality. She was the polar opposite of his wife. "Tell me about yourself, Miss Allegra Adams. What brings you to New York City?"

"Why do you ask? I don't look native?"

Ram shook his head jovially. "Not exactly."

"Well, I've been here, like, a few months now. I'm a bartender at Bobby & Eddie's on First Avenue."

"Let me guess. You're in New York studying to be an actress?"

"Nope. Can't remember my grocery list, let alone memorize lines."

"A singer? I bet you can sing. Country, maybe?"

Allegra shook her head as she chewed on toast.

"An artist?"

Allegra smiled. "Hell no. I can't even draw a stick figure."

"That's it? No 'I'm just working here until something better comes along' kind of story?"

Allegra sipped her coffee. "Why? Bartending is *the perfect* job. I sleep in every morning, I meet cool people, I make sick money—especially on the weekends, thanks to karaoke—and when I leave the bar, I don't ever have to bring work home with me. No paperwork, no e-mail. It's perfect."

"And that's what you want to do for the rest of your life?"

"Sure, why not? I'm, like, really good at it too."

Ram appreciated her honesty. He had always been surrounded with so many overly ambitious people that it was refreshing to meet someone who was happy living a simple life.

"And where is your hometown?"

"New Mexico."

"What part?"

"I'm from Albucrappy. But I'm never going back." Allegra shoveled in a mouthful of sausage.

Ram stared at Allegra while she ate, enjoying every aspect of his new, charming, unrefined friend.

Ram finished paying the cashier up front, handed Allegra her beige down coat, and held the door open against the moderately cold wind outside.

"Thank you," she said, touched by his polished manners.

"My pleasure, fair lady."

As they stood outside, Allegra shifted her weight from foot to foot, unsure of what to say next. "It was really great meeting you."

Ram smiled. "This will definitely be the highlight of my day," he said in a bedroom voice. "How can I reach you if I ever want to say hello?"

Allegra looked up from beneath her bangs. A tingle grew between her hips as they locked eyes. "I'm not sure that's, like, a good idea."

Ram's enthusiasm faded. "Why not?" His expression was seductive, almost irresistible.

Allegra blew out a warm cloud of breath against the cold air. "Look, I'm not gonna lie. I like you, Ram. I just can't be with someone who's . . . you know."

She looked at his gold wedding band.

Ram twirled the ring on his finger. "Right, I see."

"But thank you so much for inviting me to breakfast and pulling me out of that crazy store," she said as she hugged him. "Maybe we'll run into each other soon."

His long arms cradled Allegra's voluptuous body. He relished the feeling of soft, womanly curves, unlike Violet's hard, linear physique.

Allegra wanted to hold on, but finally let go. "Thank you again."

"You're very welcome, darling," he said as she turned away. "Have a wonderful Christmas."

Allegra continued walking, turning her head and waving one last time.

Ram was unable to stop watching her stroll down the block . . . Fantasizing about her strawberry-scented, waist-length hair lying beside him, as he watched it swing side to side, brushing against the back of her beige coat.

Yes, Ram was thankful to have met Allegra that day.

But even more thankful she had refused to give him her number.

FIFTEEN

LAURA WELCH didn't need a meteorologist to figure out this had been one of the hottest days of the summer. It was only Thursday, yet four people had already died from the killer heat wave that continued to sneak in and out of the city that week, and pommel those unable to escape to the breezy shores surrounding their concrete island.

Despite the crippling temperatures, Laura suggested she and Penny stand outside on the sidewalk in front of 13 East 78th Street to greet their next prospect. According to Penny, the buyer was old money moving back to New York from a stint in Los Angeles, and was ready to make an offer on a property that very day. Both were well aware the overly generous commission bonus expired in less than thirty hours— an aggressive goal for even the most talented broker.

"Can we push the other showing to four?" asked Penny, squashed into a lavender dress suit, pacing in outrageously unstable, four-inch spike heels.

"The other buyer's flying in and out of Montreal, so I think we can only push it to three thirty," she replied as she dug through her large Kate Spade purse.

"Do it, then."

Laura pulled out her smartphone and began texting. She spoke aloud as she typed. "Our—two—o—clock—is—running—late. Can—we—move—to—three—thirty?"

Penny scratched her head, anxious. "And you're sure the wife's not home here?"

Laura hit the send button. "Yes, I spoke to the younger housekeeper this morning. She said Mrs. Ramspeck is away on a long trip."

"As in gone to Europe for the summer or going to Brooklyn for the day?"

"I have no idea." As Laura spoke, a black, eight-passenger limousine turned the corner. "I think that's them."

"Good, my foundation is evaporating," replied Penny, dabbing the sweat from her top lip.

The limo pulled up beside them.

"Here we go," said Penny, speaking through her smiling teeth.

An older man in a chauffeur's hat exited the driver's side door, walked around the car, and opened the rear passenger door. The first leg to emerge belonged to a tall, thin blonde wearing a pink Chanel suit. "Lovely, Penny!" she exclaimed as her head popped out. Her toothy grin was as repulsive as her Master Cleanse breath.

Penny forced a smile. "Kinga, how are you?"

The woman hugged her aggressively. "I am well. Business is good, yah?" she said in a thick Swedish accent.

"Very good for August," she replied.

The chauffeur then helped two older women and a feminine Asian man out of the car.

Kinga turned back to the driver. "I'll call you when we're done here."

The driver acknowledged her. "I'll be circling the neighborhood. Take your time."

She swung her head back to Penny and Laura. "I'm sorry we're late. My client wanted to see the property on Sixty-Third before this one."

"We're just glad you're here," said Laura, simultaneously extending her hand while wiping sweat from her temple. "Laura Welch."

"Kinga Erikkson."

Kinga looked back at the group forming behind her. She then placed her hand on the shoulder of an eccentric, seventy-year-old woman with bright white hair and oversized purple glasses. "I would like you both to meet my client, Margaret Morgan DuPont."

"Very nice to meet you," said Penny.

"Let's get on with it. I'm starving," said Margaret as she stared at the exterior steps.

Kinga moved on to the feminine Asian man. "And this is Luke Ming, her Feng Shui expert."

He waved shyly. "Hello."

"And this is Margaret's psychic medium, Candace Cross."

"Good day, everyone," she said in an angelic voice.

Penny was not pleased. She knew psychics were the serial killers of real estate deals. "Wonderful to meet you all. Shall we begin the tour?"

Candace was hesitant. "I need a few minutes to get grounded with the energy outside, if you don't mind?"

Margaret huffed. "It's hot as hell. I'll wait for you nuts indoors," she said as she left.

Kinga rushed by her side.

Candace removed her flip-flops, placing her un-manicured feet on the sidewalk as she closed her eyes. "Ohhmmm . . . Ohhhmmm . . ."

The remaining members of the group, fully dressed in professional regalia, sweated on the sidewalk waiting for Candace to finish.

Laura looked at Penny and crossed her fingers.

Penny mouthed *kill me.*

Laura snickered.

After a full minute of loud, sweaty breathing, Candace opened her eyes and returned to the conversation. "The energy's good here. Very prosperous."

"Super. Let's go."

Penny led the group into the two-story library located on the main floor near the entrance. Its dark cherry wood bookcases were lined with antique, leather-bound classics from floor to ceiling.

Candace was overwhelmed by its majesty. Her attention was mostly focused on the fireplace, and two blue reading chairs with attached lamps, perfect spots for cuddling up with turn-of-the-century bestsellers.

Penny gestured her hands as she gave the well-rehearsed tour. "I'm not sure if Kinga mentioned this to you yet, but nearly all of the furnishings are for sale. Including this book collection, which features several first print editions, and even some handwritten copies from the early nineteenth century that were never circulated in public."

Luke turned to Margaret and spoke in a low voice. "We could put a water feature in here, perhaps a freestanding brass fountain, to balance the heavy wood energy."

Margaret nodded in response. "Good idea."

Candace walked closer to Kinga. "How old is the home?"

"I believe it was built in 1903. Is that correct, Penny?"

"Yes. And the same family lived here for eighty-nine years," she said loudly. "All good people. No bad spirits here."

"I can tell," replied Candace. "I feel good energy in this room. The family that lived here was very happy. Very loving. Very wealthy."

Penny raised her brow at Laura, who was trailing at the end of the pack. Her expression said: *No shit, Sherlock.*

The younger housekeeper, Octavia, entered the room and tugged at Laura's sleeve. She spoke with a Spanish accent.

"Yesterday, Rosa and I both try the numbers you give to me on the phone, but I so sorry, none worked."

Laura turned sharply. "Are you sure?"

Octavia nodded. "We both try to fix up the basement for you, but it's locked."

"Let's go check it out."

Laura quietly excused herself from the tour and left with Octavia.

———

Laura and Octavia stood outside the first security door, deep inside the pantry.

Laura held Penny's small notebook in her hands. "This doesn't make any sense. Penny said Mr. Ramspeck figured out the second code and e-mailed it to her. Now the first code is not working?"

Octavia's big brown eyes widened. "I don't know what happen."

"When's the last time you've been in there to clean?"

Octavia looked sideways. "Maybe"—her tongue lightly pressed against her lip—"two years ago?"

Laura was surprised. "You haven't been downstairs for two years?"

"No."

"What about Rosa?"

Octavia shook her head. "No need to clean. Just storage, mainly."

Laura looked at the notebook in defeat. "Penny is going to be *pissed*. We thought for sure we could show it today."

Octavia shrugged her shoulders. "We really try. I wish I could help."

Laura sighed. "I know you did, thank you. I guess it's just not in the cards."

Upstairs, Penny and Kinga led the group to the top of the landing in front of the master suite. Margaret held on to the final patch of railing for dear life. "I'm not climbing seven floors of stairs every night."

Kinga interjected. "You can use the elevator instead. It's practically brand-new, yah?"

"You want me to drop dead all alone in an elevator like Prince? Not me," she moaned.

"You will never be alone, Margaret. You'll always have your house staff to look after you."

Margaret waved her hand in dismissal.

Penny resumed her official tour voice. "Now, before we go in, I just want to remind everyone to use their imaginations and picture a whole new set of furniture in here."

Kinga agreed. "Please keep in mind, everything can be redone, yah?"

As Penny opened the door, Luke, who was standing at the front of the pack, caught a glimpse of something horrifying in the mirror on top of the dresser. His Adam's apple sank. His breath quickened. It was a large, brown wolf with a terrifying smile. "There's something in here," he said under his breath.

As he tried to back up, Kinga gently pushed him forward.

When he fully entered the room, he saw the wolf image was actually a reflection of a painting on the wall. "Those definitely have to come out of here," he said as he turned, pointing at the prime offender.

"Holy cow, look at this tree bed," said Margaret. "Does a lumberjack come with it?"

Candace's cheerful face drained of color. "I don't know, Margaret," she said cautiously. "The energy in this room is completely different than the rest of the house."

"I love it," said Kinga with enthusiasm as she looked around. "Very outdoors."

Luke cased the walls, zooming in on the artistic depictions of *Little Red Riding Hood* around the room. "Too many dark colors and negative images. We'll need to completely resurface this room."

"The decorator should be hanged," said Margaret. "I'd like to buy this furniture just so I can burn it."

Penny was uncomfortable. "Let's have a look at the terrace. There's a gorgeous view of Central Park from here."

Everyone followed her outside, except for Margaret, who stayed indoors. "I'm afraid of heights. I don't need to see it."

After a few seconds, Candace quickly turned back to join her. "I don't know, Margaret, this is a fantastic house, but I feel something's wrong with this room."

Margaret gave her a sarcastic look. "Maybe it's because there's a *Twilight Zone* bed in here? I could have figured that out for myself, Candace. What the hell do I pay you for?"

"Honestly, I feel there's something stronger here than the bed. I feel anger. I feel pain. I don't know what it is exactly. It's not a good energy."

Penny stepped back indoors, rushing her explanation of the terrace to interrupt Candace's conversation. "And here we have the dressing area and master closet."

Candace touched Penny's forearm. "Has anyone died in this room?"

Penny smiled. "Not one person. Every single resident passed of old age at Mount Sinai." She smiled wide, pulling that lie straight out of her ass.

Candace was first to turn the corner and enter the dressing area. She reacted strongly to the doll collection. "Here we go. *It's the dolls.*"

Margaret followed right behind her. "Easy fix. Burn them."

"Not so fast," said Luke.

"I agree," blurted Candace. "You can't disrupt an old spirit who's been here for years and expect it to leave quietly."

Penny rolled her eyes.

Kinga mouthed, *I'm sorry.*

Margaret tossed her hand in disregard. "It's just a doll collection, people. My mother had one very similar to this. Just show me the damn closet."

Penny released a sigh of relief. She reached for the closed closet door, slowly turning the knob, and opened it. "Okay. Here we go," she said, thrilled the door was unlocked.

The group poured inside the thousand-square-foot room encircled by hundreds of racks of clothing and multiple shelves of shoes. It was stuffed with so many bright, colorful garments and accessories it looked like Dylan's Candy Bar on Third Avenue.

"I thought New Yorkers only wore black," said Luke.

"Not this lady," said Margaret. "Impressive."

Penny was pleased.

Suddenly, Candace grabbed her chest. "I'm not feeling very well," she said. "May I have a glass of water?"

Luke noticed something *move* behind a rack of long coats. "Is someone in here?"

No one heard his comment. They were all concerned with Candace's health instead.

Luke approached the rack of clothing, puzzled by what could be in there.

He walked closer . . .

And closer . . .

He raised his arm . . . Preparing to part the coats to reveal what was behind—

"Water! Please!" shouted Candace, bent over, unable to stand.

Luke turned around.

Kinga rushed to hold her up.

Penny was annoyed as hell. "Let's go. There's a staff kitchen on the fifth floor." She quickly led the group out of the closet, into the dressing area, and out the bedroom door.

Luke followed behind the crowd, looking back over his shoulder several times.

Nothing else moved.

Once he caught up, he saw Penny marching the troop down the stairs to the fifth floor.

"Shoot. I left the terrace door open," said Penny.

"Yah, better close it before the mosquitoes get in," replied Kinga.

Penny gritted her teeth. She was ready to strangle the psychic for trying to kill her deal. She tapped Kinga on the shoulder. "You can't miss it. It's the second door on the right," she said cutting her way back upstairs.

Kinga led the group into the fifth-floor staff kitchen. The bright sun from the large window heated the room.

"This place needs bigger curtains," said Margaret.

Laura heard the commotion from downstairs and joined them. "Is everything all right?"

Kinga smiled, glowing from the sunny window behind her. "Just a little heat, that's all."

Luke quickly grabbed a bottle of water out of the plain white refrigerator.

"I'll take one too," said Margaret, reaching in behind him.

Luke handed Candace the water. She was pale, holding her chest as she took a sip.

"Do you need me to call 9-1-1?" asked Laura.

Kinga opened her mouth to answer when a large, *screaming* lavender blob flew down behind her, and crashed on the pavement outside.

Margaret covered her face.

Kinga was paralyzed, unable to turn around and look out the window.

Candace instantly recovered, standing ramrod straight.

Luke slowly approached the window.

Laura's mouth gaped open in fear. "Where's Penny?"

An unfamiliar female voice began screaming outside. Then another woman joined her, yelling for help.

Luke looked down at the scene below. His reaction said it all.

Kinga finally turned around to look. She gasped.

The screaming from below continued.

Laura ran to the window. She looked down and saw Penny lying on the sidewalk, with open, lifeless eyes, bleeding out the back of her smashed head, while her twisted neck, bent torso, and crooked legs smothered something attached to a pink leash held by an Indian woman screaming for help.

"Penny?" whimpered Laura.

Margaret ruffled her wings. "I think someone needs to make that 9-1-1 call now."

Two agonizing hours had passed.

Kinga, with watery mascara staining her face, was the last to enter the running limo. She held Laura's hand as the sights and sounds of sirens, ambulances, and gawkers crowded around them. She looked at Rosa and Octavia standing nearby in their maid uniforms. "If there is anything I can do," she said sincerely to the trio, "please do not hesitate to call, yah?"

Laura wiped her cheek and nodded in appreciation.

Kinga released her hand and closed the door. The limo sped off and quickly turned the corner in the distance.

Moments later, an African-American policeman approached Laura and the two housekeepers. He carefully wiped the sweat from his forehead with his sleeve. "So, we've finished talking to all the witnesses on the street, and it looks like we're ruling it an accident."

Laura nodded, unable to verbalize more than a gesture.

"And you're sure there was no one else in that room?"

Rosa and Octavia nodded.

"And according to all the witnesses we interviewed, no one saw anyone else on the balcony except the victim. We think she may have lost her footing, and in her high heels, wasn't able to stop the momentum."

Laura began to cry again, wiping her nose.

"We also checked the security of the balcony railing, and nothing was loose," he continued as the flashing lights approached from another vehicle. "But if I were you, I would have the owners get it inspected by a structural engineer as soon as possible."

"I will," replied Laura, teary-eyed.

"You also might want to take it off the market until this all quiets down."

Rosa and Octavia exchanged a look.

"That's a good idea, sir," replied Laura. "Thank you."

"Now do your best to get some rest. You've all been through a lot today. It was a freak accident, completely out of your control."

Laura whispered through her tears, "I'll try."

The uniformed officer jumped into the running police vehicle and left.

Laura stood motionless, incapacitated by the lights and murmurs of people around her, unable to release the gruesome image of her best friend, and mentor, mangled on the pavement below.

After a few moments, Octavia extended her arms.

Laura fell into her embrace, crying.

SIXTEEN

FOR ALLEGRA, finding Chloe's nine-hundred-square-foot, two-bedroom, one-bath apartment in Yorkville was like discovering a gem in the middle of a steaming heap of shit in the woods. It was a classic, six-flight, walk-up building located in the heart of the old German working-class neighborhood on Second Avenue between East 88th and 89th Streets—a mere five blocks from where she worked. To share an apartment this large for a thousand dollars a month was nothing short of a miracle, but to have two *actual* bedrooms, a full-size kitchen and a *real* living area was quite a luxury, given most living rooms in the neighborhood were instantaneously converted into sleeping dens, allowing yet another person to help cover the outrageous rent.

The quarter-floor penthouse (if one could call it that) was slightly rundown, with scuffed dark wood floors, ten-foot ceilings, and fully exposed brick walls, but it was desirable nonetheless. It had been in Chloe's family for more than thirty years, with the right to occupancy being passed to the most ambitious child of three close sisters. In fact, the apartment was still in Chloe's aunt's name, ensuring the rent-controlled bargain basement price-tag of only two thousand dollars a month.

After nailing an early morning web video shoot, Chloe spent the rest of the afternoon floating around the apartment in her summer uniform of a white tank top and baby blue boxer shorts. She opened each east and west window, excited to no longer hear the Second Avenue subway line construction in the distance, which had polluted her ears for four years until it finally opened on January 1, 2017.

Chloe plugged in as many box fans as she could near the open windows to create a breeze. Her sacred bedroom was the only room with a window-mounted air-conditioning unit, where she stored her most valuable eBay inventory—hoping the warm, dank air infiltrating the rest of the apartment wouldn't creep into her goods before shipping them out to various parts of the world.

As Chloe was plugging in the last box fan in the living room, the intercom buzzer near the door sounded. She darted down the hall and pressed the top button.

"Hi. Can I help you?"

"It's FedEx Global. I have a package for Chloe Sinclair?"

"Cool. I'll be right down."

Chloe wasn't expecting a package, but given her liberal return policy, she thought it could be from someone asking for a refund or an exchange. She tapped her way down the six-flight staircase and greeted the deliveryman with a cordial smile. "Hey, Jackson. How are you?"

"Good," he said, scanning the barcode on the legal-sized envelope. "Must be a light day. Only *one* package for you," he said jokingly. After signing, Chloe waved goodbye and made the mountain climb back up the stairs.

As soon as she returned to her apartment, she glanced down at her body and smiled, realizing she had just greeted the FedEx deliveryman wearing nothing but men's underwear.

She moved toward the dining room table and eagerly opened the package. After pulling the cardboard string, she found a computer printed note and a brown envelope.

She pulled out the note and read it carefully:

Hey Girl!

Like I promised, I have enclosed my rent for the rest of the year. I hope you can get another roommate really soon! I also gave you $$$ to ship my personal stuff to my house manager at my new address below (hubby and I are honeymooning in France for the month). Just send anything you think is important, like my keepsakes, pictures, and jewelry. You can keep or sell my clothes, makeup, shoes, etc. Just send it as soon as you can. Thanks a mil! XXOO

Allegra Martinez
c/o Hermana Maria Frances
Avenida De Las Rosas 2933
Guadalajara 44530, Mexico

Chloe then reached inside the package and pulled out the brown envelope. It was filled with crisp, new hundred-dollar bills. After counting it, she realized there were ninety-nine of them—a total of nine thousand, nine hundred dollars in cash in her hand.

Instead of celebrating, Chloe's stomach knotted. She shuffled and recounted the money between her long, dark fingers. Was it envy? Maybe jealousy? This was nearly enough cash to cover her rent for five whole months, but for Allegra, it was a drop in the bucket. Now that she's "rich as fuck."

Then it struck her.

The address said Allegra *Martinez?*

She never mentioned Mr. Big was Latino. Not that it really mattered, but it was another fact she so conveniently failed to share. *Why wouldn't she mention this?* Chloe had a thing for Latino men—Puerto Ricans and Cubans in particular. So why hide it? Was it someone Chloe had dated before? *Or is he a telenovela actor? Or a big-time drug dealer? Is that why she was so secretive about him?*

Chloe knew Allegra was no stranger to illegal substances. But when she met Allegra's pot dealer one afternoon at the bar, she saw he was a white teenaged boy who attended one of the prestigious prep schools nearby.

So, who was this mysterious Martinez fellow?

Was he married?

And if so, how did he get divorced so quickly?

Maybe he killed his wife?

Made it look like a car accident?

Then flew to New York to snatch up his mistress and marry her on the spot?

Questions flooded Chloe's brain, each one giving her greater concern than the first. Something wasn't right. Her imagination was making her sicker by the moment, and she was determined to figure out why.

She went into the kitchen and grabbed her tape gun, three flat cardboard shipping boxes, bubble wrap, and markers, then walked toward the rear of the apartment. She had not entered Allegra's bedroom since she left for a run in Carl Schurz Park eight nights earlier. But the stinging feeling in her stomach motivated Chloe to hurry up and finish the task at hand.

She entered the messy room that featured a twin-sized, hot pink comforter with white faux fur pillows, rumpled sheets, and clothes strewn throughout the floor. There were numerous empty cups, used paper plates, and soiled forks randomly scattered about. Standing tall and proud on her nightstand was Allegra's eighteen-inch purple bong she affectionately named *Beiber,* and a never-ending stash of marijuana in the drawer below it.

Chloe assembled the three cardboard boxes, placing two smaller ones inside the large one. First, she opened the white wicker dresser drawers and began feeling her way for non-clothing items. She grabbed handfuls of cheap rings, necklaces, and earrings, carefully wrapping each one in bubble wrap and placing it in a smaller box. She reached way back into the drawer and pulled out a flat, red Cartier box and opened it to reveal a gold and ruby necklace worthy of a princess. Chloe frowned, sharply jealous she had never received a gift so luxurious, but sobered at the thought it was probably bought with illegal drug money, and quickly placed it in Allegra's shipment.

Chloe continued searching for valuable personal objects, tossing broken cell phone chargers, mystery keys, and cheap drugstore makeup into the trash. As she anticipated, there were very few sentimental items, except for a stack of childhood family photos of Allegra and her two siblings.

She then spent the next hour clearing out Allegra's dresser and bi-fold closet, separating items worthy of selling on eBay and those that should be thrown out.

She literally salivated at Allegra's collection of Tom Ford, Prada, Gucci, Chanel, and Christian Louboutin, calculating in her head the thousands of dollars she would earn in the coming months from selling these highly sought-after items. When she was finished, she scanned the bottom of Allegra's closet one last time and came across a Wal-Mart shoebox hidden deep in the far corner.

Chloe reached inside and pulled it out.

As she opened the top, she saw a small red journal, and something beside it wrapped in newspaper. Chloe was stumped. She had never known Allegra to be much of a writer, but then again, she knew Allegra was a master at keeping secrets like no other person she had met before.

The red diary was brand-new, smelling of leather, with a bit of retail plastic still covering the back cover. Chloe quickly flipped through the book, noticing it was mostly empty, with only a few pages filled near the front.

She opened it to reveal Allegra's large, bubble-style handwriting with hearts and smiley faces doodled throughout.

On the first page, it read:

This Journal belongs to:
Allegra Renee Ramspeck

On the second page it read:

G Names:
Keisha
Lola
Brooke
Riley
Rebecca
Selena

On the third page it read:

B Names:
Justin
Colton
Beau
Royce
Zane
Zander

And on the final written page it read:

Possible Dates in 2019:
  April 20
  May 25
  June 15
  June 29
  July 27

Chloe was confused. *What is this Ramspeck name? Isn't her last name Martinez? What do these random first names mean? Why are all of these dates Saturdays?*

Chloe spent a good five minutes going over these questions in her head, finally arriving at the conclusion that it was none of her business. Allegra was an adult, capable of making her own decisions. And if she thought marrying Mr. Drug Trafficker and moving to Mexico was a good idea, then so be it.

Maybe this was written before Mr. Big?

But the journal is brand-new.

Chloe let out a deep sigh, concerned the ugly jealousy monster was again affecting her judgment. As someone who valued the right to privacy, she immediately felt guilty about reading Allegra's "almost" diary, even if it was only three pages long.

She closed the journal and placed it into the shipping box.

But when she looked at the item wrapped in newspaper, curiosity overwhelmed her. She unraveled it to make sure she wasn't accidentally sending drug paraphernalia overseas.

She carefully unwrapped the paper to reveal a white plastic stick with two pink lines.

A positive pregnancy test?

Chloe's heart immediately sank with frenvy. *No wonder she doesn't need her clothes. She's pregnant!*

Chloe looked at the wrinkled newspaper: It was the front cover of *The New York Times* from Friday, August 3rd. After holding the test for a few seconds, Chloe decided to re-wrap it like she found it, and placed the keepsake into the shipping box along with Allegra's other belongings.

She then carefully packed the inside of the large box with bubble wrap, sealed it with gobs of clear shipping tape, and carried it into the kitchen. She slugged the note and cash into her backpack, and headed out to make the familiar trek to the post office located two *heavy* blocks away.

A week later, a short man dressed in a yellow uniform carried a large box into an empty restaurant. He placed the package on the front bar, where a sunbaked man wearing a colorful flowered shirt was wiping down stools.

"Gracias," said the bartender to the deliveryman as he exited.

The bartender stopped cleaning and scrutinized the *USPS International Priority* shipping label:

Allegra Martinez
c/o Hermana Maria Frances
Avenida De Las Rosas 2933
Guadalajara 44530, Mexico

He did not recognize the first name, but he definitely knew the second.

He carried the box out the front door, crossing the empty, narrow street to a small building only a few yards away.

The bartender knocked on the peeling door. A young lady dressed in white answered, with rows of young babies crying in cribs behind her.

"Is Sister Maria Frances here?" he asked in Spanish.

"Yes, one minute," she replied.

The man peeked his head inside and made eye contact with a drooling, two-year-old boy bouncing in his plain crib.

A few seconds later, an elderly nun dressed in a black-and-white habit came to the front door.

The man handed her the large box. "This is for you."

"What is it?"

He shrugged his shoulders. "Probably a donation from the United States?"

Sister Maria Frances looked at the address and smiled. She immediately recognized the name *Allegra Martinez* as it was the name of a baby in her orphanage who had been featured on a local television show. The contents of the box, she thought, must be an anonymous donation made to the orphanage in her honor.

"Thank you, Antonio. May God continue to bless you."

The nun closed the door and carried the box inside.

SEVENTEEN

"AARON! STOP! Daaaad!"

A towheaded three-year-old boy smacked the remote control out of his big sister's hand and ran. The remote was connected to miniature sailboat in the sweet little armada floating on the conservatory pond in Central Park near East 73rd Street.

Little Aaron continued running, giggling his way through clusters of international tourists and children surrounding the pond. He smacked the khaki pants of an elderly man, photo-bombed a young couple by the ledge, and kicked over the tripod of a German man shooting the reflective water. He continued running, laughing, and enjoying the gorgeous, breezy reprieve from the oppressive heat that had kept him indoors all week.

Little Aaron made his final bend around the oval pond to the far West side. He immediately stopped in front of a large bronze statue of Hans Christian Anderson reading a book to a curious duck below. The statue was one of Little Aaron's favorites, but this time, it was the pretty lady and the old man with bushy eyebrows sitting behind the statue that caught his attention.

Violet waved at the small, curious child. Her wide-brimmed hat, dark sunglasses, eggplant Herve Léger dress, and coral Stuart Weitzman heels, stood out against the vibrant green background of bushes, trees, and leaves surrounding her.

"Hello, little boy," said Dr. Cohen, in his thick Jewish accent.

The boy continued staring, confused as to why such a well-dressed couple was sitting all alone on a park bench.

Finally, his big sister caught up with him, panting, out of breath. "Daddy is going to kill you. Come on." She grabbed his arm and led him away from the area, back to the other side of the pond.

Dr. Cohen flashed a radiant, yellow-toothed smile. "I just love watching children play."

Violet nodded as she removed her sunglasses. "Me too."

"Aren't you pleased I suggested we meet out here instead?"

Violet leaned forward, zooming into the busy sailboat race. She imagined herself sunning on the little wooden bow. She then scanned the impressive Fifth Avenue skyline in the distance. "You know what's ironic?"

Dr. Cohen was intrigued.

"I've lived steps away from this park since I was a little girl, and only now that I'm being forced to leave do I appreciate how beautiful it is."

Dr. Cohen angled his gray-suited shoulders. "Central Park is the most marvelous place in the world. Just look at how far people have traveled to come visit." His eyes pointed to a photographer taking pictures of a beautiful Pakistani bride and groom. He leaned back, his mustache curling upward. "Your wedding reception at the Boathouse was magnificent."

Violet smiled nostalgically. "Yes, it was."

She looked around their immediate area, noticing all the park benches beside them were empty. "We really don't appreciate what we have until we lose it. Do we?"

Dr. Cohen teetered his head. "Sadly, I think you're right."

Violet sighed. "I'm going to miss New York dearly."

Dr. Cohen removed his glasses. He cleaned them with the corner of his dress shirt, hiding his emotion. "As will I." He replaced them on the bridge of his nose. "So, where did we leave off from our last session?"

"You had asked me how I found out about the affair."

"Ah, yes. And this was a little over two months ago, correct?"

"Two months, fourteen days."

"And you didn't confront him until when?"

Fear filled Violet's eyes. Her breath slowed, and her chest rose softly as her gaze circled the concrete below.

"We can talk about that another time. For now, let's discuss what happened in the months after you discovered Ram had a mistress. Maybe start from the morning you found out."

Violet realigned her perfect posture. "Well, after I found out on the morning of June 7th, I tried to go about my schedule as usual, but I was so weak, I couldn't even leave the house.

It was as if a hole had punctured my lungs and parts of my soul began leaking out."

"And what did you tell others about why you had to cancel?"

"I told my housekeepers I was coming down with a stomach virus. I also texted the same story to Ram, and the Pure Yoga ladies I was scheduled to meet with later."

"And then?"

Violet's eyes welled. "I stayed in bed crying, and crying, for at least six hours, maybe more. Ram was due home that evening around nine, so I placed frozen masks on my face before he came in and discovered how swollen my face had become."

"Did he notice anything different?"

Violet shook her head. "No, he just thought I was ill and slept in one of the guest bedrooms downstairs. In fact, I was able to fake my illness for around three days. I was pale, swollen, vomiting. It was all very believable."

"And how did you feel during that time?"

Violet gave an austere look. "I just wanted to die, Dr. Cohen. It was as clean and simple as that. My heart ached so badly, it felt like my chest had been barreled open with two crow-bars and my beating heart was stinging as it hit the air. Just unbearable."

"And how did you cope with the intense pain over those first few days?"

"I had some Xanax left over from the other doctor I was seeing at the time, so I just took two pills every four hours and slept."

"What else?"

Violet knew what he was getting at. "You mean did I binge and purge?"

Dr. Cohen nodded.

"No, Dr. Cohen. That's all behind me. I eat healthy, watch my portions, and exercise regularly. That is how I maintain my weight. I'm the healthiest I've ever been."

"Okay, very good. And once your stomach virus was over . . . What happened then?"

Violet brushed at a leaf that had fallen into her lap. "About a week after I found out, Ram left for another business trip. It was to Brazil, I believe. I was able to catch my breath and resume my daily activities without anyone suspecting . . . much."

"Did you tell anyone else about Ram's affair?"

"No. I immediately wanted to call all of my girlfriends and cry my head off, but something inside stopped me from doing it. I'm not sure why."

"Pride?"

"Yes, perhaps it was pride. Or embarrassment. Which makes no sense, considering most of my married friends have dealt with similar situations. Except say, Antonia, who is married to a four-foot midget, or my friend Marlene, who was the one having an affair with her dog walker. I knew my friends would offer me tremendous support, yet I refused to tell anyone my secret."

"Why do you think that is?"

"I guess I didn't want to shatter my reputation. My standing in our circle."

"What is your standing in the circle?"

"I was the one who had the perfect husband. I was the one with the perfect marriage. I already earned my victim card for being the one who tragically lost a baby. Not 'Feel sorry for me because my husband is leaving me for a younger woman.' That card was already taken."

Dr. Cohen swatted a gnat that approached his nose. "So you kept your knowledge about Ram's affair to yourself. Then what?"

"Well, in the days afterward, I started reflecting on things that had happened over the prior months that I had completely missed. Like my husband suddenly taking an interest in the way he looked, waxing his chest and grooming his pubic area."

Dr. Cohen nodded. "Yes, very common signs."

"And since my husband always kept fit, I never noticed the increase in time at the gym. But I did notice he was gaining more definition in his physique and eating much healthier."

"I can see that."

"But the biggest red flag was that, around Christmas, he suddenly changed his style of underwear. Just think, fifty-three years of wearing Brooks Brothers boxer shorts, and one day, he threw out all of his boxer shorts and changed to this high-end, biker brief sort of style. I don't remember the name of the brand. It's new and all the young traders wear it?"

Dr. Cohen gestured he was unfamiliar with the brand as well.

"But more importantly, he changed with me. And that's what truly hurt the most."

"In what ways?"

Violet looked upward. "I don't know, he just changed. Like the way he looked at me. It was just *different*. Or the way he made love to me. It was like he was more masculine, more confident when we were in bed together."

"And did you see any other changes in your sex life?"

Violet was slightly embarrassed. Dr. Cohen was a father figure, and she hated talking about sex with him. "Yes, I experienced other changes too."

"Such as?"

Violet tucked her chin, shyly. "Ram suddenly became more adventurous in bed, more passionate. He wanted to try new positions. And when we did, he just seemed like he knew what he was doing."

"For example?"

Violet resisted at first, but then realized Dr. Cohen was only asking for further details to help her. "Well, he, uh, asked me to perform anal sex, which I refused, and this act where I was on my hands and knees hovering above him—"

"Sixty-nine?"

Violet turned beet red. She shuddered at the thought of an eighty-something-year-old man knowing what that was. "Yes, sixty-nine."

"Go on."

"Well, *that* I did enjoy, and while I was above him, he performed, you know, and I had an orgasm, which I almost always do when we make love, but soon afterward he asked me why I was so quiet."

"Is that unusual for you?"

"No, I'm always quiet when I climax. Which is not unusual," she said defensively. "Have you ever heard the theory that the way a woman sneezes is how she orgasms? That they're both involuntary reflexes? Well, I think that theory may be true. You know how I sneeze, Dr. Cohen."

He smiled. "A thousand little achoos."

"Yes, a thousand little *quiet* achoos. I've always been quiet, but that doesn't mean I'm not satisfied. I'm extremely attracted to my husband, and he's amazing in bed."

Dr. Cohen wiped away an itch on his nose. "Then what happened?"

"About a week later, we went out to Cipriani on 42nd Street. It's essentially a Friday night tradition for us if he's in town. We have a romantic dinner, maybe even see a Broadway show if something new comes out, but that night, for whatever reason, he didn't make eye contact with me the entire evening."

"Was he stressed about work? Or were you two fighting over something?"

"Oh, heavens, no. We rarely fight. Maybe once or twice I can remember. Heated discussions, yes, but never fights."

"So why did you think he was avoiding eye contact?"

Violet looked down at her eggplant-colored lap. "I don't know, he must have felt guilty about something. Or he was worried. Or stressed. Either way, he was far, far away. But it was stranger than that. Even though we sat through a whole three-course dinner without even sharing a glance, he drank more alcohol than usual—it was either gin or straight Patron, I can't remember—but later, when we went home, he tried to make love to me, and it felt off."

"In what way?"

Violet turned her attention to the children still playing in the distance. "He didn't look at me. He just turned me around and made love to me from behind." Violet's face saddened. "The entire time."

Dr. Cohen carefully observed Violet's facial expressions.

"Then, when he was finished, he rolled over and shut off the lamp. It was the first time we had ever been together where I felt used. I felt cheap. And to make matters worse, in the silent darkness, he asked me why we had never had anal sex before."

Dr. Cohen wiped the sweat from the corner of his lip. The strengthening sun was now bullying the breeze away. "And was that an unusual question?"

"Yes, it was, at least for us. We had never talked about it before. Or about sex, really. It was just something we did. Something we enjoyed and did whatever felt natural to us."

Dr. Cohen reflected on her statement. Thoughts ran through his head in one direction like rats in a sewer. "This all sounds very common, Violet."

Her face contorted in sarcasm. "Well, that makes me feel a whole lot better."

Dr. Cohen plowed through. "So, when did it start to feel . . . obsessive?"

Violet rolled her neck halfway. The brightening sun was becoming too much to bear. "It's when I found out her name."

"How did you discover who she was?"

"You've heard the saying, haven't you? A suspicious wife is a better investigator than the FBI and CIA combined? Well, it's true. As soon as I was done grieving, I launched into my investigator mode."

"In what way?"

"I was able to break into Ram's personal Gmail account where I read some of their coded communications. Once I saw her email address, I did a Google search, and from there, I was able to identify all of her social media accounts."

"And then?"

"And then I created a fake Facebook page of a young party boy named Daniel Frey. I sent her a friend request, and she stupidly accepted, not realizing Daniel Frey had no other friends. And just like that, I learned everything I could about her in a matter of minutes."

"Did you see Ram on her Facebook page?"

"Goodness, no. Ram believes social media is the work of the devil. He refuses to participate in any of it."

"Then, what *did* you see?"

"I saw thousands of pictures of her, and her friends. One damn photo after the next. Some were flattering, others were not. I'm sure she takes a camera with her to take a shit."

"What else?"

"I learned about her likes, dislikes, where she was employed, you name it. I know more about her than I do my own friends."

"And after that?"

"Once I knew where she lived, I would spend hours in the café across the street, watching to see if Ram ever visited."

"Did he?"

"No, he used hotels instead. The one-star Hotel Carlson was his favorite."

"How do you know this?"

"I broke into his Hotels.com account as well. Days he was supposed to be in Philly or Boston, he was actually twenty minutes away at The Hotel Carlson screwing his whore. How's that for ballsy?"

"Did you ever confront the girl?"

Violet was stoic. "Not yet."

Dr. Cohen missed the blatant lie. "Have you ever tried communicating with her?"

"She knows I know about the affair, but nothing more."

Dr. Cohen shifted his weight. The heat was starting to agitate him. "And how do you feel *right now* about all of this?"

Violet inhaled the last swig of fresh morning air. "Honestly? *I feel great.*"

Dr. Cohen was surprised. "Really?"

Violet smiled, thinking of the pinkie finger she lopped off and swallowed four days earlier. "Yes, I think I've turned the corner somehow. I'm starting to accept the situation. I know it's not my fault, and there are plenty of women my age who find love again."

Dr. Cohen angled his elbow. "That's wonderful to hear, Violet. And the selling of the house? How is that going?"

Violet's eyes sparkled. "Fortunately, not too many people have come by to look at it, so I still have a little more time before I need to leave."

Dr. Cohen was pleased with her update. "And are you still spending most of your time alone, or are you reaching out and meeting kindred spirits?"

Violet wiggled her nose. "Actually, I prefer being alone right now. I spend most of my time in my bedroom or basement. It's not hard to do, either. The house is so big, my housekeepers don't even know when I'm there."

Violet launched a silly smile, as if she just told herself a funny joke and refused to share.

Dr. Cohen scratched his ear, scrutinizing her expression. "What's so delightful, Violet? Is there something else you would like to share with me?"

Violet played innocent. "No, nothing else to report. I'm just finding my own ways to heal and staying out of everyone's way . . . Processing my situation the best I can."

A red cardinal landed on the bench beside Dr. Cohen. It twitched its beak, almost smiling. "Well, I can't argue with that strategy, if it's working," he smiled back. "I have to admit, you sound much better this morning than our last session, so all I can recommend for the coming week is that you keep doing whatever it is that you're doing."

Violet felt like a lottery winner holding an oversized check. "Thank you, Dr. Cohen. I will."

"I'll continue to check in, of course, but you know how to reach me if something urgent comes up before then."

"Of course." Violet smiled as she placed her hand on the purse beside her.

Suddenly, two NYPD police officers approached in the distance. One of them was a muscular fellow with a deep Staten Island dialect, and the other was the polite African-American who investigated Penny's accident three days earlier.

Violet was nervous. She took off her hat, placed it on her lap, and shook out her bright red, razor-cut hair.

Dr. Cohen patted his thighs, preparing to leave.

Violet tugged at his sleeve. "Let's wait a moment."

"No one will notice we're here, Violet."

The policemen continued walking toward them.

"I know. I just don't want to take any chances."

The muscular officer took a camera from his pant pocket and handed it to his partner. He then flashed one of his bulging biceps against the bronze shoulder of Hans Christian Anderson.

"You're such a douchebag," said the officer holding the camera.

"She's totally into books. She'll love this."

"Whatever." He snapped four photos, each one a different pose from the first. "There. We got it. Can we get back to work now?"

"You're such a poser."

"You're such a womanizer."

"I told you, I'm willing to share."

The black officer jokingly punched the other in the shoulder as they headed back toward the sailboat pond in the distance.

Violet watched the policemen walk well ahead of her.

She grabbed her hat, sunglasses, and purse. "I'll see you next week, Dr. Cohen."

She stood up and motioned to walk in the opposite direction of the officers.

"Of course, Violet. Take care until then."

EIGHTEEN

ALONE.

This was something Allegra Adams was not prepared to deal with: solitary confinement for hours on end. The lack of human contact, and mental and physical activity, was eating at her sanity. No Internet. No television. No phone. No music. No books. No magazines. No gadgets. No windows. No nothing.

In twenty-three years, Allegra managed to avoid electricity deprivation. She had never experienced a power outage. Or a hurricane. Or a snowstorm. Nor had she even gone camping. And although the lights and air conditioning blasted around her night and day, this was the closest thing to sensory deprivation she had ever experienced in her life.

After eleven days without stimulation, all that was left was the deafening silence of her own thoughts, and the occasional visit from her captor to empty her homemade port-a-potty, change out her bandage, or bring in junk food to eat. That's it. And when her captor did strike up a conversation, it was always a frightening discussion. Ending in the loss of a body part or the gain of a basic item necessary for survival.

For this reason, Allegra both relished and dreaded Violet's visits. She needed her ridiculous fairy tale stories to stay sane—and more importantly, her help to stay alive—but she knew the price for those interactions were extremely high.

Allegra sat against the wall in a cornflower blue and white nightgown, with a pillow and blanket rolled tightly behind her back for comfort. She sat lost in her memories, thinking about her friends in high school—trying to recall the first and last names of each person in her senior class as mental exercise.

As she did this, she inspected her legs once again, which were now filled with more splotches of red bruising. She had no idea what was causing it. She just assumed the lack of sun, vitamins, and motion was to blame.

Her body ached from lack of movement. Her bones felt rigid and tough. Her stomach swelled from too many liquids. She felt her hair layered with grease and knotted in the back of her head while she slept. She could smell herself now in full force. A body odor so strong, perhaps brought on by hormonal changes, but still unacceptable by modern standards.

The low whirring sound of the security lock grabbed her attention. She waited anxiously to see who it was, praying to any God who would listen that a fresh face would emerge.

Nope. No rescue. Not yet.

It was Violet, wearing the eggplant dress and coral shoes from the park earlier that day, holding a full blender, a clear plastic cup, and a stuffed Duane Reade shopping bag.

Allegra watched her prison guard float down the stairs like a Vegas showgirl.

"Good afternoon," said Violet. "How is your hand feeling?"

Allegra held up her bandaged left hand with four fingers. "Fine, I guess."

"Excellent," she replied with a smile. "I brought you some goodies." She placed the shopping bag at Allegra's feet and poured a light brown smoothie from the blender to the plastic cup.

"What's that?"

"It's lunch."

"What happened to all the snacks?"

Violet gave the look of a teacher. "You know as well as I do that a person cannot survive on packaged foods alone. You need protein, vitamins, and minerals. Good calories, not bad ones."

Allegra was suspicious. "You taste it first."

Violet laughed. She took a small sip of the frothy shake, over-reacting to how good it tasted. "See? No rat poison." Violet handed the drink to Allegra. "If I wanted to poison you, I certainly wouldn't go through the trouble of making you a delicious shake."

Allegra was alarmed. She knew Mad Violet was capable of anything.

"Drink."

Allegra was hesitant.

Violet crouched down, leaning inches from her face. *"Drink."*

Allegra took a small sip. Violet was right, it wasn't foul or disgusting. It had the taste of chocolate milk, brownies, Oreos, Butterfingers and Heath Bars, but there was a slight taste of something unpleasant in there. Something nutty and sour, hidden by the flavors of everything else.

Allegra handed the drink back to Violet. "Thank you, but I don't want this."

Violet's face melted. "Excuse me?"

Allegra realized her mistake. "I—I'm just not hungry right now," she said as her stomach growled loudly.

"I went through all of this trouble to make you a delicious, healthy smoothie, and you don't want to drink it?"

Allegra gritted her teeth, knowing full well that her stubbornness would have consequences. "I'm sorry, I just don't have an appetite. My stomach is sick."

Violet stared in full rage. Her amber slits glowed like a growing campfire. Her breath quickened. Her tight bird-like chest rose and fell like a gazelle ready to run toward a lion.

Allegra was mortified.

Violet's lips parted slowly as she spoke in staccato. "Well, then, I'll just leave it here in case you change your mind." Violet placed the plastic cup near Allegra's good hand.

Allegra was dumbfounded. Her troubled captor was capable of changing moods instantaneously.

Violet then dug through the shopping bag. "I bought you a few toiletries. You smell *soooo* rancid, I thought this might help." Violet tossed over a stick of deodorant. She continued digging. "And I'm sure you would love to brush your teeth, but we'll settle on this for now." She placed a medium-sized bottle of mouthwash on the floor. She dug again. "These work wonders to clean up anything." She placed a large white container of baby wipes at her feet. "And I don't know when you're due—"

Allegra panicked.

"—but I don't want you bleeding all over my floor, so here." She tossed Allegra a box of tampons.

Allegra was relieved to see the shopping bag was genuinely empty, hoping there weren't any chainsaws or machetes hidden at the bottom. "Thank you."

Violet tossed the bag aside and pulled over a chair from the dinette set. She sat directly in front of Allegra once again. "Last time, you told me about how you and Ram met. Now I want to know the story of the first time you had sex."

Allegra looked up through her bangs.

Her expression asked the question Violet was anticipating. "What? More presents? I've already given you more today than you deserve."

"I'll tell you the story," Allegra pulled on the metal chain attached to the collar on her neck, "if you take this off."

Violet chuckled. "And let you roam about freely?"

"Yes. I want to use the bathroom and sleep on the bed."

Violet's laugh intensified. "You're even stupider than I thought."

"Why? You know I can't get out of here without the combination to the door. What do you have to worry about?"

"I recall a little steak knife entering my foot the last time you were free."

"Then remove the knives. And whatever else in here that's a problem. I just want to be able to move, and maybe watch TV?"

Violet was enraged.

She jolted off her chair and pointed her finger in Allegra's face. "You don't call the shots around here, little girl! Down here, *you're nothing*! You have no rights! You have no say!"

Allegra cowered.

"And if you ever try to boss me around again, I will end this all right now!"

Allegra was concerned. Violet had never spoken like that before. What did she mean by "end this all right now" exactly? Was she planning to kill Allegra after all? Worse yet, was she planning to kill Allegra and then herself to escape punishment?

The game just took another serious turn.

"Do you know why you're here, Allegra?" The question echoed in the room as if it were the important question ever asked in all of eternity.

"Yes."

"Then tell me."

"It's because I had an affair with your husband."

"That's only partly true. What else?"

Allegra was terrified. Did Violet know her biggest secret? If so, was she going to kill her for it? "I don't know what other reason I'm here."

Violet perfected her posture, crossing her legs. "Have you ever heard the story about *The Fisherman and His Wife*?"

Allegra shook her head.

"Maybe it will explain things a little better than I could."

Allegra slumped over, shuddering at the thought of what happened the last time Violet told a fairy tale.

"There once was a fisherman who lived with his unhappy wife in a piss pot by the ocean. Every day the fisherman went out to fish, as it was their only source of food, and one day he cast out his line, and it sank deep into the ocean. As he pulled it out, a large, magical flounder appeared at the other end.

"The flounder said to him, 'Look here, dear fisherman. I beg of you, let me live. I am not a real flounder, but an enchanted prince. So what good would it do for you to kill me? I certainly wouldn't taste very good. Put me back into the water and let me go.'

"'Hold on,' said the fisherman. 'Do not waste your pleas on me. I would have thrown a talking fish back into the water anyway.' He then threw the fish back into the clear blue water, and the flounder swam to the bottom of the ocean, leaving behind a long streak of blood.

"The fisherman returned home and told his wife what had happened. She became annoyed. 'Didn't you wish for something?' she asked. 'That was a magical fish. You should have wished for a new house. Don't you think it's awful we live in this piss pot?' "

Violet kicked the orange Home Depot bucket, changing her voice with each character.

"'Go back and ask that flounder if he can get us a small hut!'

"The husband didn't agree, but heeded his wife's request. He went back to the sea, which was now green and yellow, and stood at the shore calling for the magical fish. 'Flounder, flounder of the sea. If you're a man, then speak to me. Although I don't agree with my wife's request, I've come to ask it nonetheless.'

"The flounder came swimming up to him and said, 'Well, what does she want?'

"'My wife thinks I should have wished for something when I caught you. Since she doesn't want to live in a piss pot anymore, she'd like to have a hut.'

"'Just go home,' said the flounder. 'She's already got it.'

"The fisherman went home, and his wife was standing in front of a brand-new hut. 'Come inside, Husband, look! Now isn't this much better?'

"The hut had new furniture, a kitchen, a stove, a garden, as well as chickens and ducks in the backyard. 'Now we can enjoy ourselves,' said the husband.

"'Yes, but if he can grant us this, why don't you ask for a large stone castle? Go back to the flounder and ask him.'

"'Wife,' moaned the husband. 'The flounder just gave us a hut. I don't want to ask for more favors so soon. He might not be willing to do it again.'

"'What do you mean? He'll be glad to do it. Just go back and ask.'

"So the fisherman went back to the ocean, the water now gray but calm. He stood at the shore and yelled, 'Flounder, flounder of the sea. If you're a man, then speak to me. Although I don't agree with my wife's request, I've come to ask it nonetheless.'

"'What now?' replied the flounder.

"The fisherman was distressed. 'My wife wants to live in a large stone castle by the sea.'

"The flounder sighed. 'Go home, she's already got it.'

"When the fisherman went home, his wife was standing in front of a large castle. When he went inside, the halls were filled with servants and furniture and food. 'Oh,' said the husband. 'Now, let's live in this wonderful castle and be content.'

"'I'll need to think about it,' said the wife. 'Let's sleep on it.'

"The next morning she awoke, poking the fisherman. 'Husband, get up. I want to be king and rule this entire country.'

'Oh, Wife!' pleaded the husband. 'The flounder won't want to make you king.'

The wife was angry. 'You go back to the flounder at once, and tell him what I want!'

Soon after, the fisherman, completely stressed over his wife's demands to be king, reluctantly went back to the sea, which was now black and gray. 'Flounder, flounder of the sea. If you're a man, then speak to me. Although I don't agree with my wife's request, I've come to ask it nonetheless.'

"The flounder appeared. 'What does she want now?'

"'She wants to be king,' he said shyly.

"'Go back home,' said the flounder. 'She's already king.'

"And as the fisherman returned home, he saw there were many soldiers outside. His wife was sitting on a high throne and wore a large crown made of gold and diamonds.

"'Oh,' said the fisherman. 'Now you're king, aren't you?'

"'Yes, I am,' said the wife proudly.

"'Good, now we may relax and enjoy your rule.'

"'Not exactly,' said the wife. 'Tell the flounder I've changed my mind. I now want to be emperor.'

"'Oh, Wife!' said the husband. 'I can't go back to the flounder again.'

"'Go to him now. I am your king!'"

"The fisherman went away, thinking how outrageous it would be for his wife to become emperor. When he arrived at the sea, the water was black and dense. The fisherman stepped forward and said, 'Flounder, flounder of the sea. If you're a man, then speak to me. Although I don't agree with my wife's request, I've come to ask it nonetheless.'

"'What, again?' said the flounder. 'What does she want now?'

"'Oh, Flounder,' he said, 'my wife now wishes to be emperor.'

"The flounder rolled his eyes. 'Go home, she's already emperor.'

"When the fisherman arrived home, he carefully entered the castle and saw his wife sitting on a throne twice the size of the first, now wearing a crown three yards high of diamonds and garnets, flanked by two rows of body guards.

"'Wife? Now you're emperor, aren't you?'

"'Yes, I am.'

"'It's wonderful, right?' The fisherman hesitated to ask.

"'Husband,' she whined, 'I've thought about it while you were gone, and I now want to be Pope.'

"'Oh, Wife!' said the fisherman. 'I can't possibly go back to the flounder again!'

"'I am your emperor, Husband. You will obey my commands!'

"'No, I will not go. It won't turn out well.'

"'Stop talking nonsense and go there at once!'

"Reluctantly, the husband returned to the sea again, but this time he was feeling sick and feeble. The water was now thick and black, and the horizon above him was red. He stepped forward once again, 'Flounder, flounder of the sea. If you're a man, then speak to me. Although I don't agree with my wife's request, I've come to ask it nonetheless.'

"'Are you serious?' asked the flounder. 'What does she want now?'

"'Oh,' said the man, shamefully. 'Now she wants to be Pope.'

"The flounder exhaled. 'All right. Go home. She is already Pope.'

"The fisherman went home. As he entered the castle, he saw his wife sitting on a throne two miles high, wearing three large golden crowns on her head. Numerous bishops and priests were standing around her, as well as soldiers, servants, and devotees.

"'Wife?' said the husband, astonished. 'Are you now the Pope?'

"'Yes, I am,' said the wife.

"'You must finally be happy and satisfied. Now that you're Pope, there is nothing greater.'

"'But I am sad,' said the wife. 'I have decided I want to be like God instead.'

"The fisherman was stunned. 'Wife, you cannot be like God!'

"'Oh, yes, I can. And you will ask the flounder to do it.'

"'No, I will not.'

"The soldiers advanced around him. 'Be content and remain Pope, dear wife. I beg of you.'

"'No, I won't be able to bear it. I want to make the sun and moon rise. I want to be like God!'

"The fisherman was sad. He returned to the ocean, filled with fear. The sky was now pitch-black, matching the color of the sea. He stepped forward and proclaimed, 'Flounder, flounder of the sea. If you're a man, then speak to me. Although I don't agree with my wife's request, I've come to ask it nonetheless.'

"'Well, what does she want?' asked the flounder.

"'She wants to be like God.'

"'Are you sure?'

"'Yes, she is no longer happy being king, emperor, or Pope. She wants to be just like God.'

"The flounder smiled. 'Go back home. She's sitting in your piss pot again.' "

Violet's eyes widened.

"And that's where the fisherman and his wife lived unhappily for the rest of their lives."

Allegra shivered from her navel to the top of her head, scared to death at what might come next.

Violet tucked her long bangs behind her ear. "Do you understand the story?"

"Yes," feigned Allegra.

"And which character might you be?"

Allegra shrank. "I am the fisherman's wife?"

"That's correct. You had nothing but a piss pot before you met Ram. And with each growing request—first his attention, then his gifts, his money, and finally his love—you had a wonderful thing going. A thousand women would have died to be in your position. But you, Allegra, weren't satisfied with being king or emperor or Pope—you wanted to be *his wife*. And that's how you lost it all."

Allegra looked down at the gray floor.

"What were you thinking, little girl? *You don't have the discipline to be a trophy wife!*"

Allegra looked away as Violet yelled.

"You may have caught him, but you would've never *kept* him. His business associates would have laughed behind his back for marrying such an unsophisticated, trashy girl. His social circles would have ridiculed you. His blue-blooded family would have rejected you. Our neighbors would have gossiped about you. Sales people would've gawked at your lack of class. You would had never been invited to parties, or weddings, or graduations, or bar mitzvahs. No woman would have allowed you in her home. Not the girl with the man-stealing, tramp stamp across her stripper ass! You would have never fit in! Most importantly, you're too lazy to have done what it takes to keep yourself in trophy-wife shape. Beer? Cheetos? A thirty-minute jog twice a week? No, little girl, being married to a man like Ram takes discipline, like a Marine. You would have been crushed under the pressure. Nothing comes in between you and your beauty rituals. Two-hour-a-day workouts. Manicures. Pedicures. Blowouts. Facials. Waxing. Botox. Lipo. *Because beauty is power.* And once you've lost that, you've lost everything!"

Violet's threats were meaningless; Allegra couldn't care less about any of those things. Instead, her dream was to marry Ram, encourage him to retire, and live happily ever after on a private island somewhere near Costa Rica. Their days would be filled with partying, laughing, fishing, swimming, surfing, and making love in the sand.

"I'm sorry, I really am. I just don't know how to make it up to you," said Allegra convincingly. "What do I need to do?"

Violet caught her breath. "Just tell me everything I need to know before you go."

Go? Allegra was in no condition to ask for clarification. Her body and mind were weakening with every passing moment. "I'll tell you anything you want."

"Good." Violet relaxed.

"Now tell me about the first time you had sex with my husband."

NINETEEN

BOBBY & EDDIE'S was the sort of *Cheers* neighborhood bar, where everyone knew your business before they knew your name. It was a dark, railroad-style, long, narrow space, with an old wooden bar near the front, two arcade games, two pool tables, and a smoking patio out back. Located on First Avenue between 85th and 86th Streets, it was one of Yorkville's friendliest traditions—a popular stop during the neighborhood's annual Saint Patrick's Day bar crawl. It was smaller than one would imagine for a pub in New York, with a Fire Marshall sign declaring a maximum of forty-five people, yet miraculously, it boasted three of its original opening day patrons among its regular customers.

The bar first opened in the early eighties as a working-class watering hole catering to college students, many of whom later found lucrative jobs downtown but refused to leave the area due to rent control. Some patrons married or moved away, but there were three regulars who had not: Nellie Rock, a sixty-year-old freelance news photographer, who had missed the window of marriage and kids from constantly traveling to remote places like Mozambique, Kyrgyzstan, and Estonia on assignment; Judge Richard, now fifty-five, a life-long bachelor and traffic court judge originally from Indiana, who many thought was secretly playing for both teams; and Nikola Popov, the hair dealer, who surreptitiously sourced top-quality hair from Hindu temples, Russian crematories, and Scandinavian mortuaries, selling his stash to high-end wig companies for big profits. After moving into a million-dollar studio apartment located twenty-five blocks away, Nikola still made his daily trek to Bobby & Eddie's— the place he considered home.

After thirty years of occupying the same barstools, the three eldest patrons were like a triumvirate of Indian tribal chiefs, each one maintaining their region of the bar, while welcoming transient neighbors fortunate enough to stay only two or three years. Each chief was an honored guest at the victories and losses of the extended B&E family: weddings, funerals, bar mitzvahs, graduations, and sentencings. And despite the amount of booze that freely flowed through the room, the Bobby and Eddie's tribe rarely fought, often laughed, and shared in a loneliness that only those living in the city could ever understand.

Allegra's initiation into the tribe was nothing short of serendipity. The day after arriving at the Port Authority bus station, Allegra went searching for places to live, blown away by the rental prices, which far exceeded her five-hundred-dollar-a-month budget. She sat crying on the subway, eventually telling her heart-breaking story to Nellie Rock, who was sitting beside her.

As an act of mercy, Nellie offered her couch to Allegra for a maximum of three months in exchange for daily cooking, cleaning, and walking her twin Yorkie dogs. Familiar with Allegra's résumé, she introduced her to the B&E's managing partner, Bobby Pescarelli, who was immediately taken aback by Allegra's good looks and shapely figure. At first, he debated passing her along to his friend who was always looking for "fresh-off-the-bus-ass" for his strip club, but out of respect for Nellie, he decided to keep the redheaded beauty as eye candy for his most loyal patrons.

Allegra quickly integrated into the Bobby and Eddie's family. She was down-to-earth, hardworking, and had great tits—the perfect embodiment of the bar's free spirit, sense of humor, and blue-collar charm.

Two weeks later, Allegra met Chloe, who came into the bar for Karaoke therapy after kicking her live-in boyfriend of three years to the curb. And just like that, Allegra had gone from a homeless girl crashing on someone's sofa, to a fully-employed woman living the Manhattan dream in Chloe's big apartment.

The Saturday after Thanksgiving was typically slow, a rare time when customers actually left their stools to see loved ones who berated them about their drinking behavior. It was around three thirty in the afternoon, just before the shift change of morning drunks who were trashed by four, left, and the evening drunks who started drinking at five, arrived.

Allegra wore a tight, olive green top and black tights that advertised her curvy assets when Ram—wearing a business suit and tie—entered the bar. He sat down near one of the chief's stools, while Allegra's back was turned, cashing out another customer.

Ram balanced his tall, muscular frame on the unfamiliar stool seating.

"Hi. I'm Judge Richard," said the chief, extending his hand. He was part of the Saturday morning drunk crew and was already three sheets to the wind.

"I'm Ram, nice to meet you," he replied in a deep voice.

Judge Richard looked at Ram's finely pressed suit. "Do you need help with directions?"

He smiled. "Oh, no. I was just here to say hello to her." He pointed at Allegra just as she turned around.

Her eyes opened wide. "Hey, you! Thanks for stopping by."

Ram was delighted.

"Moose, wasn't it?" she joked.

Judge Richard interrupted. "You two meet in DUI school?"

Allegra smacked his hand. "No, he's my friend, Ram. We met a zillion years ago."

Ram touched his dark-rimmed eyeglasses. "We met yesterday, actually."

Allegra smiled.

"Where at? Macy's?" The drunk judge continued inspecting Ram. "Are you a store mannequin? Your head is perfectly round and plastic."

Allegra gave Ram a look. "Judge Richard, you're wasted. Leave him alone."

Ram was entertained. "I only turn into a mannequin at night. During the day, I visit pretty girls at bars."

Judge Richard laughed heartily, then abruptly turned to chat with another victim.

Allegra leaned over the bar. Her ample cleavage was now on full display. "Wow. I can't believe you, like, came to visit me."

"Why?" replied Ram.

"I don't know. I meet guys, like, all the time, and if you don't give them your number, you never see them again." She fluffed her hair away from her shoulder. "What are you drinking?"

Ram was jubilant. He hadn't been able to stop thinking about her for the last twenty-four hours. "Why don't you surprise me with a signature cocktail?"

"*Signature* cocktail?"

"Don't all mixologists invent a special drink of their own?"

"Mixologist?"

"Yes, you're a mixologist! Impress me."

Allegra placed her index finger on her lips. "Okay. I know what I'll make for you." Her green eyes shot a come-hither look as her breasts sank down below the bar.

She pulled a small bottle of pink grapefruit juice from the ice chest below and poured it into a stainless-steel shaker filled with ice. She added one shot each of vodka, tequila, and rum, shook it loudly for seven seconds as her boobs bounced from the vibrations, then emptied the pink concoction into a tall glass and topped it with a drop of red grenadine syrup in the middle. "Here you go."

Ram grabbed the drink.

Allegra noticed the skin indentation of his missing wedding ring.

"What do you call it?"

"The Little Man in the Boat."

Ram was confused.

Allegra scrunched her eyes. "You know, *the little man in the boat?*"

Ram was lost.

Allegra's mouth gaped open. "You don't know what that is, do you?"

Ram chuckled. "No, I don't. Unless you mean the Tidy Bowl Man because it tastes like toilet water?"

Allegra threw her head back in laughter. "No, that's not it. I have no idea who that is either."

"Then what does it mean?"

Allegra was playful. "Maybe I'll show you later."

He took a sip of the cocktail and jokingly made a sour face, as if it were the worst drink ever. "Jesus Christ. I hope you give refunds."

Allegra smiled. "Not usually, but for you, I'll make an exception."

"Good. I'll take twenty more."

Ram was thoroughly enjoying spending time with his new friend.

By nine thirty that evening, Ram was on the same stool, drunker than he'd been in years.

As all new B&E initiates must do, Ram shared true, personal stories of growing up in Manhattan with the other patrons, always careful to leave out details indicating how wealthy or privileged his upbringing had been. He told memories of breaking his arm while sledding on the Great Lawn of Central Park, accidentally knocking his bratty classmate down the steep stairs of the Statue of Liberty during a third-grade field trip, and being shipped off each summer to his uncle's farm outside of Edinburgh, where farmhands charged with "toughening him up" taught him how to properly eat haggis and butcher a pig in less than five minutes.

Ram enjoyed hearing their winding stories in return, such as Judge Richard's battle with insurance companies over throat cancer; Nellie's hyena attack in Malawi; Nikola's five-some at a Russian brothel; Joe's scratch-off lottery win of fifty thousand dollars; Snakehead's 9/11 conspiracy theories; and Maryanne's sad, spinster, bottomless cup existence.

Ram enjoyed taking a small break from his insulated world of *the one percent*, bonding instead with the sad, lonely spirits who filled their days with alcohol and empty conversations. To him, this was the perfect way to stay grounded at Thanksgiving.

"How's it going, Handsome? Need a refill?" Allegra's smile was even more comfortable than before.

Ram was tired, pulling off his glasses, then scratching his eyes. "When do you get out of here?" He struggled to say his words without slurring.

"Two thirty a.m."

"Sorry, darling. That's *way* past my bedtime."

"Hold on."

One of the other bartenders, a Texan actor nicknamed Double Trouble, was drinking and socializing off-duty at the other end of the bar. Allegra approached him. "Hey, do you wanna take over my shift?"

Double Trouble was elated. "On a Saturday night? Hell, yeah."

"You don't think Bobby would mind, do you?"

"Fuck, no. Twat and I used to do this all the time." He placed his white cowboy hat onto his head. "Clock out and have fun. I'll just be here making money."

Allegra punched the clock by the register, and grabbed her purse from the bottom shelf. "All right, let's go."

Ram was startled. "You can go?"

"Yeah, DT is going to cover me. Let's party."

"Shit, okay." Ram carefully rose from his stool, slightly off balance. He was much drunker than he had expected. "Where do you want to go?"

Allegra's pea-green eyes gleamed beneath her blunt bangs. "Take me to one of your favorite places."

Ram looked up in thought. "Right, I got it. I'll call a car. My driver is on vacation."

Allegra grabbed his hand and led him to the front door.

As they prepared to exit, the customers in the bar hooted and hollered:

"Go get 'em girl!"

"Whoo Hoo!"

"Lucky bastard!"

"Mr. Clean is getting laid tonight!"

Allegra turned around and shot them the bird. "Fuck all y'all." And left.

The crowd smiled.

They *loved* it.

Ram rubbed Allegra's shivering shoulders as they waited on the sidewalk outside. "We need to get you a warmer coat, darling."

"I'm a south-western baby. Everything below sixty is freezing to me!"

A black Lincoln Town Car pulled up to the curb.

Ram opened the door. "Here we go."

Allegra hopped in, smiling like a child on Saturday morning. "Thank you."

Inside the vehicle, Ram and Allegra sat close to one another, without touching.

"Where are you taking me?" she asked.

"To the Mark Bar. Have you ever been?"

"No, is that in Soho?"

Ram smiled. "It's only five minutes away. On Madison and Seventy-Seventh."

"Oh."

"You'll love it." He placed his left hand on her thigh.

Allegra touched his empty ring finger. "What's up with that?"

Ram looked out the window, then back again. "I thought it would be rude to wear it to your workplace. I wouldn't want people thinking inappropriate things about you."

Allegra appreciated his intent. "Oh, 'married guy.'" She used finger quotes. "Right."

Ram was fully intoxicated. "Plus, I want you in my bed tonight, so I would feel guilty if I had it on."

Allegra laughed. "Yeah, right."

He gave her a *puppy dog* look. "Why not? You don't think I'm attractive?"

Allegra smiled coyly. "Of course, I do."

Ram overreacted. "Oh, you don't think *you're* attractive?"

She jutted out her chin. "I'm pretty comfortable in my own skin."

He slumped against her shoulder. "And it would feel so much better against my skin, don't you think?"

The driver's head tilted up.

"Nah, I'm only kidding. I'm honored you left work to join me. I'm pleased we have an opportunity to get to know one another."

Allegra was enticed. Underneath the sexy beast beside her, she saw a gentleness and class that was like nothing she had ever experienced before.

Once the town car reached the Mark Hotel, Ram tossed a hundred-dollar bill to the driver. He exited the vehicle and held the door open for Allegra, beating the driver to the punch.

"Thank you," said Allegra, feeling like a princess.

Ram held her hand as they walked through the white-and-black striped lobby, and turned left into the cozy hotel lounge.

The inside of the Mark Bar looked like a Hollywood movie set. Ibiza club music played in the background; sexy mood lighting highlighted the red diamond carpet and black-and-white cow-print sofas lining the walls; groups of handsome men sipped cocktails while chatting with gorgeous women wearing dresses that matched their jewels.

The Mark Bar was hot. It was sensual. A living, breathing, permanent red carpet event for some of the wealthiest people in the world.

Holy shit. Allegra immediately felt self-conscious in her casual outfit.

Ram led her by the hand to an empty yellow stool at the modern bar. "See, I told you this was a happening place."

Allegra looked around in awe, expecting the entire cast of *The Real Housewives of New York City* to emerge any second. "This place is, uh, amazing."

Ram smiled. "I've been coming here for years."

The drop-dead-gorgeous male model bartender leaned into Allegra. "What are you drinking, love?" His British accent was as slick as his thick, black hair.

"I'll have a cranberry and vodka."

"And for you, mate?"

"I'll have a gin and tonic."

Allegra twirled around in her small, confined space. "Like, everyone here is so fucking beautiful."

Ram smiled. "Which is why you fit right in."

Allegra was nervous. She felt more self-conscious about her plain olive top, black tights, and flat shoes than before. She pulled down Ram's tall shoulder, whispering in his ear. "Are you sure I'm dressed okay?"

Ram looked her over. "You're a knock-out, darling. Even if you were wearing a potato sack." His blue eyes penetrated the glass shields hiding his animal magnetism.

Allegra glanced to the side. "Aren't you worried someone might see us here?"

Ram nodded his head over to the corner, where a short, well-dressed man was groping the asses of two taller brunettes.

Allegra's mouth dropped open. "Oh my God—is that who I think it is?"

"Yes, it is."

Allegra was starstruck. It was the very married Hollywood hunk, Ben Becksdale. "Holy shit. Isn't he married to that other famous actress?"

Ram nodded his head *yes* as the drinks arrived.

"Isn't he worried about paparazzi?"

"Not here."

Allegra threw her hair back in amazement. "I must be living under a rock."

Ram handed her the cranberry and vodka, then picked up his gin and tonic.

They clinked glasses.

"Welcome to my world, darling," he said in a sexy, deep voice.

Allegra's baby-doll eyes peeked over the glass as she took a sip.

Ram had suddenly become *irresistible*.

Ten minutes before the bar closed, Ram called a limo to drive them home.

When it arrived outside, he stumbled into the back seat, much drunker than Allegra was given his six-hour head start.

"One or two stops tonight?" asked the chauffeur.

Ram and Allegra exchanged looks.

Allegra took the highroad. "Two stops. First one is on Second Avenue between Eighty-Eight and Eighty-Ninth."

Ram smiled in relief. "Good girl."

Allegra bit her lip, resisting the impulse to change her mind.

He grabbed her hand. "I had a wonderful time tonight." He kissed the inside of her wrist softly. "Thank you for spending the day with me."

Allegra melted inside.

Luckily, she was only slightly inebriated. She knew she had ten blocks to ask the wasted man sitting beside her anything she liked. "Why did you come visit me today?"

Ram rolled his eyes like a love-struck romantic. "Silly question."

Allegra straightened. "Like, you totally live this amazing life, Ram. I'm trying to figure out why you even want to know me?"

Ram slumped down in the backseat, drunk off his ass. "Because you're lovely."

Allegra wanted more. She wanted answers. "Are you happy in your marriage?"

Boom. She said it.

Ram hesitated. "My wife is a wonderful person."

Silence.

"Then why are you with me tonight instead of her?"

Ram tried pointlessly to sit up. "Oh, I see. You want to know the nuts and bolts, do you?"

Allegra felt insecure. "Well, yes, I do. I mean, before I get involved."

Ram took a deep breath as he looked out the window, watching Park Avenue buildings rush by. "I've been married almost twenty-five years, Allegra. You're too young to even understand how long that really is."

He looked toward the chauffeur.

"Were they happy?"

"Most of them, yes, but a few have been horrendous."

Allegra pursed her lips. "Like how?"

Ram sobered, looking at her directly. "Our only daughter died of SIDS a few years back. My wife hasn't been the same since. She has a lot of problems. *Mental* problems."

Allegra was shocked. She immediately felt terrible for asking. "Oh my God. I didn't realize . . . I'm so sorry."

Ram looked her straight in the eye. "My wife and I haven't been intimate for over a year. We sleep in separate bedrooms. Is that what you want to know?"

Allegra was stunned. *How could any red-blooded woman neglect the magnetic man sitting next to me?* "I'm really sorry for probing. I only wanted to understand why you're interested in me."

Ram lurched into her personal space. "It's because yesterday morning, maybe an hour or two before we met, I was alone in my townhome . . . And all I felt was loss."

Silence.

"Loss for what?" she whispered.

Ram peered deeper into her eyes. "I don't know." He leaned in closer. "I just know whatever it was, it disappeared the minute I met you."

Game over. Allegra was hooked.

She leaned into Ram's face and gently kissed him, slowly opening her mouth, gradually stroking her tongue against his.

"We're here," exclaimed the driver.

Ram and Allegra snapped up.

The driver quickly exited the car and opened Allegra's door closest to the curb.

She exited and turned around. "Thank you for an awesome evening."

Ram pretended to tip his imaginary top hat.

The driver closed the door and drove away.

As Allegra watched the red taillights turn in the distance, she stomped her foot.

Shit. I forgot to give him my number!

Fifteen days had passed, and there was still no sign of Ram.

During this time, Allegra googled his name a thousand times, reading about his family's philanthropic activities, including their funding of two libraries and a Scottish heritage museum which bore the Ramspeck name. She read about Ram's Asian/American trade company, his South American restaurant chain, and his chemical processing plant in Croatia, having to look at a map to figure out what Croatia even was.

She looked up every New York-based Ramspeck on Facebook, identifying his wife, Violet, from public pictures of them together at galas and fundraisers—leering at her designer clothes, tiny figure, and to-die-for shoes.

She found Ram's business phone numbers online, but was too afraid to call him, unsure of how he felt now that he was sober. Nonetheless, she plugged his numbers into her phone, hoping one day she would have the courage to hear he had changed his mind firsthand.

Allegra watched the front door of the bar each night, now decorated with multicolored Christmas lights and shiny silver tinsel, hoping Ram would walk in unannounced once again.

Their trip to the Mark Bar over a fortnight ago had a profound effect on her. It was like taking the red pill in *The Matrix*, making it impossible to unlearn how glamorous life is for the wealthy. She now understood why people jumped out of buildings when the stock market crashed. She now understood why people killed for it. She now understood why men would sell their souls for it.

That night didn't just change her perspective about money. It changed her DNA, *forever.*

It was extremely slow for a Sunday night.

Allegra's roommate—Chloe, the karaoke whore—had been in and out of the bar all evening. The B&E regulars secretly hated her for hogging up the good songs and singing like a true Broadway starlet. "Karaoke is about balls, not talent," said Nellie to Allegra, while Chloe was on stage. "The joy is seeing two drunk men sing 'I Got You, Babe' to one another, not watching the next Irene Cara belt 'What a Feeling.'"

Allegra agreed.

Something about the song Chloe was singing struck a chord in Allegra, forcing her to hold back tears. She didn't admit to anyone how infatuated she was with Ram, praying time would erase her memories, and make plebian life tolerable again.

Suddenly, the urge to call Ram's work number and leave a voicemail was intense. She reached for her phone below the bar, found his name, and pushed send.

"Hey, you. It's Allegra Adams. You know, the flag maker? Well, anyway, I realized I never gave you my number, so I just wanted to say hello. That's all. Call me back if you want, bye."

No sooner did she hang up the phone when it rang in her hand.

"Hello?" she asked, unfamiliar with the number.

"Allegra. It's Ram. You called?"

"Oh, yeah, *hey*. I thought I was leaving you a voicemail at work?"

"This is my private cell. I forward my calls when I'm out of the office."

"Oh, well, hey you," she said flirtatiously. "How's it going?"

"I just landed ten minutes ago at JFK. I've been in Ireland for the past two weeks."

"Oh, really?" Allegra was hopeful.

"I would have contacted you sooner, but I didn't know how to reach you."

"Oh, well, I'm pretty easy to find on Facebook. Not too many *Allegra Adams* live in Manhattan."

"Sorry, I don't use Facebook. I'm a good old-fashioned phone call kind of guy."

Allegra felt stupid.

"What are you doing tomorrow afternoon?" he asked.

Her spirits lifted. "I'm off on Mondays, so I guess I'm free?"

"Good. I'll send a car to your apartment at noon. We'll have lunch."

Allegra beamed.

"Have you ever been to Le Cirque?"

"No, I haven't."

"They have the best veal scaloppini there. You'll love it."

"Sounds great, sure."

Ram was suddenly silent on the line.

Allegra worried. "Are you still there?"

"Oh, screw it. I'm swinging by the bar right now."

Allegra was thrilled. "What, really?"

"I'll just text my wife that my plane's delayed."

Allegra's stomach knotted. "Okay."

"I just want to run my hands through that gorgeous hair of yours, if you don't mind?"

Allegra glowed. "I'll see you in a few."

"I still need to go through customs, so I should be there, say, in about an hour."

"Great, see you then."

Allegra hung up the phone. She grabbed her makeup bag and headed straight to the bathroom.

Nellie hollered from the bar. "Did Mr. Clean finally call you back?"

Allegra motioned a thumbs-up.

"Good. Go get 'em, tigress."

Allegra worked in robotic mode for the next two hours, mindlessly filling drink orders from faceless customers. She was losing hope that Ram would show up. Afraid he chickened out, she decided in advance *this* would be the first and only time he would ever leave her hanging.

Finally, her phone dinged. It was a text message from Ram:

I'M HERE. COME OUTSIDE.

> I CAN'T
> THE BOSS IS HERE
> CAN U COME INSIDE???

NOT A GOOD IDEA

> HAVE A DRINK
> WHY???

JUST CAN'T

OKAY, HOLD ON

Allegra walked over to Bobby the bar owner, who was playing billiards nearby. "I need to step outside for a minute. Is that cool?"

Bobby scanned the sparse crowd. "Yeah, just make it fast."

Allegra rushed out the door and found Ram, taller and more handsome than she had remembered, standing next to his limo. He was wearing a black trench coat with his arms and ankles crossed.

"Hey, you," he said in his deep, manly voice.

Allegra practically threw herself at him as they hugged. "Hi there," she said as she squeezed and released him. "Why can't you come inside? I'm working tonight."

Ram looked down the sidewalk. "I can't go back in there, Allegra. People will notice." His tone was serious and seductive.

Allegra furrowed her brows. "Notice what?"

"That I'm here to visit you again."

She giggled. "Oh, them? They don't care who you are! Plus, they're usually too drunk to notice anyway."

Ram looked down the other side of the block, avoiding eye contact. "What we did last time was fun, Allegra. I really had a great time, but it was *careless*. I can't do something like that ever again."

Allegra was not pleased. "What are you talking about? We didn't *do* anything."

Ram gave her a give-me-a-break look.

"What's the big deal? We ended the night in our separate homes with our clothes on?"

Ram looked at the entrance of the bar. "Did you tell anyone in there about us?"

Allegra was annoyed. "That we went out *once* and shared a little kiss? No—well, yeah. Maybe Nellie."

Ram's eyes met hers. "Just go back inside and tell everyone I ended it with you because I'm married."

Allegra slowly angered. "I don't understand, Ram. No one gives a shit about that."

He gently grabbed Allegra's shoulders. "Look, I have a confession to make. I wasn't in Ireland for the past two weeks. I was only there for a couple of days. I've been in New York the rest of the time."

Allegra eagerly waited for the punchline. "So?"

He looked to his left once again. "My wife came home the day after we went out, and I—I just didn't feel right about what happened between us."

Allegra was pissed. *Oh, now you feel guilty, asshole?* She placed her hand on her hip. "So why are you here then? So you can, like, dump me to my face?"

Ram looked down the other side of the block.

"What are you looking for? It's driving me fucking crazy!"

Ram let out a troubled sigh. His eyes locked onto hers. "I can't stop thinking about you, Allegra. I can't get you, or your beautiful eyes, or your gorgeous hair, or those fucking breasts *off my mind*, and it's bothering the hell out of me."

Allegra was stubborn. "Well, I can't stop thinking about you either. So what are we supposed to do now?"

Ram looked down the block again and then back at Allegra. "I don't know. Maybe we should forget we ever met."

Allegra scoffed. "You came all the way here to tell me that? You're such an assho—"

Ram grabbed the back of her head, pressing her lips hard against his. He moved his tongue into her mouth, mid-sentence, rolling it up against her teeth as his other hand held the small of her back.

He kissed her and kissed her.

When Ram finally let go, Allegra was dizzied by the endorphins filling her body.

He pulled off his glasses. "I'm in love with you, Allegra. We just need to find a way to do this right."

Allegra touched her lip, mesmerized by his words.

He opened the limo door. "I'll call you tomorrow." He slunk back in, ordering the driver to hurry away like a mastermind seeking world domination.

Allegra was immobile. Her heart slowed. Her body ached. No man had ever said those words to her before.

Ram's marital status was no longer an issue.

She knew that very moment. He was *the one*.

Seconds later, Snakehead stumbled outside, wrapping his fat head around the door. "Bobby says you need to come back inside now."

Allegra smiled as she looked up toward the bright moonlit sky. She inhaled a healthy dose of cold air, turned around, and went back inside the bar.

TWENTY

"YOU CAN stop the story there."

Violet's radiant eyes were now dark as crow. She uncrossed her legs, placed her pale hands against her eggplant dress, and slowly rose from the dining room chair. Her coral heels clicked against the concrete as she stood erect, towering over Allegra in her blue nightgown sitting below.

"You mean to tell me that my husband fell in love with you *before* he fucked you?"

Allegra's child-like eyes peeked up through her overgrown bangs. She thought long and hard before answering. "*Yes.*"

Violet's face tightened. Her mouth clamped shut, forcing air sharply through her nose. "Let me ask you again. According to your story, my husband, Ram, told you he loved you before you two were ever physical?"

Allegra was alarmed. Her voice softened. "I'm telling you exactly what happened, just like you asked me to do."

"*Bullshit!*" screamed Violet as she folded in half. "You're a fucking liar! My husband just used you like a blow-up doll to jerk off, that's it! That's all you are to him! A piece of shit, trailer trash, fuck-me doll!"

Allegra winced at the spit flying from Violet's tornado mouth.

"How dare you try to convince me that your relationship was some fucking Danielle Steele novel? Are you kidding me? My husband would never tell you he loved you. He's only said those words to me *twice,* and we've been married for fucking twenty-four years!"

Allegra panicked. "I . . . I thought you wanted the truth?"

Violet bent down directly into Allegra's face. Her copper hair was spiky and disheveled, glowing like it was on fire. "Yes, I want to hear the truth. But all you're giving me is cheap dollar-store fiction!"

Allegra had finally had enough. "I'm trying *to help you,* Violet. Whatever it is that made you do this to me, I don't know what it was exactly, but you must have needed to do it, otherwise you wouldn't have gone so far to get yourself in so much trouble like this. You tell me you need me to answer questions about me and Ram, and when I do, you freak out, calling me a liar, but I'm not lying—I mean, why would I at this point? I don't have anything to gain by lying, and if anything, I'm on the verge of dying at your hands, which is why I don't know what else to do but to tell you the truth—the real, whole, honest truth—exactly as it happened, *which is exactly what I'm doing!*"

Violet was shocked at Allegra's gravitas. She couldn't believe the grimy girl sitting next to her own piss pot had the balls to yell at her. She resumed her erect, perfect posture, fighting the emotion welling inside, now that she realized Allegra may have been telling the truth.

She wiped her hands down her dress. "Very well, then." She walked towards the dining room table and picked up the empty Duane Reade shopping bag on the floor.

She walked over to the kitchenette and opened the top drawer on the far left. Tears began streaming down her alabaster, taut face. She emptied the contents of the drawer—forks, knives, spoons—into the bag. She then opened the drawer below it, pulling out a pair of tongs and a can opener, and put it into the bag. She continued crying softly as she bent down and opened the third drawer below, inspected its contents, and slammed it shut. She then reached up to open the cabinet above the sink, saw there were only plastic bowls, and closed it. She opened the cabinet next to that one, now crying louder, seeing there were only paper plates, and closed it. She then opened the middle drawer next to the stove, crying as she removed a small knife and placed it in the bag. She then began sobbing, her chest rising fully up and down with every move, now opening all the cabinets and closing them quickly, one by one by one, checking the same drawers and cabinets over and over and over like a madwoman, until her sobs became violent chest heaves, her nose began spraying snot, and the tears rolling down her face became streams of water falling from her eyes until there were no more cabinets or drawers to check—she just fell to the ground, holding the shopping bag filled with items—crying, sobbing, bawling, hyperventilating, howling, wailing, and screaming for God to take the pain away as Allegra looked on . . .

Petrified.

TWENTY-ONE

LAURA, WEARING a knee-length black dress and hair swept up in a dancer's bun, tapped her bare nails next to a box of Kleenex on the conference table before her. She sat directly across from a Chinese woman in her late fifties wearing a black suit and a set of authentic pearls the size of golf balls. They both waited silently for the eighty-inch flat screen floating above them to turn on. Once it did, Ram's face appeared. His broad, white dress shirt-covered shoulders dominated the frame. The modern furnishings and messy bed behind him were different than before, but it was clear he was broadcasting from another luxury hotel room located somewhere overseas.

"Good morning, Laura. Can you hear me?" he asked.

Laura's head lifted. "Yes, Mr. Ramspeck. We can hear you just fine. I want to introduce you to our managing broker, Becky Chung."

The Chinese woman sat up straight. "Nice to meet you, Mr. Ramspeck."

"Likewise—however, I wish it was under better circumstances."

"Indeed."

Laura cleared her throat. "As I mentioned in my e-mail, Mr. Ramspeck, the initial balcony inspection came out fine, so we're clear on that front."

Ram touched the side of his glasses, relieved. "Good. The last thing I need is a lawsuit on top of everything else."

Becky squared her padded shoulders. "Miss Slovensky's extended family is well aware this was nothing more than an accident, Mr. Ramspeck. No one is blaming you or the house. I can personally assure you of that."

"Thank you."

Laura continued. "So, as we discussed, I am recommending we take the house off the market until October first for two reasons. One, it will appear as a fresh listing once buyers are settled back into the city. And two, it will allow the rumblings of this accident to die down a bit."

Becky interrupted. "Just to be transparent, Mr. Ramspeck, we are recommending this action for all of Penny's active listings. As you can imagine, we are trying to minimize the awkwardness of having prospects call in and having Laura respond with the explanation as to why she was returning Penny's calls."

Ram leaned back in his desk chair. "Yes, I understand. And I can appreciate the gravity of the situation. It must be a terrible loss for you all."

Laura looked down at the table.

"What time is the funeral today? I want to be sure the arrangement I sent will make it there on time."

"It starts at four o'clock," replied Becky.

"Good. It should be there by two, I believe." Ram folded his hands on the desk. He exhaled loudly. "Well, I really wanted to sell as soon as possible, but I can't change what's happened. I guess I'll just close on my new house as planned, and have you sell this home while I'm settling into my new place in Scotland."

Laura and Becky exchanged a hopeful look.

"Okay, let's go ahead and take it off the market."

Laura looked up. "Thank you for understanding, Mr. Ramspeck. I'll e-mail the document you need to sign to cancel the listing."

Ram was half-annoyed. "I'll sign it as soon as I get it."

Becky closed her notebook. "And if you have any questions, please do not hesitate to contact me directly concerning this matter."

"I will." He nodded. "Anything else?"

Laura shook her head.

"Not at this time," replied Becky.

"Well, I know this is a tough day for you both, so I won't wish you a good day, but know the sentiment is still there."

Laura's eyes welled. "Thank you, Mr. Ramspeck."

"Take care. Have a good night," added Becky.

Ram ended the Skype call. The screen went black.

Becky reached her hand across the table. "You did an excellent job, Laura. Penny's listings are now yours, so once you come back from leave, you can get them relisted and back on your feet."

Laura wiped a tear. "Thank you. I appreciate it."

A heavy-set man entered the conference room. He wore a shark-colored suit and tie. "May I interrupt?"

"Yes, we just finished," replied Becky.

"There's a prospect waiting in the lobby. He's asking about 13 East 78th Street? That was Penny's listing, right?"

"It's Laura's listing now," replied Becky as she looked across the table.

"I'll be out in a second," said Laura, reaching for another Kleenex.

Laura entered the marbled lobby of Sotheby's International Realty. She spotted an elderly man sitting alone, casually flipping through *Golf Digest*. He wore a navy blazer with tan pants, resembling an illegitimate Kennedy no one knew about.

Laura extended her hand. "Sorry to keep you waiting, sir. I'm Laura Welch."

"Jack Horowitz," he replied. "Pleasure to meet you."

"I understand you had some questions about 13 East 78th Street?"

"Ah, yes, I did. Is it still available?"

"Technically, yes. Yes, it is."

"Good. I want to buy it." The man pulled a checkbook from his interior jacket pocket. "I'll pay the full asking price. Twenty-five million, was it?"

Laura was stunned. "I'm not sure we're able to show the property today—"

He gestured his hand. "I don't need to see it. I've been there a dozen times with my wife. We're friends of the Ramspecks."

Laura opened her eyes. "Oh."

"My wife has always loved their home, and when I saw on the local news that somebody died during a real estate showing, I thought, why not buy it for her?" He leaned in closer to whisper. "My housekeeper told me Ram and Violet are getting divorced, so I thought, why not surprise my wife for her birthday and get the home she's always admired."

Laura raised her thin brows. "Of course, that's what *wonderful* husbands do."

"How soon can we close? Can we do it before September eighth? I'm throwing my wife a big party at Orsay's that night. I want to wrap up the house key and give it to her in front of everyone. It'll make a big splash."

"Uh, yes, since it's an all-cash deal, I believe we can do that. If you're willing to buy the property as is, without a full inspection, of course."

Jack gestured his hands to say *no problem*. "I'll need someone to sell my penthouse on Lex and Eighty-Third after we move in, so we can talk about giving you that business as well."

Laura's somber mood lifted. She had just gone from earning a fifty-thousand-dollar base salary to nailing two million dollars worth of commission in five minutes.

She smiled, believing Penny was orchestrating the deal from above. "Sounds great, Mr. Horowitz." She touched his arm. "Let's go into my office and work out the details."

"Terrific."

TWENTY-TWO

VIOLET SAT on the padded bench in her master bathroom. Her high, dry, cracked forehead was fully exposed by the tight white headband pulling back her hair. Rings from the movie star dressing room lights reflected in her eyes as she removed the smeared black mascara from her swollen face. Her nose was pink. Her cheeks were puffy. Her red lipstick had seeped into fine lines surrounding her mouth, like tiny blood creeks feeding a blood ocean. The top of her eggplant dress was wet from the tears shed freely earlier in the basement.

Her gold iPhone sat next to her on the marble countertop, plugged into the wall charger. It rang a familiar tone. A photo of a smiling dark blonde in her late thirties once again appeared with the words LISA HOROWITZ above it.

Violet looked down at the phone, waiting for the little gray *voicemail* box to appear. Once it did, she hit the icon and played the message on speaker:

"Violet. It's Lisa again. I'm *so damn* worried about you! I have no idea where you are, or what you're doing? I haven't heard from you in weeks! Well, the main reason I'm calling is that I heard from Anna that, uh, you and Ram are getting divorced? Is that *true*?"

Violet jerked as if she were poked with a Taser.

"I'm just as shocked as you are, so I can understand why you need some alone time. But I wanted to let you know I'm here if you need anything. Maybe talking about it will help? Or maybe we can do a girl's trip to St. Barth's again? Or Martha's Vineyard? I'm good with either. You choose, my treat—"

Violet ground her teeth. Her breathing intensified through her nostrils.

"I also understand Ram bought a castle in Scotland and is moving next month, which must be *devastating*, I'm sure. I assume you're going to stay here in New York, but no one's seen or heard from you, Violet. We're your friends, and we're here to help . . ."

Violet elongated her neck, trying to extract more oxygen from the air. She had no idea Ram had purchased another home, or worse yet, was planning to leave the country.

" . . . I also have some big news I'm not sure you're going to like, but I want you to hear it from me first before anyone else tells you."

Violet's heart began racing.

"I pray it doesn't hurt our friendship, Violet."

She stared at the phone screen, anxious.

"My new housekeeper let me in on a little secret a few minutes ago. Apparently, my husband *bought your house* for my birthday. It's supposed to be a big surprise at my party next month—which I still hope you can make—but Gloria filled me in ahead of time."

Violet was frozen.

"I just pray this doesn't come between you and me, Violet. I *cherish* our friendship."

She couldn't believe her ears.

"I have no idea what your plans are after the closing, so I also wanted to tell you that my baby sister—you know the one who just graduated from NYU? Well, she accepted a job in DC and is sub-letting her studio apartment on East 57th in case you're interested. It's got a view of a brick wall, but it's modern and super comfortable, so let me know. Okay?"

Violet was fuming.

"Call me when you get this message! I want to make sure everything's Kosher between us. You're a dear friend, Violet, and I don't want to lose you. Call me back. Bye."

Violet ripped the phone out of the charger.

She threw it against the mirror.

It bounced back onto the counter.

She screamed, picked it up, and threw it again.

The screen smashed as it fell onto the floor.

She began hyperventilating.

She ripped off her headband and threw it into the sink.

She ran into her bedroom, circled the floor several times, hitting the bedpost trees, slapping the brown silk curtains, growling and snarling like a wolf in heat.

Suddenly, she stopped. Her face was expressionless. She carefully removed each coral shoe from her dainty feet. When she was finished, she took off like an Olympic sprinter and ran outside her bedroom door.

She pounded down the seven flights of stairs like a Beethoven piece readying soldiers for battle. She passed by both housekeepers undetected—Octavia on the fifth floor, too busy talking to her sister on the phone; and Rosa, with headphones, vacuuming on the third floor—landing hard on the wooden surface of the first floor, near the kitchen.

She licked her lips as she plucked the shiny Austof-Reed meat cleaver from the wooden block, batted open the pantry door, and punched her way down the two security doors with lightening by her side.

When she arrived in the basement, she tiptoed down the final set of stairs to Allegra, lying on her side, comatose and sleeping on a pillow, covered by her precious army blanket.

Violet stood in silence with the meat cleaver in hand. Her mouth was sealed shut. Air raged through her nostrils like a horse ready to attack.

Allegra sensed heavy breathing and slowly opened her eyes to see the maniac standing above her—a menacing silhouette lit from behind.

Allegra sprang into a sitting position, slamming her back against the wall.

Violet grabbed a handful of Allegra's long, cinnamon-red waves.

She swung the meat cleaver down, chopping off the entire side of Allegra's hair, cutting a small part of her ear in the process.

"Ahhhhh!"

Allegra put up her hands in defense as Violet swung the meat cleaver again, slicing into Allegra's forearm, hitting the bone.

"Ooouuuch! Stop!"

Violet pulled out the cleaver from Allegra's arm, then grabbed another long piece of hair, cutting it so closely it grazed Allegra's scalp, causing it to bleed.

"Stop! I'll do anything you want!"

Violet then pulled another chunk of Allegra's hair, hacking it off in one shot.

"Please! Stop doing this!"

Violet reached behind Allegra's head, pulled another handful of hair, knotting it up into her fist, slicing it sideways just millimeters from her head.

"I'm sorry! I'm *so sorry!*"

Both of Allegra's arms were now gushing blood all over the floor. She squeezed her eyes shut as Violet pulled her overgrown bangs tightly, hacking the whole thing off in one sweep, leaving a quarter-inch of red fuzz above her brows.

Allegra cried for mercy. "Please, Violet! Stop! We can talk about it!"

Violet ignored her pleas. She continued hacking off the rest of Allegra's hair—pulling, wrenching, yanking, slashing, ripping, and cutting—until nothing remained on top of Allegra's head but bloody patches of skin with random strands of long, red hair sprouting throughout.

Allegra looked like a Barbie Doll massacred by a demented child.

She cried hysterically as she buried her face into her knees, with blood running from her scalp onto the floor, both gashed elbows shielding her face from continued blows.

Finally, Violet stopped.

She raged as she panted, breathing like a monster who had just destroyed a city. She threw the meat cleaver to the ground, pulled up the skirt of her eggplant dress, and removed a pair of red silk panties.

Allegra did not see what Violet was doing. Her head was still buried in her knees, begging and pleading for her life.

Violet, bare from the waist down, placed her hairless vagina in front of Allegra's bald, bleeding head. "I will destroy you," she said in a deep, growling voice. She then pulled Allegra's four-fingered hand from the air, shoved it between her legs, and used it to rub her clitoris.

"I will *fucking* destroy you!" she growled again, this time in a malevolent voice.

Allegra did not fight.

She did not struggle.

All she wanted to do was *die*.

Just kill me quickly, she thought, as Violet pleasured herself with her limp, bleeding hand—mocking the act more than enjoying it.

After a while, Violet silently climaxed, then backed away. She pulled her eggplant dress down from her waist and retrieved her panties from the floor.

Allegra was lost. This was more than she could handle.

Violet patted down her dress and wiped her long bangs away from her face. She then walked over to the kitchenette, opened the top left drawer, and removed a small key. She walked back over to Allegra, who ducked into a ball as Violet came closer.

"Please! No more!"

Violet tugged the metal chain attached to Allegra's dog collar, yanking her vacant green eyes into the air. Violet inserted the key into the small lock behind it, throwing the sweaty dog collar to the ground.

Allegra rubbed the front of her bare neck. Her bondage was gone.

She was finally *free to move* around.

Violet picked up the meat cleaver from the floor, and went back up the stairs. "There's a First Aid kit in the bathroom," she said with her back turned, exiting the security door.

As soon as Violet was gone, Allegra counted to a hundred, praying this wasn't some sort of trick. When Violet didn't return, she picked up the long strands of red hair scattered by her feet, hugging it tightly in a final goodbye.

She then wobbled into the mysterious bathroom ten feet behind her. She flipped on the lights and looked into the mirror, seeing her reflection for the first time in nearly two weeks.

Allegra looked like a dying cancer patient.

She was bald. She was bleeding. Random strands of long hair sprinkled around her head. Red splotches and pimples covered her pastel, childlike face. The whites of her eyes were yellowing. Her nose and lips were swollen. Her teeth were dull gray.

The image in the mirror was unrecognizable. She was a monster. An unlovable, unfuckable, unbearable monster.

Ram would never love her like this. It would take years to recover her natural beauty.

Violet had won.

And if it weren't for the tiny soul growing inside her belly, Allegra would have drowned herself in the bathtub that night.

Somehow, though, she found the strength to pull back the shower curtain. She reached inside, turned on the water, and crawled into the steaming hot paradise. She washed herself with a fresh bar of soap, carefully missing the gashes and wounds covering her entire body.

When she was finished, she stood naked on the vinyl tile, air-drying without a towel. She searched the empty cabinets, finally discovering the SURGICAL SURVIVAL KIT below the sink. She opened the kit and searched for oint-ment, bandages, and gauze—anything that would dull the stinging, throbbing pain radiating in hundreds of places above her waist.

And then she saw it: a sharp, brand-new, #22 scalpel with a three-inch blade.

Suddenly, Allegra's will to survive *returned*.

TWENTY-THREE

"VIOLET? Are you still with me?"

Dr. Cohen waved his hand in front of Violet's face as she watched the rain hit the sidewalk in plump, full drops. She was hypnotized by the random pattern of the rainfall, leaving empty voids between each splash stain, creating a gray and beige houndstooth pattern along the familiar Park Avenue walkway.

"Violet? Can you hear me?"

The distinctive smell of new carpet aggravated her senses. She finally returned, snapping away from the window and back toward Dr. Cohen. "Where's Sparkles?"

His face saddened as he pointed upwards. "She crossed the rainbow bridge before me."

"Oh, I'm so sorry, Dr. Cohen. You must be heartbroken."

He fanned his hand. "No need to feel sorry for me, Violet. I'll be seeing her again very soon," he said with a sincere smile. "As for you, I'm quite concerned about your periods of withdrawal. Is this occurring frequently?"

Violet struggled to pay attention. Her mind's eye burned with the image of Allegra on the floor, balled up like a frightened armadillo. "No, not as much as before. I just have a lot on my mind."

"What is weighing on you so heavily today?"

Violet looked down at the new carpet which had changed from when she was last in Dr. Cohen's office. The outdated, beige and brown semi-shag was now flat and checkered with primary colors of blue, yellow, and red.

"You were talking about the months leading up to your confrontation with Ram?"

"Yes. What about it?" Her bold eyes diverted to a six-foot-wide, colorful painting hanging beside her. It was a gargantuan scene of rainbow-inspired paint splashes with multiethnic children dancing on either side.

Violet lifted her index finger and traced the rainbow paint colors thrown violently against the innocent canvas. "Is that new?"

"Ah, yes," he said, regrettably. "It's part of the daycare moving into the building. This will be the new administrative office as of September fourth."

"I forgot. School's back in session after Labor Day."

Dr. Cohen was morose. After spending more than fifty years in the same location, it was difficult for him to leave. "Yes, yes, it is."

Violet studied the poorly painted faces that made the dancing children look like cookies baked in an oven. "Very odd."

Dr. Cohen nodded in agreement. "Now, let's get back to you. We've already covered the worst part, the moment you discovered the affair—"

"Oh, no." She shook her head emphatically. "That's *not* the worst part, Dr. Cohen."

He picked up the pen and legal pad from the glass coffee table by his shins. "Go on."

Violet extended her bony collarbone, emphasized by the neckline of her MaxMara dress. "The worst part came afterward. Pretending not to know." She crossed her legs in the opposite direction. "Do you know what it's like watching your spouse tell lies about where he's going, whom he's meeting, what he's doing—day after day—dozens of ridiculous stories a week, knowing that he's lying to you?"

Dr. Cohen chewed on his pen. "No, I have never experienced that personally."

"Your mind wanders into terrible places, Dr. Cohen. Routine, daily tasks become almost impossible to complete." She looked at the floor. "You literally become *obsessed*. It clouds everything you think about the past, present, and future because all you can do is think about how they touched, how they laughed, how they shared body fluids, how long has she been there, what went wrong, what did I do—"

"Do you still love Ram?"

Violet was offended. "Of course, I do. We've been together for more than half of my life. He's a part of me, part of my family, like a parent or a brother. I cannot separate him from me, or me from him—I feel like we're Siamese twins being ripped apart by an amateur surgeon in a back alley. I'm falling apart."

Dr. Cohen raised his pen. "Roughly sixty percent of all long-term marriages experience infidelity at one point or another. Many of them—especially those that have reached the twenty-year mark—can survive. In some cases, it makes couples stronger. All is not lost, Violet."

"But this affair was different." She tucked her bangs behind her ear. "I've lost Ram forever."

"Why? Because he cared for her?"

"No. Because he *loved* her more than me."

Dr. Cohen was intrigued. "Did he tell you this during the . . . confrontation?"

"No. *She* told me."

Dr. Cohen reacted. "You spoke to Allison?"

"You mean Allegra."

"Yes, Allegra. You confronted her? When?"

Violet looked away from Dr. Cohen and toward the over-stuffed bookcase by the front door. "I can ask her anything I want about the affair. She's completely under my control."

"Violet, this is a traumatic event." Dr. Cohen's eyebrows moved so rapidly, it looked like gray caterpillars were bouncing on top of his spectacles. "I don't think you should confront the girl in any way. It will only make matters worse. It will just complicate your recovery."

"Too late."

"Violet, what have you done?"

"Nothing major," she answered wryly.

"It's important we remain honest here. How did you connect with Allegra?"

"I met with her in person."

"Is she aware of what your husband has done to the both of you?"

Violet fibbed. "Yes."

"And what took place during your meeting?"

"I just asked her a few questions about how it all started. Again, nothing major."

"What was her response? Was she cooperative or combative?"

"Oh, she was very cooperative. Remorseful, in fact."

"And did you discover any new information?"

Violet nodded her head. "Oh, yes, quite a bit. For instance, Ram lied to her about our sex life. He told her we had been sleeping in separate bedrooms and hadn't been intimate in years."

Dr. Cohen was not surprised. "It's very common for cheating spouses to fabricate sexual problems in order to alleviate the guilt for the third party participant."

"Yes, and she's stupid enough to believe it. And then she went on to tell me—" Violet's eyes welled. "Never mind, it's all fairy tales anyway."

Dr. Cohen wrote something on his legal pad.

"The bigger news is that Ram sold our townhome. To Lisa Horowitz—one of my very best friends—no less."

Dr. Cohen raised his eyes. "Really? Allegra told you this?"

"No, I heard it directly from the traitor's mouth." she swung her long, copper bangs away from her eyes. "Lisa was always jealous of me. Figures."

"I see." He continued writing.

"Oh, and it gets better. Ram already bought an estate in Scotland and is moving there next month."

Dr. Cohen stopped writing. "Why?"

"I think *you know* why."

He caught her hint. "Of course. Running away from the mess he created."

"Exactly."

The two stared at one another in silence, unsure of where to go next.

Dr. Cohen stated his most pressing concern. "Consequences follow us beyond death, Violet. It's very important you remember this."

She rolled her eyes. "Another religious lesson?"

He placed his pad on the table. "My gut tells me you're contemplating something drastic." His Jewish accent blossomed with that final word. "I want you to stay connected to me until this urge subsides."

Violet turned back to the rainstorm outside. "Oh, I see where you're heading now."

Dr. Cohen removed his glasses. His tone turned serious. He leaned into his thigh as he spoke with passion. "Violet, I know exactly what you've done."

Her eyes connected to his. He had never spoken to her this way.

"It's time you let Allegra go. *You must let her be free.*"

Violet was terrified. "What do you mean?"

"You must let her go as soon as possible. If you don't, I may not be able to protect you from what comes next."

"What are you talking about?" Violet played possum, despite the rapid-fire pounding of her heart.

"You must release her from the guilt she feels from breaking your marriage apart. No more contact. No more questions. Release her from the guilt and see how much better *you* will feel."

Violet sat quietly for a moment, realizing Dr. Cohen was speaking metaphorically, not literally. "Oh, I get it. I will."

"Are you sure you can forgive her?"

"Yes."

"Very sure? Because it's essential for your recovery."

"Yes, I'm quite sure."

"Good." Dr. Cohen wrote something down.

Violet smiled nervously, masking her guilty breath like a person who kept driving after causing a five-car pile-up on the highway.

TWENTY-FOUR

NELLIE SCROLLED through her smartphone while sitting at the main bar of Bobby & Eddie's. It was difficult for an award-winning photojournalist to suddenly be left out of the action due to the lack of interest in international events, and her recent double bunion foot surgery.

The last summer Nellie had worked had been filled with media red meat: ISIS terror hits on Orlando, Paris, and Nice; the ethnic war in Syria; racial clashes between inner city residents and police; and out-of-control protestors outside Trump and Clinton rallies. Now with the election over, the airwaves were filled with soap-opera monologues about Russian mobsters, paid-off porn stars, and the stream of White House firings that made *everyone* nervous.

Instead of catching the incredible emotion of current events, Nellie sat on the sidelines like a common citizen, forced to digest complex global issues by consuming tiny, bite-sized blurbs beamed into a miniature handheld screen. She longed for the days of being in the center of the action, snapping away at the horrors of humanity, while feeling the exhilaration of force-feeding moral lessons to unsuspecting diners back in the USA.

Nellie's usual sidekick—a half-empty glass of cheap Chardonnay—sat quietly in front of her as she scrolled, ignoring the drunk bar mates around her.

"You're addicted to your phone," said Judge Richard, bombed by one o'clock that Saturday afternoon.

"We're all addicted," said the bartender, Double Trouble, as he cleaned out glasses with a dry rag. "Don't listen to him, sweetheart."

Nellie raised her head. "Do I ever?"

Chloe Sinclair entered the bar wearing a scandalous outfit of a spaghetti strap top and shorts so tiny, the bottom of her dark, flawless butt cheeks peeked through.

"Oh, look, it's Mariah Carey," whispered Nellie to the men beside her.

Chloe made a beeline for the empty stool in the corner. "Hey, Nellie. Hi, Judge Richard."

Both mimed hellos in return.

"What are you drinkin', sweet cakes?" asked the bartender.

"I'll have a Diet Coke. Thanks."

The bar patrons turned their heads in unison, as if an alien had appeared out of thin air. Usually, the only people allowed to abstain from drinking alcohol at D&E were those who were in recovery or pregnant, and even they got shit for it.

"No mojitos today?" asked Nellie.

Chloe fluffed her natural, curly hair. "I can't. I have a second callback at three o'clock, so I need to stay sober. I'm just here killing time so I don't freak myself out over it."

The bartender sprayed her boring Diet Coke into a plastic cup with ice. "What's it for?"

"It's a commercial for the new Honda Civic."

"Can you even drive a car?" asked Nellie.

"Of course not," replied Chloe. "I'm a New Yorker."

"Well, break a leg, sweet thing. This one's on me." The bartender handed her the soda.

Nellie cheered up. "Actually, I'm glad you're here, Chloe. The boys and I were just talking about you an hour ago."

"Yes, we thought about chipping in on a present for Allegra," said Judge Richard.

Nellie tapped the top of her glass. The bartender pulled out a five-dollar bottle of wine and refilled it. "Right, it's a 'fake wedding and a baby' present. Do you have her new address?"

Chloe was flabbergasted. "You guys *knew* Allegra was pregnant?"

The crowd all nodded their heads.

"Didn't you?" added Nellie.

"Well, yes, I mean, I found out later," she said embarrassingly. "So, what was the deal? Who's this Martinez guy she married?"

Nellie and Judge Richard exchanged a look.

"Martinez? I thought she ran off with Mr. Clean?" asked Nellie.

Judge Richard was puzzled. "Me too. Tall guy with the bald head?"

Nellie scratched the top of her salt-and-pepper hair. "His name was . . . It's the same name as that Scottish museum on Fifth and Ninety-second?"

"Ramrod?"

"Eehh, that's almost right."

"*Ramspeck?*" asked Chloe.

"Bingo!" confirmed Nellie. "His last name was Ramspeck. Allegra called him 'Ram.' There we go."

Nellie clinked glasses with Judge Richard.

Chloe slumped in her stool. "I'm so confused."

"Why, honey?" asked Nellie as she sipped her Chardonnay. "He seemed like a great guy to me."

"I don't know. . . I mean, Allegra left for Mexico without taking her wallet, or her purse, or her ID? How did she even get on a plane without a passport? And I know she doesn't have one because we couldn't go on a cruise together because of it. Then she didn't contact me for four full days. It worried the shit out of me so much, I even went to the police."

"We were all worried too, until you called Bobby and told him what happened," added Judge Richard. "People in love do impulsive things, Chloe. Plus, I don't think you need a passport to fly on a private jet, do you?"

"Oh, that's right, he was into that *flying everywhere on a private jet* thing," said Nellie.

"And if you *do* need a passport, she probably got one within twenty-four hours. It's not hard if you're willing to pay up."

Chloe walked closer. "Can you check and see if she was ever issued a passport, Judge Richard?"

"You're that concerned, huh?" asked Nellie.

Chloe nodded her head.

Judge Richard pursed his lips. "I know someone who could do that for me, but I'll need her social security number, city of birth, and birthday too."

Chloe agreed. "I have it somewhere at home. It's on my lease application."

Nellie made a face. "I think you may be overreacting *a tad*." She sipped her drink. "It's all pretty explainable, when you break down the details."

Chloe became animated. "Well, the big issue for me was that I received this letter in the mail asking me to ship all her stuff to Mexico, which I did, but then when I sent a text to give her the tracking number, her phone was, like, out of service."

"So why is that odd?" asked Nellie, before taking another sip. "Maybe *hubby nuevo* got her a new phone with a Mexican number?"

"Good point, Nellie. You should be a detective."

"I know, right?"

"I don't know, it just feels strange. First, she gives off the impression she married some baller Mexican named

Martinez, then she writes *Ramspeck* in her journal, like she was already married."

Nellie and Judge Richard shared a laugh. "That's cute, but Allegra can't possibly be married yet. How long does it take to get divorced in New York, Judge?"

"With his kind of money, *at least* a year," he responded. "Most judges insist on a legal separation of twelve months before finalizing a divorce."

Chloe scrunched her face. "I don't get it. Why would she take off and lie to me?"

Nellie smiled. "For Christ's sake, Chloe, she got *knocked up* by a *married* man! Not something you want to advertise. I would have hauled ass and gone upstate myself."

The bartender leaned in and joined the conversation. "Maybe the wife killed her?"

"You're a sick son-of-a-bitch," said Nellie. "Just shut up and pour me another drink."

The bartender laughed.

"*The wife*? Never thought about that. Must have been big news to her," added Judge Richard. "Do you have the address where you sent Allegra's belongings?"

Chloe thought for a moment. "Yeah, it's in my backpack."

Nellie tapped her fingers on the bar. "Good, because I'm dying to Zillow the house and see how much it's worth."

Chloe held up the printed note that came with the money. "Here it is." She handed it to Judge Richard.

"I don't have my reading glasses." He immediately handed it to Nellie.

Nellie looked at the paper. "Hey, I know where this is. Allegra lives in the touristy part of Guadalajara." She entered the address into her smartphone. It popped up on Google as *La Bruja Restaurant & Bar* in Guadalajara, Mexico.

"Now that's odd," said Nellie.

"What?"

"You sent all her personal belongings to a restaurant?"

"Maybe that Ram fellow owns it," chimed Judge Richard. "Didn't she say he owned a chain of restaurants in South America?"

"Oh, true, she did. Damn, you've got a good memory for an alcoholic," said Nellie.

"Thank you." He smiled, missing the slam.

Nellie wiped the corner of her mouth. "You see? Everything is good, Chloe. Allegra just ran off to Mexico with her married boyfriend, so they could have their baby in peace while he gets a divorce in the States. Not a big deal. Just a typical Manhattan love story."

"Can we call the restaurant to make sure?" asked Chloe.

Judge Richard shrugged his shoulders. "It can't hurt. You speak Spanish, don't you?"

Nellie bent her wrist. "What the hell. I still have global minutes on this thing." She dialed the number that appeared on the Google search.

Nellie took another gulp of wine as the line rang in her ear.

"Buenos Dias. Habla Ingles? . . . Oh, you do, great. I was calling to speak with Allegra Adams? . . . How about Allegra Martinez? . . . Is there anyone named Allegra associated with your restaurant? . . . Do you know if the owner's last name is Ramspeck? . . . Oh, I see." Nellie looked at Chloe and Judge Richard. "Okay, thank you so much for your time. Adios."

She hung up.

Nellie wrinkled her forehead. "No one knows Allegra there. And the owner is an eighty-year-old Mexican woman who's been the chef for fifty-five years."

Chloe placed her hands on the bar. "See?"

"Are you sure the address is right?" asked Judge Richard.

"I'm positive. They accepted the package addressed to her," replied Chloe.

Nellie scratched her head. "Maybe we should check on that passport thing, Judge. What do you think?"

"It couldn't hurt. I'll do it first thing in the morning," he replied. "I should know something by Wednesday night, so stop back by the bar," he said to Chloe.

"I will, thank you."

Chloe felt vindicated as she took a sip of her Diet Coke.

Finally, everyone knew that 'darling Allegra' was a *total* liar.

TWENTY-FIVE

OCTAVIA, the housekeeper, reclined in one of eight midnight blue, memory-foam luxury recliners in the sixth-floor media room. Her dark, virgin hair ponytail hung off the back in a carefree manner as she licked the salt off her fingers from finishing a bag of Lay's potato chips.

The over-the-top entertainment center featured a 1940s-era red popcorn stand and a real movie theater projection screen from a boutique picture house that burned down in Chelsea years ago. The concept for the space was left over from the days Violet led *The Murder House Book Club*—a short-lived intellectual project that quickly turned into an informal movie night after discovering most UES wives preferred watching the movie versions of novels instead.

Violet abandoned her book club in 2007, along with most of her other social endeavors in the months leading up to her daughter's adoption, using the room only twice after Briar Rose's untimely death.

Octavia cradled a gray ostrich feather duster in her lap, a souvenir given to her by Mr. Ramspeck after his trip to Australia earlier that year. She crossed her ankles in the air, watching the CNN live broadcast of protestors outraged by yet another AR-15 fueled mass shooting at a local high school. She had become so accustomed to seeing the same sign-wielding marchers, she failed to catch which shooting they were at, and instead relished the moment to refresh her toes that had gone numb from cleaning non-stop since seven that morning.

Rosa entered, defiantly removing her hot pink earbuds. "What are you doing?" she asked Octavia in Spanish. "We're not done yet."

"I'm taking a little break. Come sit with me and watch the news."

"Did you finish dusting the library?"

"Yes. It's all done."

"How about the guest bedrooms?"

"Done."

"And the master suite?"

Octavia shot her a look of defiance. "I'm not going in there alone again." She returned her gaze to the screaming people with anti-gun t-shirts on screen.

"You have to. It's your job. You haven't touched that room in two weeks."

"Who cares? We're both unemployed in four days."

Rosa sucked in her lips. "*I care.* I'm not going to lose my one-year's pay because you don't want to dust his bedroom. We have to leave this house spotless. So move your pretty little butt up there and do it!"

Octavia drank from a bottle of orange Fanta soda as the sound of gunshots fired through the television set. Pure chaos developed on screen. "You think I forgot what happened last time?"

"Octavia, it must have been someone from the sidewalk talking, and their voice traveled up to the room. You're just making excuses."

Octavia threw her hands in the air. "I'm not crazy, Rosa! That demon doll said my name. It *said my name* and winked at me!" She exaggerated her expression as she winked in demonstration. "I swear on my poor mother's grave."

Rosa rolled her eyes. "Jesus Christ. Not this again."

Octavia lifted up in the recliner. "How about I do the kitchen for you if you dust the bedroom for me?" She waved her prized duster in the air. "I'll buy dinner tonight too."

"I don't want to do it."

"Why not? If the demon doll is just my imagination?"

"Because, it's not my job. I do my job, you do yours. That's how it works."

"Then let's skip it. Mr. Ramspeck won't notice. Men never do."

"Mrs. Ramspeck will notice the dust when she gets back. She always checks."

Octavia waved her hand. "She won't notice either. She's too"—
she motioned her finger in a circle around her temple—"*crazy*."

"Go dust the room now, or I'm telling Mr. Ramspeck that
your boyfriend drank all his expensive liquor and replaced
it with the cheap stuff that comes in plastic bottles."

Octavia slapped the armrest. "Okay, okay, I'm going."

Rosa crossed her arms. "Good."

"But I'm leaving the door wide open, and you better come
get me if I start screaming. Okay?"

Rosa gave a rare smile. "You have my word."

Octavia slowly unlocked the door to the master suite, leaving
it wide open after she entered.

"Hello? Is anyone here?"

She gripped the feather duster handle like it was a deadly
weapon.

As she crept in, her gaze followed the lines in the wooden
floor, purposefully avoiding the *Little Red Riding Hood* paintings with ghostly eyes that followed her every move. The
three scenes she hated in particular were the one that showed
the wolf dressed in a powder blue bonnet and nightgown,
grinning in bed; the one where Little Red is depicted mid-
scream as the evil wolf bites her ankle; and the one where
Little Red and her real grandmother share a blanket of the
wolf's pelt while napping near the fireplace. In that painting,
Octavia could have sworn she could see the diabolical face

of the wolf within the flames of the fireplace. This hidden image, out of all the other haunting items in the room, was the scariest one by far.

Octavia walked directly to the brown silk curtains ahead of her. She forcefully parted the pair that led to the terrace, causing a cloud of dust to fly into the air and gracefully fall to the floor. The indirect sunlight filled the chamber with as much positive energy as it could offer, but the dark vibe of the room sucked it up faster than a black hole.

Octavia was becoming annoyed with herself. She was a fierce señorita who had faced more dangerous things than possessed dolls while growing up in Roatán, Honduras, including being mugged twice, and witnessing a man execute his adulteress, eight-months-pregnant wife with a machete on the dirt road in front of her shanty home.

Octavia squeezed her soft waist as she talked herself into facing the fear, carefully avoiding eye contact with the monstrous tree-post bed and its creepy branches crawling up the ceiling. Instead, she focused on the filthy dresser and writing desk, lamenting having to dust the entire room while she was so exhausted at the end of the day.

She looked directly through the wood archway leading to the main dressing area, knowing the last time she breached that threshold—the day before Penny's death—the oversized, blonde doll with the red cape and plaid dress, spoke to her in that room, telling her something she could not bear to repeat. She told Rosa what had happened that evening, leaving out the full message told to her by the doll, but no one else. And when Penny mysteriously fell off the balcony, and police officers invaded the room, she pleaded with Rosa to tell Mr. Ramspeck about the encounter, but Rosa refused. At least for now, Octavia knew the doll would be sitting on the middle shelf near the center of the display, where she and Rosa left it, waiting for a new visitor to arrive to start chatting away.

Octavia inhaled a desperate breath, choosing to face the doll head on before turning her back on it while cleaning the rest of the room. She considered gently putting it away in the back of the main closet, or placing a towel over its face like her sister would do when their pet parrot, Houdini, wouldn't shut up during the night.

She grasped her feather duster, placing one foot in front of the other, walking in a straight line toward the open archway. *It's only a doll. It can't hurt you,* she thought. *Only four more days of work, and then I'll be able to do whatever I want for a whole damn year.*

As Octavia approached the threshold, she spoke aloud in the best English she could command. "Hello, little doll. I'm leaving soon, so no need to—"

The doll was sitting on the floor, grinning.

Octavia screamed.

Rosa heard her from the kitchen.

Octavia dropped her feather duster, ran outside the dressing area, slammed her shoulder into the tree-bed post, continued running out the bedroom door, down the stairs, and into Rosa's arms, who was standing on the third-floor landing.

"My God, child! What happened?" asked Rosa.

"Did you put that doll on the floor?"

"No, child. I haven't been in there."

"Don't play with me!"

Rosa was concerned. "I promise you, I haven't been in that room. What happened?"

Octavia pulled away from Rosa and continued down the stairs.

Rosa followed.

"Tell Mr. Ramspeck whatever you want because I'm leaving."

"What? Octavia!"

Rosa followed her through the main foyer.

Octavia cried as she went into the front closet, pulled out a denim purse, and slung it around her shoulder. "You were a great boss. A little bitchy at times, but you taught me a lot, and for that, I thank you."

"What are you doing? Don't quit now. Please."

Octavia gave a sad smile as she looked back over her shoulder, slammed the door shut, and left forever.

TWENTY-SIX

ALLEGRA MADE up her mind. She had a plan. *To win.*

Using a fully functional toilet; taking twice-daily, hot showers; brushing her teeth with dollar-store toothpaste; washing her face with discontinued soap; wearing warm, clean nightgowns; and sleeping five full nights on the soft, king-sized bed transformed Allegra's failing will to live into an *anima* ready to crush the competition on any survival reality show. This was it. The moment Allegra decided she wouldn't give up. The moment she declared she would walk out of the infamous basement safe room of 13 East 78th Street—alive and healthy—as a wife, mother, and millionaire, all in a year's time.

This was her hit reality show: *Survive, Allegra.*

And the prize if she could make it to the season finale?

The man she loved. The baby she wanted. The name she coveted. The house she adored. The fame she desired. The money she earned. The legacy she deserved.

Violet had been extremely quiet over the last five days. She was only visiting twice a day now to deliver fresh clothes, and pitchers full of what Allegra called *obnoxious smoothie*—the strange concoction of protein milk, Oreo cookies, Heath bars, and the unpleasant, unfamiliar taste of the sour ingredient Allegra simply could not pinpoint. But whatever it was, it was keeping her energy up, clearing her severely pimpled and blotched face, and helping her thrive in a sunless environment of steel, concrete, and sin.

Since gaining her freedom to move about, Allegra spent most of her days looking through the steel cabinets, inspecting every corner, top, and underbelly. She found numerous, useless supplies, such as cans of corn, peas, olives, chicken, tuna, spam—all inedible without a can opener—and barrels of water that could keep her alive for one hundred eighty days. Her goal was to identify every potential weapon she could use to launch her upcoming attack on her captor, unable to find anything more vicious than the #22 scalpel from the Surgical Kit and an ergonomically designed heavy can of beans Allegra planned to use as a sledgehammer. Anything more valuable—or in this case, dangerous—must have been under lock and key in the digitally secured walk-in refrigerator and freezer, or the wooden hope chest with a large Masterlock keeping its treasures tight. Although a scalpel and a can of beans wasn't much, Allegra was convinced it was enough to knock Violet into unconsciousness so that she could slit her jugular vein and pound her head in, uninterrupted, ensuring the monster would never wake.

Allegra needed to get as fat as possible to survive the potentially long period of starvation with Violet dead. She worried if the fetus growing inside her would survive, but given Mother Nature's tendency to root for the underdog, she felt it was a risk worth taking.

Especially since her rescuers must only be days away. They had to be. Someone must have noticed she was missing by now. Chloe. Ram. Bobby. Nellie. *Someone.*

Someone must have noticed she left her purse in the apartment.

Someone must have noticed she didn't show up for work at the bar.

Someone must have noticed she wasn't answering calls or texts.

Someone must have seen Violet take her from Carl Schurz Park.

Or kidnap her out in the open.

Or whatever happened that night she was running.

Someone must have seen Violet drag her inside the townhome.

The neighbors? The housekeepers? Security cameras outside?

Someone must have seen my photo plastered on television. Or on flyers in Yorkville. Or on the Internet. Or Facebook?

Someone must have noticed I am missing by now.

So, where the fuck is everybody?

Allegra's thoughts raced faster than her heartbeat, making her feel nauseated. She immediately changed the subject of her inner dialogue, focusing instead on changing into the fresh, white nightgown folded on the dining room table. It had long sleeves, an empire waist, and was longer than the others, with a hem that almost reached the floor. It was a lovely, comfortable garment, but wouldn't work for her secret nighttime exercises.

Four days ago, after Violet made her second and final obnoxious smoothie delivery of the day, Allegra started practicing sprinting up the stairs to the coded door. She would stand casually at the bottom of the steps, pretending to be going off to bed or to the bathroom, imagining Violet at the top of the landing, with her back turned, entering the combination into the keypad to the right of the exit. She would wait for the perfect moment after Violet opened the door—when she could sprint up the stairs, smash Violet on the head with the can-of-beans sledgehammer, and make a run for it.

Brilliant idea. Or at least she thought so at the time.

But the biggest discovery over the past several days was the book, magazine, and DVD cabinet closest to the antiquated television in the lower left-hand corner of the room. Allegra had never been much of a reader in school—in fact, it was the activity she enjoyed the least—but given her solitude and crippling lack of mental stimulation, she was thrilled to find what appeared to be used New York Public Library copies of *The Great Gatsby, Anna Karenina, The Catcher in the Rye, Catch 22, Moby Dick, The Picture of Dorian Gray,* and so many more. Each one had a list of unrecognizable names listed in the inner front pocket and check out dates going as far back as 1973, but in some strange way, Allegra felt a bond with those imaginary people. David Lorcheinstein. Mary Cosby. Alejandro Vega de Moreno. She visualized how each person looked. How they spoke. Where they lived. And what was going on in their lives when they read that particular library book.

She was convinced not one of them was going through what she was. That was the one thing she knew for sure.

Though a non-reader, she was devouring almost a book a day—impressive even by bookworm standards. And if anything positive were to come from this horrific ordeal, it was that Allegra would never again take for granted the magical simplicity of a hard printed book that could transport her out of any undesirable situation, any time she liked.

The one item Allegra avoided in the safe room was the bathroom mirror. She tried to place a pillowcase over it but did not have anything to fasten it securely. She assured herself that the less she looked at her patchy/bald head, cut arms, and nine fingers, the better. She wanted to cherish the way she looked before her imprisonment—the way a family member would refuse to see a corpse, preferring to remember the way their loved one looked when they were alive.

Amazingly, Allegra was positive enough to convince herself her hair would grow back, her cuts would heal, and that a pinkie finger was a useless digit anyway. It was this extraordinary talent to see the positive in the direst of situations that set Allegra apart from most other millennials. Her naive tendency to believe that *good will always triumph over evil* is what fueled her to carry on, though in the end, it ultimately blinded her to the most stunning revelation about Violet she could have ever imagined.

Allegra sat at the dining room table, wearing her white nightgown, as she started to read the third chapter of *Lord of the Rings: Volume One*. She was amazed to see the scratched-up, three-book set in the cabinet, never once realizing that an author gave birth to one of her all-time favorite movie trilogies—a literary masterpiece that took J.R.R. Tolkien *twelve years* to finish and a Twitter reviewer *twelve seconds* to demolish.

The low whirring sound of the door unlocking was Allegra's Pavlovian bell to close her book, slump in the chair, and look feeble. Naturally, she assumed it was Violet. But even if it was the police, she wanted to look as weak and helpless as possible, to make for better rescue footage captured by the body cameras they would be wearing.

Violet glided down the stairs wearing a watermelon pink Michael Kors dress and white Givenchy platform sandals.

She held a full blender filled with the obnoxious smoothie, an empty plastic tumbler, and a bag from Party City.

"Good morning," said Allegra cheerfully, hoping it was still daylight.

Violet returned her enthusiastic greeting. "Good morning— well, afternoon. It's almost one o'clock." She placed the blender and cup on the dining room table next to Allegra's book. "What are you reading?"

"*Lord of the Rings.*"

"Funny, I've never read the book or seen the movies."

"I bet you would like this. You know, given your knowledge of fables and stuff?"

"You mean fairy tales. Fables are different."

"How so?"

"Fables are straightforward stories meant to teach children moral lessons. There are no hidden messages. A fairy tale, however, conjures a world of magic, highlighting stories of good versus evil, and allows the reader to ultimately decide if a moral lesson exists or not."

Allegra was captivated by Violet's answer. "Did you, like, study that in college or something?"

Violet nodded her head. "Yes, I majored in English Literature after dance. I was studying to be a professional ballet dancer at Julliard before I was accidentally dropped on stage and broke my ankle." She looked down at her right shoe.

Allegra took note.

"It was serious enough to end my career at your age. But that's all in the past now."

Allegra smiled warmly. She sipped her obnoxious smoothie, determined to win the gold medal in Olympic mind-fucking. "Thank you. This is delicious. Please keep them coming."

Violet looked Allegra over, noticing she had gained weight—at least ten pounds, maybe more—over the past two weeks. "Good. I'm glad you like them." She lifted her finger in the air, thrilled to know her plan of making Allegra fat was working. "I almost forgot. I bought you these." She reached into the Party City bag and pulled out three packages of synthetic, colored wigs. One was hot pink, the other was electric green, and the third, shocking blue. All three had the same picture on the front of the package and were the exact same style: chin-length bob cuts with bangs, most commonly seen at university Halloween or bachelorette parties.

Allegra grabbed the hot pink wig, bewildered by its purpose.

"I thought you might want something to cover your head now that it's scabbing. It's just a little . . ." Violet touched her chest, repulsed. "A little hard to look at."

Allegra swallowed the insult with an iron stomach. "Oh, okay, sure. I'll wear them."

Violet was gracious. "Good." She motioned to go back up the stairs as Allegra tore open the pink wig package.

"Don't you want to hear the rest of the story anymore?"

Violet stopped. "Which story?"

"The love story of Ram and Allegra."

Violet smiled victoriously. "No, I think I've heard enough for now."

"Are you sure? I mean, I haven't told you anything yet about the way we fucked every Tuesday and Thursday night while you were out doing yoga. . . or how we ran into your friends *all the time*, let's see, I met Gretel at The Carlyle . . . your personal trainer, Anna, at Serafina . . . and your pals, Lisa and Jack, at Le Cirque . . . or how Ram allowed me to pick out a necklace at Cartier for my birthday . . . or about the night he made love to me in your funky tree bed." She puckered her lips. "Nope. I don't think we've covered *any* of that."

"What did you just say?" Violet was incensed.

Allegra sipped her smoothie like a juvenile delinquent who just tricked her teacher into getting fired. "I'm not sure how much more information you're, like, looking for? I'll tell you the whole story. Or part of the story. Whatever you want to hear."

Violet turned around and pulled a seat out from the dining room table. "Go ahead, then. Tell me."

"There's so much. I mean, like, where do you want me to start?"

Violet gnawed her lip. "How long were you two together?"

Allegra looked up at the florescent lights as she thought out loud on purpose. "Let's see, Ram and I met on Black Friday last year, then we officially started dating December 11, we got engaged August 9—which is, ironically, the day before you and I met—and since we technically haven't broken up, I would guesstimate we've been together about eight months or so."

Violet angered. "You can't get engaged to a man who's married."

"Well, you know what I mean. He asked me to marry him over the phone from China, so it counts for something in my book."

Violet was pissed. "Since you're so freely sharing information today, tell me how you and Ram were able to meet up so many times behind my back."

Allegra thought for a moment, looking for a good place to pick up the story. "Yeah. I can explain that. It was easy."

TWENTY-SEVEN

THE CHILLY December wind made Allegra dance from side to side in front of her apartment on Second Avenue. She anxiously waited for Ram's limo to arrive, checking her QVC *Today's Special* watch multiple times as six o'clock drew closer.

She wore a vintage patchwork rabbit fur coat once owned by her hippie grandmother, tight jeans, and black pirate boots. Her waist-length, cinnamon-red hair was as gorgeous as ever with the cold, dry air nurturing her waves like the New Mexico heat never could. She was fully made up and accessorized to the extreme, with a cross-body purse and an overnight bag, excited to spend her first sleepover with Ram, and ecstatic to not be single during the holidays.

It was the day before Christmas Eve, and Allegra could not wait to visit the famous Fifth Avenue holiday store displays and the gargantuan Christmas tree at Rockefeller Center. Despite the threat of terrorism plaguing major cities around the globe, the spirit of Manhattan was cheerful and optimistic, best personified by the theme of happy families celebrating life in the mind-blowing windows of Macy's,

Barney's, Bloomingdales, Nordstrom, Neiman Marcus, and the almighty mother ship of Upper East Side fashionistas, Bergdorf Goodman.

At this point, Ram and Allegra had only been seeing each other for two weeks, having consummated their relationship during Ram's lunch hour at the Pierre Hotel the day after he admitted his love for her. Due to his busy schedule, they were only able to meet three other times in various hotels for sex, each quickie lasting no more than an hour. Until now, Allegra was content with this arrangement, but she was utterly giddy at the prospect of spending an entire night with her newfound love.

Earlier in the day, Ram mustered the courage to lie to Violet, pretending he needed to fly to Washington, DC, to put out a business-related fire the next morning. Ram was finally over his initial bout of extreme paranoia, having just acquired a *domestic girlfriend,* as he called it, preferring to keep his previous extra-marital affairs short, casual, and most importantly, overseas. Ram's confession to having cheated on Violet at least twenty times over the course of their marriage did not concern Allegra, for she valued his decision to tell the truth, feeling their inherently deceitful relationship needed to be built on a solid foundation of unconditional honesty with one another, if it were to ever succeed.

Allegra's elderly neighbor across the street waved hello as he left his building dressed as Santa Claus. She waved back as Ram's black stretch limo pulled up to the curb.

The driver exited and opened the door. "Good evening, Miss Allegra."

"Hi, Eric."

She dropped into the backseat of the black ship of greed, greeting Ram with a pale pink lipstick stain on his cheek. "Hey, you!"

The smell of new car leather filled her senses.

Ram held two dozen red and white roses in his hand. "Hello, darling. These are for you." His deep voice was as seductive as his perfectly tailored black suit.

Allegra pretended to smell the scentless roses. "Thank you. They're beautiful." She placed them in the vase nested inside the long bar lining the vehicle.

"Where to, Mr. Ramspeck?" asked the driver.

"Let's hit Rock Center first, then shopping."

"Aye, aye, Captain." The driver rolled up his privacy shield and disappeared.

"How was your day, gorgeous?"

"It was great! I got a manicure, a pedicure, and a massage." She spread out her fingers with hot pink polish on the tips. "Thank you for arranging it for me."

"You are very welcome."

Allegra leaned her shoulder on the black leather seat, facing Ram. "I'm so excited about tonight, I wasn't able to sleep a wink. Where are we staying?"

"It's a surprise, darling. You'll love it, I promise."

She licked her lips in the most appealing way. "I can't believe I'll have you until the sun comes up. What a special treat." Allegra looked into his eyes.

His expression hardened. "So, what did you tell your roommate about what you were doing tonight?"

"Oh, Chloe? I just told her I was going to be out all night and not to worry."

"Good . . . And you didn't mention me by name? Right?"

Allegra threw a sarcastic look. "No, I call you Mr. Big, just like Carrie does in *Sex and the City*. I already promised you. No one knows about us, except your driver," she said, smiling.

"Good because discretion is the key to us being together. Everything I've ever worked for could crumble in an instant if my wife ever found out about our relationship."

Wife. Allegra pouted inside. She hated that word.

Ram reached down into the side bar, where an open bottle of Dom Pérignon chilled on ice. "Let's have a little bubbly to celebrate the occasion, shall we?" He poured two glasses, handing one to Allegra.

"Cool. I've served this, like, twice in my life. Been dying to taste it."

"How about a toast?"

Allegra smiled. "Do another Scottish one. *Please*?"

Ram squinted one eye as he thought hard to remember a good Scottish toast. His Uncle Bernard—whom he spent every summer with from the ages of seven to nineteen—was famous for two things: teaching Ram how to slaughter pigs, and reciting traditional blessings that everyone else had forgotten. "Okay. I've got one." He cleared his throat.

"May those who love us, love us. And those who don't love us, may God turn their hearts. And if he doesn't turn their hearts, may he turn their ankles, so we will know them by their limping," he said in a dead-ringer Scottish accent.

Allegra paused, waiting for the punchline. "What does that mean?"

Ram chuckled. "I have no idea."

They clinked glasses, kissed, and drank.

Ram picked up a letter-sized manila envelope sitting beside him. It was about a half-inch thick, with a metal closure in the back. "This is for you."

"What is it?"

"You'll see."

Allegra placed her champagne glass down on the side bar, and opened the envelope filled with papers: a welcome letter from Ram's global trading company, a w-2 form, a direct deposit application, a confidentiality agreement, and a schedule of Violet's weekly exercise and salon appointments.

"Is this a job application?"

"No, it's a new-hire packet. Congratulations. You're my new Personal Shopper." He smiled wryly.

Allegra was confused. She read in the welcome letter that her new salary was a thousand dollars a week—twice the amount she was making in tips as a bartender. "You want me to work for you?"

Ram smiled. "No, Allegra, you won't actually be *working* for my company. It's just the best way for me to transfer funds into your account, and it explains why you have my credit card in case someone ever asks."

Allegra was lost.

"You saw what happened with President Trump's lawyer, didn't you? Can't be too careful with these things."

"What things?"

Ram tapped the envelope still in her hands. "There's more inside."

She pulled out two credit cards—a black American Express Centurion Card and a silver Platinum Visa. Both had ALLEGRA ADAMS embossed along the bottom.

"The black card has no spending limit, so be *extremely* careful with that one. But salespeople will jump through hoops when you show it. Plus, it has the best concierge service in the world and can get us tickets into any event, even if it's sold out. And, of course, you'll receive invitations to Fashion Week and a few other exclusive events."

Allegra was floored. "Wow. That's pretty cool."

She continued shuffling through the papers, stopping at the non-disclosure agreement, which she began reading. The paragraph that immediately caught her attention was:

IF THERE IS A BREACH OR THREATENED BREACH OF ANY PROVISION OF THIS BINDING AGREE-MENT, IT IS AGREED AND UNDERSTOOD THAT THE DISCLOSER SHALL HAVE ADEQUATE REMEDY

*IN MONEY OR OTHER DAMAGES FROM THE RE-
CEIVER AND ACCORDINGLY SHALL BE ENTITLED
TO INJUNCTIVE RELIEF OF NO LESS ONE MILLION
DOLLARS PER INSTANCE OR OTHER PUNITIVE
DAMAGES TO THE HIGHEST EXTENT ALLOWED
BY NEW YORK STATE LAW.*

Her eyes widened. "Does this mean you'll sue me for a million dollars if I tell my sister?"

Ram bowed his head like a puppy. "Allegra, darling, you make it sound so awful when you put it like that."

"But I'm right, aren't I?"

Ram ruffled his lips. "Darling, I have a lot to lose, okay? I'm risking everything—my inheritance, my reputation—so I can be with you. Please understand this is how it has to be, otherwise I won't be able to continue."

Allegra looked at the black AmEx card in her hand. She once saw Kim Kardashian use it on her reality show to buy a Lamborghini for Kanye West.

She instantly feared she had pissed Ram off. "I understand where you're coming from, really, I do. It's not a problem. I promise."

"Good."

"I'll sign everything when we get to the hotel tonight."

Ram drank from his glass. "That's my girl."

Allegra's guts were reeling inside. Her intuition bell was ringing louder than the screaming cabbie beside them.

She pulled out the paper listing Violet's salon appointment and exercise calendar. She couldn't believe how jam-packed it was: Manicures every Friday at ten. Facials every Monday at four. Massages every Wednesday and Saturday at two.

"And what's this schedule for?" she asked.

"Those are the *only* times you may contact me when I'm not at the office or on the road. It's vital you keep all written communication professional. No selfies, no Facebooking, no Tweeting, no Instagraming, and especially *no sexting*. I'm trusting you with my future."

Allegra looked down at the paper again. She clicked her tongue. "Holy shit. Your wife works out from seven to ten every Tuesday and Thursday night? That's, like, three hours straight. What about dinner?"

"I think there's a half-hour break in between classes for a juice bar visit, but yes, that's dinner for Violet. It's mostly social time with her girlfriends."

"Wow. That's pretty dedicated."

He curled up by Allegra as an Uber driver honked loudly at their limo for cutting him off. "So on Tuesday and Thursday nights, if I happen to be in town, we'll get a room. I'll make a standing reservation at The Mark Hotel, since they know how to keep their mouths shut."

Allegra was uncomfortable with the idea.

"Please adjust your work schedule accordingly."

Allegra's romantic feelings were escaping her body. "I take it you want me to quit the bar too?"

"Heavens, no. I think it's a perfect cover, otherwise people will start questioning who's paying your rent. It's even better if you work exclusively weekends and holidays. This way you'll be free for me during the week, and it'll keep me from worrying about what you're up to on Saturday nights."

Suddenly, the business end of being a mistress didn't sound so fun.

"Wait. I'll be alone *every* Saturday night?"

"Darling, you realize we won't be able to spend weekends together, don't you? Christmas, New Year's, Valentine's— you'll have to ride out most holidays on your own. I'll need to be home. That's how it works."

Allegra conjured a plastic smile. "No, I understand. I get it."

"However, I can tell you that if everything works out between us—and I honestly think it will—I'll go ahead and buy a large studio apartment where we can meet up anytime. You can live there as long as you like."

"For how much a month?"

Ram laughed. "It would be rent-free, darling. You're so silly sometimes."

Allegra welcomed the possibility of having her own place *rent-free*. Chloe's shopping addiction and banned food list was driving her crazy. "Actually? That would be awesome."

"They're a few buildings going up on Third Avenue. I'll take a look at the floor plans and get you something with a balcony. Are you afraid of heights?"

Allegra's eyes lit up. "No."

"Good. I'll get you a high floor with a great view. It probably won't be ready for a year or two, but new is always better."

Allegra was stoked. A brand-new studio apartment in a high-rise building with a doorman, pool, and workout room was all she ever dreamed about the second she arrived in New York. "That. Sounds. *Amazing*. I love the idea, babe!" She kissed him on the lips. "Thank you."

"Good. I could tell you were a smart woman." He kissed her back, sticking his tongue in her overly receptive mouth.

She pulled away abruptly. "Wait. Aren't there laws against sleeping with the boss? Can't I get in trouble for this?"

Ram laughed. "First of all, *you* wouldn't get into trouble, *I* would. Secondly, my company is privately held. I own one hundred percent of the stock, so I pretty much get to do whatever I want, as long as it's legal. And thirdly, it would only be illegal to sleep with the boss if you filed a sexual harassment complaint, which you probably wouldn't do since your real job was to be my girlfriend in the first place." He laughed again. "You're a riot, darling."

"Oh, right on." She gave a quarter-smile. Her eyes glanced away, focusing instead on the city buildings flashing outside as they approached Fifth Avenue.

Out of nowhere, Allegra's enthusiasm faded.

Ram noticed. "What's the matter, love?"

"It's nothing, really."

"Come on. What happened to our *unconditional honesty* policy?"

Allegra stared vacantly out the window. "Well, it's just that, I don't know, something doesn't feel right."

"What part doesn't feel right?"

"You know, this whole thing feels, like, so *businessy*. I mean, it's not romantic."

Ram was annoyed. He took the envelope back from Allegra's lap. "A million other girls would give their left pinky finger for a Black Card with their name on it. We can always return to the way it was, Allegra. I have no problem, whatsoever."

She quickly realized her mistake. "No, I'm excited about all of this, babe. Really, I am. It's just that . . ."

"What is it? I can tell you're disappointed about something?"

"No, it's just that I've never done anything like this before. It's all very new."

Ram refilled Allegra's glass with more champagne. "Honestly, if you don't like the idea, I can scratch the whole thing. But I won't be able to help you with the rent or give you money . . ."

Allegra looked closely at the label of Dom Pérignon as he poured. She realized her whining was about to jeopardize her one and only chance at hitting the lottery. "No, it's fine, babe. I swear it. I was just a little confused by all the paperwork." She took a large, classless gulp and continued pleading her case. "Seriously, Ram. I didn't expect anything from you. Not money, or credit cards, or fancy gifts, and definitely *not* an apartment." She held his hand. "Honestly, this is all blowing me away. Thank you." She kissed him on the cheek. "I am truly grateful."

Ram was pleased to see she had finally come to her senses. "You have no idea what you're getting yourself into, do you, darling?"

Allegra bit her nail. "I don't even know a side chick, let alone how to be one."

Ram leaned in to kiss her. "And that's exactly *why* I picked you."

———

The limo drove down the magnificent lighted holiday route of Fifth Avenue. Store displays with dancing Santas, elves, snow queens, ice princesses, and reindeer were abundant.

The world's most expensive fashion, furs, and jewelry flooded Allegra's senses as the stores flashed by her in the window. She even caught sight of her dream store, Tiffany & Company, which dwarfed in comparison to the colossal, glittering snake wrapped around the Bvlgari building nearby.

The limo turned right and arrived at Rockefeller Center on West 50th Street. Gold and silver flags led the way for mobs of tourists who filled the plaza, mostly around the iconic ice rink overseen by a golden Prometheus, and the multicolored, hundred-foot Norway spruce, which was the second tallest it had been since the tradition started in 1933.

"Wow. This is insane!" said Allegra as she stepped out of the limo. "Come on, let's get closer!"

Ram gave the driver instructions before exiting. "Just look at that tree. Absolutely beautiful."

Allegra turned around. "Are you sure we won't run into anyone you know?"

Ram was calm. "My circles completely avoid tourist traps during the holidays."

"So where do you want to go?"

Ram pointed at the packed ice skating rink.

Allegra twirled her hair. "You remember I was born and bred in the desert. Right?"

Ram laughed. "You've never been ice skating before?"

Allegra shook her head *no* like a five-year old child.

"Trust me, you're going to love it."

———

Ram and Allegra laughed, non-stop, for eighty-two torturous minutes as he mostly skated backwards while holding on to Allegra's forearms.

They talked and giggled about common first-date topics: favorite foods, favorite movies, and their favorite childhood Christmas memories, proving Ram and Allegra were as different as two people could possibly be.

Ram shared his funny story of growing up a lonely, only child and begging his parents for a pet for Christmas at the age of six. When he woke up that cold Christmas morning, he ran down the stairs to the largest of twelve trees in the townhome, seeing the usual mountains of presents, and his favorite animal of all time: a live, baby koala bear shivering in a silver cage.

It was love at first sight.

Ram named his koala bear "Skipper," after the television show *Gilligan's Island*, and quickly made it his best friend. But after loving and hugging it for a total of five days, he begged the butler to anonymously call animal rescue after it had bitten everyone in the house—including him—at least twice.

Allegra returned with the heart-breaking story of her mother taking a third job as a waitress at Denny's in order to afford Gameboys for her three children, the Christmas before Allegra turned eight. Her mother was already working two jobs—one as a cashier at Wal-Mart and the other as a cashier at Shell Gas Station—both part-time gigs, since full-time work was impossible to find for a high-school drop-out who left school to give birth to her second child.

This memory was particularly joyful for Allegra. It was the last Christmas her mother was beautiful and sober, for the following spring she met the man on the graveyard shift who would expose her to methamphetamines to stay awake, and heroin to fall asleep—the two substances that would ultimately end her life.

"See, you're getting the hang of it," said Ram, almost crying tears of laughter from watching Allegra's goofy, exaggerated fear of the ice.

"Don't worry, babe. Paybacks are a bitch," she replied, moments before falling flat on her ass and dragging Ram, cackling, down to the ice with her.

Afterward, they returned to the limo, still amused and feeling the warm holiday spirit from the growing crowds behind them.

"Where to next?" asked the driver.

Ram looked at his gold and diamond presidential Rolex. "Our first stop is Tom Ford on Madison and Seventieth, and then we'll hit Christian Louboutin between Seventy-Fifth and Seventy-Sixth." He popped open a new bottle of Dom Pérignon chilling on ice. "Time for new suits, new dresses, and new *heels*." He rubbed his hand along Allegra's cheap, synthetic leather boots as he kissed her passionately.

Allegra was bursting under her skin. *This is fucking awesome.*

The drive up Madison Avenue was equally, if not more, beautiful than their drive down Fifth Avenue. Allegra opened the window to feel the cold, fresh air on her face as they swooshed by the holiday displays of Hermes, Longchamp, Chanel, Alexander McQueen, Givenchy, Kate Spade, Tory Burch, and Prada, finally stopping in front of Tom Ford New York.

Ram held Allegra's hand as she exited the limo. "Have you been here before?"

"No."

"You'll love it. He's the sexiest designer in the world."

As they entered the ultra-modern boutique, a six-foot black woman with an exotic accent greeted them at the door. "Mr. Ramspeck, always on time."

"Imanka." He kissed her on both cheeks. "How are you, darling?"

"I'm fabulous. And who's this pretty lady?"

Allegra beamed like a groupie, holding on to Ram's sleeve.

"This is Allegra, my new assistant."

Imanka was animated. "Like Allegra Versace? Very pretty name. And gorgeous hair." She extended her hand. "Enchanté. I'm Imanka. And before you ask, I'm from the beautiful city of Abidjan, Ivory Coast, in West Africa."

Allegra smiled. *She must have mind-reading powers.*

The store was empty except for a well-dressed Asian woman at the cash register. It was obvious Ram had arranged a personal shopping appointment.

He straightened his red tie as he looked at Imanka. "Can you put together a nice package for her? I need five outfits suitable for dinner and cocktail parties."

"And for your handsome self?"

"Show me what's new this season."

"Wonderful." A young, sharp-dressed Latino man suddenly appeared by Imanka's side. "Raphael will be at your service." She then took Allegra by the hand, whisking her away to the back of the store.

Allegra looked back over her shoulder, confused.

Ram just smiled and waved.

Allegra stripped down to her black bra and panties, waiting anxiously in the softly lit dressing room by herself.

Imanka returned with an armful of dresses. "You like green, yes?"

Allegra nodded. "It's my favorite color."

"Good, because green, purple, and black look ravishing with your hair." She held up a tiny, emerald, one-shoulder cocktail dress. "I hope this fits. The biggest size we carry in the store is size eight."

Eight? That's your biggest?

"Oh, that should work, " said Allegra nervously.

Imanka looked her body up and down. "You would be a four if it weren't for those curves. Very hard to find off-the-rack designer clothes for an hour-glass figure, but I'm sure we can squeeze you into something."

Allegra suddenly realized why Violet worked out so much.

Imanka placed the green dress over Allegra's head, tugging it down past her D cup breasts, barely zipping up the back, given her full backside.

"So how long have you been dating Ram?"

Allegra was taken off guard. "Sorry?"

"I can always tell when a *special friend* comes in." She said the words in slow motion. "You're not his assistant, are you?"

Allegra immediately remembered the confidentiality agreement. "Uh, no—I mean, yes. *Yes*, I'm his personal shopper. Or assistant."

Imanka was not fooled. "I understand your situation very well," she whispered into her ear. "I too have been a special friend, but with a very famous man." She turned Allegra toward the mirror. "Which is why I'm forty-three, never married, and have no children."

Allegra had no idea how to respond. Instead, she reacted to the image in the full-length mirror. The one-shoulder, body hugging, short green dress made her waist look five inches smaller. Her body looked *amazing*.

"No wonder he's crazy about you," said Imanka, sincerely.

"Thank you."

Imanka bent over, whispering into Allegra's ear. "Just don't ever let the clock run out."

Allegra smiled nervously, looking at the dangling white price tag underneath her armpit as a diversion. The dress cost $2,900.

Imanka returned to her animated self. "This one's definitely a yes. I have five more for you to try. Let's keep going."

Ram and Allegra stood at the front counter while Imanka placed their purchases into black TOM FORD garment bags. "And that should be everything, Mr. Ramspeck. Today's total will be $33,241.09."

Allegra silently gasped.

Raphael held up a large black and gold handbag with the letters TF on the front. "This just came in. It's sold out in Europe, and we only have three left."

Allegra was in love.

Ram noticed. "I'll take two."

"Same style?" asked Raphael.

"Yes. Just give me the other one in a bright color."

Raphael pulled the second bag in scarlet red.

Allegra was flabbergasted. "I think the black one's enough," she said politely. "I wear the same purse all the time."

Ram shot her a look.

Allegra's heart sank to the floor. She realized the second bag was for Violet.

Imanka recalculated the total. "That'll be $41,229.73"

Allegra suddenly remembered her grandmother telling the story of how she bought her two-story home in 1968 for $41,000. Now she was watching a man purchase clothing for the same amount.

Ram looked at Allegra. "Well?"

Allegra was confused.

"Aren't you going to pay?" he joked.

"Oh, yeah, sure." Allegra pulled out the black credit card from her beat-up purse and handed it to Imanka.

Imanka looked at her with condolence while running the card. "Please sign here, Miss Adams." She handed her a leather portfolio with a pen and receipt inside.

Allegra felt like a celebrity being asked for an autograph. "Thank you."

Imanka and Raphael grabbed the heavy garment bags and went out the front door as Ram and Allegra followed.

The driver opened the limo door, helping Imanka and Raphael place the purchases inside.

"That's everything. Good luck with your new wardrobe," said Imanka to Ram.

He kissed her on both cheeks. "Have a lovely Christmas, darling."

Imanka smiled. "You too, handsome. I look forward to seeing you—and your stunning *assistant*—again very soon."

The limo continued five blocks north on Madison Avenue, stopping in front of Christian Louboutin. Glittering red, gold, and silver shoes sparkled in the flawless store window.

Allegra's jaw dropped to the floor. She didn't recognize the name, but she definitely recognized the shoe. *Oh, my God. It's the red-bottomed heels everyone wears on Real Housewives.*

Ram checked his iPhone since he placed it on silent while ice-skating. He became visibly annoyed. There were four missed calls. Three of them were from Violet.

"You go inside and ask for a new pair of boots and at least three pairs of heels. Make sure one of them is black," he said with authority.

"Aren't you coming in?"

"No, I have to make a few calls for work."

"Okay."

Allegra exited the limo and stepped inside the busy store, all by herself, intimidated by the skeletal customers prancing around in five-inch stilettos. The shocking red carpet, the same signature color as the bottom of Louboutin's shoes, practically blinded her.

She looked at the women in the store. *I'll never be able to walk in those things,* she thought to herself.

"May I help you?" said a well-dressed man with platinum hair and dark roots.

"Yes, I'm looking for a new pair of boots and some heels."

His eyes scanned her cheap watch, Target purse, and flat feet. "Anything in particular?" His undertone was ruder than his actions.

"I need at least one pair of heels in black."

He gestured at the white wall of sexy shoes sitting in cubbyholes. "Have a look, and let me know if you see anything you like," he said abruptly before walking away.

Allegra felt inadequate. Unwanted. Unwelcome.

She walked over to the shoe display and grabbed a pair of sky-high black leather platform pumps. She then flipped over the red sole and saw the price: $875.

She tried to get the attention of the flippant salesman, who was busy chatting with the security guard about his lame stepmother and how he dreaded hosting her and her two ugly daughters for the holidays. "Excuse me?" she said several times before getting up from the bench and approaching him. "I'd like to try these on. Size nine."

The salesman shot her a look. "I'll see what I can find." He finished his story to the security guard, slowly breaking away.

Allegra reacted. She pulled out the Black Card from her beat-up purse. "You take American Express, right?"

The salesman's eyes did a double take. He straightened his shoulders. "Of course, we do. We love our American Express customers." He gently took the shoe from her hand. "The *Bianca* is an excellent choice—it's our most popular style. What size do you wear again?"

Allegra felt slightly more powerful. "Nine."

"And you want it in black?"

"Yes. Bring me every color you've got," she said, now in control. "I also want to see the sparkling red shoes from the window."

"Absolutely."

"Oh, and bring me the hottest boots you make as well."

"Sure, right away." He extended his hand. "I'm Jonathan, by the way. You are?"

And just like that, every single bit of doubt magically left Allegra's body.

Thirty minutes later, Allegra returned to the limo with three full shopping bags in hand.

"How did you do?" asked Ram.

"Oh my God, I bought a great pair of boots and, like, five pairs of heels—I hope you don't mind—but I totally know you're going to love what I picked! I don't think I can walk in them yet, but I'll definitely practice. I promise."

Ram chuckled. "Oh, darling, those shoes aren't for walking." He kissed her on the lips. "They're for *strutting* that sweet ass of yours."

He grabbed her hips. "Don't ever lose that ass, or your beautiful tits." He kissed her breast. "Promise me you'll never go on a diet."

Allegra laughed. "Good, because I'm *starving*."

The limo continued eleven blocks north, stopping at the corner of Madison Avenue and East 77th Street, directly in front of the Mark Hotel.

"Are we eating or are we staying here?" asked Allegra.

Ram relished hiding his surprise. "Both."

"But don't your friends eat here all the time?"

"We're not going *inside* the restaurant."

Allegra was slightly disappointed. She enjoyed her one and only time at the Mark Bar so much, she was dying to try the adjoining Jean-Georges restaurant. "I get it. We're getting room service so we don't run into anyone you know."

Ram swung his head side to side. "Something like that," he said, smiling.

A bellhop brought a pushcart to the car and opened the door. He held Allegra's hand as she exited onto the curb. After Ram stepped out, the bellhop loaded the shopping bags onto the pushcart and disappeared.

Ram and Allegra walked across The Mark Hotel's signature black-and-white striped lobby floor, over to the front desk to check in.

A gay man with skin tanner than whole wheat toast cheerfully greeted them. "Welcome to The Mark Hotel. My name is Bradley. Are you checking in?"

"Yes," replied Ram.

"Is this your first time staying with us?"

"No, sir. It is not."

"Excellent. We're glad to have you back, Mister . . . ?

"Ramspeck."

"Wonderful, Mr. Ramspeck." He clicked his jaw out several times while clacking away at the keyboard. "Ahhh. Here you are." He looked at Allegra and smiled as he picked up the phone. "Hello, Niles. Mr. Ramspeck has arrived." He turned back to Ram. "What time would you like dinner to be served?"

"As soon as possible, please."

"Wonderful." The clerk picked up the phone again. "Yes, this is Bradley from the front desk. Our penthouse guest has arrived and would like dinner as soon as possible."

Allegra's eyes widened as she turned toward Ram.

"I told you I had something special planned," he whispered. Allegra was bowled over. "Thank you so much."

"*Balthazar Ramspeck the third!*" yelled a man who stood ten feet away. He was in his early sixties, wearing light blue sunglasses and a scarf around his neck.

"Vittorio?"

"Ciao, vecchio amico! I thought that was you."

Ram embraced the man, patting him hard between the shoulder blades. "I thought you moved back to Milan?"

"I did. I came back to spend the holiday with my daughter," he said with an over-dramatic Italian accent. "We have dinner reservations at nine o'clock. You should join us."

Allegra was petrified. All she could think about was that damn confidentiality agreement.

Vittorio hawked her down. "And this beautiful thing? Who is she?"

Ram and Allegra answered at the same time: "This is my personal shopper, Allegra." "I'm his assistant, Allegra."

"Which one is it? Assistant or shopper?" Vittorio laughed. "Never mind, I ask too many questions." He grabbed a piece of Allegra's long, red hair. "Such a beauty." He turned to Ram. "You should get her on the"—he pressed his nostril as he snorted—"diet. It does wonders for the baby fat."

Allegra was taken aback. *Did he just say I'm fat?*

Ram laughed and slapped Vittorio's shoulder. "You've spent way too much time with supermodels." Ram pulled him closer. "Allegra, this is Vittorio Marconi. He's a legendary photographer in the fashion business."

"Two hundred eighty-nine magazine covers and counting," he said proudly.

Allegra barely smiled.

"No, honestly, it takes the baby fat right off. Coke diet, not the other way around," he laughed.

Allegra was not impressed. "Oh, that's nice."

A white-haired butler arrived, gently interrupting the conversation. "Excuse me, Mr. and Mrs. Ramspeck. Pleasure to meet you," he said in a pitch-perfect British accent.

Vittorio raised his brows. "Mr. and Mrs.?" He shrugged his shoulders. "Well, not my business. I need to be going anyway."

He gave Ram a hug as the butler patiently waited. "Boun Natale. Send my love to Violet." He turned to Allegra. "Ciao, Bella."

Ram waved goodbye without a care in the world as Vittorio disappeared into the adjacent Mark Bar.

Allegra was concerned.

"Don't worry. He's the biggest player on the planet," said Ram.

"I don't like him. He's rude."

"What, Vittorio? He's a sweetheart."

Allegra shot him a look. "Really?"

The butler waited for her to finish speaking. "Are we ready to view your suite, Mr. Ramspeck? Mrs. Ramspeck?"

Ram and Allegra nodded their heads.

"Very well. Please, follow me."

———

The butler rode with Ram and Allegra in the elevator. "Have you been to The Mark Hotel before, madam?"

"Yes, I've been to the bar, but I've never stayed here."

"Well, your husband has treated you to a very special gift this evening."

Allegra was giddy. She especially enjoyed how the butler kept referring to Ram as her *husband*. "Cool. I'm super excited!"

Ram smiled.

The butler continued his speech. "Our grand penthouse opened only five months ago. It is the largest and most expensive hotel suite in the world. Twelve thousand square feet of pure, indomitable luxury."

Allegra turned to Ram, stupefied.

Ram was excited. "I've been dying to stay in this suite, darling. Now I have a good reason." He kissed her on the forehead.

The elevator doors opened.

The butler continued talking as they strolled down the hall. "The penthouse occupies the top two floors of the building, which was originally constructed in the art deco style of architecture in 1927. The suite features five custom bedrooms, six full bathrooms, four fireplaces, two powder rooms, two wet bars, a library lounge, a chef-worthy full-size kitchen with appliances by Gaggenau and Miele, and a living room with a twenty-six-foot ceiling that can be converted into a grand ballroom."

Allegra was floored. "*A ballroom?*"

"See, darling? I told you I picked a special place."

The butler stopped in front of the entrance. "Every piece of furniture has been hand selected by the legendary designer Jacques Grange." He opened the black double doors. "You are the thirty-eighth and thirty-ninth guests in the world to stay in this room."

Allegra's green eyes popped out of their sockets. "Wow!"

The foyer was as large and bright as a hotel lobby, with a dark wood floor and a black iron staircase to the right.

Allegra was amazed. She had never stayed in anything larger than a standard Comfort Inn hotel room before. The idea of staying in the world's most expensive suite was hard to process. "I'm, I'm speechless."

Ram appreciated her reaction.

The butler led them around the rest of the cavernous residence decorated in chic colors of cream and beige. When they arrived in the kitchen, a professional chef waved hello as he cooked, while two female servers dressed the twenty-four-person dining room table with white linens and silver nearby.

Hundreds of red and white roses occupied the center of the table.

"This is all for me?" she asked, feeling like Belle from *Beauty and the Beast*.

"Yes, darling." Ram kissed her on the lips. "Merry Christmas. May all of your dreams from this point forward come true."

Allegra beamed back. "As long as I have you, Mister Ramspeck, *they will.*"

The butler continued his tour, walking Ram and Allegra into the bright, white living room featuring a baby grand piano and soaring ceilings. "Those doors lead to the two-thousand-five-hundred-square-foot terrace, which overlooks the Metropolitan Museum of Art and Central Park. We typically serve dinner outside, but we thought it was too cold this evening."

Allegra grabbed Ram's hand and squeezed it tightly. "No problem."

The butler wrapped up his tour. "Your bags will arrive shortly after I leave, and you will find the master suite just ahead on the right. If you prefer another color scheme for the bed linens or need them changed for any reason, please ring me by phone. I'll be staying down the hall and will be up all evening, completely at your disposal."

Ram was impressed. "Thank you, Niles." He pulled out his wallet and gave the butler five one hundred-dollar bills.

"Thank you, sir. Very kind of you."

The butler made his way to the front door.

Allegra turned to Ram in complete awe, with tears welling in her eyes. "No one in my entire life has ever treated me like this. You are my guardian—"

Ram put his finger on her lips. "Shhhhhh. I love you, Allegra. You don't have to thank me every two minutes." He kissed her softly, holding her chin. "It makes you sound unworthy."

The dark-haired server interrupted their moment of romance. "Excuse me, Mr. and Mrs. Ramspeck. Dinner is served."

———

Allegra sat at the north end of the elegant, twenty-four-person table fit for the Windsor family. She finished her last bite of cake, the perfect ending to the most fabulous six-course, mini-dish dinner she had ever consumed: lobster bisque soup, Caesar salad, prosciutto-stuffed chicken with fennel-crusted potatoes, spicy lobster pasta with grilled chimichurri halibut, pan-seared rib-eye steak with ricotta gnocchi, sautéed spinach, fresh-baked bread, and a miniature chocolate lava cake for dessert.

Ram threw his napkin on the table in defeat. "I give up. I'm done."

Allegra rubbed her belly. "I can't possibly eat another bite."

Ram lifted himself from the table, walked down the long line of chairs, then bent down and kissed her. "Now, since I won't see you again until January eighth, this is our Christmas and New Year's Eve combined. But sadly, I only have three more presents left to give you."

Allegra was embarrassed. All she had for Ram's Christmas gift was a Brooks Brothers gift certificate in her purse.

"Three more presents? I think you've done enough, babe."

Ram led Allegra by the hand into the master suite at the end of the hall. As she walked into the simple, tasteful room with a king-size bed and a floating gas fireplace, she saw a large cream-colored box with a red bow on top of the comforter.

"Another gift?" asked Allegra, feeling overwhelmed.

As she unraveled the bow, she saw the words LA PERLA printed on top. She opened it to reveal a sexy black lace bustier and a garter belt with black stockings.

"That's why I wanted the black heels," he said slyly, groping her from behind.

Allegra held up the bustier. "I hope I can fit into this after that meal."

Ram jokingly put his finger in his mouth and gagged. "There's always the option."

"You're crazy," she said, ignoring his suggestion.

She grabbed his hand and placed it between her jeans. "You feel that?"

"What?"

"That little button that's dying for you to play with it?"

Ram was getting hot. "What about it?"

"That's 'the little man in the boat.' The one I named my cocktail after."

Ram smiled. "I'm going to need one while you get changed." He kissed her wet lips. "You put that on while I pour the drinks, and get the music started."

———

Familiar Christmas tunes played softly in the living room. The unmistakable holiday smells of pinecones, cookies, and fireplace permeated the air.

Ram was crouched down behind the bar, having just placed something underneath the sink, when Allegra reappeared in her La Perla lingerie gift set. Her big boobs, small waist, and shapely hips made her look like Jessica Rabbit on the cover of *Hustler Magazine*.

"Wowzie," said Ram as he rose to his feet.

She twirled around. "You like it?"

Ram walked over to Allegra as she threw her arms around his neck. "You bet I do."

He wrapped his large hands around her tight waist, holding on to the small of her back as she pressed her ample breasts into his strong chest.

"I love you," she said before launching her mouth onto his. "This is the most romantic night of my life. I can't believe you've done this all for *me*."

Ram kissed her back strongly, as she let her torso go limp, surrendering to the alpha male who was holding her floating body mid-air.

"I'm glad you like it, darling. Merry Christmas."

The doorbell rang. It was so loud, it echoed through the entire suite.

Ram broke away from the kiss. "They're early."

Allegra's arms fell to her side. "More butlers?"

"No, darling. It's your last two presents," he said eagerly as he left the room and headed to the front door, at the opposite end of the floor.

Allegra waited for him to leave. She then hurried over to the bar, stumbling twice in her four-inch heels before pouring herself a full glass of Grand Patron Tequila. She drank nearly half the glass in one shot, shuddering as it burned down her throat. She then took mini-gulps of the remaining tequila, drinking it as fast as she could while Ram was away, determined to get mildly drunk before making love, since the large dinner had washed her champagne buzz away.

Allegra heard female voices chatting and laughing with Ram in the hallway as they approached the living room area. She quickly downed the final shot.

Ram returned, standing in between two tall, gorgeous women in Burberry trench coats. They looked like Victoria's Secret supermodels dressed like spies. The one to Ram's left was Scandinavian with long, straight blonde hair, and the one to his right was Latina with dark brown beachy waves. "Allegra, I'd like you to meet Sapphire and Alexis."

The girls waved. "Hello." "Hi."

Allegra was instantly embarrassed about her revealing outfit, placing her hands over the see-through lace covering her nipples. "I'm sorry, I wasn't expecting company."

Sapphire, the blonde super spy, untied her trench coat. "Don't be shy, sweetie. That's why we're here."

Allegra was baffled. *What?*

"She's much prettier than you described on the phone," said Alexis to Ram, while removing her coat and handing it to him.

Both ladies were wearing ultra-sexy lingerie and high heels, just like Allegra.

"Merry Christmas, darling!" said Ram enthusiastically.

Allegra faked a smile. "Can I talk to you for a moment, *alone?*"

"Of course, darling. Come with me." Sapphire handed her coat and purse to Ram. "Ladies, please help yourselves to a drink."

"Take your time."

"We're here all night."

The supermodels strutted their mesmerizing bodies to the bar. Side by side, they looked like six-foot extraterrestrials from another dimension—too gorgeous to be human.

Ram and Allegra walked down the hallway.

Allegra whispered through her teeth. "Holy shit, what is this?"

"It's your last two presents, like I promised."

"You're fucking kidding, right?"

"Why? What's the matter?"

She walked faster, pulling him inside the closest guest bedroom. "I thought tonight was going to be special—it's our first time waking up in the same bed!" She stomped her foot. "*Who are these people?*"

"Darling, there's five goddamn bedrooms in this suite. They won't be sleeping with us when we're done."

Reality hit Allegra like a bullet. *These women are hookers.*

He caressed her hair. "Is this because you're a little scared? You've never been with another woman, have you?"

Allegra once kissed her brother's girlfriend in high school and hated it. "No, it's not that, it's just, this whole evening was *so romantic*, it was like a dream come true, and I thought it would be about you and me for the entire night."

Ram threw the trench coats on the bed. "Beautiful bodies pleasuring one another *is* romantic."

"No, it's not."

Ram was pissed. "You want me to ask them to leave? After I've blown a hundred grand on you today?" His tall, daunting nature was intimidating. "I just handed the girls five thousand dollars each to give you the night of your life. And now you want them *to leave?*"

Allegra feared his anger. "No, I don't."

"Are you sure? If not, tell me now because I don't want you stopping everything in the middle of our party and embarrassing me."

Allegra was hurt by his words. But the little girl who watched her mother cry every time she traded food stamps for drugs, instantly feared losing the peace of mind Ram's money would bring. "Okay, I can do this. I won't embarrass you."

"Are you sure?"

"*Yes*, I'm positive." The tequila suddenly kicked in. "Just let me have a few drinks first."

"I've already got that covered," he said, circling the room.

"I'm sorry I even brought it up. Okay?"

Ram's tone lowered. "You know, I'm concerned you might not be able to handle a man like me, Allegra."

"No, *I can*. I can handle you, Ram. I promise."

He shook his head while looking at her sitting on the bed. "I'm not that different than any other man in my situation. Do you realize this?"

Allegra had no clue what he was talking about. "Yes, yes, I do."

Ram leaned forward. "There isn't a man on this planet with my net worth who doesn't suck every bit of pleasure out of life. Trust me. I know a lot of them."

Allegra was petrified. "Yes, I understand. I get it."

He shifted his foot. "*You* are my one and only girlfriend. But you have to realize that I have varied appetites, and I need to know right now that you will accept them without any judgment or complaint. Do you follow me?"

Allegra felt like a child being scolded. "Yes."

"Some nights it will be just us. Other nights, I will invite my friends."

Allegra prayed her reaction was not visible on her face. "Okay."

"Sometimes it'll be a woman—or two or three—and sometimes it'll be a man. To me, a beautiful ass is a beautiful ass. It all depends on my mood, and you'll just have to accept that."

Allegra's brain froze. *Did Ram just say he sleeps with men?*

He pointed in the air toward the living room. "Those women are the best in the business. They're professionals. They know what they're doing. They know you're my girlfriend and they *respect* you. They will always ask your permission first before touching me. That's how it works."

Allegra fought back tears. "Okay."

"They're not here to replace you, Allegra. They're here to *pleasure* you. What's wrong with that?"

Allegra lost her ability to think. "Nothing, when you put it like that."

Ram caught his breath. "So . . . are we good now?"

Allegra was heartbroken. Her fairy-tale romance just took a hellish turn, and she was willing to do whatever Ram wanted to get it back.

She grabbed his head and kissed him softly. "I love you unconditionally. And if this is what makes you happy, then I want to be a part of it."

Ram was relieved. "Are you sure?"

"Yes."

"No backing out mid-stream?"

"No."

"Good. That's my girl." He kissed her quickly. "Now, let's get you some party supplies. I can tell you're going to need it." He held her hand as they exited the guest bedroom, walked down the hall, and re-entered the living room.

"Is everything fine?" asked Sapphire, sipping vodka.

"Yes, we're all set now," replied Ram.

Alexis adjusted her stockings. "This music is cheery. I adore the holidays."

Ram walked over to the ladies, went under the bar sink, and pulled out a large mirror tray with a razor blade, a short straw, and two eight-balls of cocaine lined up in rows.

Ironically, Bing Crosby's "White Christmas" began playing throughout the room.

Ram placed the tray on the bar, with Sapphire and Alexis smiling on either side. "Darling, it's your party. You go first."

Allegra drew a deep breath. Until now, she had avoided hard drugs after watching her mother spiral into nothingness.

"Dar-ling?" he repeated in a singsong voice.

Allegra exhaled silently. She walked over, took the straw, and snorted the shortest line. She immediately threw her head back, sensing the soft, powdered chemical taste filling her nasal cavity. Happiness entered her head, falling farther down the back of her nose, into her throat, down to her core.

Within seconds she felt good. She felt confident. She felt sexy.

Instant self-esteem.

She walked over to Sapphire, wiping away a blonde tendril of hair before kissing her on the mouth—orally transferring remnants of powdered courage from one tongue to the other, before placing the straw in Sapphire's hand.

Ram was delighted. "That's my girl," he said as he rubbed the back of Alexis's thigh.

"Let the sleigh rides begin."

TWENTY-EIGHT

"YOU SHOULD be a novelist. Your ability to make up shit is amazing."

Violet sat back in the dining room chair, rubbing the top of her watermelon pink dress under the table. "You honestly think I believe you? That Ram's secretly gay and hosts expensive orgies with hookers and cocaine?"

"He's bisexual, not gay." Allegra's silly pink wig made her look fifteen years old.

"That's where you screwed up, little girl. Ram can't stand homosexual men—plus, he's a total cheapskate. He would never spring for prostitutes or an expensive hotel suite."

Allegra shrugged her shoulders. "Believe what you want."

Violet sneered. "Plus, I doubt he's ever touched a drug in his life. I begged him to try a marijuana cigarette with me once in college, and he refused."

Allegra tried not to laugh. *What a dork.*

"My husband may have bought you dresses and shoes. Yes, *that* part I believe. But the rest of it? One hundred percent bullshit. You are the biggest liar I have ever met."

Allegra lifted her bandaged hands in the air. "Go ahead. Think what you want." She flipped the pink bangs out of her baby-doll eyes. "I appreciate your belief in my ability to create, like, a crazy story off the cuff, but I don't have a creative bone in my body. The reason it sounds like I'm lying is because everything I told you has been happening behind your back for years, and your mind literally can't"—she did an impression from *A Few Good Men*—"you can't handle the truth!"

Violet lifted herself up from the table, annoyed.

"The saddest part is that you don't even *know* your husband. Not as well as I do."

Violet turned her back.

Allegra ignored her cold stance, pouring the final serving of obnoxious smoothie from the blender container instead. "Would you like some?"

Violet shook her head *no*.

"That's right, you don't eat. Totally forgot."

Violet turned around. Her face remained stoic. "I can't imagine Ram springing for a big night every time you two had sex."

Allegra nodded while she swallowed the drink. "Oh, no, you're right. That was the *only time* Ram went all out. We had nothing but totally shitty hotel rooms after that."

Violet looked away. That was exactly how Ram would have played it.

She tried hard to ignore the memory of Ram returning from his DC trip with scratches on his back, or the red Tom Ford purse he gave her for Christmas.

Allegra held her finger in the air. "You're right, Ram is very cheap. But the good news is that he never scrimps on hookers—especially the guys. He was paranoid as fuck about them being, like, totally clean, you know?"

Violet was not comforted by her words.

"He never used a condom either. With me or any of us, in case you didn't figure that out already."

Violet's stomach turned. Ram refused to use condoms when they were dating too. Her ankles became weak. "I see." She walked to the bottom step, turned, and crossed her arms. "You eventually signed those confidentiality papers, I assume?"

"Yep. I signed everything the next morning."

"So, you're breaking your contract by telling me about his affairs?"

Allegra erupted in laughter, sarcastically gesturing her hands like a model showcasing a brand-new prison cell. "Sure as hell looks that way, doesn't it?"

Violet silently continued up the stairs, stopping halfway.

"Then tell me this, Allegra. If Ram is as sexually deviant as you describe, why on earth would you even want him?"

Allegra licked the smoothie mustache from her upper lip. "Because it got me off. Especially watching him fuck other guys."

Violet felt ill. "You're such a whore."

Allegra raised her glass. "Here's to all the whores in the world," she said before taking a big gulp. "Especially the ones locked up in basements."

Violet shook her head in disgust as she continued to the top of the stairs.

Finally, it hit her. "Wait. How do I know you're not just making these stories up so I get disgusted with Ram and let him go?"

Allegra was as calm as a Hindu cow. "Violet, you have a choice. You can choose to believe me, or not believe me. It's totally up to you." She adjusted her wig. "You asked for the truth, and I'm giving it to you—the whole truth, just as I experienced it."

Allegra gave a smartass smile. "He's either your husband or he's not."

Silence.

Violet was speechless, processing Allegra's last line over and over in her head.

He's either my husband or he's not?

Her breath stalled.

Her stomach growled.

Acid crawled up the back of her throat.

She punched the security code and quickly shut the heavy door behind her.

As soon as the lock finished resetting, Allegra slammed the empty glass on the dining room table in victory.

She had accomplished her goal.

Gotcha. Bitch.

TWENTY-NINE

"DO YOU remember what time he said to meet here?"

Nellie was on her fifth glass of cheap Chardonnay for the evening. Staying out past four o'clock was rare, especially on Wednesday nights, when the professional crowd invaded Bobby & Eddie's for the Humpday Happy Hour special.

Chloe sat beside her wearing a professional gray pantsuit. "Judge Richard said they'd be here by six. What time is it?"

"Six thirty-five. My pumpkin is expiring at this youngster ball."

"You can leave if you like." Chloe sipped her mojito. "I don't have anything planned tonight, so I can stay—oh, wait, Judge Richard!"

Judge Richard and another man appeared near the front door. His mystery guest looked straight out of a 1980s cop series, with spiky gray hair, beady blue eyes, and a pot-holed face.

Nellie waved him down.

Judge Richard eagerly approached. "Ladies, I would like you to meet my good friend, Elliot Fish, retired NYPD homicide detective and now private investigator."

"Nice to meet you." Nellie extended her hand flirtatiously. "Fish? Like the TV show *Barney Miller*?"

"Yes, unfortunately."

Chloe extended her hand. "I'm really excited you could meet with us."

"Likewise." He flagged down the bartender. It was the owner, Bobby, filling in for Double Trouble, who had an audition for an *Oklahoma* revival earlier that day.

Elliot ordered two beers, then turned toward Chloe. "Can I buy you a drink?"

Chloe opened her mouth but Nellie responded. "I'm drinking Chardonnay, and she'll have a mojito."

Elliot gave Bobby the full drink order, placed his credit card on the bar, and cleared his tar-lined throat. "Judge Richard filled me in on your case. It's definitely interesting."

Chloe was neurotic. "Do you think we're overreacting, or is this something we should be worried about?"

"Before I answer your question, I want to confirm a few items first. I want to make sure the Judge has his facts straight." He pulled a tiny notebook and pen from his back pocket.

"I never forget a case detail," said Judge Richard in defense. "Those brain cells are still kicking."

"Okay," said Chloe politely. "Please ask me whatever you like."

Eliot wiped his mouth. "You said your roommate, Allegra Adams, left on what day, exactly?"

"Thursday, August 9th. She went for a run in Carl Schurz Park around five-thirty p.m. and never came back."

"So, she's been missing for three weeks?"

"Well, if she's even missing. We're not sure."

Elliot grumbled. "As I understand it, your roommate was depressed for a few days, but then received a mysterious phone call that changed her mood before going out for her run?"

"Yes, that's correct. I think she was in a serious fight with her boyfriend earlier in the week. Whatever it was, it had her really upset. She wasn't eating or talking. She even called in sick to work. But while she was getting ready to go out running that night, she received a phone call that made her crazy happy. I heard her scream out of joy from the other room, but when I asked her what was up, she said she couldn't tell me yet, but it was good news. Then she left, smiling all the way out the door."

"Can you check her phone records to see who called her?" asked Nellie.

"Yes, it's a lot harder than it used to be, but I have my ways." He turned back to Chloe. "And what did she have with her when she walked out the door?"

"As far as I can remember, she had her iPhone, earbuds, armband, and house keys. In addition to her clothes and shoes, of course."

"What was she wearing?"

"She always wore two sports bras when she ran because her chest was so big." Chloe looked up, recalling the last time she saw Allegra in detail. "That night, she had on a black tank top and long, black biker shorts that stopped just above the knee."

"What color were her sneakers?"

"They were multicolored. Bright neon colors."

"Okay." Elliot wrote down notes in his tiny notebook. "Did she take her ID?"

"No, I found her driver's license in her wallet later. Along with all of her credit cards, money, gum, you name it."

"And where is the wallet now? Can I take a look at it?"

Chloe glanced at Nellie nervously. "I sent it to her in a box. Along with the rest of her belongings."

"To a fake address in Guadalajara," added Nellie. "Bad idea. We know."

Bobby served everyone their drinks. Judge Richard impatiently grabbed his beer, not wanting to miss a single question.

"Okay, let's back up," said Elliot. "Your friend goes jogging with nothing but her iPhone and keys, then goes missing for how long before she contacts anyone?"

"Four days."

"Okay. So your friend goes jogging—with no extra clothes, money, or cards—takes off with her boyfriend to Mexico, gets married, and calls you four days later?"

"Well, almost. She texted me."

"Can I see those messages?"

"Sure." Chloe navigated through a few screens and handed him her phone.

Elliot glanced over the texts. "Does anything about these messages seem strange to you?"

"Not really."

"Did she send you any pictures from the wedding?"

"No."

"Any pictures of the wedding ring?"

"No, she said she couldn't upload photos because they had bad Internet or something."

"Did she post any pictures from Mexico on social media or anything after August 9th?"

"The last thing Allegra posted on Facebook was a sad face on August 8th. That's when she was depressed. The day stamp is listed on her timeline."

"Did you, or anyone she knows, talk to Allegra *by phone* after August 9th?"

Chloe felt stupid. The more Elliot asked her questions, the more she realized she should've gone back to the police sooner. "No, not that I know of. She even asked me to call Bobby and tell him she wasn't coming back to work because he didn't know how to text."

"That's troubling right there." Elliot wrote down more notes. He handed Chloe's phone back to her. "Take a closer look at those text messages. Is that how she writes? Her manner of spelling and expressing herself?"

"Yeah, I think so."

Elliot sighed. "Okay, tell me about a letter you received from her?"

"Yes, a few days later, I received a note in the mail with money—"

"Did she sign the note?"

"What do you mean?"

"With her signature. Or was the whole thing printed off a computer?"

"It was printed."

"How much money did she send you?"

"Nine thousand, nine hundred dollars."

"Smart move because it's problematic to ship anything over ten grand. And what did you do with the cash?"

"It was part of her rent, so I'm holding on to it. Also, I had to use a big chunk to ship her stuff off to Mexico."

Nellie chimed in. "This is the part that worries me, Detective Fish."

"Not a detective anymore, but I'll admit I miss being called that."

Nellie smiled.

"Anyway, back to your story. So you packed up all of her personal effects and shipped it to the wrong address in Guadalajara?"

Chloe frowned. "Yes. Turns out it was a restaurant and no one knows her there."

"But they accepted the package?"

"Yes."

"And what was in it, exactly?"

"I shipped her purse, wallet, jewelry, journal, phone chargers, cameras, photos—anything that seemed important. But she didn't want her clothes or shoes. She said I could sell those. Which I did, on eBay."

Elliot was disappointed. "So, basically, you shipped off all the evidence."

Judge Richard raised his brows. Nellie looked to the floor.

"Yeah, I guess so," said Chloe. "Is that bad?"

Elliot stretched out his chin, choosing not to comment. "Who's her next of kin?"

"Her mother's deceased, and she never knew her father. But she does have a brother and sister in New Mexico."

Bobby wiped the bar nearby and interrupted. "Are you guys talking about Allegra? Is something wrong?"

"No, we're just making sure she's okay," responded Nellie.

"No big deal," added Judge Richard.

Elliot continued. "Do you have their contact info?"

Chloe shook her head. "I have no idea how to find them. Adams is a very common last name."

Bobby interrupted. "I've got her sister's number. It's listed as Allegra's emergency contact on her job application. I almost called when Allegra went AWOL a few weeks ago."

Elliot pointed at Bobby. "That's what I'm talking about. Thank you."

Bobby left the bar and walked toward his office in the back.

Chloe became emotional. "So, I really screwed up, didn't I? By sending away all her stuff?"

"We're not done yet, so hold on before jumping to conclusions. Allegra may be alive and well, but what you're describing to me sounds a little suspicious."

"How suspicious?" asked Nellie.

Elliot turned serious. "More than two thousand people go missing *every single day*. That's eight hundred thousand people a year. But the majority of them don't send cash in the mail to get their evidence thrown away. Looks to me like somebody went through a whole lot of trouble to make everyone think she just took off. This may turn out to be a homicide case."

Judge Richard and Nellie gasped simultaneously.

"My God. What makes you say that?" asked Chloe.

"I had a chance to check on her passport yesterday. Allegra doesn't have one. Nor has she ever applied for one. Even if she traveled by private jet, she's gonna need a passport, unless it was a plane that flies under the radar to smuggle drugs, but that's an entirely different scenario."

Chloe was shocked.

"Unless I confirm someone, *anyone*, actually spoke with her either on the phone or in person after August 9th, I'm going to consider this a missing person's case. People simply don't leave without their wallets. Not willingly. No matter how romantic the proposal might have been, every young lady in America would have the forethought to swing by their apartment, grab their most important belongings before going on a plane—if she even went on a plane. Which I highly doubt."

"Who would do such a thing?" asked Judge Richard. "Everybody loved Allegra. She was a fantastic bartender."

Elliot pulled his earlobe. "Does she have any enemies? Any stalker ex-boyfriends?"

Nellie, Chloe, and Judge Richard exchanged looks, all shaking their heads *no*.

"The girl was a sweetheart. She didn't have any enemies," added Nellie.

Elliot smiled wryly. "But she was carrying a married man's baby when she went missing? Is that correct?"

"Yes, that's true," said Chloe. "I found her positive pregnancy test in the closet. But no one knows who the father is."

"I do," said Nellie with confidence. "Allegra told me the night she found out. It's the married guy, Mr. Clean. She was waiting for him to return from a business trip to tell him in person. But he's definitely the father."

"Then that's where my investigation will start."

Nellie scratched her head. "But what if Allegra was attacked by a stranger in the park?"

"Right, like those two girls who were raped and killed while jogging?" added Judge Richard. "What if she's a victim too?"

Elliot folded his arms. "It's a decent theory, but highly unlikely. If there's been foul play, whoever did it obviously knows her well enough to mimic the way she writes. Either that or they studied her closely for months. Again, this is only *one* possible scenario. She could very well be on a Mexican beach with her husband, someone she just met online. Some guy none of you know about."

Judge Richard swallowed his drink. "But your instinct is telling you otherwise?"

"I'm afraid it is."

"What if she's still alive and being held against her will?" asked Nellie.

"That too is a possibility. However, there's no ransom note, and murder is more common than kidnapping. It's much cleaner."

Chloe turned green. "I think I'm going to be sick."

Nellie rubbed her back. "Don't beat yourself up, kid. You didn't know."

Elliot continued writing in his notebook. "So, what's the name of the married boyfriend she was bragging about?"

"Somebody Ramspeck. His nickname is Ram."

"And he lives here in New York?"

Nellie answered. "Allegra mentioned to me once that she went to his townhouse on East 78th Street. It stuck in my mind because that's the street where all the residents go balls out with Halloween decorations, right?"

"Yes, I took my granddaughter trick-or-treating there a few years ago," added Judge Richard. "It was packed."

"Okay. Ramspeck on East 78th, that shouldn't be hard to find. I'll talk to the guy and see what he says." Elliot's pen ran out of ink.

Bobby returned to the bar with a red file folder in hand. "Can I borrow a pen?"

"I'll do you one better. Here's her HR folder," said Bobby as he handed Elliot the file. "Fuck the Labor Department. I don't feel right about her running off either."

"Excellent. Now I have a place to start." Elliot drank his beer. "But we still have to talk about fees. A missing person case usually runs about two hundred an hour, but since you're not the family and just a group of friends, I can do it for a hundred and fifty plus travel and expenses, with a two-thousand-dollar retainer."

Nellie was floored. "Well, nice knowing you, Elliot."

"No way you can do this pro bono?" asked Judge Richard.

"I'm sorry, man. You have no idea how many times I get asked that question."

"What happens if you find her and she's okay?" asked Chloe.

"Well, the minute I find out she's alive and well, I stop looking and you get whatever's remaining in your retainer."

Nellie was skeptical. "Yeah, but we're only her pals. Two thousand is a little—"

"I'll pay it," volunteered Chloe. She had just made over four thousand dollars by selling Allegra's dresses on eBay. "It's her money anyway. Might as well put it to good use."

Judge Richard felt guilty. "I'll throw in another five hundred if you go over the retainer," he said. "Allegra was a good girl."

Nellie felt pressured. "Okay, count me in too."

Elliot was satisfied. "That's enough to get me started, unless I have to go to Mexico to knock on a few doors, which I'll only do if I have to." He held up the file folder. "I've got everything I need to get started. Who should be my main contact moving forward?"

Nellie pointed at Chloe. "She's the one paying."

"Good, let me log your number into my phone here, and I'll start making calls first thing tomorrow morning."

THIRTY

NATURALLY ILLUMINATED during the day by a domed glass ceiling, the Celeste Restaurant inside London's famed Lanesborough Hotel is an alluring display of 18th Century decor with heavy white moldings, Wedgewood blue walls, antique gold furniture, side-by-side chandeliers, and hand-carved friezes depicting Greco-Roman images of domesticated life gone awry.

It was nearly two o'clock on the Friday before Labor Day.

With most American business travelers away for the holiday, the dining room was unusually empty, except for a traditionally dressed Indian couple, an African prince, and Ram, who dined alone.

He sat on a gold sofa with a table in front of him, with blue and gold pillows to support his aching back, as he finished his late lunch of smoked lamb neck with spring onion and green pepper coulis. He finished reading the last article from that morning's *Financial Times*, taking a well-deserved break from business dealings as he rested before flying to New York on Monday to face the reality of his crumbling personal life.

He dabbed his lips with a linen napkin when his phone began to vibrate on the table. The name LAURA WELCH appeared on the screen.

"Good morning, Laura. How are you?"

Laura sat at Penny's old desk at Sotheby's Realty in New York. She wore a red Prada suit, and her dark hair was down and styled. "Do you have a second to speak?"

"Yes, perfect timing. I'm just finishing lunch. I stopped in London for a few days before heading back to New York."

"Good. I won't take much of your time, then. The reason for my call is that I have set the closing for Friday, September 7th at three o'clock. Will that work for you?"

"That's what, a week from today? It's coming up rather quickly."

"I know. We had to move mountains to get Title to close so soon."

"Do I need to be present for the closing?"

"No, you can sign the papers on Tuesday, like we planned. I just want to make sure your movers will be finished with the house and ready for the final walk-through on Thursday."

"Movers?" Ram was taken aback. "I haven't been able to reach my wife and discuss any of this with her yet. She's still angry about the divorce."

Penny sipped her Starbucks latte. "I'm sorry to hear that."

"I've left at least twenty voicemails about her need to find a new place, but she hasn't spoken to me in weeks. I'm willing to rent her an apartment for at least a year. I just need to hear back on whether she's staying in New York or moving to Florida to be closer to her parents."

Laura was happy to hear the ex-wife might be shipped down South. "I agree. Absolutely makes sense to speak with her first."

"I'll be back in New York on Monday, so I'll talk to Violet then. But it doesn't give me a great deal of time to arrange for movers. Can we postpone the closing a couple of days?"

"Unfortunately, Mr. Horowitz said his only condition was that we close before September 8th so he could give the keys to his wife for her birthday. We already accepted his offer. The deposit is in escrow. It's all set."

Ram stabbed the final piece of lamb neck on his plate. "I see. Well, I guess I'll just have to figure it out."

"Now, keep in mind, if you need to put your items in storage, we work with a fabulous company in New Jersey that can move everything in one day. They specialize in storing high-end items, and we've never had any complaints. They're miracle workers."

"That's good to know."

"In fact, I think it may be your best solution moving forward, until you and your wife can work out the details as to where she would like you to send her clothing."

Ram reacted. "That's exactly my point. I've just been so busy with work that I haven't had any time to deal with the divorce. I've been waiting until I get back to New York."

"Completely understand, Mr. Ramspeck. That's what I'm here for, to help you through this entire process. Getting full asking price without an inspection is a dream come true. Jack and Lisa are elated to be living in your home. I think it's a win-win for all."

"Yes, I agree."

"And how are the renovations coming along with your new home in Scotland?"

"Beautifully, actually. I had a chance to visit yesterday. Hard to wire a castle from the 17th century for WIFI, but we're getting there."

Laura glimmered at her desk. *Wow, a castle.* "Outstanding. I wish you all the luck in the world. And if it gets too lonely, you always have a friend in New York who's willing to visit." Laura bit her tongue for being so forward. "Professionally, of course." She rolled her eyes. *That's even worse!*

Ram was flattered by the flirtation. "I have fifteen empty bedrooms. You and your girlfriends can visit anytime."

Laura smiled as she nervously tapped a pen on the glass desk. "So, I'll go ahead and arrange for the storage company to swing by Monday morning to give you an estimate. Does that sound good to you?"

"That should work. I'll be home the entire day dealing with the move."

"And I'll come by on Tuesday to have you sign the papers for closing."

Ram was hesitant. His gut was telling him something was wrong. "Great, see you then." He hung up the phone before Laura could continue with her predictable pleasantries. She was mid-sentence as the call abruptly ended.

A male server wearing white gloves came by with a silver pot. "Would you care for more coffee?"

He exhaled loudly. "How about a Bloody Mary instead?"

"Certainly."

The phone vibrated again. Ram answered it without looking.

"I just realized, I still need to get the door codes from Violet—"

"Hello?" a man's voice was on the other side. "Mr. Ramspeck?"

"Yes, speaking. May I ask who's calling?"

"My name is Elliot Fish, and I'm a private investigator from Manhattan. Did I reach you at a good time?"

"Uh, yes. I'm in London right now. What is this about? Are you with the police?"

"No, sir. I'm a retired homicide detective with the NYPD."

Ram's stomach fell on the word *homicide*.

"I've been retained by Miss Chloe Sinclair to investigate the disappearance of Allegra Adams."

Ram's heart sank. "Disappearance? I thought she eloped and moved out of the country?"

Elliot was surprised. "So you knew Miss Adams?"

"Yes, of course." Ram looked around the room, focusing on the three diners surrounding him. "Can I call you back at this number when I return to my hotel room? I'll be there in ten minutes."

"Surely. I'll be expecting your call."

Ram sat on an exquisite powder blue bedspread under an ivory canopy. The large bedroom suite was filled with so many antiques, it looked as if he were living at the Smithsonian.

Ram called back the last number listed on his phone.

Elliot answered. "Hello?" He was in his Bronx apartment wearing a plain shirt and seventeen-year-old polyester trousers.

"Yes, Mr. Fish. This is Balthazar Ramspeck returning your call."

Balthazar? No wonder everyone calls him Ram. "Is this a better time to speak?" Elliot kicked his dirty shoes onto his metal desk.

"Yes, much better. I prefer we have this discussion in private. I have a feeling I know what you're going to ask me."

"I understand. By the way, I'm in my apartment next to the A/C, so if it get's a little loud, let me know. Can't get reception anywhere else in this joint."

Ram was impatient. "So what's wrong with Allegra? Is she all right?"

"Well, that's what I'm trying to figure out, Mr. Ramspeck." Elliot searched for his pack of Marlborough Reds on the desk. "How long have you known her?"

"We had an affair for about seven months, give or take."

Elliot was surprised at Ram's honesty. He expected it would take at least ten minutes to persuade him to come clean. "I must remind you, Mr. Ramspeck, you're under no obligation to speak to me. This is a civil investigation, not a criminal one."

Ram's low voice crumbled. "Yes, I know."

Elliot lit a cigarette. Smoking two packs a day at fifteen dollars a pack, it was the one and only vice that kept him years from retirement. "You sound very upset."

"*I am* very upset. Allegra destroyed my life."

Elliot blew smoke at the purring A/C. "How's that?"

"Nearly a month ago, my wife found out about our affair and confronted me over the phone. When she asked me to choose between her and Allegra, I asked my wife for a divorce."

Elliot took a deep drag. "Must have been a shock to the system."

"Yes, it was. I told her I was in love with Allegra, and there was nothing she could do to salvage our marriage."

Elliot raised his brows. "That must have been devastating news, I'm sure."

"Truth is, our marriage had been over for years before I met Allegra. It was only a matter of time," he said defensively.

"I divorced three women myself, Mr. Ramspeck. Not judging you in any way." Elliot slumped in his chair. "So what happened next?"

346

"I immediately called Allegra and told her what happened. I asked her to marry me over the phone and promised I'd take her to Tiffany's to pick out a ring when I returned to New York. I was in China at the time."

"And what was her reaction?"

"She was thrilled, especially since we had been fighting a few days before that. Allegra was sick of being a mistress and threatened to leave me."

"So the timing was perfect."

"Yes, I guess one could say that. I didn't have the heart to bring it up to Violet first, so when she confronted me, it was the right moment."

Elliot pulled his earlobe. "If you and Allegra were so happy, then how did she destroy your life?"

Ram removed his glasses and placed them by his side. "It was the strangest thing. After Allegra accepted my wedding proposal, she stopped talking to me for about three days. No calls. No texts. Just complete silence. Then one night, I received a series of texts that said she changed her mind. That I was 'too old and boring', and that she had met someone her own age—Jose Martinez I think his name was. She said she eloped with him and moved to Mexico."

"Funny, that's the same story Allegra's sister told me on the phone."

"Mr. Fish, I destroyed my marriage of twenty-four years so Allegra and I could be together. And for what? My wife won't even return my calls. She's left me. I'm about to lose half my fortune for nothing."

Elliot took notes at his desk. "How did your wife find out about the affair?"

"I'm not sure. All I know is she knew Allegra's full name, birthday, and address. She screamed those details to me on the phone."

"And you never thought to deny it?"

"At that point, I had no choice but to be honest. I was in love with the girl. I wanted to marry her."

Elliot hesitated on sharing the next fact. He extinguished his cigarette in the overflowing bud tray. "We have reason to believe Allegra was pregnant before she disappeared. Were you aware of this?"

His throat cracked. "Pregnant?" Ram was speechless.

"Mr. Ramspeck?"

Ram slowly replaced his glasses on his nose. "Was it mine? Or the man she ran off with?"

Elliot ran his hand through his spiky gray hair. "According to witnesses at Bobby & Eddie's, Allegra claimed the baby was yours."

"She talked to other people about me?"

"Yes, I'm afraid so. Two witnesses claimed to have met you in person."

Ram grabbed a fistful of bedspread as he spoke. "It's true. I met a few of her friends when I went to the bar *one time*."

Elliot shuffled his papers. "So why do you think Allegra had a last-minute change of heart? To not marry the father of her child?"

Ram wiped sweat from his forehead. "She said she didn't want to go through a lengthy divorce; that her new boyfriend wanted to marry her right away." Ram fought back emotion. "After I popped the question, I warned her that my divorce could get long and nasty. That it might take a few years before we could have a big wedding. And I was right."

"Did you speak to her on the phone, or was all of your communication by text?"

"She broke up with me via text. Allegra never liked speaking on the phone."

Elliot wrote that down. "Can you send me screen shots of all of your communications with her? I need to get a sense of how she wrote."

"Unfortunately, I deleted them. I deleted her as a contact altogether. I couldn't bear to see her words ever again."

Elliot quietly pounded his fist on the desk.

"The kid broke my heart, Mr. Fish."

Elliot feigned sympathy. "I can only imagine." He reached for a second smoke. "Have you heard from Allegra in *any* *way* over the last two weeks? E-mail? Messaging? Anything?"

"No. I tried calling her phone several times to see if I could change her mind. I left a few voicemails, but then the number ended up disconnected."

"Right. The number is no longer in service."

"Elliot, I need you to be straight with me." Ram leaned forward, almost falling off the bed. "Is there something I should be worried about? Am I in danger? Or my wife?"

"No, Mr. Ramspeck, I don't see how that could be the case."

"I still love her, you know. I only want the best for her, even if it means being without me."

"Allegra touched a lot of people, Mr. Ramspeck. She seems like a very nice girl."

Ram lifted from the bedspread and began pacing the room. "I just wish I wasn't about to lose my shirt when my wife finally shows up."

Elliot's ears perked. "What do you mean *shows up*?"

"My wife. She's practically disappeared."

Elliot straightened in his chair. "What's your wife's name again?"

"Violet."

"And when was the last time she spoke to you?"

"About three weeks ago."

Elliot's lungs struggled to get oxygen. "And what was her disposition when she confronted you about the affair?"

"She was angry. She was yelling. She was as hysterical as any other woman would be."

Elliot flipped through several papers. "You wouldn't happen to remember what day that was, do you?"

Ram stopped to look at the ivory drapes. "Yes, I do remember the date. I had just finished a major trade deal in Beijing when she called me. It was Thursday, August 9th."

Elliot's beady blue eyes lit up. "Thursday, August 9th. You're sure?"

"I'm positive. It was the second worst day of my life. A little hard to forget."

Elliot lit another cigarette. "Do you know what time, approximately, she called you?"

Ram opened the drapes and saw it was raining outside. "Let's see. Her call woke me up in the middle of the night, so it had to be early afternoon for Violet."

Elliot pulled his earlobe again. "Mr. Ramspeck, do you have any reason to believe your wife would have confronted Allegra on that day?"

Ram hesitated.

"Mr. Ramspeck?"

"Why do you ask that?"

Elliot knew he struck a nerve. "I'm just trying to figure out who spoke with Allegra the day she may have gone missing."

Silence.

"Honestly, I'm not comfortable answering that question without my wife being present."

Elliot shut off the A/C. "Can you tell me why? This is really important, Mr. Ramspeck."

Ram cleared his throat. He carefully constructed his words like a defense attorney discussing a guilty client. "My wife has a history of mental problems. And depression. I'm afraid this might make her appear to be culpable in some way."

Elliot felt a tingle run down his spine. "Did she say anything in particular that worried you?"

Ram stared out the foggy hotel window. "My wife didn't take the news well. That's all I can tell you at this point."

"Did she threaten to hurt Allegra?"

Ram motioned to hang up the phone. "I'm afraid this is heading in a dire—"

"*Mr. Ramspeck.*" Elliot's tone sharpened. "We're not entirely certain, but we have reason to believe someone was impersonating Allegra when she texted you, which means she may be deceased or in serious danger. If you have any feelings left for this young girl, any information you share now can make all the difference."

Ram's heart thudded.

"You're heading for divorce court either way, Mr. Ramspeck. Holding back information to protect your wife will do you no good if something happened to Allegra. You might even be held accountable if you don't share it with me or the police in advance."

Ram exhaled loudly. "I really don't feel good about this."

"Please, Mr. Ramspeck. The more you tell me, the more I can help Allegra."

Ram ground his jaw. He thought long and hard about sharing his secret.

"Please, Mr. Ramspeck. I'm a grown old man. Don't ask me to beg."

Ram held the curtain as he took a deep breath. He could no longer protect his wife's pristine image. "The last thing Violet said to me on the phone was that if I sold our home and went through with the divorce, she would kill herself and take Allegra with her."

Boom.

Elliot fell back into his chair. His chest expanded. "Has your wife ever threatened or attempted suicide before?"

Ram's eyes fell to the flowered carpet. "Yes, she tried to kill herself twice after our daughter passed away."

Elliot's heart beat loudly. "Where is your wife now? May I speak to her?"

"I don't know."

"Is she home?"

"Maybe. My housekeepers recently moved out, so I have no clue."

"Can you give me her phone number?"

"I don't know if that's a good idea."

"Mr. Ramspeck—"

"I'll be home early on Monday. I can arrange a meeting then."

"Mr. Ramspeck, we may not have that kind of time. This is *extremely* important. I need to speak with your wife as soon as possible. Can you fly home sooner?"

Ram let go of the curtain. He felt a momentum building he was no longer able to contain. "Yes. I can have my jet ready by tomorrow morning."

"Good. Please call me the second you land in New York."

Twenty minutes had passed. Ram was distraught beyond all measure.

He rinsed his face with cold water in the hotel bathroom. The reflection of his blue eyes pierced the mirror as his mind raced and his breathing took on a foreboding rhythm.

He grabbed an embroidered washcloth from the brown marble countertop and patted the remaining water from his bald head and angled face.

He walked back into the bedroom, picked up the phone lying on the roll-top writing desk, and dialed Laura Welch.

"Sotheby's International Realty. May I help you?" Laura finished chewing the last bite of her gluten-free Panini sandwich.

"Hi, Laura. It's Balthazar." His voice was low and melancholy.

"Yes, Mr. Ramspeck. Did you receive the e-mail I just sent you? The storage company—"

"Look, I've just received some extremely difficult news about my wife."

Laura panicked. This was not the kind of phone call she was expecting. "My goodness, is everything okay?"

"I'm not exactly sure yet. All I know is that I want to cancel the sale."

Laura's chest exploded. Two million dollars in commission was at stake. "What do you mean, Mr. Ramspeck?"

"I don't want to sell my townhome. I'm not moving."

Penny had warned her of nuclear bombs like this, but she never believed it could happen with her first million-dollar client. "But, Mr. Ramspeck, you were so eager to sell? What about your castle in Scotland?"

"I'll keep it. Or flip it. I don't care. I'm not moving."

Laura's mouth gaped open.

"Please send me a bill for any expenses you may have incurred."

Laura was nauseated; she had just signed a lease for a brand-new Porsche that morning. "Mr. Ramspeck, please reconsider. This is an excellent time to sell—"

"My mind is made up. Please tell Jack and Lisa I'm terribly sorry."

Ram hung up the phone.

Laura was left holding silence to her ear.

"Mr. Ramspeck? . . . *Mr. Ramspeck!*"

THIRTY-ONE

FOR THE FIRST time in years, Violet was the only soul in the house.

Or at least, she pretended to be.

It was early Saturday morning, ten minutes before seven o'clock—two days before Ram was scheduled to return home from his month-long business trip in Asia.

Violet twirled a pirouette on the ancient Persian rug in the two-story library, balancing her slight weight on the tips of her toes like her days attending Julliard. She wore a white Dolce & Gabbana flowing skirt—a sharp departure from her usual constricting shift dress silhouette—which made her feel like the dancer she was born to be.

It was a rare occasion for Violet to be barefoot in the house, an even rarer occasion to be in the most lavish room without housekeepers, houseguests, or a husband to watch her glide like a swan from corner to corner.

She was upbeat, for it was the day she planned to get revenge for Allegra's heart-stabbing stories about her husband. It was her turn to tell Allegra about the night of August 9th. The night Allegra had completely forgotten. The night she went running, fell down the rabbit hole, and into Violet's basement.

With Ram coming home in less than forty-eight hours, Violet knew it was her final chance to launch a blitzkrieg.

She floated across the dark teak floor to the kitchen and opened the refrigerator, plucking out a bottle of water. She appreciated Rosa had left it fully stocked before her last day of employment. The formerly bare shelves were now filled with whole milk, orange juice, soda, brownies, pies, watermelon, pasta, and cheese—all foods Ram would enjoy upon his return, and would make any nutritionist cringe.

Violet picked up a stack of freshly laundered nightgowns she had placed on the breakfast bar shortly after waking. Allegra's wardrobe had grown to five outfits, with the short cornflower blue and lilac purple nighties always being her favorites.

Violet entered the pantry, ignoring the catcalls from junk food as she walked past them, begging to be opened and consumed like sirens seducing sailors into crashing through rocks.

She punched in the two door codes and emerged into the brightly lit room that had become a second home now, numb to the buzzing sound above her head from the fluorescent light threatening to go on strike.

She saw Allegra fast asleep in the bed, completely covered from head to toe with the warm, ivory comforter. Her deep sleep, light snore, and expanding chest were visible even as she lay beneath the covers.

The dining room table was littered with empty bags of chips, used plastic cups, random magazines, and the VitaMix blender container, which held remnants of the obnoxious smoothie from the evening before.

Violet placed the stack of folded nightgowns on the opposite end of the crumb kingdom. She walked over, took a whiff of the dirty blender container, and recoiled, as it was starting to rot.

As she began removing the rubbish, she saw Allegra had left a magazine open to the last article she was reading. It was from a 1986 issue of *Good Housekeeping*.

THE FIRST YEAR: WHAT YOU DO NOW WILL AFFECT YOUR BABY FOREVER.

BY DR. BENJAMIN SPOCK

Violet flipped through the pages, scanning the tips outlined by the famous pediatrician, noticing pictures of young mothers with padded shoulders holding infants, curious as to why Allegra would even be interested in reading the article.

Suddenly, it dawned on her. *No, it can't be.*

Violet threw the trash back onto the table and marched into the bathroom. She opened the cabinet door beneath the sink, moving items aside, and pulled out the unopened, untouched box of tampons she had given Allegra more than three weeks ago.

Violet was petrified. *Allegra hasn't gotten her period.*

She then inspected the white toilet seat she had cleaned the day before, looking for the last piece of evidence that would confirm her suspicion. As she lifted the seat, she saw several specks of dark brown matter. She carefully scraped it with her fingernail and held it to her nose.

It was the familiar smell of her old friend *vomit.*

She can't be. No!

Violet became dizzy. She fought to maintain her balance, falling slowly to the ground as she held the toilet bowl. She felt as if an invisible spear had broken her ribs. Unable to breathe, unable to move, her mind raced, processing decades of failure to get pregnant, failure to respond to fertility shots, failure to carry IVF embryos, failure of twenty-nine months of adoption applications, failure of keeping her baby girl alive . . . Failure of *becoming a mother.*

Violet wanted to end it all. Right there, in that very moment.

But instead, she managed to stand erect and quietly returned to the main room. She picked up the blender container and walked barefoot up the stairs as Allegra continued sleeping.

As she re-entered the pantry, her eyes became glassy.

Why stop now, Violet? We all know the end is near.

The voices continued in her head.

None of this is your fault. You deserve a treat.

More and more the voices teased her—the colorful, food-porn sirens on the shelves, sandwiching Violet in between the walls of her own personal hell.

And that's when she broke. Just like she had every other morning and evening since Allegra had been locked away in that basement.

She rushed into the kitchen and placed the blender container on its base.

She pulled out a large plastic tumbler, filled it with whole milk, drinking it as fast as she could. *Milk always makes it smoother on the way out,* she thought to herself. *It's your last one. Make it epic.*

She pulled out the aluminum tray of six brownies, stuffing each one into her face between gulps of milk. When she was finished, she dashed into the pantry, scanning the sirens around her. She took a red package of Chips Ahoy cookies; a yellow package of Golden Oreos; a green container of Pringles; an orange bag of Cheetos; and a black bag of Smartfood white cheddar popcorn.

Her arms were filled with snacks as she walked back into the kitchen, sat at the breakfast bar and *ate it all in one sitting . . .* Shoving and cramming each morsel of processed food into her mouth, as her skin tingled, her heart sprinted, and her veins danced with adrenaline. She particularly loved the high from being able to gorge alone without anyone discovering her—feeling the heroin-like numbness take over her body once the massive doses of chemicals and insulin hit her bloodstream and brain.

When she was finished, she opened the freezer, and pulled out a pint of Ben & Jerry's New York Super Fudge Chunk ice cream for dessert. When she was done, she returned to the freezer, forcing down a second pint of Chunky Monkey, gagging as the final banana-filled spoons met her mouth, reaching her point of Nirvana.

Unable to fit another bite into her tiny body, she stood up from the counter and rubbed her round, extended belly, pretending she too was carrying a child. She spoke to her imaginary fetus—Baby Hansel—saying how much she loved him and couldn't wait to meet him, secretly sad that he would need to emerge in five minutes, and even sadder this would be their last visit.

When she was ready, Violet held the blender container in one hand, bent over, and stuck two fingers from the other hand down her throat. The roof of her mouth was scarred from growing nails and the top of her knuckles raw from purging at least two times a day, *every day.*

Her stomach knew the routine. She convulsed in one strong movement, like a full-body orgasm emptying at least a pound of the thick, brownish-gray matter into the container. She forced her hand down farther, waiting for the next wave to hit. And it did. Emptying more matter until the container was filled three quarters of the way. When she was finished, she placed the container on the counter, and dry heaved over the sink until she was sure she had emptied completely.

Afterward, she rinsed her mouth with water from the faucet, ignoring the uncomfortable pressure behind her eyeballs, as she stood upright to regain her composure. She reached over and grabbed a container of Serious Mass Weight Gain Powder in Chocolate, adding two scoops to her fresh vomit, and the remaining milk from her glass before pressing the SMOOTHIE button on the VitaMix.

And just like that. Another batch of obnoxious smoothie was made.

As the blender pulverized its mystery ingredients, Violet carefully cleaned the breakfast bar of crumbs, containers, and bags, wrapping all evidence in paper towels before throwing it into the trash. When she was finished, she took a clean plastic tumbler from the cupboard, grabbed the full blender container, and went back downstairs to feed Allegra her daily breakfast.

When Violet arrived in the basement, Allegra was awake and freshly showered. She sat at the dining room table reading *Oprah* magazine, wearing her favorite cornflower blue nightie and mismatching blue wig. Allegra's face was rounder and glowing, her weight gain becoming more evident by the day.

Violet approached with the blender and empty cup in hand. "Are you hungry?"

"Oh, yes. Thank God, I'm starving."

Violet poured Allegra the first glass. "Did you sleep well?"

Allegra's eyes fixated on the blender as Violet poured. "Yes, I did. No dreams. Just pure sleep." She then took a large sip of the vomit-smoothie, relishing the taste. "Umm. The more chocolate, the better."

Violet smiled. "Good. I'll keep that in mind."

THIRTY-TWO

THE COOL AND breezy September weather was completely different than the August heat that plagued city dwellers the week before. Elliot Fish wore a light brown jacket as he walked west on East 78th Street, admiring the blonde European tourists coming from the Met Museum almost as much as the architecture of the stately townhomes glued side by side, until he reached his destination of 13 East 78th Street.

Standing at the bottom of the ten-step staircase, he took a moment to appreciate the antique white, neo-classical facade of the intriguing Ramspeck home—particularly the Roman Corinthian columns that framed the bowed doorway, having studied construction at The City College of New York before transferring to the police academy after his second semester.

He walked up the staircase, immediately noticing that the black cast iron gate guarding the front door like medieval prison bars, was closed and locked. He walked on the other side of the gate, looking for an external door buzzer. Once he found it, he pressed it several times.

No one came to the door. *No maid? No house manager?* Elliot was puzzled. In his experience, owners of places as fancy as this always required at least two staff members to be home.

He placed both hands on the cast iron bars and rattled the gate loudly, scanning the overhang for security cameras, hoping that some type of motion sensor would spot him.

Nothing.

He inspected the gate closer, taking note of the pile of *New York Times* and *Wall Street Journal* newspapers thrown between the bars and accumulating in front of the door.

It looked as if no one had lived there for months.

Elliot pulled his earlobe, thinking of what to do next. He walked back down the steps and looked up toward the higher floors filled with flowerboxes of dying red geraniums. He casually looked through the windows to see if he could spot anyone inside, having to wave reluctantly to suspicious tourists whispering behind his back as they passed by.

After a few minutes, Elliot finally gave up. He realized he wouldn't be able to speak with Violet until Ram returned home from London later that night. Refusing to be patient, he pulled out his cigarettes, lighting one up as he dialed a number on his cell phone.

An old-fashioned beige landline phone rang several times before a uniformed police officer, sitting at a desk overflowing with burrito wrappers, answered it. "Watchowski speaking," he said with a mouth stuffed with food.

"Good morning, John. It's Fish."

Watchowski was in the middle of inhaling his third break-fast burrito. "You must have ESP. I was just about to call you."

"Yeah? What did you find?"

Watchowski looked around the precinct; it was filled with empty desks. He lowered his voice, making sure no one was eavesdropping. "You know that number you had me look up?"

"Which one?"

"The surgeon who thinks his wife's banging his brother?"

"The Rothschild case. What about it?"

"I finally traced the number that keeps calling the wife at two in the morning while the doctor is at work . . . It's her personal trainer."

Elliot took a drag from his cigarette as he walked north on Madison Avenue. "It's always the damn trainer."

"Or the nanny, or the dogwalker, yadda, yadda, yadda. I have his address if you need it. He lives in Hoboken."

"Good, e-mail it to me. I'll snap a few pictures of the wife leaving his place and we'll call it a day."

"Got it."

"How about the Adams case? Did you look that one up yet?"

"Just finished. I've got the records right here." Watchowski held the burrito in his mouth as he shuffled through a stack of papers. He held up a single page with the words CTN: CELL TOWER NETWORK OF NEW YORK printed across the top. His eyes scanned down the table of phone numbers, call times, and tower locations. "Okay. The Adams girl received only one phone call around five thirty p.m. on August 9th. The number was from a TracFone."

"A disposable phone?"

"You got it."

Elliot took a deep drag of his cigarette as he continued walking. "Where did the call come from?"

"It was local. It pinged the tower on East 67th."

"Maybe it was her pot dealer." Elliot avoided eye contact with a homeless girl and her baby on the corner. "How often did she call?"

"This was the one and only call from that number. But here's where it gets strange. I looked up the TracFone records, and Adams was the one and only call it ever made."

Elliot stopped walking. "Can you tell me who registered the phone?"

Watchowski grabbed his plastic cup filled with more ice than Sprite. "The phone's sold in every bodega in New York. I can't trace it."

Elliot blew out a cloud of smoke. "Who did the Adams girl contact after the 9th?"

"You were right. She didn't make any outgoing calls or text messages until four days later. But on that day, she sent a shitload of texts to five different numbers within a ninety-minute period."

"Can you give me that list?"

"I'll e-mail it to you as soon as we hang up." Watchowski took another bite of his burrito, with scrambled eggs hanging from the side of his mouth. "And like you suspected, the Adams phone wasn't used again after the 13th. It was shut off by Verizon on the 20th due to lack of payment."

"Right. Her roommate said she was terrible about paying bills, even if she had the money." Elliot wiped his brow as he stepped into the street to hail a taxi. "Can you tell me on what day the phone traveled to Mexico?"

"Mexico?"

"The texts she sent on the 13th. Which tower picked her up in Guadalajara?"

Watchowski hit the bottom of his drink with a straw, making a loud slurping sound. "Her phone never left the Upper East Side, Fish. Those messages she sent pinged the same tower as the TracFone. The one on East 67th."

Elliot's eyes jolted open. "Shit. She's still here."

Watchowski wiped his mouth. "Guess your gut was spot on." He tossed the salsa-stained napkin onto the floor by his feet. "Giuliani was right. You should've never retired."

An empty taxi sped by. Elliot furiously shot him the bird. "Remember to say that at my funeral, will you?"

Watchowski stood up to unfasten his belt. "Are you gonna call it in, or do you want me to do it?"

Elliot kicked the curb as he watched full taxis fly past him. Being the only son of a die-hard Irish cab driver, he stubbornly refused to use Uber, Lyft, or any other *amateur* taxi service. "No, I'm gonna figure out what happened to the

Adams girl first. If I call it in now, they'll just let the case grow weeds under the missing kid files."

"That's truth right there." Watchowski smiled. "You know, I envy you. No red tape. No captain. I think of going private all the time."

Elliot was out of breath as he crossed the street. "You can't leave, John. I need someone on the inside to do my dirty work."

Watchowski ate the last tater tot that fell onto his desk. "Dirty work? Like taking client thank you gifts off your hands? By the way, that Harry Potter show was out of this world. Martha gave me the best blow job of my life when we got home."

Elliot panted as he continued walking east, heading toward the 77th Street subway stop on Lexington Avenue. "Just keep digging for me, man. We're the only hope that Adams girl's got," he said, struggling for air. "Let's pray we find her alive."

THIRTY-THREE

VIOLET APPROACHED the entrance of Dr. Cohen's office building on the corner of East 83rd and Park Avenue. She looked like a 1950s Hitchcock character with dark sunglasses and a floral scarf wrapped around her head that matched her blue blouse, flowing white skirt, and burgundy Jimmy Choo heels.

The exterior signage had been replaced with an expensive gold-embossed sign that read: IVY LEAGUE DAYCARE ACADEMY.

As she entered the building, the smell of paint and plastic whacked her senses like a bat cracking a speedball.

She knocked on Dr. Cohen's door, now labeled ADMIN-ISTRATIVE OFFICE.

Dr. Cohen meekly answered, holding a small cardboard box filled with memorabilia. "Violet?" His thick Jewish accent was stronger than ever. "How wonderful to see you!"

"I'm glad you're still here."

He opened the door wider. "I was just gathering a few items before I leave. Please come inside."

Violet noticed the room had been completely transformed from the drab, outdated, '70s psychiatrist office into a Candy Land board game acid trip. "I wasn't sure if you left already."

"I'm leaving tonight." He exhaled loudly. "But I'm very glad you came by." His eyes were as warm as a crackling fireplace.

Violet motioned to sit at one of the four new red desks in the room.

Dr. Cohen stopped her. "I'm not sure that's prudent. They don't know I'm here."

Violet awkwardly stood back up. "I just came over to say goodbye. And to thank you for all you've done."

Dr. Cohen bowed his head humbly. "That's very sweet, Violet. I will always worry about you." He reached out and gave her a hug.

Violet fought back tears as she held his frail, decrepit body in her arms.

Dr. Cohen released Violet, holding her in front of him like a grandfather inspecting his first grandchild. "How are you feeling these days? Is your eating schedule still working as planned?"

"I haven't binged in almost a year. Thank you for asking."

Dr. Cohen smiled like a proud parent. "And your situation with Ram? Do you think you'll be able to move on from that as well?"

Violet faked a happy face. "Yes, I'm making progress every day."

"Good, I'm very pleased to hear it," he said as he kissed her forehead. "The hardest lesson for humans to learn is that we must let other people live their own lives, take their own paths, and make their own mistakes."

Violet nodded as he spoke, scanning the room one last time, noticing how much larger it looked with primary colors throughout.

Dr. Cohen's eyes saddened. "You know how to reach me, Violet, so if you should need anything at all, please find me. I only want the best for you."

"Thank you, Dr. Cohen," she said as she hugged him again tightly. "Good luck with your trip. Stay well."

"You too."

Violet cried both happy and sad tears. Saying goodbye to the one and only man who stood by her side since childhood was utterly overwhelming. She quickly released him from her grip, turned, and prepared to exit.

On the way out, she noticed a beat-up brown leather suit-case sitting behind the front door. It was the same suitcase her father owned years ago. The one she gave Dr. Cohen for his birthday when she was twelve as a way to keep her father's memory alive.

"You still have the suitcase I gave you?" she said, halfway out the door.

"Why yes, it's my favorite."

Tears ran down Violet's face. "That's amazing," she said while leaving.

Dr. Cohen followed her out into the empty hallway. His tone became more serious. "You were right about Hell, Violet."

She turned around. "Excuse me?"

He caught up with her. "Do you remember the first time you came back for therapy? You asked me if I believed in Hell."

"Yes, what about it?"

Dr. Cohen adjusted his glasses as if he were about to say the most important thing anyone has ever said in the history of psychiatry. "You said Hell wasn't a place or a destination, but an energy force. An evil force that lives around us, beside us, *inside of us.*"

Violet wasn't sure where he was heading. "Yes. I remember saying something along those lines."

"Well, you were right. There is no Hell outside of the one on this Earth. We make our own hell *within us.*" His eyes deepened with wisdom. "So please keep this in mind as you make your final decisions."

Dr. Cohen looked at Violet as if he knew her deepest and darkest secrets, which made her nervous. As a young girl, she always suspected he could read her thoughts. "Thank you. I'll keep that in mind," she said faintly as she pushed open the building door.

"Good."

Dr. Cohen smiled wide as Violet left, waving goodbye as she walked onto the sidewalk. As soon as he closed the door, she noticed a young tree near the front entrance with a small plaque beneath it. It was covered with freshly fallen leaves from the tree.

She knelt down and brushed away the foliage to reveal a gold plaque that read:

IN LOVING MEMORY OF
SIMON L. COHEN, M.D.
March 26, 1930 - April 19, 2018

A final tear fell down Violet's cheek as she stood up. She reached into her bag, replaced her dark sunglasses on her face, and headed into the CVS pharmacy one block west.

THIRTY-FOUR

ANGELO'S BARBERSHOP pumped Reggaeton music in the Latino neighborhood of East Harlem, located forty blocks north of the Ramspeck home. It was a fun and festive Saturday morning tradition, with dozens of young men in white tank tops lined up outside—like Roman senators visiting a public bath—to discuss politics, sports, and women, all under the guise of a haircut and a beard trim.

Rosa and Octavia could faintly hear the music from their IHOP restaurant booth located on the corner of Lexington Avenue and East 126th Street. Rosa wiped away a small stain of triple-sugar black coffee from the chest of her velour sweatsuit, while Octavia looked on wearing a new cashmere sweater with jeans.

A young Hispanic waitress approached with two plates of breakfast. "Here you go. Do you need hot sauce for your eggs?" she asked Rosa in Spanish.

"I'm good. You?"

Octavia shook her head. "I'm fine."

The waitress waved her hand. "Just flag me down if you change your mind."

Rosa dug into her western omelet as Octavia's eyes followed the waitress until she disappeared.

Octavia slapped her hands on the table. "Thank you so much, Rosa. You have no idea how much I prayed about it." She looked at the packed duffle bag by her feet. "There's no way I could go back to that house."

Rosa tore a piece of toast with her teeth, like a bull tearing the tights off a matador. "I wasn't going to throw your things in the garbage," she said after swallowing the piece whole. "It was the right thing to do."

Octavia smiled as she took a bite of her strawberry pancakes. "Oh, I received my one year's pay in the bank yesterday. What do you call it again?"

"Severance pay," replied Rosa in English.

"Yes, that's it. I really needed that money. Thank you so much."

Rosa eyed Octavia's expensive cashmere sweater. "It's nothing," she said, sipping her coffee. "So what do you think? Do you want your old job back or not?"

Octavia furrowed her thin, painted brows. "Are you sure he's not selling the home now?"

"I'm positive. He called me last night and said we can have our old jobs starting on the 15th of September. We can keep the money he already gave us too. Which is very nice of him."

Octavia sucked a piece of strawberry. "Are you going back?"

Rosa nodded her head while chewing. "I'm going to visit my son in Ponce for ten days before I move back in."

Octavia looked at the group of teenagers, who were being loud at the breakfast bar. "Mr. Ramspeck is such a nice man, but *her*?"

Rosa puckered her lips. "The wife's not coming back. She's too angry."

"Did Mr. Ramspeck say so?"

"He told me she's definitely moving out, maybe to Florida. But hey, things can change at any time with a divorce. She can always move back in. That's the risk we take."

"I know." Octavia sipped her orange juice. "What's sad is that the pay is really good. And Mr. Ramspeck is a very sweet man. But the devil lives inside his bedroom."

Rosa rolled her eyes. "Again with the doll."

"Is it gone yet?"

Rosa huffed. "Mr. Ramspeck said all of Violet's things are still there."

Octavia reached her hand across the table. "Rosa, I'm not lying to you. The doll didn't just say my name, it actually *spoke to me*. And I think it had something to do with that real estate lady falling off the balcony."

Rosa gave a sarcastic look. "If it's so powerful, how come it has never talked to me? I've cleaned that bedroom a thousand times."

Octavia shrugged her shoulders. "I don't know. Maybe it's scared of you. You're much scarier than me."

Rosa drank her coffee, ignoring the veiled insult. "What did the doll tell you, *exactly*? Tell me the truth."

"No, I'm too afraid to repeat it." Octavia took one last bite of her pancakes and reached into her denim shoulder bag. "I've made up my mind." She pulled out a set of keys and placed it in front of Rosa's plate. "I'm not going back to that crazy house. Please tell Mr. Ramspeck I appreciate his offer, but I'm going to accept the job with the Horowitz family in Bridgehampton instead."

Rosa chewed another piece of toast. "So you're willing to make less money because of a doll?"

Octavia placed a twenty-dollar bill on the table, and stood up, leaving her half-eaten stack of pancakes on the plate. "Thank you again, Rosa. You were a fantastic boss."

"Come on, Octavia, at least finish your breakfast. You don't have to leave."

Octavia shook as she grabbed the stuffed duffle bag, fighting the urge to run. "All I can tell you, is be careful in the basement. Don't ever go in there alone. It's too dangerous."

Rosa stopped eating. She rolled back her shoulders, giving Octavia her full attention. "Is that what the doll told you?"

"No."

"Then what did it say, Octavia? This game is getting old."

Octavia slung her bag over her shoulder and quickly sat back down on the edge of the seat. "That day, when it talked to me? It was like what, the day before that lady died?"

"Yes, I remember."

"Well, I was on my way to Mrs. Ramspeck's closet to hang a few dresses I picked up at the dry cleaners, and when I walked past the dressing area, I heard somebody whisper my name."

"Did you recognize who it was?"

"No. It was a little girl's voice."

"Go on."

"So when I turned my head to see who it was, there was nobody there. Only the dolls."

"And then?"

"I moved back toward the closet and I heard my name again, but this time, I could tell for sure it was coming from one of the dolls."

"I'm surprised you didn't run away."

"Oh, I wanted to, but I couldn't. It was like I was being pulled by a tractor beam against my will. Whatever it was that came over me, I walked closer and closer to the dolls, until the big, blonde one in the middle started smiling at me." Octavia's hands were trembling as she spoke. "It's impossible for her porcelain face to smile—her mouth is painted on."

Rosa saw the fear in Octavia's eyes. She was beginning to believe her. "Then what happened?"

"As I got closer, my heart was pounding through my throat because I've never been so scared in my life . . . Then, when I was right in front of the doll, her mouth didn't open, but there was a voice inside her." Octavia bit her lip. "She spoke to me in English."

"This could be important, Octavia. What did she tell you?"

Octavia rolled her neck, debating whether or not to trust Rosa with information that could forever label her a troublemaker. Finally, she gave in.

"The doll said in a child's voice, *'Please help me. I'm buried in the basement.'*"

The hair on the back of Rosa's neck stood on edge.

Octavia's brown eyes were as wide as plates. "And then it *winked* at me!"

Rosa crossed herself like a good Catholic. "Jesus Christ. The devil's child."

"That's what I've been saying!" Octavia grabbed Rosa's arm. "Please don't tell Mr. Ramspeck what I told you. I don't want him to give me a bad reference."

Rosa took the warning seriously. Upper East Side women were especially paranoid of Latina housekeepers practicing Voodoo, Santeria, or Candomblé in their homes. This was the kind of thing that could end a housekeeper's career as soon as word got out. "I promise, I won't tell a soul. Your secret is safe with me."

Octavia was relieved. "Thank you so much, Rosa. You have no idea how glad I am to hear you say that." She released her arm and stood back up. "Just be careful. Stay away from that doll, and never go down to the basement. Will you promise me?"

Rosa nodded her head. "Trust me, I'll never go down there again. I'll tell Mr. Ramspeck we saw rats in the pantry."

"Good." Octavia bent down to give Rosa an awkward hug. "Be safe. And God bless."

"You too."

Octavia walked away and left the restaurant.

Rosa looked outside the window and watched Octavia walk along the sidewalk . . . Finally, the tension began releasing from her body . . . Holding tight to her secret, that the doll told her *the exact same thing* the night before she moved out of the Ramspeck home.

THIRTY-FIVE

AS SOON AS Violet left the basement, Allegra took five deep breaths and counted to twenty.

She waited patiently for the whirring sound of the door lock resetting itself to stop. She removed her blue wig—revealing a horrifying head of red fuzz alternating with oozing brown scabs—threw her ruse of reading *Oprah* magazine to the side, and resumed her escape training regimen of a hundred push-ups and multiple sprints up the stairs, three times a day.

After she was finished, she was extremely winded. Completely exhausted. No longer able to combat the fatigue of pregnancy and lack of nutrition, recognizing the day she needed to act would come sooner than she was ready for. Luckily, she had enough water in the big blue survival barrels to stay alive a good six months—unsure if it had an expiration date and unwilling to find out if it did. She had gained at least fifteen extra pounds, ready to withstand the potential starvation if her escape did not go as planned, ready to gamble and weather the next thirty days in extreme conditions, unless she could find a can opener or knife that would open the tinned foods mocking her in the steel cabinets.

Allegra was both mentally and physically determined to stay in the basement until someone—*anyone*—would come to her rescue.

That very second, Allegra decided tomorrow morning would be *the day*. The day, like so many others before it, when Violet would unsuspectingly sneak into the basement to give Allegra fresh clothes and obnoxious smoothie while she slept. But this time, Violet's jugular vein would meet the sharp, three-inch blade of the #22 scalpel she had forgotten in the first aid/surgical kit beneath the bathroom sink.

Yes, tomorrow was going to be the end of Allegra's imprisonment. No matter how risky. No matter what the outcome. Either way, she would be free of Violet *forever*.

The cornflower blue nightgown stuck to Allegra's growing body, soaked with sweat from working out. She quickly removed it, placing it on the back of a dining room chair, hoping it would dry before Violet's return later that evening. She took the long, clunky, white nightgown from the folded stack on the table, placing it over her head and onto her body, deciding to save the short, pink nightie for her big run the following day.

Post workout, Allegra downed the rest of the obnoxious smoothie. By now, she was immune to the mysterious, sour taste she was never able to properly identify, caring very little about its ingredients, considering it had not killed her the fifty or so times she had drunk it before.

As Allegra moved away from the dining room table, her limbs became weak; her eyelids became heavy. Although she had only been up two hours, she walked back to the bed, searched for the scalpel hidden between the mattress and box spring, placed it under her pillow, and dozed off for a mid-morning nap.

As soon as she closed her eyes, she began to dream. Her unconscious mind, finally relaxed enough to confess, released the vivid memory of the week leading up to her capture . . . Including the unspeakable fight with Ram that ended with the biggest surprise of her life.

THIRTY-SIX

"HELP, BABE! There's *a roach* on the pillow!"

Allegra screeched as she jumped out of bed with only a dingy white sheet covering her glistening, satisfied body at The Hotel Carlson—a one-star theater district dump widely known for its transient clientele and random disappearances of young back-packing foreigners recruited into the underground sex trade.

"Ram! Help! It's gross!"

Ram shut the water off to his weak-pressure shower. "Kill it yourself," he said from the tiny bathroom a few yards away. "It's only a bug."

Allegra watched the arrogant pest sashay across the pillow like a model on a catwalk. "You're fucking crazy! *You* kill it!" she screamed back.

Ram stepped out of the shower, wrapped a towel around his chiseled waist, and marched into the damp room he had occupied for the last two hours. He snatched a heavy *Guest Services* book from the nightstand and squashed the foreboding insect in one hit—splattering its brown furry legs on the pillow, where Allegra's head lain seconds before.

"There. It's done," said Ram in a deep, ominous tone. He threw the book on the floor and walked back into the bathroom.

Allegra took notice. Her stomach flipped in fear as he marched past her without making eye contact.

Tonight was a total disaster.

It was meant to be a private celebration the day before Ram left for a month-long trip to Asia to close two mergers that would double his net worth.

But instead, it was a catastrophe.

Allegra thought their weekly Thursday evening rendezvous would be the perfect opportunity to share her big surprise. The surprise she learned about the day before, when her late period and a pee stick changed her life in an instant. She was so happy she wanted to call Ram immediately, but chose to wait to make the exciting announcement in person, as they were making love.

Probably not the best timing, she thought to herself. The words "I'm pregnant" exploded from her lungs as Ram made love to her from above. He continued until he climaxed, but was unusually silent. Solemn. As far from 'bursting with joy' as any father could be.

He's too stressed to think about having a baby and having to explain the situation to his wife, she rationalized. *Bad timing. That's all this is.*

While Ram brushed his teeth, Allegra threw on a green St. Patrick's Day T-shirt and light blue denim jeans, purposefully leaving off her uncomfortable bra and thong panty, too sore and tired after cumming three times to move another inch.

Once again, Ram entered the bedroom, but this time he was naked. He quickly stepped into his blue underwear as if an imaginary fire alarm rang outside.

Allegra began to worry. "I take it you're not happy about the baby."

Ram turned and gave a cold look. "What married man *would* be?" He reached for his black dress pants, hastening his speed.

Allegra knelt on the corner of the bed, watching him dress. "I know it's shocking. Trust me, I totally freaked out yesterday too, but this is something we should celebrate." She gently touched his forearm. "You should be really excited about being a father for the first time!"

Ram was offended. "I *was* a father, Allegra. Get off my back." He jerked his arm out of her grip.

Allegra was embarrassed. She had forgotten about his adopted daughter, Briar Rose. She quietly begged God to change his attitude. "Look. We don't have to tell anyone right away. The baby's not due until next April. That'll give us plenty of time—"

"There will be *no baby.*"

Allegra was stunned. "What?"

"I want you to terminate the pregnancy while I'm away. There's a clinic on East 70th Street. Use my credit card."

Allegra's face crumbled.

"And don't wait until the last minute. The earlier you do it, the better for your body."

She was heartbroken. "You want me to go to an abortion clinic? I can't believe you're saying this!" Her voice grew louder. "I thought you *loved* me!"

Ram forcefully grabbed her shoulders.

"Ouch, you're hurting me—"

"I do love you, Allegra, but we're *not* having a baby!" He let her go. He clutched his white dress shirt from the floor and snaked his long, bulky arms through the sleeves.

Tears streamed down Allegra's face. Her mascara ran as far as her lips. "You can't do this to me, Ram. You just can't!"

"No, Allegra, *you* can't do this *to me*! I'm the one who has everything to lose here, not you! You lied about being on the pill. It's your lie. It's your problem!"

Allegra cowered as he screamed at her. She had never seen him angry before. And with his large stature and loud, deep voice, he was as scary as a blackout in a horror movie.

"But *I was* on the pill," she said meekly. Her statement was true. But what she failed to add was that she often forgot to take it. "I didn't lie to you."

Ram finished buttoning his shirt. "We can't have a baby together. At least not now."

Allegra sniffled. "If not now, then *when*?"

"I don't know, Allegra! Just not now!" His negative energy sent mutant shock waves that bounced off the peeling gray wallpaper.

Allegra felt like she had been run over by a bus. The man she adored, the man who treated her like gold, was now as cold as a cadaver because she was carrying *his life* inside her.

Allegra's anger soon outweighed hurt feelings.

She flipped her hair, pissed off at his reaction. "Fine. I'll just tell your wife I'm pregnant. See how she likes it."

Ram's blue eyes grew large. "What did you just say?" His enormous, menacing frame approached Allegra.

"That's what you're afraid of, isn't it? Can't go out tonight because of Violet. Can't call me back because of Violet. Can't text me for a week because I'm on vacation with Violet," she said in a whiny, child-like voice. "Well, I say *fuck Violet!* I'm having this baby, and there's nothing either of you can do about it!"

Ram's hot breath turned into a storm. "Don't you ever threaten me again, Allegra. Or this will all be over!"

"Fine! Let it be over!" She grabbed her black Tom Ford purse from the dirty gray carpet. "Have a nice flight to Beijing. Or Tokyo. Or whatever country you're ass-kissing next, asshole!"

Allegra stormed out sobbing, slamming the door.

Ram threw his briefcase across the room, leaving a deep dent in the wall.

The next afternoon, Allegra lay in bed crying, writing baby names in her red journal, hoping the act would bring about a more positive outcome from the Universe.

As she wrote, she carefully monitored her iPhone on the nightstand. She knew Ram's private flight was scheduled to leave at five o'clock that evening.

She checked her phone every ten minutes to see if Ram had texted or called.

He had not.

"Are you okay?" asked Chloe as she peeked her head into Allegra's bedroom. "Shouldn't you be at work?"

Scared to death Ram would sue her for divulging information about their relationship, she decided to withhold the truth. "I called in sick. I have the flu."

"That's a bummer, I hope you feel better. Look, I'll be working on my eBay stuff in the living room, so holler if you need anything."

Allegra's face was red and swollen. "Thanks, I will."

Two days later, Allegra sat alone on the sofa, eating Cheese-Its and mourning the loss of the one and only man she ever loved. She attempted calling him a hundred times, always chickening out at the last minute, demanding in her head that he needed to call her first, apologize, and beg her back.

She spent the last twenty hours binge-watching *House of Cards*, resonating with the recurring scene of actors Kevin

Spacey and Robin Wright sitting by an open window, sharing a single cigarette as their married characters conspired to take over the world.

It was then she realized she was throwing away the greatest opportunity of her lifetime: The opportunity to rocket out of generational poverty by raising a blue-blooded baby with a child support payment that could support her entire family in New Mexico.

She wiped her drizzling, runny nose and gathered the courage to dial Ram, knowing it was late morning in Beijing.

The phone rang four times before he picked up.

"What is it?" Ram's voice was cold and impersonal on the other side. He walked along a busy sidewalk, towering over the crowd of shorter, dark-haired citizens rushing to work.

"Hey, babe. It's me."

Ram was silent for five seconds. "What do you want?"

"I want to tell you that I love you. And that I love this baby whether you do or not."

Ram's eyes shifted. He was more concerned with arriving at his meeting on time. "Okay?"

"I also called to remind you that you can make, like, a totally different choice, you know?"

Ram accidentally stepped on an Asian teen's foot. "Sorry." He continued walking with purpose. "Meaning what?"

Allegra bit her nail on the sofa. "You can always divorce Violet and marry me."

Ram was silent. "Allegra, I just want things to go back the way they were."

Allegra's pea-green eyes darkened. "So, no matter what I do, you're not going to accept this baby. Are you?"

Ram fluttered his lips. "Look, Allegra, I'm not good with kids. I've lived fifty-three years of my life without having any of my own, and quite frankly, I've never regretted a moment of it."

"So, that's why?"

"Yes, and the fact that I'm an only child, and my ninety-six-year-old father has a clause in his will that I will be excluded if I ever father a child out of wedlock."

Allegra squeezed her eyes in pain. His words cut her like rusted razor blades. "So, I guess this is it between us?" She secretly prayed his answer would be *no*.

Ram softened. "It doesn't have to be the end, Allegra. It's up to you."

She sat straight up on the sofa. "So, what you're saying is that if I get an abortion, you still want me, but if I keep the baby, you're dumping me?"

Ram's voice fainted to a whisper. "I'm afraid so."

Allegra could not believe her ears.

Her lips suddenly foamed like a wild banshee. "Well, rot in hell, asshole, because I'm going to tell the entire world about our affair! I'm gonna tell your wife and post online what a deadbeat dad you are, refusing to man up and take responsibility for your own child—"

"Allegra, calm down—"

"No! I will not calm down! I've heard of big shot dicks like you before, but I never imagined *you* were one of them!"

"Allegra! Don't end it like this—"

"Fuck you! I hope you enjoy your trip because your *whole fucking life* will be fucked when you get back on Labor Day!"

Allegra hung up. Her bloated face fell into her hands, sobbing hysterically.

Ram held the silent phone to his ear, stunned.

He looked both ways, then crossed a busy street filled with cars, bicycles, and pedestrians.

When he reached the other corner, he called her back.

Allegra wiped away tears and gathered herself before answering. "What do you want, deadbeat?"

"Are you serious about telling my wife?"

Allegra hesitated. "Yes, why?"

"Can you at least have the decency to give me the chance to tell her first? After all I've done for you, I at least deserve that."

Allegra pursed her lips. "Why should I be merciful? You're dumping a pregnant woman."

"Because she's an innocent victim in all of this. I should be the one to break the news, not you. But I need time. I'm scheduled in back-to-back meetings until Sunday."

Allegra relished the moment. For the first time in their relationship, she was the one with leverage. "Okay. You've got until Monday morning, my time, to tell her. Otherwise, I'm knocking on your front door and spilling the beans myself."

"Thank you. I'll address this with Violet as soon as I can." Ram's voice was oddly humble. "Take care, Allegra. I'm sorry it has to be this way."

Allegra was devastated. "Take care, babe."

Ram ended the call.

After being cocooned for a week, Allegra finally felt physically well enough to exercise. The women in her family had a tendency to gain as much as eighty pounds during pregnancy, instantly making Allegra paranoid about her swelling thighs—ready to combat the anticipated weight gain head on.

It had been two full days since she last spoke to Ram, yet somehow, she was still optimistic he would eventually come to his senses. Convinced his love for her would outweigh reason. Outweigh the displeasure of divorce. And outweigh the reduction of his hard-earned fortune by half.

Allegra believed that once Ram saw their newborn baby for the first time, he would leave his wife and choose his new family over his barren past.

It was almost five thirty in the evening. She was already thirty minutes late for her most lucrative weeknight shift at Bobby & Eddie's bar. She had missed nearly a week of work, but with more than twenty thousand dollars in savings from Ram's pretend job, she was hardly worried about getting fired or finding a new gig.

Chloe practiced lines for an upcoming audition in the living room as Allegra dressed in her bedroom. She changed from her lazy housedress into two sports bras, black bike shorts, and a black, fitted tank top. As she sat on the edge of the bed lacing up a pair of crazy-colored running shoes, her iPhone rang. The screen name was UNKNOWN CALLER.

Something inside Allegra urged her to pick it up. "Hello?"

"Allegra, it's Ram."

She flew backwards into an upright position on the bed. "Ram? Where are you calling me from? My phone didn't show your name."

"It's a new number. Where are you?"

"I'm at my apartment. Why?"

Ram sighed relief. "Great. What are you doing this very second?"

Allegra was confused. "I was just about to go running in Carl Schurz Park. Why?"

"Come outside. *Now.*"

A smile slowly grew on Allegra's face. Perhaps her prayers came true. Perhaps there was an expensive apology present waiting for her outside. "Okay?"

"Come outside your building now." Ram hung up.

Allegra beamed. She grabbed her phone, armband, and house keys. She pranced toward the front door.

Chloe noticed. "Hey, you look a million times better."

Allegra was giddy. "I just got some great news, that's all."

"Where you off to?"

"I'm heading to the park for a run. I'll be back in an hour." Chloe was indifferent. "Cool. I'm going out with Raven tonight, so don't stay up late."

Allegra pulled open the front door. "No worries. Have a good time!"

She jogged down the five flights of stairs, passed the wall of metal mailboxes, and battered through the building door.

Ram was standing outside at the end of the external staircase, dressed casually in a plain blue T-shirt and jeans. He stood next to a running yellow cab, holding a dozen red and white roses in one hand, and a small black box in the other.

Allegra was overwhelmed with happiness. She pinched her thigh, praying this wasn't a dream. As she walked closer, he opened the Tiffany & Co. box and dropped to one knee.

Inside the box was a gleaming, four-and-a-half carat cushion-cut solitaire.

"Allegra Renee Adams. Will you marry me?"

Allegra almost fainted. She touched her chest, unable to breathe from joy. "Oh my God, Ram! *Yes!*"

His eyes were void of emotion. "Please forgive me for being such an asshole."

"I do! I forgive you!" Allegra threw her arms around him.

Ram adjusted his glasses. "I told Violet everything. I asked her for a divorce, and she agreed."

Allegra squeezed Ram tighter as she seized the ring and placed it on her finger.

She stared at the beat-up yellow taxi and the Sikh driver who was ignoring their moment. "Where's the limo? And Eric?"

Ram tilted his head. "I wanted this to be a surprise." He smiled. "Let's go."

"Wait. I'm not dressed right." She turned to go back into the building. "I need to get my purse—"

"No, no, you're fine the way you are. Come on. We'll be back in an hour or two."

"Where are we going?"

"You'll see."

Allegra smiled, knowing Ram's surprises were the best in the world.

He opened the back door of the cab. "After you."

Allegra angled in, scooting as far as she could, making room for Ram beside her. There was an open, black bottle of Freixenet Cordon Negro in a plastic ice bucket with one plastic champagne glass on the torn leather seat.

"Second stop?" asked the driver. His white turban was as tall as the headliner.

Ram placed his hand on Allegra's thigh as she gazed at her engagement ring from every angle.

"The corner of Fifth and Seventy-eighth."

Allegra looked at the label as she poured herself a glass of champagne, completely forgetting that a pregnant woman should abstain from drinking alcohol. Instead, she was busy wondering why Ram bought a twelve-dollar bottle for such a special occasion.

"Where's your glass?" she asked.

"I'm not drinking tonight. Too much paperwork later."

Allegra shrugged one shoulder.

She looked out the cab window while she drank the golden bubbles . . .

Toasting herself for convincing the man she loved to choose *her*.

THIRTY-SEVEN

ALLEGRA'S EYES sprang open.

She was lying facedown, with her face buried in the ivory pillow. *I never made it to the park*, she thought in revelation. She looked at her left hand with four fingers and one scabbed stump. *Where's my fucking ring?*

Violet must have it.

Allegra rolled over. Her eyes blinked at the harsh fluorescent lights in the ceiling. She then sat up, startled to see Violet sitting at the table, quietly watching her sleep.

"I didn't know you were here," said Allegra.

Violet said nothing.

Instead, she slowly reached for the shining metal cleaver on the table. She extended her left wrist as she gently swung the meat cleaver across it, slicing down, barely scratching the skin. She repeated the move, this time, slicing up. She repeated the motion again, slicing up, slicing down—like an enthusiastic violinist—over and over, scratching only the surface of her skin, drawing minimal blood, as if practicing for the real performance.

Allegra panicked. *Mad Violet has lost it.*

Violet remained silent . . . casting an evil smile as she practiced slicing her wrist.

Allegra broke the stillness. "Violet, what are you doing?"

Violet stopped and looked up. The spots where her amber eyes once lived were now cavernous holes. She resumed swinging the shining cleaver above her wrist, shooting flashes of light as it reflected the bulbs from above. It was moving and swaying, deeper and deeper, like a pendulum inching closer and closer to slashing her wrist wide open.

Allegra was baffled. She spotted a CVS pharmacy bag and a Clearblue Digital Pregnancy Test Kit sitting on the table beside Violet.

Shit.

Allegra clandestinely reached under her pillow and placed the scalpel in her long sleeve. She rose from the bed, moving in slow motion, like a worried camper afraid to startle a bear.

Violet's eyes fixated on her wrist while she spoke. Her voice was high, like a young girl. "You remind me of one of my most favorite Grimms Brothers fairy tales as a child," she said, while carving hundreds of thin red lines into her skin.

Allegra was too frightened to answer.

Violet stopped and made eye contact, placing the meat cleaver in her lap. "It's called 'How Some Children Played At Slaughtering.' Have you heard it before?"

Allegra grasped the scalpel tighter, hiding it behind her hip. "No. I haven't." Just by the title, Allegra knew something terrible was about to happen.

Violet transferred the cleaver from her right to left hand, now practicing the pendulum slicing motion on her right wrist. "Well, let me share it with you . . ." She cleared her throat, returning to her normal, adult voice.

"There once was a farmer who had a beautiful wife and three sons. One day he needed to kill one of his pigs for supper. So, early that morning, he slaughtered a pig in the barn as his two eldest sons sat on a haystack and watched him. He sliced the pink creature's throat ear to ear." Violet motioned the meat cleaver across her neck. "And watched it run around in circles until it bled out and died.

"Later that afternoon, while their father was out plowing the fields, the children decided to play farmer and animal. The eldest son said to the other, 'You be the little pig, and I'll be the farmer.' He then took the shiny knife his father had left, and slit his little brother's throat from one side to the other.

"Their mother was upstairs, bathing the youngest child in the house. When she heard the cries of her dying son, she immediately ran downstairs and into the barn. Upon seeing what had happened, she took the knife out of her son's throat and was so enraged she stabbed the heart of the child who had killed him. She then quickly ran back into the house to tend to the child she left in the bathtub. But while she had been gone, the baby slipped under the water and drowned.

Now, the woman became so desperate after losing all three of her children, she went back into the barn, found a horse rope, and hanged herself from the rafters.

"When her husband came back from plowing the fields and saw his entire family had perished, he became so despondent, he fell to the ground and died of a broken heart."

Violet grasped the meat cleaver in her hand. "The end." She slowly lifted herself from the chair and approached Allegra, who was standing at the side of the bed.

Allegra held the scalpel tightly as she approached. "I don't get it?" Her plan was to keep talking to Violet as a distraction.

Violet came closer. "You don't understand the moral of the story?"

Sweat rolled from Allegra's patchy red and brown scalp. "No, please tell me what it means."

Violet stopped a foot in front of Allegra. Her amber eyes glowed with insanity as she held the cleaver to the side of her white, flowing skirt. "The moral of the story is that even one thoughtless, selfish, bad decision has a domino effect . . . Until everyone in the story *dies.*"

She swung the meat cleaver at Allegra's shoulder.

Allegra ducked out of the way.

She swung it again, missing Allegra's head by an inch.

Allegra popped up, and drove the scalpel deep into Violet's forearm, slicing it vertically.

Violet dropped the meat cleaver. "You stupid bitch!" She grasped her bleeding arm. "Look at what you've done!"

Blood trickled through Violet's fingers as she squeezed her wound tightly.

Allegra picked up the meat cleaver from the floor, and threw it far into the corner, out of reach. She grabbed Violet by the hair, turned her around, and placed the scalpel blade against her jugular vein. "You're walking me out of this house *now!*"

Violet threw her elbow into Allegra's stomach. "Go to hell!"

Allegra yanked Violet's hair as she absorbed the impact. "Do that again, and I will cut your throat!" She dug the scalpel deeper into Violet's neck. "Walk me up the fucking stairs! *Now!*"

Petite, starving Violet was no match for Allegra's strength and determination to be free. She tried to wiggle out of Allegra's choke hold, unable to move without the blade sinking deeper into her neck. "You can't leave, Allegra. It's too late."

Allegra screamed as she jerked Violet's head backwards, ripping handfuls of copper hair into her fist. "Fucking walk!"

Violet complied.

Allegra pushed Violet up the stairs, like a bank robber walking a hostage into the street. "Now punch in the code!"

Violet hesitated. "You're not getting out of here."

Allegra slapped the side of Violet's face with her free hand. "I'm done playing! Let's go!"

Violet reluctantly entered the numbers 0-3-1-5-2-0-0-7.

March 15, 2007. Allegra committed the date to memory in case her first escape attempt failed.

The familiar whirring sound of the door unlocking made Allegra's strength grow exponentially.

The light turned green.

They moved forward, as the first door closed behind them.

They stood in the dark corridor.

"Keep going!" yelled Allegra as she pushed Violet up the second set of stairs.

At the second door, Violet paused. "You can never leave this house, Allegra. They won't let you."

"*Who* won't let me? The fucked-up voices in your head?"

Violet's body went limp as she entered the numbers 0-5-1-6-1-9-9-4.

May 16, 1994. *Got it.* The door lock whirred. Allegra's body released a flood of endorphins at the sound of freedom. The light turned green. "Open it!" she commanded.

Violet opened the door.

Allegra was too eager to notice the blinding light of the junk food pantry, or that Violet's arm was bleeding all over the floor. "Keep going!"

They hurried through the kitchen, then the hallway, and through the foyer, until they reached the back of the front door.

It had an old-fashioned antique keyhole as well as two modern locks above it.

"You'll never leave," said Violet. "It's too late." She laughed.

"Fuck you! I'm going home!" Allegra threw Violet against the door twice, smashing her thin body and sculpted nose into the eyehole. She then threw her onto the ground, kicking her multiple times in the midsection as she screamed. "You—crazy—evil—bitch!"

Violet lay in the fetal position, laughing wickedly. "Go ahead. Leave. See what happens."

Allegra focused her attention on the door. She turned the knob, unable to move it. She then turned the top locks counterclockwise, and then clockwise, unable to hear the click of liberty she was dying for.

"No, no, no, no—"

"I told you. It's too late," said Violet from the floor.

Allegra yanked the gold knob with all her might, unable to comprehend why the door remained locked from the inside. "Please God! Let me out!"

Violet cackled like the evil queen from *Snow White*.

Allegra walked over to Violet, still curled and giggling on the ground. She kicked and kicked and kicked her in the face, until she stopped laughing.

Blood from Violet's broken nose ran on the teak wood floor.

Allegra turned and continued trying to open the door, crying in desperation to get out. "Why won't this open? Why!" She pounded her fist. "Help!" Her voice grew louder. "Call 9-1-1!"

Allegra pulled the knob harder.

Violet cast a demonic smile as she wobbled her way back up to her feet—enjoying the vision of Allegra's full body weight pulling the knob fruitlessly.

She hunched over. "Maybe you need a key, little girl."

Allegra turned around. "Give it to me."

Violet wiped the blood from her nose and smiled. "*Never.*"

Allegra held the scalpel high in the air. "Get me the key or I'll kill you right now."

Violet moved closer, still off balance from the beating. She closed one eye and leaned in, like a fearless madwoman ready to end the world. "It's too late, Allegra. *I won.*"

The movement of Allegra's long white sleeve gave Violet enough time to dash away as she swung the scalpel, grazing Violet's cheek.

Violet ran into the farthest corner of the kitchen and pulled out the largest Austof-Reed knife from the butcher block.

Goddammit. Allegra realized she had lost her advantage.

Violet held the knife by her lips. "Now, we can stand here and play sword fight, or you can go back down to your cell and take a pregnancy test for me . . . like a good little girl."

"Fuck you." Allegra flipped the scalpel in her hand.

Violet walked closer to the foyer. "I've already come this far, Allegra. What makes you think I won't go all the way?"

Allegra noticed the staircase was a ten-yard dash away. "Good luck, bitch." She sprinted toward it, skipping steps as she ran up the stairs in her long, cumbersome nightgown.

"You stupid whore!" Violet quickly removed her burgundy heels and ran up behind her, barefoot.

Allegra kept running, desperately trying to figure out where the lowest balcony was. She ran into the second-floor landing, looked at the workout room and laundry, and continued running up the stairs.

Violet was quick on her heels. "You can't win, Allegra! Let it go!"

Allegra continued scurrying. The only room she remembered the one time Ram brought her here was the master bedroom on the top floor. She remembered it had a large terrace.

But she could never survive the jump.

Allegra entered the third floor, running into the second guest bedroom, and hid under the bed.

Violet stopped at the third-floor landing. "Ah-leg-rah," she said in a singsong voice. "Where are you, little girl?"

Allegra readjusted her body under the bed, ready to cut Violet's Achilles tendon, take her down, and stab her heart with the scalpel.

Violet walked into the first guest bedroom, holding the stainless steel knife close to her chest. "Al-leg-rah . . . Come out, come out, wherever you are . . ."

She checked the closet. Nothing.

She continued searching the room, changing her voice to sound like a little girl. "But, Violet, what big ears you have?" She changed her voice to sound like a mean, old wolf. "The better to hear you with, my dear . . ."

She checked under the bed. Nothing.

"But, Violet, what big eyes you have?"

Allegra could hear Violet's madness in the adjoining room.

"The better to see you with, my dear . . ."

Violet walked into the hall, toward the second guest room, continuing her one-woman show. "But, Violet, what big teeth you have?"

Allegra swallowed as Violet entered the room.

"The better to eat you with, my dear!"

Allegra could see Violet's arthritic feet from her viewpoint. Her heart raced.

"I know you're in here, little girl. I can smell you . . ."

Allegra's breath halted.

"Because you smell like fear . . . And you *taste* like it too . . ."

Allegra held the scalpel in her hand as Violet walked closer and closer to the bed.

Violet cast a beastly smile. "I should know. Little girls like you taste *yummy*."

BAM!

The loud noise of the front door slamming shut reverberated throughout the house.

"Shit. Ram's home," whispered Violet in her normal voice.

Allegra was petrified. If she screamed for help, Violet would kill her before Ram could make it up the stairs.

Violet suddenly ran out of the room and locked the door.

As soon as she left, Allegra rolled from under the bed, rocketed to her feet, and pulled the knob. "No, no, no!" She pounded at the wooden door furiously. "Ram! Help! I'm in here!"

There wasn't a second to waste.

Allegra ran to the opposite side of the room, looked out the window, and saw the headlights of Ram's limo pull away from the curb in front of the house. She banged at the black cast-iron bars, screaming for help. "Eric! Eric! I'm up here! Help me!"

She looked at a small chair by the desk, then shook the bars again. Her heart pounded, knowing that even throwing the chair through the window would not help her escape.

Ram was her only hope.

She returned to the locked bedroom door—screaming, yelling, and screeching his name, pounding, beating, and clobbering the exit with all her strength.

"Ram! Ram! I'm up here! Help me!"

Allegra screamed for three full minutes, into exhaustion. She knew there had to be a better way.

She looked around the 18th-century decor, scanning for something she could use as a key to open the old-fashioned lock. A bobby pin? A nail? She prayed to God to give her a solution.

She closed her eyes and asked Him to lead the way.

Suddenly, it came to her: *The desk.*

She pulled out the top middle drawer, and found a large ornate black key.

Oh my God. Thank you.

She used the key to unlock the door, carefully opening it to see if Violet was close by.

She held the scalpel blade in front of her body as she approached the third-floor landing—ready to kill on sight.

Out of nowhere, she felt insecure. Scared to death of what Ram would think once he saw her scabby head, maimed hand, and monster thighs.

Then it dawned on her. *What if Violet kills him?*

Her memory flashed back to Violet saying the slaughter fairy tale was about bad decisions leading to a situation where *everybody dies.*

"No!" she whispered loudly.

The house was silent.

Allegra tiptoed down three flights of stairs, looking for signs of Ram and Violet on the first floor below.

They were nowhere to be found.

Allegra looked around the foyer. She saw seven Louis Vuitton suitcases parked by the front door, yet the blood Violet had dripped from her sliced wrist and broken nose had magically disappeared.

She tried to open the front door again, hoping Ram left it unlocked.

But it was still locked.

Think, Allegra. Think!

Exhausted and dying of thirst, she walked over to the refrigerator in the kitchen. She opened the door to see it was packed with fresh milk, six brownies, oranges, apples, meats, and new lettuce—fully stocked, as if Rosa had been there hours ago.

Allegra pulled out cranberry juice, drank it quickly, and carefully replaced the bottle without making a sound.

Where the fuck are they?

She continued creeping through the kitchen, to the pantry door, and opened it.

She looked inside and saw the heavy stainless steel door to the basement was wide open.

"Oh my God! They're in there," she said aloud, fearful for Ram's life.

Allegra walked through the open door, into the dark corridor, with the scalpel in hand, unsure of what she would find next.

She reached the second security door. It was closed.

She remembered the code. *March* 15, 2007.

As she entered the numbers into the keypad, her stomach did backflips.

Maybe I shouldn't. Something's wrong.

But she couldn't see another way out. Ram was her only hope.

Allegra pressed enter. The light above the keypad turned green.

She slowly opened the security door and quietly stepped onto the landing.

She carefully pulled the door shut to minimize the noise.

She looked below to the hellish prison she had spent the last twenty-two days in.

No one was there.

But the steel security door to the walk-in freezer was *wide open.*

Allegra quietly marched down the steps, holding the scalpel in one hand and the long hem of her nightgown in the other. "Ram?" she said meekly.

As she reached the bottom of the stairs, her heart battered through her chest, fearing the worst had already happened. "Ram? Is that you?"

She continued walking toward the freezer, looking back over her shoulder, scared Violet would sneak up and attack from behind. "Violet?"

No one was there.

Allegra took two more steps, peeking her head around the open door and into the walk-in freezer.

As she looked inside, she saw Ram removing a folded white letter from a frozen, dead woman's hands.

Allegra was *terrified.*

She peered closely at the frozen body, sitting in an upright position with her head leaning against the corner of the stainless steel room. Beneath the ice, she made out copper-red hair . . . A long, sequined evening gown . . . And small, frostbitten feet.

It was Violet's dead body.

"Boo!" whispered a voice behind Allegra as she jumped.

Violet smiled and laughed. "*Surprise!*"

Allegra began hyperventilating. "What? I-I don't understand—"

Violet's beaten face erupted in laughter. "I totally had you fooled, didn't I?"

Ram closed the freezer door with the letter in his hand.

Allegra turned to him, shocked. "Ram?"

"Oh, he can't hear you, little girl," said Violet, smiling.

Ram punched the code into the keypad of the walk-in refrigerator next door.

Allegra couldn't breathe. She couldn't process what was happening.

She ran over to Ram, grabbed his wide shoulders, and shook his back. "Ram, please! Help me!"

Violet laughed hysterically. "You really are stupid, aren't you?"

Ram opened the large steel door to the walk-in refrigerator.

The distinctively fruity, rotten smell of decaying human flesh burst through the entrance.

Ram gagged, covering his mouth with his dress shirt, as he entered the room.

Violet pinched her nose, remaining outside the door. "Pee-yew! You smell like shit!"

Allegra's face turned green. She held her breath, trying not to inhale the rancid odor as she followed Ram inside.

He spotted the huge burlap sack in the back of the chilly room.

Violet spoke nasally through her pinched nose. "Now here's the good part. Watch closely."

Allegra's eyes felt as if they were forced open with toothpicks, able to see everything he was doing.

Ram fought the urge to throw up from the stench, moving quickly to the back of the room. He bent down and carefully unraveled the rope cinching the top of the sack. He then pulled the sack down, revealing a sleeping woman's cinnamon-red hair, pale face, and slumped shoulders.

It was Allegra's dead body.

Allegra stared at the incomprehensible scene. *It can't be.* The scalpel fell from her hand, bouncing several times on the concrete floor.

Ram looked at the body's angelic, sleeping face with sadness in his eyes. He ran his finger along her hairline—kissed her cold, decaying forehead—rose to his feet, and left the room, *walking straight through Allegra* on his way out.

Allegra gasped, feeling a burning hot sensation as he stepped through her body.

Violet slapped her on the back. "Well, at least he gave us our own rooms."

Allegra turned around, incredulous. "Am I—?"

Violet nodded her head. "Finally. A girl remembers."

Ram went up the stairs, opened the security door, and left the basement.

Allegra zombie-walked in her long white nightgown to the dining room table. She pulled out a chair, sat down, and buried her head in her hands.

Violet followed behind, tossing her white flowing skirt like a flamenco dancer.

"I don't understand. I feel exactly the same way as I did before. I get hungry, I get tired, I feel pain—I feel *alive*."

"Me too."

Allegra pounded the table. "And why can you leave the house and I can't?"

Violet grinned. "It's because you never thought to walk *through* the door."

Allegra scratched her itchy head. "But you always used the codes?"

Violet waved her hand. "That was just for appearances. The longer you thought you were alive, the more information I could get."

Allegra sat back in the chair, blowing air from her lips. She was more interested in learning about her death than Violet's motives for keeping it a secret. "Why are we both still here? Aren't we supposed to go somewhere? I want to see my mother."

Violet raised her index finger. "Now *that* part I haven't figured out yet. I have no idea what comes next."

"Great." She placed her head back in her hands, squeezing her temples hard in frustration. "So, what are we supposed to do now?"

Violet rotated her palms. "I guess we wait for *something*." She shrugged her shoulders. "I have no idea."

Allegra slapped the top of her thighs. "Why can't I remember what happened?"

Violet crossed her arms. "It's probably from the drug he gave you."

"*He* gave me?" Her baby-doll eyes looked up. "I thought *you* were the one who did this to us?"

Violet placed her hands on her hips, contemplating telling Allegra about the night she was murdered. "Oh, what the hell. You already know how the story ends."

THIRTY-EIGHT

VIOLET PLUGGED her gold iPhone into the wall charger beside her.

She sat in a strapless bra and panties at her make-up vanity, putting the final touches to her dramatic red lipstick, false eyelashes, and extravagantly spiked hair. After two difficult weeks of witnessing Ram's mysterious mood swings and bizarre behavior, she was relieved to have a noble reason to get dolled up and spend quality time with her friends.

It was Thursday, August 9th, the night of the annual Upper East Side Autism Awareness Gala, for which she served as co-chair for the third year in a row. She had just spent the last two hours laughing with her professional glam squad—a married, transgender couple who specialize in hair and makeup—who had her in stitches about their thoughts on genderless bathrooms. Even though they had left fifteen minutes earlier, Violet still chuckled at their jokes spontaneously.

Now that she was ready from the neck up, she went into the dressing area, where a single item hung from a portable dress rack near the center of the room.

It was a sequined, royal blue, one-shouldered, floor-length Marchesa couture gown.

Violet was *in love* with that dress. Not only did it cost the same as a compact car, it was a miracle size 0. A size she hadn't been able to achieve for years. A size that was the blue ribbon prize for three weeks of starving.

She was even more thrilled when she learned the venue for the black-tie affair had been changed last minute from a private mansion in Sag Harbor to The Peninsula Hotel's *Salon de Ning* rooftop, located only twenty-three blocks away. Since Ram was out of the country, she preferred staying in the city, dreading having to suffer the three-hour limo drive to the Hamptons alone.

Violet walked over to her Little Red Riding Hood porcelain doll collection—as she often did—paying special attention to a different girl every time. She would ask them questions about their day, how they were feeling, and if they were happy living in her home. She imagined the little girls responding in different children's voices and accents:

Yes, Mommy.

No, Mumsy.

Si, Mama!

But tonight, Violet was in a rush, expected to arrive a full hour before the other guests to ensure the evening's events went smoothly. She slipped into her gown and grabbed a sky-high pair of silver crystal Christian Louboutin shoes from the closet.

She headed down the staircase barefoot, holding her shoes, unable to walk in heels down the steps due to her tight-fitting gown.

As she approached the first floor, she saw the front door lock turning.

A burglar?

No one she knew was expected home. Ram was in China. Octavia was tending to her sick mother in Honduras. And Rosa was staying the night with her daughter in the Bronx, as she had done every Wednesday and Thursday night for the past eleven years.

Violet was terrified. She held one of the heels as a weapon and hid in the library before the front door swung open.

"Holy shit, I can't believe you're taking me here again!" said Allegra loudly, laughing behind Ram as he entered the foyer. "You're so fucking ballsy."

"Why? This will all be yours soon."

What? Violet peeked her head around the corner and watched Ram and Allegra enter. She had known about the affair for over a month and had seen Allegra's pictures on Facebook, but this was the first time she heard her voice or laid eyes on her in person.

Allegra plopped the red and white roses into a vase with no water. She then held the empty black bottle of champagne in the air as she twirled around. "I don't know what's in this cheap shit, but I'm sure feeling it."

Ram grabbed and kissed her. "That's why I bought it."

Violet hid again, afraid Ram could see her.

Allegra sported a drunken expression. "Where is everybody?"

Violet peeked her head around the open archway, unseen. She spotted Ram oddly dressed in a blue T-shirt and jeans, and Allegra in her black workout clothes.

"Let's see." Ram placed his finger on his lip, pretending to think. "Everybody's gone."

Allegra laughed, almost falling over. "Where's the wife?"

Her question confirmed Violet's suspicion. *The whore knows he's married.*

Ram pulled Allegra by the arm toward the kitchen. "She's in the Hamptons tonight for a fundraiser."

Allegra began slurring her words. "Is that all she does? Goes to parties? Hey, wait. Do I have to go to parties too?" She stumbled over her own foot.

Violet's ears bled.

Allegra regained her balance. "Wait. Am I, like, totally slurring?"

Ram smiled wide. "No, darling, you're just drunk with happiness."

Allegra twirled again, dancing and looking at her huge engagement ring. "I can't believe we're getting married!"

Violet almost threw up at the sight of the shiny rock on Allegra's finger. She carefully placed her glittering shoes on the floor, and moved behind the staircase, following the illicit lovebirds like a Russian spy.

Ram and Allegra disappeared into the pantry.

Violet could still hear their voices.

"Where are you taking me?" asked Allegra. "And why aren't you drinking tonight?"

Ram easily pushed open the heavy door. "Like I said in the cab, I have a lot of paperwork to do tonight, darling. I'll catch up later."

He and Allegra disappeared into the basement.

Violet moved into the pantry, high on *catching him in the act* adrenaline. "This is it. Time to confront my husband," she whispered aloud.

She waited in the pantry for seven long minutes, giving them time to get naked, while fighting the temptation to rip open and gorge every bag of chips in the room until she felt numb.

When Violet was ready for the big showdown, she struggled to remember the code to the first security door.

Finally, she remembered it. *Right. Our wedding date.*

She plugged in the code and opened the door.

She walked down the steps, through the dark corridor, holding the hem of her gown to avoid tripping.

As she reached the second door, her heart fell. She remembered the eight-digit code like it was yesterday. *The day I lost Briar Rose.*

She drew a tremendous breath before entering the code and pushing the door open, bracing herself for what would be the second most heart-breaking scene of her life.

As soon as she stepped in, the grunting sounds of Ram making love to Allegra poisoned her ears.

She carefully closed the door, moving as quietly as possible.

As she descended the basement stairs, her eyes zoomed into the lower left-hand corner, where the bed was. At this vantage point, Violet could only see the top of Ram's bald head and broad shoulders, curious as to why he left his shirt on.

Ram's grunting voice became emotional as he spoke through each thrust. "This—hurts me—more—than having—to silence—my own daughter."

Violet felt as if she had been struck by lightning.

She ran down the remaining steps, flew around the corner and saw Ram—fully clothed—thrusting his hands into a pillow over Allegra's face.

"Ram!" she screamed. "What the hell are you doing?"

He jumped out of his skin and turned around. "Violet? I thought you were away?"

He slowly pulled his arms from the pillow . . .

While Allegra's naked torso and limbs beneath his body remained motionless.

Violet covered her face. "Jesus Christ! What have you done?"

Ram wiped sweat from the top of his head and chuckled. "I know this looks terrible, but—"

"What *did you say* about silencing our daughter?"

Ram squirmed in every direction, ignoring the question. "Look, Violet, I did this for us. She was planning to destroy our marriage."

"*Destroy our marriage?*" Violet walked closer to the bed. "Are you trying to kill Allegra?"

"You *know* her?"

"Yes, I know everything about her, you son of a bitch!" She tore at her hair. "You even bought her an engagement ring?"

Ram pulled the ring from Allegra's limp hand and held it in the air. "It's fake, Violet. I paid twenty bucks for it at the airport." He placed it in his front pocket.

Violet slapped her mouth in horror—this was premeditated murder in the first degree.

She started walking backwards.

Ram menacingly approached her. "Now, calm down, darling. It's not as bad as you think."

"But why did you kill our baby girl? She never did anything to you! She was innocent!"

Ram sighed as they locked eyes.

"Tell me! Why?"

Ram rolled his eyes. "Because I *hate* screaming babies, Violet. I need my sleep. You know that."

Violet's ankles went weak. She sank to the ground. "No, not Briar Rose."

"She wasn't even our blood, Violet! My parents refused to put her in the will. She would have been an outcast!"

Violet folded in child's pose on the floor, sobbing. "I knew it wasn't SIDS, I just knew it. My baby girl," she wailed. "*My baby girl!*"

Ram couldn't stand her grief. "Get up, Violet." He pulled her up by the arm.

"No, we need to help Allegra!" Violet broke from his grip and ran to the side of the bed.

She removed the ivory pillow covering Allegra's naked body. Her eyes were closed. Her mouth gaped open.

Allegra was no longer breathing.

She had passed out from the triple dose of Rohypnol—the mind-erasing date rape drug Ram had put in the champagne before she entered the taxi.

Violet touched Allegra's wrist.

Nothing.

"Oh my God, Ram! You *fucking killed* her!"

Ram motioned to calm her.

"What have you done to our perfect lives, Ram? *What have you done?*"

"I have a plan," he said calmly. "We'll move her to the freezer."

"What?"

"Yes. Since you and I are the only two people in the world who know the security codes, we'll move her to the freezer, and no one will ever find her for as long as we live."

"*What?* I can't believe you're even saying this!"

"Tomorrow we'll send out text messages from her phone, telling everyone she met some guy online and eloped to Mexico. I even know how to convince her roommate to ship her things to a foreign address. No one will ever tie her to me."

Violet was fossilized.

"No one will even suspect she's missing, Violet. She has no family. No friends. Nobody gives a shit about her. It's the perfect plan."

Violet reacted. "Have you lost your fucking mind? We *have* to call the police!"

Ram grabbed the back of his neck. "That's not what we're doing, Violet."

She wiped her face, smearing the red lipstick. "Yes, we're calling the police, Ram! And you're going to tell them about Allegra *and* Briar Rose. You're going to tell the truth about *everything!*"

Ram laughed in disbelief. "You're not serious, are you?"

Violet stepped around Ram, fearful of what he might do next. "If you loved me, you would do this. I'll get you the best lawyer on the planet." She moved backwards, stepping right into the dining room table. "I won't leave your side, Ram. I promise."

Ram laughed uncontrollably. "Lawyer?" he snorted. "You're such a goody two-shoes, Violet. It kills me."

She frowned. She had literally run out of tears. "But I thought you loved me, Ram? Why? Why throw it all away like this?"

Ram's blue eyes looked like two soulless marbles.

"I need to know, Ram. Do you *still* love me?"

He invaded her personal space, towering an entire foot over her petite frame.

"I do love you, Violet. It's just that I love myself more."

He lifted Violet by the hair—dangling her toes two inches from the floor.

"Ram! Please! Stop!" She writhed from the pain of her hair ripping at the roots.

He dragged her across the concrete floor to the freezer, gripping the top of her head, holding her at a distance while he entered the security code to open the door.

"Ram! Please, don't do this!" Violet punched and kicked as he held her away from his body.

As he opened the door, an eerie cloud of cold mist escaped, as if evil had been set free.

He threw Violet far inside the room and quickly locked the door.

He hit a red button on the keypad labeled EMERGENCY TWO-WAY LOCK—a bonus safety feature considering the door was originally designed to contain nuclear power plant accidents.

Inside the freezer, Violet sat on the unbearably cold floor, unable to stand up in her long, royal blue, sparkling gown.

She crawled her way to the entrance, lifted herself up by the handle, and pummeled the door with her fists. "Ram! Please don't do this! I love you! I forgive you! I forgive everything!"

But Ram could not hear her pleas.

He had already left the basement.

She looked at the digital thermometer on the wall. Ironically, it matched the size of her dress: Zero degrees Fahrenheit.

Violet knew it was only a matter of time.

The arctic air viciously froze her nose, fingers, and toes within minutes. Her alabaster skin took on a purplish-blue tinge, succumbing to the freezing temperatures quicker than most, due to her lack of body fat.

Violet shivered uncontrollably as she hobbled to an empty corner and sank down against the wall . . . Freezing at first, then burning so hot, she attempted to rip her gown into pieces . . . But was too weak to move her arms and legs . . . Until the cold returned, fusing the mascara on her eyelids closed . . . Feeling the excruciating pain from her extremities turning black and her organs hardening inside . . . Praying that God would take her into His Kingdom quickly . . . Or convince her husband to have mercy on the woman who loved him unconditionally.

God chose the former for Violet.

But before taking her final breath, she managed to part her blue, frozen lips and utter the only words that ever mattered to her . . .

"*Briar Rose*."

THIRTY-NINE

ALLEGRA WIPED a small tear from the corner of her eyelid. She had no idea Violet had endured so much turmoil in what appeared to be the ultimate *Housewife* lifestyle. She better understood the underlying reasons for her transition from an insecure, weight-obsessed, young ballerina into a vengeful, finger-swallowing, mentally unstable monster.

"I'm really sorry about your daughter." Allegra's words were sincere.

"Yes, me too."

Allegra bit her lip. "So, at what point did you figure out you were, you know . . ."

"Dead?"

Allegra nodded her head.

Violet rocked up and down on her toes. "Well, I knew something was different when I woke up in the freezer the next morning feeling warm and toasty. My hair was wet, but otherwise, I felt great." She held the back of the chair. "But what really convinced me was when I saw the shoes I left upstairs by my feet, and a letter in my hand. Obviously, I didn't write the letter."

"A suicide note?"

Violet nodded sadly.

"Ram wrote it?"

Violet nodded again. "He must have put it in my hand after I passed away."

Allegra shook her head. "Damn, that's cold."

Violet cracked a smile at the pun.

"What did it say?"

"It said I was sorry for killing you . . . That I did it because I couldn't live knowing my husband was leaving me for a younger woman. It even had an apology to my parents for causing them so much pain."

"Wow."

"Heartbreaking, I know."

"And then you found me next door?"

Violet's bleeding face toughened. "You couldn't imagine how angry I was when I first saw you sleeping in the sack. I couldn't believe *you* were the cause of all of this."

"*Me?* Ram was the one responsible, not me!"

Violet rolled back her shoulders. "Allegra, you knew Ram was married the minute you met him. You knew the danger. You knew the risk of hurting others. There's a reason why it's called a marriage *vow* . . . *It's because when a vow is broken, horrible things happen.*"

Suddenly, the moral of Violet's fairy tale was revealed.

"That's bullshit!" Allegra got up from the table, offended. "I was an innocent victim in all of this, just like you! I had no idea what he was capable of!"

Violet crossed her arms. "You died because you were a home-wrecker, Allegra. A mistress. A sidepiece. A careless, soulless whore who got pregnant by a married man."

Allegra had suffered enough from Violet's vitriol. After weeks of agonizing torture, she refused to endure any more insults from the woman who had tricked her into captivity.

She threw her arms in the air and screamed toward the ceiling: "God, are you there? Hey, God! If you can hear me, I want to *leave* this fucking place *now!*"

A loud boom thundered above.

Violet and Allegra looked up, bewildered.

"What was that?"

"I don't know."

A tiny white light, the size of a flashlight in the dark, appeared just below the ceiling.

"What on earth is that?"

"I don't know."

The tiny light quickly grew to the size of a plate, and then a tire, before occupying the entire ceiling and rotating in a swirling fashion like a whirlpool.

Within seconds, it looked like a hurricane on a satellite map, made of the brightest, most loving light in the Universe.

"Whoa," said Allegra. "Did I do that?"

Violet was in awe. The light from the hurricane was like the sun, but not blinding. Instead, it was warm and inviting.

She looked at her hands. The age spots that were once there had suddenly disappeared. Her nose instantly mended. Her skin radiated in the pure, beautiful light.

Allegra's skin started to glow as her long, wavy red hair and missing finger reappeared. Her body returned to its perfect state. She stared at her waist in amazement.

Violet grabbed Allegra's shoulder as they watched the hurricane of light transform them into the most perfect versions of their physical bodies. It felt as if they were being touched by God . . . feeling and basking in *pure love*.

Suddenly, the real-world whirring sound of the basement door unlocking echoed through the room.

Violet and Allegra's heads snapped in unison toward the door.

"It's Ram," said Allegra. "We need to hide."

Violet's eyes were glued to the top of the stairs as Ram and Elliot entered the basement.

"It's time to go, Violet," said an old man's voice from behind.

She turned around and saw Dr. Cohen carrying a brown beat-up suitcase, standing beside a beautiful redheaded woman, glowing in the hurricane light.

"Dr. Cohen?"

"*Mom?*"

Allegra's mother looked healthier and more alive now than ever before. Her shoulder-length cinnamon-red hair was undeniably the same as her daughter's. "It's time to leave, pea baby."

"Mom!" Allegra tackled her mother, hugging her tightly. "I've missed you so much!"

Allegra's mother smiled as she stroked her daughter's hair. "I know, baby, I know. I have so much to tell you."

Ram, Elliot, two uniformed officers, and three men wearing NYC Police Crime Scene Unit jackets funneled down the stairs carrying metal boxes, folded stretchers, and forensic equipment.

"We need to go now," whispered Dr. Cohen as they all stepped out of the way of the police.

Elliot ran his hand through his spiky gray hair. "I already gave the suicide note to the lead forensics officer upstairs." He touched Ram's arm. "It's just a formality, Mr. Ramspeck. We understand this is a murder-suicide. But if you need a copy of the letter, I can arrange it."

Ram pretended to cry. "No, I never want to read it again. Her parents will be devastated." His gripping performance as the remorseful, cheating husband who lost the two women he loved, was Oscar-worthy. He entered the door code and opened the freezer to reveal Violet's dead body inside.

The police officers standing behind him remained stoic. It was their third cadaver of the night.

Elliot pulled his earlobe. "Hmm. This is only the second time I've ever seen suicide by freezer. Very strange, but I've seen stranger."

Ram fought back alligator tears. "I had no idea asking for a divorce would lead to this. I begged her to go back to therapy. It's all my fault."

Elliot placed his hand on Ram's shoulder. "Mr. Ramspeck, when a person is hurting this badly, all the therapy in the world won't cure them. When a soul is ready to leave, there's nothing any of us can do to stop it. At least she's no longer in pain."

As Elliot said those words, the swirling white whirlpool above began shrinking.

Allegra's mother held her daughter's hand. "Are you ready, pea baby?"

"Yes, Mom. Let's go." Her perfect white smile glowed as she gave Violet one final look. It was the look of *forgiveness*.

Violet nodded in response.

Dr. Cohen reached his hand out to her. "Come with me, Violet. Your father is waiting. We have to go now."

She stepped backwards, moving toward the staircase. "I can't leave my home, Dr. Cohen. I'm staying."

The whirlpool shrank more and more as Allegra and her mother slowly transitioned from solid bodies . . . into transparent figures . . . until they faded away.

The whirlpool was almost closed.

"Please, Violet. It's now or never!" Dr. Cohen extended his hand as far as he could. "There's nothing left for you here, Violet. There are no second chances to leave. Come with us!"

She ignored him as she walked up the stairs, stepping through a NYPD officer, who shivered as their souls briefly intertwined.

She looked back over her shoulder and smiled. "You will always be family, Dr. Cohen." She waved. "I love you. Take care."

Dr. Cohen's body began fading as he retracted his arm and gripped his suitcase. He reluctantly accepted Violet's decision to stay among the living. "Good luck, Violet . . . You will always be the daughter I never had."

Dr. Cohen waved one last time before disappearing into the light.

When he left, the whirlpool had completely vanished with him.

Violet watched from the top of the basement stairs as they took crime scene photos of her body, now lying in a stretcher outside the freezer below.

She smiled, nostalgic of the wonderful forty-nine years she had on this Earth . . . quietly laughing about how much time she had wasted perfecting that frozen, worthless corpse.

She turned around, walked through the first security door and into the dark corridor.

She floated up the stairs in her flowing white skirt, went through the second security door, and into the pantry.

She floated through the kitchen, and past the foyer—spotting a rookie officer stretching yellow caution tape near the front entrance.

She grazed the railing with her hand as she continued floating up the main staircase, ascending higher and higher until the chaos below grew silent as she reached the seventh floor.

She entered her bedroom, casually touching the tree bedpost, feeling like a Monarch butterfly that's finally escaped its cocoon.

She moved into her dressing area . . . floated toward her doll collection . . . and smiled.

Suddenly, her body faded from a solid figure into transparency . . .

Finally morphing into a white mist that entered the large, blonde Little Red Riding Hood doll near the center of the display.

The doll's blue eyes opened wide.

Her eyelashes fluttered.

Her painted mouth curved into a smile . . .

And Violet *winked* us all goodbye.

THE END

AUTHOR MESSAGE

AFTER SPENDING years as a screenwriter in Hollywood, I made the life-changing decision to move into the literary world so I could tell my stories directly to you—the audience—without interference from directors, producers or studio executives.

And I can tell you after writing VIOLETS ARE RED that *I am here to stay.*

If you enjoyed reading this novel as much as I enjoyed writing it, please take the time to share your thoughts on Amazon and Goodreads . . . Honestly, it would mean the world to me!

The greatest gift you can give an author is to take the time to write an honest review about their novel. Reviews are what make or break a book, no matter what the topic or genre.

I have a number of titles lined up over the next several years and would love to stay in touch.

Please visit my website to sign up for my VIP READER LIST to learn more about upcoming book releases, signings, and giveaways at:

WWW.MYLOCARBIA.COM

OR FOLLOW ME ON SOCIAL MEDIA:

TWITTER: @MyloCarbia
FACEBOOK: /AuthorMyloCarbia
INSTAGRAM: @mylocarbia
GOODREADS: mylo_carbia

Forever grateful to you, my *Ghost Babies.*

Mylo Carbia

THE QUEEN OF HORROR

ALSO BY THE AUTHOR

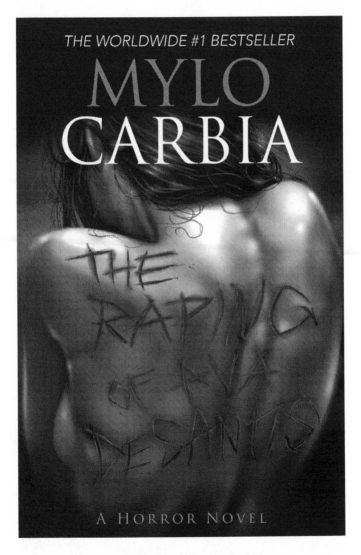

AVAILABLE WHEREVER BOOKS ARE SOLD
WWW.AVADESANTIS.COM

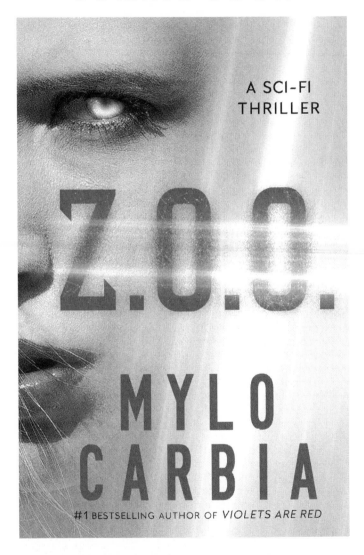

COMING SOON

A SCI-FI
THRILLER

Z.O.O.

MYLO
CARBIA

#1 BESTSELLING AUTHOR OF *VIOLETS ARE RED*

WWW.ZOOTHENOVEL.COM